THE
CONGRUENT
DRAGON

Book Three of the Congruent Mage Series

The Congruent Mage Series

www.CongruentMage.com

The Xenotech Support Series

www.XenotechSupport.com

Dedication

To the wonderful people of the
Atlanta Radio Theatre Company
for all their support and inspiration.

I'd also like to acknowledge the stirring words
of the *Song of the Shieldwall* by my friend Debra Doyle,
gratefully referenced with her permission.

Cover and Map designs by Dan Paulson

ISBN-13: 978-0-9978319-4-8

Spiral Arm Press
1725 Carlington Court
Grayson, GA 30017

www.SpiralArmPress.com

Chapter 1

The Great Green Dragon

"What. Is. That?" asked Merry.

"Fly higher," shouted Nûd from Rocky's back.

Merry and Eynon were side by side on their flying disks, close to Nûd and Rocky. The wyvern was already following Nûd's recommendation and gaining altitude. Eynon and Merry did likewise until they were a hundred feet up and could witness the scene below unfolding.

They watched as the floor of the quarry buckled and split, revealing a huge, green-scaled monstrosity. The triangular tail-tip they'd taken for a vertical piece of slate was arcing through the air at the end of the sinuous length of the creature's massive tail. The tip looked like the barbed head of a hunting arrow and the tail itself had a thicker diameter than the oldest oak in the Coombe. Rocks from the quarry floor were sloughing off the beast's back, crashing down into piles of jagged stone. Eynon thought the shifting rocks must sound like the waterfall back in Melyncárreg would, if boulders, not water, were rushing over it. A cloud of greenish dust was rising from the quarry and chunks of rock as big as milk cows were sailing skyward, tossed up by snapping layers of stone.

An errant green-soapstone missile struck the bottom of Eynon's flying disk and knocked him sideways. Chee was hanging vertically, clutching Eynon's neck and hair. Eynon was surprised by the impact. One of his feet slid out of the leather strap holding him on his disk and for a few moments he flailed like a giant had picked him up and was pinching his ankle between a thumb and forefinger, shaking him. Rocky swerved to avoid a soaring boulder nearly as big as he was and Merry's flying disk rattled as a dozen smaller chunks of rock struck the bottom of her disk like extra-heavy hailstones.

"Higher!" ordered Merry.

Nûd and Rocky complied.

"I'm trying," said Eynon. He maneuvered his flying disk underneath him again and stuck both feet securely into their straps. Chee still gripped Eynon's hair and his legs were wrapped around his neck. The raconette's long tail was flicking back and forth under Eynon's nose, distracting him. Eynon stroked Chee's back with one hand and disengaged his familiar's feet from his neck with the other. Then he ascended to join Nûd and Merry.

More of the monster was visible now. Vast wings, like a batsnake's, but oh-so-much larger, were now exposed. They were a lighter shade of green than the beast's tail and tucked against the creature's broad back. The part of the beast they could see shook like a dog tossing drops of water from its back, if the water was blocks of fractured stone big enough to build cottages. The monster's scaled tail snapped back and forth, cutting through the cloud of green dust and making Eynon, Merry, and Nûd *very* glad they were out of its range.

"What do you think it is?" Eynon asked Nûd. "You've read through the library at Damon's Academy."

"You should be able to tell us the name of this sort of beast, even if you only looked at the pictures," said Merry.

Nûd gave her a hurt look that turned to a smile when he saw her eyes dancing and realized Merry was teasing.

"You mean you don't know?" Nûd teased back.

"I think *I* do," said Eynon. "They're in all the best stories."

"And on the prows and sterns of the Bifurlanders' longships," said Nûd.

"Except those have gold scales," said Eynon.

"And they're a *lot* smaller," said Merry, who had met the young Bifurlanders, Sigrun and Rannveigr and their friends, a few hours earlier on the battlefield along the Brenavon.

"It could be a wyvern," offered Nûd.

"No," said Eynon. "I can see it has *four* legs, not two."

"There's no way anything that big could be supported on two legs like a hawk's," said Merry. "Wyverns can only grow so big."

"Look!" shouted Nûd. "The wings are unfurling!"

Like a flutterby emerging from its chrysalis or a ship preparing its sails, the monster's wings slowly extended and snapped out to their full length.

You could fit Haywall's milking barn under one of them, thought Eynon.

A thick but nearly translucent green membrane stretched along the wings' supporting framework.

They do look like a batsnake's wings, Eynon considered. *Or bat wings in general.*

He could see ropy blood vessels as well as bones inside them. Their liberation stirred up eddies in the green dust, sending more of it swirling high enough to reach Nûd and Merry and Eynon. Chee sneezed and Eynon cast a transparent shield of solidified sound around them all to keep the dust away.

I should have done that earlier, thought Eynon.

The raconette patted Eynon on the head, as if confirming Eynon's observation. Merry brought her flying disk close enough to Eynon's to overlap, so she could hold his hand. Together, with Nûd on Rocky a dozen feet above, they stared down as the monster's wings flapped twice, then snapped into some sort of ready position.

The great beast's torso was halfway out of its stone prison now. Individual scales on its body were as big as knight's shields, at least where they could be seen. The scales weren't a uniform green. Instead, they were iridescent and reflected the afternoon sunlight like new leaves in spring after a rainstorm. There was enough room on the creature's broad back for a good-sized inn and a stable.

A long neck, still mostly buried, was visible heading toward the southern end of the quarry. Eynon saw villagers from Wherrel gathered to the east, observing the scene from the gap leading into the Coombe. He spoke to Merry and the two of them built a double-layered wall of solidified sound across the opening, protecting the onlookers from flying debris. Eynon was glad his family didn't live nearby.

Then the neck came free, like the deep roots of a weed, with rocks rather than dirt giving way as it came to the surface. It was long and even thicker than the creature's tail. It curved up, an arch filled with tension. That tension suddenly released as a wedge-shaped green head with a toothy mouth large enough to swallow Rocky whole snapped out of the quarry's stone floor.

The monster's head moved left and right, using long-dormant muscles. Intelligent dark-green eyes with vertical black pupils blinked in the sunlight. Their depths seemed to spin in a hypnotic pattern. Four massive legs pulled themselves out of circular holes in the rock and the creature's full dimensions were revealed.

It isn't the size of Fercha's tower, Eynon realized. *It's bigger!*

The head on the end of the long neck rose to regard the young observers. Without conscious thought they all descended to match its eye level. Merry squeezed Eynon's hand and Chee tightened his grip on Eynon's hair. Nûd and Rocky kept their station close above.

First, the monster looked at Merry, then Eynon. It seemed interested in Eynon's red magestone but didn't linger. Then it noticed Nûd. The beast's huge eyes held Nûd's for a dozen heartbeats. It spoke.

"Son of Tamloch," said the great green dragon. "Is it time?"

Chapter 2

Two Thousand Years

"Time for what?" asked Nûd without thinking.

"Time to fight the Roma," said the dragon. "Have they invaded Orluin at last?"

"Uh," said Eynon. Merry gave Eynon a look that said *Let me handle this.*

"Before we discuss military strategy, shouldn't we introduce ourselves?" asked Merry. "My name is Merry, and my fellow wizard is Eynon."

"Nûd is the name of the man on the wyvern—his name is Rocky," said Eynon.

"Chee!" said Chee, clutching Eynon's ear with one hand-paw while madly waving the other.

"And Eynon's small companion is Chee—he's a raconette," said Nûd with a smile. "What's *your* name?"

"I," said the dragon, waiting to confirm everyone's attention, "am Viridáxés."

"You're very big," said Merry.

The dragon stretched his wings and bent his long neck, so his head could regard his body. His eyes turned this way and that to take in every aspect of his vast bulk, and he seemed to preen before replying.

"Indeed," said Viridáxés. "Thank you for your kind words, dear lady. I *am* big, aren't I? If you'd like, you may call me Viridáxés Mór."

"Viridáxés the Great," said Nûd.

"Yes, my king?" asked the dragon. The huge creature paused from admiring its size to focus on Nûd.

"I'm not the..." Nûd began.

"Shush," said Merry, cutting Nûd off. "He wasn't asking you a question, O Great and Mighty Viridáxés. Nûd was just restating your words in the fashion they're spoken today."

"How long have I been sleeping?" asked Viridáxés. "It must have been quite long for me to have grown so large."

"When were you buried beneath the quarry?" asked Eynon.

"Master Mage Séanoll planted me here in the thirtieth year after the First Ships landed in Orluin," said Viridáxés. "He feared the Roma would follow the Ériu west and wanted an unstoppable weapon to use against them."

"In that he most certainly succeeded," said Merry.

"But the Roma..." said Eynon.

"Are determined foes," said Merry. "Tamloch is indeed fortunate to have you as an ally."

"You've been asleep for over two thousand years," said Nûd.

"So long?" mused the dragon. "Master Séanoll thought it would be only a few centuries. That explains it."

"Explains what, O Great One?" asked Eynon.

"Why I'm so big, of course," said Viridáxés. "I'm tremendous."

"Indeed you are," said Nûd. "How big were you when you were planted?"

"Barely the size of the wyvern you ride," said Viridáxés. He lifted his head until it was even with Rocky, who stared back at the dragon unflinchingly.

Rocky is brave, thought Eynon. *Considering that Viridáxés could swallow him in two bites.*

"What did you eat below the quarry to grow so huge?" asked Eynon.

Merry rolled her eyes.

"You are a mage and you do not know?" asked the dragon, turning its giant head toward Eynon. "I shall have words with your master about failing to teach you the proper lore of dragons."

Eynon offered a contrite bow, tipping his flying disk a few degrees forward. "My apologies, Your Magnificence," he said.

Viridáxés snorted, sounding a bit like a geyser erupting in Melyncárreg. "If what you say is true, I have been soaking up magical energy from the magestones in this quarry for two thousand years, growing larger and larger until summoned by a royal son of Tamloch. The Roma will not dare to stand before me."

"You are mighty beyond compare," said Merry without exaggeration. "Sadly, much dragon lore has been lost over the centuries. There are few dragons even a tenth your size left in all of Tamloch and Dâron, and they mostly avoid humankind."

"There never were many dragons," said Viridáxés, making a sound something like a sigh or a broken forge bellows. "And Dâron treated theirs better than we did in Tamloch. I expect that's what happens when you accidentally eat a miscellaneous royal prince."

"You personally?" asked Nûd.

"Alas, yes," said Viridáxés. "Though as I said, it was an accident and he was eleventh in line for the throne, not that I'm claiming his position in the succession as an excuse."

"Of course not," said Merry.

Nûd held his stomach, looking a little green.

"What do dragons usually eat?" asked Eynon, trying to change the subject to help his friend, but not succeeding.

"Aurochs," said the dragon. "At least on the far side of the Ocean. Cows and wisents mostly, on this side, before I went to sleep."

Viridáxés stretched his neck back toward his tail and moved it in broad arcs with his head upside down. Nûd, Eynon and Merry could hear monstrously large vertebrae pop like sheets of ice breaking on the Moravon in the spring. A few seconds later, the dragon's head was back in place, staring at Nûd. Two nostrils the size of flying disks flared and sniffed.

"Don't worry," said Viridáxés. "I'd never consider eating anyone likely to be king." The dragon sniffed again. "You're third in line—no, second. Your father is a wizard and out of the succession. I can smell it."

Nûd frowned. "How can you tell something like that just by sniffing?" he asked.

"Séanoll enchanted me to serve the crown of Tamloch," said Viridáxés. "There's a mark that is passed unbroken from fathers to sons across generations in the royal line."

"That doesn't make any sense," said Merry. "How can a royal family's line last two thousand years without being broken? What if a queen slept with a groom, or a prince was switched for a pauper's son at birth? The old tales are full of such things—and what about ruling queens?"

"Not in Tamloch," said Nûd. "Bastard kings before queens, the saying goes. Ruling queens only happened in Dâron."

"I know not the *how* of it," said Viridáxés, "but I expect Séanoll enchanted the Tamloch royal line to run true and unbroken, so I would always know my master."

"Wizards can do that?" asked Eynon.

"Maybe," said Merry. "We can ask Fercha or Damon later."

"Later," said Eynon, his eyes fixed on the dragon.

"Tell us more of dragon lore, Your Immensity," said Merry. "Is it true dragons can breathe fire?"

"Truly, much has been forgotten if fear of dragon's fire has faded," said Viridáxés. "Aye, dear lady, dragons can breathe fire. Internal congruencies not only help us fly and support our great size, they also give us access to many other powers of wizardry. I can exhale cold winds, spit lightning bolts, and shoot out blasts of flame ten times my length." Viridáxés turned his head and looked back toward his tail. "At least I think so," he said.

"Wow!" said Eynon.

"Wow…" said Nûd softly. He put his hand on his forehead.

"Could you show us how you breathe fire?" asked Merry, pitching her voice to sound half her fifteen years. "Please, *please?* That would be amazing!"

"As you wish, child," said Viridáxés. "You will want to move back."

At Nûd's direction, Rocky moved back a hundred feet without turning around, like a giant black hummingbird in flight. Eynon and Merry joined Nûd and Rocky on their flying disks. He smiled to see Chee imitating Merry's face as she had implored the dragon to demonstrate his powers.

Viridáxés curled his tail around his haunches, lifted his front legs off the ground and extended his neck skyward, pointing up like an arrow. A rumbling sound came from the base of his throat, sounding like stampeding wisents. Rocky echoed the sound in his chest.

It was only a whisper in comparison. The dragon's neck seemed to pull down into itself, then pop upward. Viridáxés mouth opened wide and a column of green flame as broad as Eynon's outstretched arms erupted into the sky. It roared like a thousand mountain lions and extended high enough for the top of the column to be out of the humans' unaugmented sight. They could feel the heat of the flames from a hundred feet away. It was hotter than standing beside a swordsmith's furnace.

The tower of flame stopped after a few seconds. Viridáxés closed his mouth and resumed standing on four feet. He brought his head back to its previous level and smiled—as much as a dragon's reptilian mouth could smile—showing off teeth the size of scimitars.

"Bravo!" shouted Merry. "Stupendous!"

Eynon whistled, then added, "Truly spectacular!"

Nûd was holding the sides of his head and rocking back and forth slowly. His mouth was open, but he wasn't saying anything. Chee was hiding behind Eynon's neck making frightened *chee-chee-chee-CHEE* cries. Eynon reached up to stroke the raconette's fur. It helped.

"My fire is hotter than a flaming mountain! My anger, more powerful than a hurricane! My wings blot out the sun!" bellowed Viridáxés.

Merry, Eynon and Nûd listened in awe.

Viridáxés rumbled a different sort of sound deep inside. Eynon took it to be amusement.

"I hoped I'd be big enough to use those phrases," said the dragon. He snapped his wings out and shaded the humans with one of them. "I've been waiting two thousand years for the chance."

Merry clapped. Eynon joined in. Nûd didn't. His expression reminded Eynon of a man who'd just lost his dog.

"Well," said Viridáxés. "Where are the Roma? Where is the king of Tamloch? When do we leave?"

Merry answered. "The Roma and the king are far from here," she said. "We need to confer with more senior wizards to determine the best course of action and maximize the impact of your arrival."

"That is how it should be," said Viridáxés. The dragon looked around. "I don't see any cows or wisents nearby. Perhaps I will settle back down on my bed of magestones to soak up more magic as a substitute?"

"That sounds wise," said Merry. "We will withdraw a short distance to give you peace and quiet while you rest and will have something to eat ourselves. We'll wake you when we have further news."

"Excellent," said the dragon. "Breaking free from all that rock was tiresome work. We can find the king of Tamloch after I close my eyes for a bit and take a nap."

He yawned, revealing teeth as tall as Nûd and Eynon before settling his massive body down onto the shattered stones of the quarry. Boulders slid out of his way like so much scree. He curled around in a spiral with his tail wrapped around one side of his body and his neck around the other and began to sleep. Soon green-tinged clouds of steam rose rhythmically from his nostrils.

Nûd and Rocky followed Eynon and Merry as they flew over the low mountain east of the quarry. They hovered for a few moments to encourage the onlookers to go home, then landed on a fallow field south of Wherrel. Eynon and Merry hugged each other, with Chee soon inserting himself between them for comfort and reassurance. Nûd joined them, with Rocky close behind. The wyvern showed no interest in flying off to find a deer or fat ewe. Merry and Eynon moved a foot apart and Chee jumped up to Eynon's shoulder, clutching the hair below Eynon's cap with its fresh sprig of holly.

"Now what?" asked Eynon. He shook his head and stared at Nûd. Merry did the same.

"Why are you looking at *me?*" asked Nûd.

"He's *your* dragon," said Merry.

Chapter 3

Haywall

Nûd's voice cracked. "What do you mean, *my* dragon?" he asked.

"You're a royal son of Tamloch," said Merry. "That sounded really important to Viridáxés. If anything happened to Túathal and Dârio you'd be king of Tamloch as well as Dâron."

"I'm not interested in being king of anywhere," declared Nûd.

Eynon noticed his friend was sounding different—less like a rusty hinge and more like Eynon's father's mellow baritone.

"I don't know if that matters to Viridáxés," said Merry. "I *do* know I'd be much happier with him following instructions from you or Dârio than Túathal."

"Uh huh," said Eynon. "He's so *big*. And so *green*."

"That's why I'm so worried," said Nûd. "We've got to keep Viridáxés away from Túathal. He's *so* huge and *so* powerful that even with Tamloch's army routed, Túathal could use Viridáxés to turn Brendinas and Tyford to rubble."

"Whatever we do," said Eynon, "we can't let the dragon know that the Roma already settled in Orluin fifteen hundred years ago."

"Certainly not," said Merry. "They're our allies."

"Why does your voice sound different now?" Eynon asked Nûd.

"What do you mean?" replied Nûd without his typical vocal creak.

"You don't sound like a gate that needs oil anymore," said Merry.

Nûd tilted his head and recited one of Ealdamon's epigrams that was particularly apt under the circumstances. "Always keep your head around dragons, or they may keep yours for their own amusement." He rubbed his chin and looked back at Merry and Eynon. "What do you know?" said Nûd. "I *do* sound different."

"Maybe it's because you've been away from Melyncárreg?" suggested Merry. "I remember the air being dry there."

"That could be it," said Nûd. He was speaking slowly, as if trying to hear his words as he spoke them.

"I think it's the sulphur," said Eynon. "Breathing sulphur-tainted air all your life can't have been good for your voice. I expect you're starting to sound like you would have sounded if you hadn't spent most of your life in Melyncárreg."

"Maybe," said Nûd.

"Chee," said Chee. The raconette jumped from Eynon's shoulder to Rocky's back and rubbed his stomach.

"I think Chee has the right idea," said Eynon. "We've got a lot to talk about and there are better places than a farmer's field to do it. Haywall isn't far. We can fly over there, have some lunch, and decide our next steps." Eynon covered his mouth as he yawned. "I don't know about you, but I'm so tired I'm about to fall over. Maybe I can even get in a nap."

"Sorry for keeping you up and distracting you last night," said Merry, teasing Eynon by blowing him a kiss with both hands.

"Stop that!" said Eynon. "It was a very pleasant distraction, and well worth the associated sleep deprivation."

"Ahem," said Nûd. He tried to tap his foot impatiently, but the sole of his boot was muffled by the soil of the fallow field. "I think going back to your home in Haywall is an excellent idea."

"Because you want to see my sister again," said Eynon.

"I just saw her," said Nûd. "I'm more interested in lunch. I didn't get much sleep in the last few days either." Nûd yawned. "I need a nap, too. If I'm not careful, I could sleep for a week."

"So long as it's not with my sister," said Eynon. He grinned at Nûd and the big man poked Eynon's ribs with two fingers.

"Who Braith decides to sleep with and when she decides to do so is *her* business," said Merry. She poked the ribs on Eynon's other side.

Eynon pulled his elbows in protectively. "I know, I know," said Eynon. "You can both stop."

"I won't give you cause to worry," said Nûd. "She's a sweet girl and I like her, but it's not going farther than that."

"Good," said Eynon.

Nûd rubbed his stomach, imitating Chee. Merry mirrored Nûd's motion with her right hand.

"I get it," said Eynon. "Follow me. If we hurry, I can help my folks make us something to eat."

* * * * *

The mid-afternoon sun was bright as its rays streamed through the oiled parchment window of Eynon's parents' cottage.

"Tell me again about the wisents," said Braith as she helped clear the lunch dishes. She lingered next to Nûd while she transferred his plate to a carved maple tray. "That was a brilliant idea," she said, putting her mouth close to Nûd's ear.

Recognizing Braith's ploy to get him to turn his head so their lips would be only inches apart, Nûd continued to face Eynon across the table. Eynon grinned and Nûd answered.

"It was Eynon's really," said Nûd. "I said we should come up with a surprise of our own. Eynon's idea was to stampede the wisents into Tamloch's army."

"Fercha created the wide gate to transport the wisents to the battlefield," said Merry. "Nûd collected the magestones we used to power the wide gate."

"Chee!" said Chee who was tossing a fat acorn up and down with his feet in the middle of the table while leaning against a small dense loaf of dark rye bread Glenys, Eynon's mother, had given him.

"Yes," said Nûd. "You helped collect magestones, too. Thank you."

Chee nodded and pulled his lips back to show two rows of white teeth. Braith laughed. She balanced her tray in one hand and rested the other on Nûd's shoulder.

"I'm impressed by your team effort," she said. Braith squeezed Nûd's shoulder and circled the table to clear Merry and Eynon's plates. She listened to the continuing discussion as she scraped them into a pail by the side of the sink. The leftover food—what little there was of it—would help feed their pigs.

"Now we have a bigger problem to deal with," said Merry.

"I still can't believe a dragon bigger than Haywall's milking barn was sleeping under the quarry west of Wherrel," said Daffyd, Eynon's father. He was standing on the other side of the sink from Braith, cutting a dried apple and honey pie into slices. *"How long* had it been there?"

"Almost two thousand years," said Nûd, shaking his head slowly from side to side.

"Let sleeping dragons lie," said Glenys from the side of the cottage's main room away from the kitchen and hearth. "That's what my grandfather used to say, though I never knew why."

"There haven't ever been dragons in the Coombe as far as I know," said Daffyd, "though I've heard rumors of trappers seeing ones three times as big as that wyvern of yours out west in the Borderlands, by the three rivers."

"Trappers' tales are as reliable as old Athican stories about headless men with faces in their stomachs," said Merry.

"Or ones who hop about on one giant foot," added Nûd.

"Scoff if you want," said Daffyd, "but I know one of the trappers who said she saw a dragon unfurl its wings on top of a mountain just beyond the point where the three rivers meet. She's not the sort of person to exaggerate."

"Unlike your account of a dragon big enough to crush all of Haywall if it landed in our square," noted Glenys.

"We're not making up *this* dragon," insisted Merry.

Eynon jumped in, providing a distraction. "It was kind of you to arrange places for us to sleep if the dragon keeps dozing and we can stay the night, Mother."

"What are the odds of that?" whispered Braith.

Glenys let her daughter's comment pass. She was fluffing a pair of pillows on a makeshift mattress stuffed with straw on the floor near Braith's bed and caught Eynon's eye. "This should do for you and Merry," she said. "I've found a real bed for Nûd with a neighbor."

"Thank you," said Nûd and Merry simultaneously.

Eynon smiled at his mother, then glanced ruefully at Merry. He was glad his mother had found them all places to sleep, but there wouldn't be any lovemaking for him and Merry tonight with his sister a few feet away and his parents sleeping in the loft above. He also admired the deft and oh-so-polite way his mother had ensured Nûd and Braith wouldn't be under the same roof once the sun went down—*if* they stayed the night, that is.

Glenys gave her son a knowing smile. Eynon hoped Nûd would be boarding with Glynneth, an older honorary "aunt" of his who lived one cottage down and baked delicious sweet cakes.

Eynon pitched his voice so both his parents would hear. "I appreciate you feeding us lunch and putting us up on short notice," he said.

"We're glad to have you and your friends," said his mother.

"Of course," said Daffyd. "This is your home. You're always welcome here—and thank you for keeping your wyvern away from the cows."

The corners of Merry's mouth turned up and Nûd couldn't hold in a laugh. "Eynon is nothing if not considerate," he said.

"And polite," said Merry.

"Chi-*chee,*" said Chee. He pulled off a chunk of the dark bread and began to chew.

"Can I see the dragon in the quarry?" asked Braith as she carried slices of dried apple and honey pie to the table.

"Is it wise?" Daffyd asked Eynon.

"I think it's a good idea not to confuse Viridáxés by introducing him to too many people," Eynon replied.

"That's for the best," said Nûd.

Merry's mouth was full of pie, so she only nodded vigorously. They'd all agreed on the way to Haywall that they didn't want more people in Dâron learning that Viridáxés was loyal to the royal family of Tamloch, or that the dragon's perceived mission was destroying the Roma. Nûd had asked Eynon and Merry to be especially careful not to say anything about his own royal lineage to Braith and they'd agreed.

"The dragon could eat you," said Glenys. "They're supposed to be particularly fond of maid..."

"If you complete that sentence, I'm leaving with Eynon and Merry and Nûd in the morning," said Braith. "I'll start my wander year early and move to Tyford, or even Brendinas."

"Yes, dear," said Glenys, sounding contrite. "I'm sorry. That went too far."

Daffyd rolled his eyes at his wife and smiled at his daughter. He picked up the pail of dinner scraps by the sink and crossed to stand beside Glenys.

"We'll go out and tend to the outdoor chores for an hour or so to give you young people a chance to talk," he said, putting his unencumbered arm around his wife's waist. He gave Glenys a kiss and steered her toward the cottage's door. "I'll see to the hogs and you can feed the chickens. I've got a few projects in mind for the cottage, too."

"I know we just had lunch, but since we don't know when or if you'll have to leave, I'll plan an early dinner," said Glenys.

"Thank you," said Eynon quietly. "I'll help cook."

Braith smiled at her father and tried hard not to look at her mother.

"Don't eat my pie," said Daffyd as the door began to close.

"Or mine," added Glenys, pushing it shut behind her.

Braith and Eynon laughed. Merry and Nûd joined in.

"Sit," said Eynon, indicating that Braith should sit next to Merry, not Nûd. She did, reluctantly, and gave Eynon a look that said *I know what you're trying to do.*

"If I can't go see the dragon, the least you can do is let me listen to your plotting," said Braith.

"We're not plotting," said Merry. "We're planning."

"If we were plotting," said Nûd, "we'd do it after dark."

"It won't be dark for five or six *hours,*" said Braith.

Little sisters, thought Eynon.

"What do we do now?" asked Merry. She turned her head to Nûd, then Eynon.

"We have to contact one of the senior wizards," said Eynon.

"Who?" asked Nûd.

"The only one we *can* contact is Doethan," said Merry. "Eynon has a communications ring for him."

"Not exactly," said Nûd.

"What do you mean, not exactly?" asked Merry. "Eynon has a ring to reach Doethan. I gave him back the one he gave me."

"No, no, I know that Eynon can reach Doethan," said Nûd. "It's just that he's not the only senior wizard we can contact."

The big man reached his hand inside the neck of his shirt and pulled a silver chain over his head. He held the chain out over the middle of the table. Two gold rings threaded by the fine silver links swung hypnotically back and forth, hanging from Nûd's fist.

"*Chee-eee-eee...*" said Chee, his eyes moving back and forth, following the rings' motion.

"What are those?" asked Eynon.

"Communications rings, obviously," said Merry.

"Correct," said Nûd. "One for Damon and..."

"One for Fercha," completed Merry.

Nûd nodded.

"Wow!" said Eynon.

"Damon gave me one, so I could reach him if I ran into problems while maintaining trails at Melyncárreg," said Nûd. "I've used it a few times. I've never used the one Fercha gave me."

"I'm sorry," said Merry.

"Not everyone has parents as nice as Eynon's," said Nûd.

"Why didn't you contact one of them when you were attacked by the basilisks?" asked Eynon.

"Umm..." said Nûd. "I'd like to say that I wanted to prove I could survive on my own without their help. Unfortunately, I was so busy trying to stay alive that I forgot I even had them."

"Oh," said Eynon. He tilted his head and grinned at Nûd. His friend grinned back.

Braith tugged on Nûd's arm. "Who *are* all these people?" she asked.

"Wizards," said Eynon. "More senior wizards."

"You've only been a wizard for a week or so," said Braith. "Every wizard has to be more senior than *you.*"

Little sisters—they keep big brothers humble, Eynon mused. He nodded to Braith and said, "True enough."

"Now we have a decision to make," said Merry.

"What's that?" asked Braith. She leaned forward to stare at the pair of rings on Nûd's left hand.

Nûd tilted his hand so the rings caught the early afternoon light.

"Who are we going to call?" he responded.

Chapter 4

The Battlefield

"Look out, Your Majesty!" shouted Duke Háiddon.

A trio of wisents, stragglers following the main body of the stampeding herd, were attracted by King Dârio's flapping light-blue surcoat. Provoked by the movement, all three large, shaggy bovines decided to charge Dâron's young monarch as he walked across the battlefield to examine an equally large animal—an odd-looking giant deer Damon had called a flathorn that had broken a foreleg and was writhing on the ground nearby.

Dârio sidestepped one onrushing wisent but was struck a glancing blow by the flank of another as it rumbled past him like a runaway supply wagon. The impact knocked Dârio back and flipped him into a reverse somersault. He ended up face down with a mouth full of grass, only inches away from an odoriferous oval of wisent dung. Dârio pulled his knees under him and sat up, then stood and drew his sword—no small feat wearing a heavy coat of plates. That proved to be a mistake, as the glint of afternoon sunlight on the sword's bright steel caught the eye of the third wisent. The beast lowered its head, pawed the ground, and sped toward Dârio, breath steaming from its nostrils.

"Guards! To your king!" Duke Háiddon commanded.

Three men and two women in royal livery who'd been waved off by the king earlier now ran toward Dârio. Their young liege was holding his sword in front of him, hoping to discourage the charging wisent with its point, but ready to dance out of its way if possible. It was clear the guards wouldn't get there in time. To nearly everyone's surprise, seconds before it reached the king, the wisent stopped and fell to the ground with a long Roma *pilum* lodged deep in its thick neck.

Quintillius waved to Dârio, who bowed to acknowledge the Roma governor-general's throw. Dârio dispatched the wisent with a swift blow to its neck, removed the spear, and threw it back to Quin. The pilum's shaft quivered in front of the tall Roma leader.

"Thank you," said Dârio. "Excellent aim."

"You as well," said Quintillius, sweeping his hand forward to reference the spear's wooden shaft. The point of the pilum was embedded in the sod two feet in front of the governor-general's left boot. Quin pulled the weapon out of the ground and handed it to the guard he'd borrowed it from a few moments before. He winked at the woman whose face was mostly hidden by her helmet, then turned and walked out to join Dârio, Duke Háiddon, and Dârio's five guards beside the dead wisent.

"The kill is yours, Your Excellency," said Dârio. "I'll have the meat sent to your camp for your soldiers, the head stuffed and mounted as a trophy of your prowess, and the hide turned into a robe to keep you warm on cold winter nights."

"That's very kind of you," said Quintillius, "but don't worry about the meat. Feed your own soldiers. There are so many wisents near our lines that I'm sure my troops will quickly tire of eating them." The tall Roma leader grinned at Dârio. "I'll be glad to take the head and robe, though. It will impress my children."

"Not your wife?" asked Duke Háiddon. The corners of his mouth turned up and his eyes were merry.

"She's not easily impressed," said Quintillius, offering a wry smile.

The duke and Dârio laughed. They were both aware of Laetícia's formidable reputation as Occidens Province's spymaster.

Dârio took a dozen paces to stand near the injured flathorn. He danced in, avoiding the creature's oversized antlers, and cut its throat with the edge of his sword to end its suffering. The beast went still.

"Perhaps your troops will enjoy tasting something *other* than wisent?" offered Dârio. "This beast will be yours as well—and its mounted head."

"I wonder if it will taste more like beef or like venison?" asked Quintillius. He stroked his chin with one hand.

"Only one way to tell," said Duke Háiddon. He gave instructions to one of Dârio's guards to summon cooks to dress the carcass.

"I'm very pleased with your battle strategy," said Quintillius, nodding toward Háiddon and Dârio. "It's not often Roma's legions come to a battle and take no casualties."

"Quite true," said Háiddon. "Dâron's young king is wise beyond his years."

"And exceedingly lucky," said Dârio. "It pays to have talented friends."

Duke Háiddon gave Dârio a half-bow. King Bjarni chose that moment to join them, accompanied by three broad-shouldered warriors from the Bifurland fleet carrying round shields and double-bladed axes. Dârio, Quintillius, Háiddon, and Bjarni stepped a few paces away to gain a modicum of privacy.

"Welcome back," said the duke to the king of the Bifurlanders. "How goes the effort to round up Tamloch's soldiers along the southern edge of the ice?"

"As well as can be expected," said King Bjarni. "They were glad to board our dragonships as prisoners to avoid being trampled by wisents."

"We had much the same reaction from the Tamloch soldiers we let pass our shield wall on the east bank of the Brenavon," said Quintillius.

"Engineers and wizards from all three of our territories are turning the island in the river into a stockade," said Duke Háiddon. "The Bifurlanders are cutting down trees while Dâron soldiers are setting them upright in holes dug by Roma wizards."

"Thank you both for your assistance," said Dârio. "We can get a lot done quickly when we work together."

"You're quite welcome," said Quintillius. "The work is going fast, and we won't have to worry about keeping the prisoners fed, since there are still hundreds of wisents on the island, too." The tall Roma leader's eyes danced and he traded smiles with the others. Then he took a deep breath and his expression grew serious. "The sooner we get the situation here in hand, the sooner King Bjarni's fleet and my legions can return to Nova Eboracum to counter the Tamloch fleet."

"We're working as fast as we can," said Dârio. "You can count on Dâron to add troops for Nova Eboracum's defense."

"It should be quite a surprise for the Tamloch fleet," said Bjarni.

"I'll say," said Duke Háiddon. "They won't expect our forces appearing on a flotilla of five hundred dragonships, all raining arrows and javelins down on them."

"Are you sure the Bifurland fleet can get there on time?" asked Dârio.

"Mafuta and Fercha assure me it can," said Quintillius. "They've figured out a way to build a wide gate across the river."

"Marvelous," said Dârio. "Where *is* Fercha, by the way?"

"Didn't you see her?" asked Duke Háiddon. "She went south to the Dormant Dragon with Verro, Doethan, Ealdamon, Astrí, that young wizard with dark hair attending Túathal, and a few others. Verro's wizards lifted Túathal on overlapping flying disks and floated him off to the south in the direction of the inn an hour ago."

"I missed their departure," said Dârio. "How did Túathal look?" Dârio couldn't find much filial concern for a man he'd despised most of his life, even if Túathal actually *was* his father. Then again, he didn't look forward to the prospect of ruling Tamloch as well as Dâron if Túathal died. *It would be like trying to get cats and dogs to share a food dish,* thought Dârio. *Or wildcats and wolves.*

"Not good, Your Majesty," said Duke Háiddon. "King Túathal's face was the blue-white color of thick snow and his hands were as cold as the ice on the river."

Dârio tilted his head quizzically at the duke.

"I didn't touch him, My Liege," said Háiddon. "But Salder did and I trust his word. He's Baron Derwen's son, out on the Upper Rhuthro. They make marvelous cider."

Dârio nodded and Háiddon continued.

"Salder worked as a spy for Dâron in the court of King Túathal," said the duke. "Dâron owes Salder a great debt. He gave Túathal the sleeping draught that allowed us to capture him."

"Was he also responsible for *poisoning* Túathal?" asked Dârio.

Duke Háiddon's eyes stared at the ground and he moved uncomfortably from side to side. "Ummm... Your mother..." he began.

Dârio flashed a rueful smile.

"Say no more, Your Grace," said the young king. "I should have realized my mother would be close at hand when someone's been poisoned. Is she being questioned?"

"Verro was escorting Princess Gwýnnett south to the Dormant Dragon personally," said Duke Háiddon. "I assume interrogating her is high on his agenda."

"No doubt," said Dârio. He shook his head quickly, as if to clear it, and stared at the duke. "Since when is the Master Mage of Tamloch allowed to question a princess of Dâron?" Dârio asked. "Did I miss something? Did we *lose* the battle to Tamloch?"

"Of course not, sire," said Duke Háiddon. "The circumstances were a bit, *uh,* unusual."

"I'm sure they were," said Dârio, still fixing the duke with his gaze.

"Say rather that your mother went south with Fercha, Doethan, Ealdamon and Astrí," said Duke Háiddon. "Verro may well have been in their custody."

"Right," said Dârio, drawing out the word and accepting the fact that those particular goats were already out of the shed.

"Fercha took responsibility," said Duke Háiddon, "and Queen Carys said it would be all right."

"You've spoken with the queen?" asked Dârio. "You've told her about our victory?"

"I have, Sire."

Dârio noticed the gold ring on the duke's right hand and smiled. The Old Queen had her fingers—and the rings on those fingers—in many pies around the kingdom and beyond its borders.

"Did you also tell her what Túathal said about being my father?"

"I did," said Duke Háiddon.

"What was her response?" asked Dârio.

"She said *thank you,*" the duke replied.

"Oh," said Dârio. He muttered under his breath a few times before speaking. "Why couldn't I have had a more admirable father?"

"You *did,*" said Duke Háiddon, softly.

"That's spoken true, youngling," said King Bjarni. "It's a wonder you're not a monster yourself with such a sire."

"Some back in Brendinas might say that I am," said Dârio. "I owe what good sense I have to the duke here," he continued, slapping Duke Háiddon's shoulder.

"Along with help from Prince Dâri, Fercha, the Old King and Queen Carys," said the duke.

"That's all well and good," said Quintillius. "I'm sure you're kind to dogs and small children. We can sort that out later and worry about who's the rightful king of Tamloch tomorrow. For now, we need to focus on preparations for gating back to Nova Eboracum before sundown."

"My troops and ships can be ready in an hour," said King Bjarni. "We've already escorted the Tamloch prisoners to the island stockade. You can start loading legionnaires aboard sooner than that. We'll pull our longships up against the east bank to make the process easier."

"Excellent," said Quintillius. "I'll send Felix south to find Fercha, so she can help Mafuta build the wide gate across the river."

"Very good," said Dârio. "I'd like to ride along with him, if I may?" The young king tilted his head toward Quin.

"Certainly," said the governor-general.

"I appreciate it," said Dârio. "I want to hear what Verro is able to extract from my mother. I may be able to help him tell fact from fiction."

Chapter 5

The Dormant Dragon

"I like this Roma custom," said Dârio, standing on the back of the flying disk Felix was expertly directing.

"What custom is that?" asked the tall young wizard.

"Wide belts for wizards," said Dârio. "Especially ones with built-in straps."

"We've found it makes it easier for passengers to fly securely," said Felix, "and some wizards dislike strangers' arms around them. They'd prefer to reserve that level of intimacy for individuals they chose, not ones forced upon them."

"I respect that opinion and will encourage the wizards of Dâron to adopt the practice," said Dârio. "The leatherworkers' guild will appreciate it as well." Dârio admired the belt Felix was wearing. It was black, tooled to show round purple-dyed circles, like Roma magestones. Four straps were riveted to the back of the belt, making it easy for one or two people to hang on and fly without worrying about falling off.

"How long do you think it will take for your wizards to start wearing wide belts?" asked Felix over his shoulder.

"Not long at all," said Dârio. "I'm going to commission wide belts for every member of the Conclave and give them as gifts at midsummer. They'll be in kingdom colors and I expect all but a few contrarians will wear them."

Felix laughed. "There are only a few contrarians among Dâron's wizards?" he asked. "Quintillius should be so lucky."

"Oh? I thought the Roma were a well-organized and highly-regimented people," said Dârio. "At least that's your reputation."

"You're right, at least when it comes to military matters," said Felix, "but not in anything outside that sphere. Roma are driven by duty and honor—but we're also motivated by self-interest, just like any other people. Wide belts are a military requirement for wizards.

We wear them because it helps us transport soldiers or couriers, and we're never sure when we might be pressed into service."

Dârio could see muscles in the young wizard's neck tense up.

"Are there other reasons?" he asked.

"Yes," said Felix. "The loops are also helpful for certain *qua-qua* maneuvers."

"*Qua-qua?* That three-dimensional game Roma wizards play?" asked Dârio.

"Correct," said Felix. "It's not considered good form, but sometimes a group of up to four wizards will join into a single wall, holding their belt handles, and slam into single wizards on the opposing team, knocking them down a level. The tactic is called a *sweep,* and some purists insist it is ruining the game."

"Fascinating," said Dârio. "I had no idea. Are *you* a purist?"

Felix laughed again. "Not at all. Most of them are too old to play any longer. I'm still young and have been pleased to *sweep* my opponents many times. There's nothing more satisfying than knocking a fellow wizard..."

"Look!" said Dârio. "There's Arthábben—and there's the Dormant Dragon."

The small village twenty miles below Brendinas along the river and close to the battlefield was a collection of a few dozen cottages with blue-slate roofs. The inn, at the south end of the village, was its largest building. It was even larger than the two long, low structures Dârio spotted. He took one of them to be a communal cow barn but didn't recognize the purpose of the one near the river. From the air, they could see three stone docks just east of the undetermined building. They extended out into the Brenavon with fishing boats of various sizes alongside them.

"Where should I land?" asked Felix.

"In the inn's courtyard," replied Dârio. He could see two small children playing some sort of skipping game on the slates covering the courtyard.

"Shall we give the children a show?" asked Felix. "Hang on and lean out," he said, without waiting for Dârio to answer.

From a hundred feet up, Felix began to rotate his flying disk, spinning it faster and faster, like a double-winged maple seed pod descending. The tall young wizard's purple cloak flapped out in the wind, contrasting with Dârio's light-blue surcoat. Dârio even managed to draw his sword with his right hand while leaning out and holding on to the Roma wizard's belt with his left. The sword sparkled in the afternoon sun like it was made from ice crystals. Dârio hoped they looked impressive.

Two feet from the ground, Dârio hopped off the flying disk and bowed to the girls. Felix touched down lightly and flipped his flying disk up into his hands with an artful bit of footwork. He stowed the flying disk on his back and snapped his arms out to maximum extension, letting his robes catch the strong breeze off the river.

The girls had watched the descent and landing with wide eyes. Once Dârio and Felix were both on the ground, the girls looked at each other and shrugged.

"Are you supposed to be the king?" asked one girl who seemed almost indistinguishable from her sister. "Momma Coegi said you were the king."

"When is the wyvern coming back?" asked the other girl. "Doethan said we could ride him."

"Your mother's right, I *am* the king," said Dârio. "I'm glad to have you both as my steadfast and loyal subjects." He bowed, then slid his sword into its sheath in a fluid motion.

The second girl turned to the first one. "What does steadfast mean?" she whispered.

"I don't know," the first girl whispered back. "Just smile and bow."

While the girls smiled and bowed, Dârio tried to hide a grin and Felix raised one of the sleeves of his purple robe in front of his mouth so the girls wouldn't be able to see his expression.

"The sick man is inside," said the first girl. "He's on one of the tables in the common room."

"Momma Gwest said we should play out here and stay out of people's way," said the other. "Are we in *your* way?"

"Are kings people?" the first girl asked the second. "What about wizards?" She scrunched her eyes and tilted her head, staring at Felix. "Where are you from?"

"Nova Eboracum in Occidens Province," said Felix.

"You're really tall," said the first girl. "And you must be a Roma. Roma are good soldiers. My name is Plenna and I want to be a soldier when I grow up."

"Practice with your weapons every day when you're older," said Felix, "and for now, try to do what your mother tells you. Soldiers have to learn to follow lots of orders."

"We have two mothers," said the other girl. "My name is Mercha and I want to be an innkeeper like Momma Gwest."

"Both are worthy roles," said Dârio. "Can you tell us who is inside the inn?"

"The sick man in fancy green robes, the tall wizard in plain green robes..." began Plenna, as if reciting from a list.

"The wizard lady who was here yesterday with red hair that looks like a dandelion," said Mercha, "and the old grumpy wizard without much hair."

"Damon," said Dârio.

"Uh huh," said Plenna. "He went in a few hours ago, but we haven't seen him in a while. We haven't seen the short, older wizard-lady wearing a hood who held his hand since she went in, either."

"Astrí," said Dârio with a smile.

"We did hear a loud *pop* though," said Mercha.

"It was a funny sound," Plenna added.

"An *ad hoc* gate," said Felix as an aside to Dârio. "Laetícia makes a similar sound when she gates out."

"Doethan is here, too," said Plenna.

"We want him to give us another ride on his flying disk," said Mercha.

"The high lady with strands of pearls in her piled-up hair..." continued Plenna.

"Princess Gwýnnett," supplied Dârio.

"She's a *princess? Ick!*" said Mercha.

"She's also my mother," said Dârio.

Mercha didn't reply, she just looked at Dârio then lowered her eyes and moved her head slowly from side to side. Dârio often shared the same expression when dealing with his mother. He shrugged.

"Anyone else?" Dârio asked.

"A nice lady wizard with brown hair," said Plenna. "She was taking care of the sick man in green robes."

"And her boyfriend," said Mercha. "She was mad at him, though."

"What makes you think he was her boyfriend?" asked Plenna.

"The way he kept making cow-eyes at her while she ignored him," said Mercha.

"Maybe," said Plenna. "I wonder what he did to make her mad?"

"I don't know," said Mercha. "But I hope we find out."

"Me, too," said Plenna. She put her hand on her chin and rubbed it. "I almost forgot. The *pothy-carry* is inside, too. He brought medicine."

"Apothecary?" asked Felix.

"Uh huh," said Plenna. "He came downriver in his boat. It has a grinding thing for herbs painted on its bow and he docked at one of the piers in the village. Mercha and I led him here."

"He came in a vessel with a pestle?" asked Felix.

"If that's what you call the grinding thing," said Plenna.

Felix could see both girls playing with the new word on their tongues.

Dârio tried one last time before the girls were too distracted. "Have you told us about everyone inside the inn?"

"Uh huh," said Mercha. "All the guests, anyway. Momma Gwest sent the rowdy wizards in green down to the drying shed with a small cask of ale to get them out of the way."

"Drying shed?" asked Dârio.

"For fish," said Felix. Growing up along the sound between Insula Longa and southern Tamloch, he'd understood the girls' reference immediately.

"Oh," said Dârio. "The odd building by the river. Of course."

"We don't let the cows near it," said Plenna.

"It makes their milk smell bad," said Mercha.

"And we can't have that," said Felix. "Thank you, ladies. You've been a big help."

"You're welcome, good wizard," said Plenna.

"Please, call me Felix," he said, smiling.

"I'll be sure to remind the wizard with the wyvern about your ride," said Dârio.

"Yay!" shouted both girls. They jumped up and down and made happy sounds, then split apart and circled around Felix and Dârio, heading for the far side of the courtyard. Mercha repeated *the wizard with the wyvern* while Plenna kept saying *the vessel with the pestle* for several iterations, then the girls switched phrases.

Dârio looked at Felix. He raised an eyebrow and the corner of his mouth a tiny fraction. The wizard returned the gesture.

"After you, good wizard," said Dârio, moving his hand toward the main door of the Dormant Dragon.

"No, after you, Your Majesty," said Felix. He took three broad paces, extended one of his long arms, and opened the door.

Chapter 6

The Common Room

Dârio entered with Felix right behind him. The common room was bright, with afternoon sun streaming through the inn's western windows. Several robed figures clustered around a table, hiding who or what rested there. King Dârio was confident he knew the object of everyone's attentions.

"How is Túathal?" he asked. "Will he live?"

"I don't know," said Verro, who turned to face the young king. Tamloch's master mage's expression was grave.

"He'll live," said Uirsé, a young, brown-haired wizard who didn't waver in her attention to Túathal. "Once someone brought me my kit I gave him *two* healing potions for the poison's effects on his body." She took a dark glass phial from a middle-aged man with a long black beard and scarred hands. Dârio stepped forward and peered down to see Uirsé holding up Túathal's head and pouring the phial's contents down the king of Tamloch's throat. Túathal swallowed, reflexively.

"What was that, a *third* healing potion?" asked Felix from a point above and behind Dârio's right shoulder.

"No," said the man with the long black beard, "Two of those should be plenty. This contains various herbs and tinctures, but it's mostly finely-ground charcoal."

"To draw out the poison," said Felix.

"Precisely," said the bearded man. "We can only hope that it will soak up enough of the poison before it can completely enter his system."

"Thank goodness you could get here quickly," said Uirsé. She pulled the empty phial away from Túathal's lips then gently lowered his head back to a pillow on the planks of the table. "It was a stroke of luck that you were nearby," she said, nodding to the bearded man.

"Herophilos Bodégash, at your service," said the man. "I was staying with friends north of town, doing some fishing and dabbling in alchemical research when suddenly two armies showed up a mile from the place. It was disconcerting—then an hour ago one of the villagers from Arthábben started pounding on the door and shouting I was needed at the Dormant Dragon to help heal a sick man."

"Are you a hedge wizard?" asked Felix. "Do you know healing magic?"

"I, young man, am an *apothecary,*" said Herophilos, looking up at the Roma wizard. "I know the substances of the natural world and the workings of the human body. The proper application of one to the other can cure nearly any ill."

"If so, I thank you for your assistance," said Dârio.

"If so," said Bodégash. His face began to turn red and he looked ready to splutter a full-on tirade at King Dârio, but Felix diverted him.

"Your first name is Athican," he said. "Is it the one you were born with?"

The apothecary's puffed up manner abruptly deflated. "If you must know," he said quietly, "my parents named me Jubble. I gave myself the name of *Herophilos* after a famous Athican physician."

"That's understandable," said Felix. "I'd change my name too, if my parents had done something like that to me."

Herophilos seemed to warm a bit and smiled at Felix, then the young king got his attention.

"You're a doctor as well as an apothecary?" asked Dârio. He didn't know quite what to make of the man—he was evidently skilled, but carried a log, not a chip on his shoulder for some reason.

"I'm no wizard," said Herophilos, "but I do know something about healing."

"Particularly regarding poisons," said Uirsé. "He's the author of *Poisons and Their Antagonists.* Copies of it circulate in Riyas and beyond, not just in Dâron."

"So you're a treasure of my realm," said Dârio. "I'm *very* pleased you were close at hand."

Herophilos beamed and swelled in response to his monarch's praise.

"How was the fishing, by the way?" added Dârio.

"Not so good until that huge fireball went off yesterday afternoon," said the apothecary. "After that, I filled my creel with trout in less than an hour and landed a river sturgeon almost as big as my boat."

"Good for you," said Dârio. "What's *your* prognosis for your patient?"

"Observe his face," said Herophilos. "Notice he's no longer pallid and his breathing is more even." He touched Uirsé's shoulder and she leaned back so Dârio and Felix could see Túathal's face and chest. Tamloch's king did look better—though that still left a lot of room for improvement.

"Fetch me cool cloths," ordered Uirsé.

Salder, who'd been standing on the far side of the table, bowed and said, "Yes, my love," before running off to find Gwest, the innkeeper, and fulfill Uirsé's request. The dark-haired wizard scowled at Sal's retreating back, then shook her head and offered a small smile.

Dârio and Felix shared a quick glance. After listening to the girls outside in the courtyard, the young king was rooting for Salder, and he expected the tall Roma wizard was as well.

Fercha stood next to Verro on the far side of the table. Dârio and Felix walked around the table to stand beside them.

"It's good to see you again," said Felix.

Fercha nodded at Felix. "Good to see you as well," she said. "Does Mafuta need me for the wide water gate already?"

"She does," said Felix.

"So, Dârio, why don't you just order the fleet to return to Riyas," said Verro. "Túathal named you his son and heir. With him incapacitated, you *are* the heir to Tamloch."

"Will you join me to meet the Tamloch fleet's grand admiral and confirm my claim?"

"I won't be leaving my brother's side," said Verro. He put his arm around Fercha and gave her a hug. "Go, my love," said Verro. He tilted his head a few inches and whispered something in her ear. Fercha nodded.

"Do you think they'll be fit to work magic?" she said.

"Send the apothecary over to the fish-drying shed with some phials of charcoal," said Verro. "That should sober them up."

"Right," said Fercha. She smiled and pulled Herophilos aside. After speaking softly with the bearded man for a few minutes, Dârio saw Herophilos nod, grab a leather bag, and leave by the front door. Fercha returned and kissed Verro with enough intensity that Felix and Dârio looked away. She left the common room like the apothecary, accompanied by Felix.

"Good luck," said Dârio. Felix raised a hand to acknowledge the king's sendoff, but Fercha seemed too single-minded to hear. Verro and Dârio were left side by side, looking at Túathal on the table.

"He's looking better," said Verro.

"He is," said Dârio. "I can see the improvement, even in the short time I've been here."

"I thought he was dying," said Verro.

"Is he really my father?" asked Dârio.

"He is," said Verro. "I ran my own set of consanguinity tests to confirm it."

"That means you're my uncle," said Dârio. "Fercha seems fond of you."

"You could say that," said Verro. "She married me."

"That's not a guarantee of affection," noted Dârio.

"No, it's not," said Tamloch's master mage. "If it helps, she married me *before* Nûd was conceived."

"I don't think that matters to me one way or the other," said Dârio, "but it does mean that Nûd is the rightful king of Dâron, though he doesn't want the job."

"Why so?" asked Verro. "It's strange that I don't know anything about my son."

"And I don't know anything about my father," Dârio replied. "I don't know much more about Nûd than you do. I met him yesterday afternoon on board the Bifurland flagship."

"Oh," said Verro. "Why do you think he's not interested in being king?"

"Because he told me as much," said Dârio. "Nûd is an odd duck."

"If he grew up in Melyncárreg with Damon for company, he'd have to be," said Verro. "Sometimes Damon is too clever for his own good. I've heard stories about the way he trains apprentices, like sending them out to a valley full of basilisks to find their magestones."

"That sounds far too close to sending them to die to me," said Dârio. "Damon didn't seem deliberately sadistic to me."

"Oh, the apprentices weren't in danger of dying," said Verro. "At least not according to a defector I interviewed. Damon has a gate to the valley and would step in to save them from being eaten if they were turned to stone."

"Kind of him," said Dârio. "He didn't keep a statue garden behind his castle?"

Verro chuckled. "Maybe he does, but not from what my source said. Besides, petrification from the gaze of a basilisk only lasts for an hour or two. It wears off on its own, if you're not eaten first."

"Good to know," said Dârio. "Speaking of interrogations, where's my mother and were you able to get her to tell you anything about the poison?"

"She's upstairs in a private room," said Verro. "Doethan is with her. Salder gave her more of the sleeping potion after I talked to her and she's going to be out until morning."

"What did she tell you?" asked Dârio.

Verro led Dârio away from the table where Túathal was resting and over to a far corner of the common room.

"She said she'd been plotting with my brother for years," he whispered. "Túathal was going to make her his queen, then abdicate in your favor and rule both kingdoms through you, with your mother's potions helping him control you."

Dârio shook his head in disgust. "Nothing you could tell me about my mother would surprise me."

"I was aware of Túathal's agenda, but not about *her* plans," Verro continued. "After Tamloch's army was routed by the wisents, Princess Gwýnnett must have decided that ruling both kingdoms through you without Túathal's assistance would have given her a stronger position."

Dârio let out a long stream of air. "What can I do with her?"

"There are only two options," said Verro.

Dârio stared at the green wizard.

"Death, or exile."

"I was hoping you'd provide another alternative," said Dârio. "I'm not going to kill my own mother. I may have had to play at being a monster, but I'm not one."

"Good," said Verro. He looked over at the table where Uirsé was tending Túathal.

"Had he crossed the line?" asked Dârio.

"Probably," said Verro. He took a calming breath. "No, definitely. I let personal loyalty blind me to what he had become."

"So," said Dârio. "Exile for them both?"

"Together," said Verro. "They'd be fitting companions for each other."

"Where?" asked Dârio. "Far to the west? In a deep cavern?"

"Perhaps," said Verro. "Or on an island."

"You won't try to rescue them?"

"No," said Verro. "It seems clear that you'd make a far better king for Tamloch than my brother."

"That's not a high bar," said Dârio.

Verro nodded and smiled. "True enough," he said. "You can set a new standard."

"Will you help me—uncle?"

"I will," said Verro.

Then the relative calm of the common room vanished when they heard a woman's high-pitched scream.

Chapter 7

Savory Pies

Dârio sprinted for the stairs while Verro called after him.

"Let me know if you need help," said the green mage to Dârio's back. Footsteps on treads were the only response. A second scream resounded as Dârio reached the top of stairs, making it easy for him to identify the room where they were coming from. It was two doors down on the right. Dârio turned the handle and put his shoulder to the door but it didn't open. It felt like the heavy oak portal was bolted from the inside.

"Open up! Open up!" shouted Dârio. He banged his fists against the portal.

"I've got everything under control," said Doethan's muffled voice. "There's nothing to worry about."

"Save me, son!" said Princess Gwýnnett from the far side of the door. "He's killing me!"

Dârio stopped pounding on the door and stood back. He'd been dealing with his mother long enough to know he trusted Doethan more than Gwýnnett. For that matter, he trusted the lowliest street sweeper in Brendinas more than his mother.

"Is there anything I can do?" asked Dârio.

"You could bring me some chicken-and-egg pie if the cook has made more," said Doethan. "I'm getting hungry."

Dârio felt the muscles in his shoulders relax. If Doethan was more concerned about his stomach than Gwýnnett things couldn't be that bad on the other side of the door.

"I'll check," said the young king.

"Don't leave me!" screamed Gwýnnett. "He's poisoning me!"

"Then I'm sure the two of you will enjoy comparing techniques," said Dârio. He stomped down the hall and imitated a heavy tread going downstairs before walking on tiptoe back to the door to his mother's room. He leaned in and put his ear to the door. It wasn't often he had a chance to hear his mother talk when she wasn't the one in charge. Dârio was pleased that a narrow gap in the door's planking let him hear the conversation on the other side clearly.

"It's time for you to go back to sleep," said Doethan. "You're upset. You need your rest."

"I *don't* need to rest. I've been asleep for hours," said Gwýnnett. "I know the potion that blasted boy used and one dose should only be good for half an hour. How much have you given me?"

"Not enough, apparently," said Doethan. "You're still awake."

"Of course I'm awake, you idiot," said Gwýnnett. "You don't think I didn't build up a tolerance to the most common poisons and potions, did you?"

"It's not something I ever gave much thought to," said Doethan. "I much prefer working with potions that heal, rather than harm."

"That's why you needed Ealdamon to save you in the Conclave," said Gwýnnett. "Hibblig would have beaten you into a stain on the floor if *he* hadn't interfered."

"I remember things differently," said Doethan. "You've trained your spies to only tell you what you want to hear."

"Nonsense," said Gwýnnett. "Now untie me and let me go. I've got to see to Túathal."

"You've done more than enough for Túathal already," said Doethan. "You *could* help by telling me the exact poison you put in his goblet..." Doethan's voice trailed off.

"Why would *I* poison Túathal?" said Gwýnnett. "We're going to be married, you know."

Dârio sighed. Was his mother really losing her mind or was she as crazy as a fox, hoping to lull Doethan into underestimating her. Dârio had dealt with Gwýnnett all his life and *he* couldn't tell. He softly stepped down the hall and downstairs to the common room, where he shrugged his shoulders in response to Verro's inquiring glance. Verro replied with an answering shrug. It was a gesture Princess Gwýnnett often inspired.

A moment later, Dârio entered the kitchen. Coegi, the cook, was checking a wisent haunch roasting on a spit in the hearth. It seemed a few of the huge beasts Eynon had driven onto the battlefield had wandered south to Arthábben and been conscripted for locals' dinners.

"Do you have any more of that delicious egg-and-chicken pie, dear lady?" asked Dârio. "Doethan said he'd appreciate a slice, and truth to tell, I'd enjoy one myself."

"Sorry," said Coegi as she gave the spit a turn, causing a few drops of fat to sizzle on the coals. "There's no more egg-and-chicken pie, but I made two similar pies filled with bacon, eggs, green onions, and cheese." She pointed with her free hand. "They're on the counter behind you."

Dârio turned and saw the pies. They had delicately fluted crusts and smelled wonderful.

"I'm sure these pies will be a more than adequate alternative," said Dârio with a smile. "They seem like all the elements of a hearty breakfast in one slice."

"Our guests haven't complained over the years," said Coegi. "There's a knife in the block to your right for cutting and turned wooden plates in the cupboard to your left."

"Thank you," said Dârio. He took three small plates from the cupboard and found a sharp knife where Coegi had designated, then cut three generous slices from one of the pies and put each one on a plate. He thought Doethan and his mother might appreciate some cider to go with their pie. "May I have a tray, some mugs, and a pitcher of cider, please?" he asked.

"Of course, Your Majesty," said Coegi.

"Call me Dârio."

"Yes, Your Majesty." Coegi smiled. "There's a pitcher of cider in the cold box. Please ask Doethan if he could put a spell on a second one before he leaves, if you would. It would be a big help. There are goblets and a tray in the closed cabinet below the cupboard."

"Thank you again," said Dârio. "I'll have to pay for you to visit Brendinas to teach *my* cooks how to make your marvelous savory pies."

"That's very kind of you," said Coegi. She wiped a drop of sweat from her forehead and smiled. "You're very polite for a king, Dârio," she said. "Not at all like the stories I've heard."

"I'll take that as a compliment," said Dârio.

"How is your mother?" Coegi inquired. "Those screams were disconcerting. The children were worried, and so was I."

"I'm very sorry about Gwýnnett," said Dârio, surprised at how much his words resonated. Psychological pain washed through him as he realized he was effectively an orphan, with a father he didn't know and a mother he didn't respect. For a moment, he wished Túathal and Gwýnnett would both die and end his pain—then he was consumed by shame at his thoughts. *Does it make me a monster to wish my monstrous parents dead?* he considered.

He pushed down his pain and glanced at Coegi. The cook hadn't noticed his detached expression. Dârio took slow breaths and submerged his feelings in the mundane task of stacking plates, goblets, and a pitcher full of cold cider on a tray.

"There are napkins in the drawer," said Coegi.

"Thanks," said Dârio. He took three napkins and saw they each were decorated with childish embroidery in bright colors. All the designs were variations on the blue dragon painted on the wall of the common room. Dârio smiled. Plenna and Mercha must have done the stitching. The child-like honesty of their needlework reassured him about Dâron's prospects for the future.

"Dario?" asked Coegi.

"Yes?"

"Will you pay for all four of us to come to Brendinas? Gwest and the girls as well? Gwest's uncle can come down to mind the inn while we're away."

"Of course," said Dârio.

"That would be very nice," said Coegi. "I'd like the girls to see the capital."

"I'll see you all have a guided tour of the palace," said Dârio, "and will make sure Plenna has a chance to see a training session for the royal guards."

Coegi gave Dârio a smile twice as bright as the glowing coals on the hearth. "That's very kind of you," she said.

"It's all self-interest on my part," said Dârio. "I want to enjoy your delicious pies in the palace, not just on my visits to the Dormant Dragon."

"Of course, Your Majesty," said Coegi.

They both laughed and Dârio left the kitchen, laden tray in hand. Verro nodded in his direction as he stepped into the common room.

"How's Túathal?" asked Dârio.

Uirsé answered, not Verro. "Much better," she said. "He's sleeping peacefully. I think he's past the worst of it."

Verro abruptly sat on a bench and slumped, looking like an unstrung longbow. Dârio understood how he felt—he'd had to stay strong, at least in public, while feeling drained. He remembered how he felt when Prince Dâri, the man he thought of as his father, had died two years ago. It was a relief to be able to show weakness. He put his tray down on the table behind Verro and touched his new-found uncle's shoulder.

"There's savory pie and cold cider in the kitchen," said Dârio. "You and Uirsé would both benefit from something to eat and drink."

"I'll fetch some in a minute," said Verro. He rubbed his forehead and stretched his long limbs. "Everything was alright upstairs? The screams weren't important?"

"Just Gwýnnett being Gwýnnett," said Dârio.

"I'm worried about how my brother will react when he wakes and realizes his grand plans have gone awry," said Verro. "Part of me doesn't want to be here when he does."

"I feel the same way," said Dârio. "I don't even want to see my mother when I take this tray to her room." The young king sighed and took a seat on a bench opposite Verro. "Want to fly us west and go hunting with me on a royal preserve?" asked Dârio.

"You know the answer to that," said Verro. "Spending time getting to know you would be wonderful, but we both have responsibilities." Verro sat up straight and stared at Dârio. "What do *you* want, nephew? Do you *want* to rule Tamloch? I dare say you'd do a better job of it than your father, much as I hate to sound disloyal to my brother, but he's never done much to encourage loyalty."

"What do *I* want?" asked Dârio. "I want to be a good king—of Dâron or Tamloch or both together. Uniting the kingdoms *might* avoid a good deal of strife in the years to come, if Tamloch's people and nobles would accept me, and if Nûd truly doesn't want the throne of Dâron."

"Sounds like we need to learn the answer to that question before either one of us can move forward," said Verro. "And I want to get to know my son. I still can't believe Fercha kept him from me all these years."

"I'm not thrilled with Fercha, either," said Dârio. "Apparently, she knew that Túathal was my father, and so did Astrí and Queen Carys. The three of them are not on my list of favorite people right now. Speaking of Astrí, where is she? And where's Damon? I thought the two of them came south with the rest of you?"

"It was very crowded in the inn. They saw Túathal was in good hands and left a few hours ago," said Verro. "They didn't say where they were going. Damon just made an *ad hoc* gate and they left."

Dârio shook his head and laughed. "That means you're the only one of my master mages left to advise me."

"I'll try my best," said Verro.

"I appreciate it," said Dârio. "Once I've delivered this food to Doethan and my mother, I can eat my own slice."

"And I'll get something to eat and ensure Uirsé eats, too," said Verro.

At that moment, Salder rushed through the back door of the inn carrying a bucket full of wet cloths.

"Sorry it took me so long," he said. He delivered the cloths to Uirsé and the two of them worked together to position them on Túathal's face and forehead.

"Just a moment," said Dârio. He returned to the kitchen, cut another slice of savory pie and collected another goblet.

Verro watched him with a question in his eyes.

"Salder," said Dârio. "Get some cider and pie from the kitchen for yourself and Uirsé. Verro and I are going upstairs to see my mother."

"As you wish," said Verro. He looked back at his brother, shook his head slowly, and followed Dârio up the stairs.

Chapter 8

Gwýnnett's Room

Dârio held the tray while Verro knocked twice on the door to Gwýnnett's room.

"Let us in," said the king. "I've brought you pie and cider."

"Who's with you?" asked Doethan from the far side of the door.

"Verro," said Dârio.

"Would it be easier for you if I opened the door?" asked Verro.

Dârio wasn't sure if Tamloch's master mage was addressing him or Doethan. Part of his mind wondered if there was a way to craft locks that wizards couldn't open.

"No, I'll get it," said Doethan's voice, a bit muffled by the thick wood.

A few seconds later they heard a key inserted and turned. The door opened and Doethan welcomed them into the room, which was larger and better furnished than the usual accommodations at an inn, though the Dormant Dragon *was* the first major stop on the main road from Brendinas to the southern provinces, fiefs and baronies.

Dârio estimated the room to be twenty feet long by fifteen wide, with a pair of large, leaded-glass windows as tall as a man in a broad alcove on the outer wall across from him. To Dârio's left was a canopied bed large enough to sleep four comfortably, or six on a busy night with lots of travelers passing through. There was space for another guest to sleep on the padded seat in the nook below the windows and the king assumed the room could hold still more people if there were slide-out trundle beds beneath the canopied bed.

Both of the tall leaded-glass windows were open to let in the warm afternoon air. Dârio spotted a fat tabby tomcat warming himself in a sunbeam outside on the west side of the window ledge. The cat regarded Dârio with one eye and yawned. *Even a cat can look on a king,* thought Dârio. He smiled, thinking about the good-hearted nanny who'd first shared that saying with him back when he was five. It was several years before he understood what it meant.

Only one person occupied the big bed at present—Dârio's mother, Princess Gwýnnett. She was nestled under a well-padded down quilt. The young king was surprised by her appearance. His mother's face was softer and gentler than he remembered. She usually looked like a predatory bird, an angry goshawk or sharp-beaked harpy eagle. Now, asleep, she looked more like a resting dove. Dârio shook his head slowly, wishing such a transformation could be permanent. He couldn't remember a single instance of his mother being kind to him, or to anyone for that matter, without an ulterior motive.

"There wasn't any egg-and-chicken pie, but Coegi made bacon, egg, cheese and green onion pies instead," said Dârio, handing the wizard the tray.

Doethan put it on top of a flat-topped chest and poured three mugs of cider. Each man took a mug and a plate with a slice of pie.

"Smells good," said Verro.

"Tastes good," said Doethan, biting off the end of his slice.

"Did she give you much trouble?" asked Dârio, pointing to the sleeping princess with the tip of his pie wedge.

"What do you think?" Doethan replied with a smile. "You were standing outside the door earlier and heard her ranting." He was alternating bites of pie and sips of cider.

"I thought I was being discreet," said Dârio. After a large bite of pie, he decided that Coegi would have to teach the palace cooks *this* recipe, too.

"Wizards have excellent hearing," teased Doethan. "When we choose to."

"I'll keep that in mind," said the young king.

"Thank you for guarding her," said Verro, licking his fingers. "Forgive me, nephew, but I was close to strangling Gwýnnett when I interrogated her. Your mother can be difficult."

"Tell me about it," said Dârio. "I've had to put up with her all my life."

"She seems peaceful enough now," said Verro. "What did you give her?" he asked Doethan.

"The same herbs Salder gave her earlier," said Doethan. "I plan to keep dosing her over the next several hours whenever she starts to wake up."

"The potion won't hurt her, will it?" asked Dârio. He was eying the slice of pie he'd cut for his mother, since it seemed she wouldn't be eating it.

"No, it's completely harmless, with no deleterious side effects," said Doethan. "I've used it to keep patients quiet for several weeks at a time while they recover from serious injuries. She'll be fine."

"I'm glad to hear that," said Dârio. "For now, I'm just glad I don't have to listen to her complaints and insults. We can let her wake when we've figured out what to do with her."

"You mean where to send her into exile?" asked Verro.

"I guess," said Dârio. "It's all so confusing. I need to exile her, and Túathal as well, though they're not my biggest worry. I'm the rightful heir to Tamloch, but *not* the rightful king of Dâron, and my cousin who *is* the rightful king is nowhere to be found. Should I try to rule both kingdoms separately? Or unite them under a single crown? It's a lot to think about."

"I can see why you don't want to worry about your mother as well, with so many other things on your mind," said Verro.

"Not that I can *help* thinking about her," said Dârio. "Having my own mother commit treason gives me a lot to think about."

"*Did* she commit treason?" asked Verro. "Her actions sought to *expand* your authority by making you king of Dâron *and* Tamloch."

"Under Túathal's thumb," noted Dârio.

"Then why did she poison my brother?" asked Verro.

"I see what you mean," Dârio replied.

"She thought you would be easier to control than Túathal," added Doethan.

"And she'd be right about that," said Dârio. "Especially if I forgot to test everything I ate or drank."

"The pie and cider are safe to consume, in case you were wondering," said Doethan with a smile.

"Hah!" said Dârio. "So much for my constant vigilance. I thought I wouldn't have to worry with my mother unconscious."

"It wouldn't be wise to stop having what you eat and drink

inspected," said Doethan. "Your mother is brilliant in her own way and is capable of anything. She engineered your very existence..."

"With help from my brother," said Verro.

"And she maneuvered things to have you rule two kingdoms..." Doethan continued.

"With help from my brother," Verro repeated.

All three men showed tight smiles.

"Fine," said Dârio. "She didn't commit treason, but I certainly can't have her remain in the kingdom where she could stir up trouble. Would the two of you ward a small island where she could be sent into exile?"

"I would," said Doethan.

"So would I," said Verro. "As I promised earlier. If my brother lives, it would be best to isolate him there as well. There are several candidates off the coast of Tamloch—the Isle of Vines and Bucket Island, for example."

"I'd rather have them closer to Dâron," said Dârio.

"There's an island near the mouth of the Moravon," said Doethan. "It's not on the fastest route to Tyford and is big enough to have plenty of game. I camped there once as a lad."

"What's it named?" asked Dârio.

"Weasel Island," said Doethan.

"Sounds perfect," said Verro. He gave a small laugh.

"There aren't any birds left on the island because the weasels ate their eggs," said Doethan.

"We can relocate my mother and Túathal there once he's recovered," said Dârio. "When should we make the formal announcement about Túathal naming me his son and heir?"

"Today," said Verro. "On the battlefield. Without delay. Duke Néillen and I heard Túathal. So did quite a few others. We can restate your claim for all the Tamloch nobles and field commanders."

Dârio rubbed his chin and nodded.

"I'd emphasize being named his heir, but not his son," said Verro. "We don't want to confuse your claim on the throne of Dâron until we've had a chance to talk to *my* son."

"That's good advice," said Dârio. "I hope we can get Nûd to accept his birthright."

"When we go back to the battlefield I can encourage Duke Néillen to join me in reaching out to Grand Admiral Sónnel," said Verro. "Perhaps the two of us together can get him to call off the naval attack on Nova Eboracum."

"Let's hope that works," said Dârio.

"The Roma have been good allies," said Doethan. "I don't want to see them—or the Bifurlanders—lose good people."

Dârio and Verro both held up their mugs to signal their agreement.

Princess Gwýnnett moaned softly. She shifted on the bed and settled closer to the edge near the king and two wizards. Verro stepped beside Gwýnnett and put two fingers along her neck to feel her pulse.

"It's still strong," he said. Then Verro's eyes went wide. *Too strong,* he realized.

Dârio noticed the tomcat leave its perch on the window ledge and leap from the alcove to the bed. The feline's teeth were bared and the hair on his back was standing up. The tomcat turned to face the tall leaded-glass windows and hissed. The young king's eyes flicked toward the windows, but then were drawn to another movement on the bed. Dârio watched, wide-eyed, as Gwýnnett's hand shot out from under the quilt. A sharpened fingernail on her right little finger jabbed into the flesh of Verro's forearm and bit in like a tiny dagger, drawing blood. Gwýnnett sat up and Verro's body went stiff and toppled on the bed like a falling tree landing in the spot she had recently occupied.

Doethan heard the tomcat hiss again, louder this time, and took a step back as he saw Hibblig and two other broad-shouldered wizards in striped robes fly in through the open windows. The intruding newcomers landed their flying disks on the room's wooden floor with a trio of loud thumps.

Two seconds later, Doethan was knocked to the floor when Hibblig's fist collided with his jaw. One of Hibblig's companions held Dârio in place with a constricting sphere of solidified sound. The big wizard instructed the third intruding wizard to make sure Doethan stayed down and crossed to Gwýnnett.

The princess turned one corner of her mouth up in a sneer. She took Hibblig's elbow and paused for a moment to mock the others.

"I've found it pays to build up an immunity to common potions," she said. "Too bad Verro didn't do the same."

Hibblig boarded his flying disk and Gwýnnett stepped on behind him, putting her arms around Hibblig's waist in a familiar way that made Dârio feel even more uncomfortable than present circumstances warranted. The disk rose and slowly flew out the tall leaded-glass windows that were open to let in the spring air. The remaining pair of wizards in striped-blue robes followed. Dârio heard the tomcat hiss again and yowl as they departed. Seconds later, the sphere of solidified sound holding him in place disappeared with a snap of in-rushing air.

"Are you all right?" Dârio asked Doethan as he helped the wizard to his feet.

"I'll live," said Doethan, rubbing his jaw. "But I'd better see to Verro. He doesn't look good." He stepped to the bed and took in Verro's rigid form, then felt the Tamloch wizard's neck and grimaced. "Looks like distilled basilisk-gaze venom," said Doethan.

"Blast!" said Dârio. He moved to the open windows and stared out at the silhouettes of three flying disks rapidly heading south. It was too late to do anything about them now.

He checked the angle of the sun. It wasn't too far past noon— there *was* still time for the other items on his plate. He needed to revive Verro, return to the battlefield, claim the throne of Tamloch, and stop the invading Tamloch fleet. Dârio hoped Fercha's mission to gate the Bifurlanders' ships to Nova Eboracum harbor would be successful, but ultimately unnecessary.

"Verro!" came a shout from Uirsé below. "Come down here. Túathal is waking up."

Dârio noticed a strange, distracted look on Doethan's face. The wizard's eyes moved to stare at his left hand. One of his rings was pulsing.

Chapter 9

Expect the Unexpected

"Did you hear me?" shouted Uirsé. "What's going on up there? Who's making all that noise?"

"We heard you," replied Dârio, raising his own voice. "We need you up here right away. Have Salder stay with Túathal. Verro's petrified."

"Verro?" shouted Uirsé. "I'll be right up!"

A few moments later, Dârio heard footsteps on the stairs and Uirsé entered the room carrying two leather bags, one tooled with a mortar and pestle design—from the apothecary, Dârio expected.

Uirsé saw Verro's unmoving body on the bed, took two steps and sat beside him. Doethan was now in a far corner of the room, conversing with someone through the circular interface of a communications ring.

"How long has he been like this?" asked Uirsé.

"Only a minute or two," said Dârio. "Doethan said it was distilled basilisk-gaze venom."

"I said it *looked like* distilled basilisk-gaze venom," said Doethan, temporarily turning away from his ring's interface.

"How do you distill a basilisk's gaze?" asked Dârio.

"From the blood of its victims," replied Uirsé. The expression on her face made Dârio feel like he was the only person on this side of the Ocean unaware of that fact.

"Is there anything you can do for him?" asked Dârio.

"We could just wait for it to wear off," said Uirsé. "Assuming that's what it is. I agree with Doethan, that's the most likely cause, at least from what I've read."

"What else could it be?" asked Dârio.

"First, tell me how it happened," said Uirsé. She put her hand inside the neck of his robes and felt his chest. "He's still warm. That's a good sign."

"Things were a little confusing here," said Dârio. "Hibblig and two other wizards in my mother's faction broke into the room and took her."

"I noticed she was missing," said Uirsé. "Losing your mother is rather careless of you—and who's Hibblig?"

Dârio took Uirsé's rebuke in stride. "Hibblig is an over-muscled wizard who wants to be Dâron's master mage. From what I heard, he'd defeated Doethan in a duel in Dâron's Conclave to claim the title until Ealdamon returned to put him in his place."

Doethan turned his head and spoke again. "He hadn't defeated me. I was holding my own and had him right where I wanted him."

"Whatever," said Uirsé, waving her free hand dismissively. "Tell me how Verro was poisoned."

"Envenomed," said Doethan from his far corner. "Probably."

Dârio shook his head. Uirsé rolled her eyes.

"I'm not exactly sure *what* my mother did," said Dârio. "She grabbed his arm and he fell on the bed."

"Which arm?"

"The right one, I think."

"Help me move him," Uirsé commanded, sounding like a senior physician, not a junior wizard. Together, Uirsé and Dârio removed Verro's flying disk and adjusted his body so that he was on his back and positioned as if he were sleeping in the bed instead of sprawled across it. Uirsé pulled back Verro's right sleeve and inspected his arm.

"Here it is," she said, pointing out a small, half-moon-shaped bruise to Dârio. The skin around it was an odd shade of gray— more like stone than flesh.

"What does it mean?" the young king asked.

"It means your mother *did* administer distilled basilisk-gaze venom," said Uirsé.

"How long will it take to wear off?"

"A few hours," said Uirsé. "Victims are usually eaten much sooner than that."

"I don't see anyone here planning to eat Verro," said Dârio. He spared a second to glance at the tomcat who was now casually grooming himself at the foot of the bed. The cat looked back at Dârio and raised his upper lip, showing long sharp teeth. Dârio smiled at him and resolved to keep a close eye on the feline.

Uirsé said, "Hah!" and noted the tomcat's teeth as well.

"Two hours will be far too long," said Dârio. "Verro and I have to tell the Tamloch army I'm Túathal's heir and stop a naval invasion of Nova Eboracum as soon as possible."

Uirsé put the leather bag on the bed next to Verro. "I'd better try something faster then," she said.

"Please," said Dârio.

Uirsé's eyes moved from Dârio's feet to the top of his head. "What kind of a king would *you* be?" she asked.

"A far-better one than Túathal," said Doethan, turning away from his remote conversation again.

Uirsé smiled a tight smile. "I'll cure Verro quickly for his own sake, not yours," she said. She reached into the leather bag and pulled out a tiny phial about the size of the last two joints of her delicate little finger.

"What's that?" asked Dârio.

"Immolation Bird tears," said Uirsé. "They're quite rare, and they'll wake anything."

"I thought Immolation Birds were only in children's stories," said Dârio. "Are you telling me they're real?"

"They're real enough," said Uirsé, "and they're quite a problem for foresters during the dry season. The reason they're rare is because their tears not only counteract basilisk-gaze venom, they also rekindle desire in men and women."

"Given that, I'm surprised there are any Immolation Birds left on this side of the mountains," said Dârio.

"I never said there were," Uirsé replied. She gently opened Verro's immobile mouth and put one drop from the phial on his tongue.

For a few seconds, nothing happened. Uirsé took Verro's hand and tried to curl his fingers around hers, but they were stiff and unmoving. Dârio could see very small movements as Verro's chest rose and fell.

A dozen heartbeats later, Uirsé smiled when Verro's fingers bent of their own accord. Tamloch's master mage squeezed Uirsé's hand and his eyes snapped open. They seemed full of panic, as if his mind was trapped inside a body it couldn't control, which wasn't far from the truth.

"Be patient, you're under my care," said the brown-haired wizard. "You've been petrified, but I've given you a counteragent and you'll be fine in a few more minutes."

Verro's eyes calmed and his chin shifted down in a hint of a nod.

"See," said Uirsé. "Your muscle control is already returning."

Dârio put his palm on Verro's shoulder. "You're in good hands, uncle," he said. "We'll head north as soon as you've recovered."

Verro nodded again, his chin moving farther this time.

"I have to talk to Doethan," said Dârio. "But I'll be nearby on the far side of the room if you need me."

This time, Verro smiled, or at least the corners of his mouth turned up slightly. Dârio smiled back and walked over to stand behind Doethan, where he could see who was on the other side of the communications interface. It was Merry and Eynon, with Nûd behind them. All three looked worried.

Don't we all, thought Dârio.

Eynon was speaking, and the young king heard his own name mentioned.

"Dârio has to come to the quarry west of the Coombe right away," said Eynon. "His claim to Tamloch's throne is ahead of Nûd's."

"Is Túathal still alive?" asked Merry. "It would be better for all of us if he wasn't."

"Túathal is alive," said Dârio. "He's even waking up. What's going on?"

"Hello, Dârio," said Eynon. "It's a long story. Doethan can tell you more. You need to get here as fast as you can."

"I can't come west right now," said Dârio. "I have to help our Roma allies by stopping an attack from Tamloch's fleet."

"This is a much bigger priority," said Merry. "Much *much* bigger."

"It can't be helped," said Dârio. "I'm headed back to the battle-field as soon as Verro recovers."

"Recovers from what?" asked Nûd. "Was my father hurt?"

"Yes, unfortunately," said Dârio. "My mother petrified him when she escaped."

"Gwýnnett escaped?" asked Merry.

"Will he be all right?" added Nûd.

"He'll be fine," said Dârio. "Uirsé gave him a counteragent and he should be back to normal in a few minutes."

"Thank goodness for *that,*" said Nûd.

"Hibblig and two other wizards from Gwýnnett's faction flew in and took her," added Doethan.

"That explains the red mark on your jaw," said Merry. Doethan nodded, rubbed his chin, and winced.

Dârio heard footsteps behind him but didn't turn. He assumed Verro was back on his feet and had come to join him.

"You should come back to the battlefield, Nûd," said Dârio. "Verro and I need to talk to you. You've got some big decisions to make and so do we."

"Bigger than you think," said Nûd. "For the sake of all Orluin, *don't* let Túathal wake up."

Dârio saw Merry and Eynon's eyes grow large. Nûd opened his mouth to warn Dârio, but it was too late.

"Why don't you want me to wake up?" asked Túathal from three steps behind Dârio.

The young king turned around and saw Túathal was still wearing his magnificent green robe with hundreds of quatrefoils picked out in gold thread. He held a broad-bladed kitchen knife to Salder's throat. It looked like the one Dârio had used to cut slices of pie. From the corner of his eye, Dârio could see Uirsé's body slumped on the bed on top of Verro.

"Let him go!" shouted Merry through the communications interface. She seemed ready to jump across the miles like it was a gate and wrestle the knife away from her brother's neck.

"Tell me why it's so important I shouldn't wake up, and I may release him," said Túathal. His upper lip pulled back in a false smile. "Do you know why, my boy?" he asked Dârio.

"They didn't have a chance to tell me," said Dârio. "What did you do to Uirsé?"

"Nothing permanent as yet," said Túathal, "though she deserves to die for failing to check the wine in the goblet this traitorous fool served me. I just gave her a dose of sleeping powder." He tilted his free hand, drawing attention to a large ring with a small open storage compartment.

"I'm not a traitor, and neither is she," said Salder, taking care not to jostle Túathal's arm as he spoke. The knife was perilously close to vital arteries. "I have always supported Dâron, and Uirsé knew nothing about it. She trusted me."

"So did I," said Túathal, "as much as I trust anyone. That makes you a traitor—to *me*."

Túathal moved the knife blade along Salder's neck, leaving a row of tiny red drops where the metal broke the skin. He leaned in toward the communications interface, focusing on Merry.

"Tell me what's so important that you want me asleep instead of awake," Túathal restated. "What big, *big* news do you have to share?"

"Don't tell him," said Nûd.

"She has to," said Eynon. "Salder is her brother. We can figure out another way to stop Túathal."

"I doubt it," said Túathal. "Now talk."

Doethan nodded imperceptibly at Merry. She started the story about flying west to find Nûd, then the communications interface began to deteriorate. First, every other word was unintelligible, then the entire circle filled with grainy clouds until the interface faded away, leaving a point of light in its center before disappearing completely.

"You think you're clever, don't you, wizard," said Túathal, addressing Doethan. "Not clever enough, though. I arrived in time to hear *Coombe* and *quarry,* so they must be where my brother's raid captured green magestones." Túathal raised his voice. "Wake up, brother! Push that wizard wench off you and let's get out of here. I don't know what's in that quarry, but it sounds like it will help me win my kingdom back."

Dârio calculated angles, trying to determine a way to stop Túathal without costing Salder his life. He couldn't find one.

"Verro, stop dawdling," said Túathal. "We need to leave."

"That's unfortunate," said Verro from the bed. "Alas, your queen-to-be, Gwýnnett, chose to petrify me before she left the inn a few minutes ago. It will be more than an hour before the effects wear off. I'm not going anywhere." Uirsé's body, at right angles to his, held him in place.

"Gwýnnett will get what *she* deserves soon, too," growled Túathal. "How will I get out of here now, I wonder?"

"There's a permanent gate to Brendinas off the kitchen," said Verro. "You have enough spies in Dâron's capital to figure something out from there."

"Very true," said Túathal. "Or I could make my way to Fercha's townhouse and take the gate the two of you use for your liaisons—if you'll give me the code phrases needed to enter her townhouse and trigger the gate."

"Glad to, brother," said Verro, "but you'll have to come to me, so I can whisper them in your ear. We don't want the world to know how to gate from Brendinas to the royal palace in Riyas."

"Wise as always," said Túathal. "Keep your distance," he said to Doethan and Dârio. They stayed on the far side of the room while Túathal shoved Salder over to where Verro lay on the bed.

"I would appreciate it if you'd move Uirsé," said Verro. "Her weight makes it hard for me to breathe."

"I have a better idea," said Túathal. He removed the knife from Salder's throat and positioned it next to Uirsé ribs. "You move her," he told Salder. "Pick her up and hold her. If you're holding her, you won't be able to attack me." Túathal spun the knife around in his hand. "Once you've moved her, the balance on this blade is good enough that I can throw it and strike her heart before you can stop me."

Salder nodded and didn't say anything. He stood behind Uirsé's body, put his arms under her shoulders, lifted her upright, and dragged her away from the bed. He stroked Uirsé's cheek with one hand.

Túathal leaned close to Verro so his brother could whisper the passwords.

"I'm sorry I can't take you with me," said Túathal. He touched a ring on Verro's finger. "I'll let you know when I'm back in Riyas."

"I—think—not," said Verro. Tamloch's master mage wrapped his hands around his brother's neck and began to squeeze.

Chapter 10

Fercha and the Fleet

Fercha's mind was still turning in circles like a dog chasing its tail over the morning's events as she guided her flying disk north and east to the river. Her thoughts whirled at the new possibilities now open to her and the people she cared about. Túathal might be dying and was certainly deposed as king of Tamloch. Dârio was acknowledged as his son and rightful heir. That was a surprise, Fercha considered, smiling at her own capacity for amazement.

On top of all that, her own long-held secrets were secrets no longer. She was revealed as Princess Seren's daughter and her son Nûd shown to be the true king of Dâron. She hoped Nûd would muster the confidence to assume his birthright. For that matter, Verro no longer backed his brother and was acting like an ally, not an enemy. That change was something she'd long hoped for, but not expected.

Does that mean we really might have a life together? Fercha mused. *After so many years of hiding, could it be possible?*

She put that thought aside on a high shelf in her mind and gazed down to search the dragonships on the Brenavon for signs of Mafuta and Felix. As expected, she saw flashes of purple among the dark furs and saffron-dyed shirts of the Bifurlanders on the flagship. Combining ego and exuberance, she corkscrewed her flying disk around a hundred feet above the flagship's tall mast until she was even with the crossbar holding its tightly furled sail, then she descended like a falling falcon to land on a bare spot of deck between the Roma wizards and Bifurland's seated king and queen.

"Ooo!" said Rannveigr from her spot on a thick fur between the thrones.

"Nice flying," said Sigrun, sitting beside her friend.

"Thank you, girls," said Fercha. She smiled and bowed to King Bjarni and Queen Signý, then turned to do the same for Mafuta and Felix. Fercha was surprised to see Quintillius, the governor of Occidens Province, standing between the two purple wizards. Quintillius was an inch or two taller than Felix, but more filled out and muscular.

"*Salve!*" said Quintillius.

"Hail!" Fercha replied. She continued turning and nodded to three wizards across from the Roma in richly embroidered amber robes with deep hoods who attended Bifurland's monarchs. The trio made Fercha uneasy, which she assumed was their intent. *Mystique can be a powerful tool,* she considered.

King Bjarni stood and opened his arms in a gesture of welcome. "I'm glad you're here," he said. "Mafuta tells me you've figured out how to build a gate that will get my fleet directly to Nova Eboracum harbor."

Sigrun, his young daughter, bounded up and hugged Fercha, then she stepped back, looked up, and started talking nonstop in a high piping soprano.

"Can you really make a magic gate through *water?* What about the magestone dust? Won't it wash off in the current? How can you make it big enough for ships and their masts to pass through?"

Rannveigr, Sigrun's friend and cousin, joined her fellow golden dragon rider and kept the questions going when Sigrun paused to take a breath.

"Does weight matter? Ships are so much heavier than soldiers. What has to be at the other end of the gate? Does it make a difference if one end is salt water and the other fresh?"

Fercha considered taking a step back, but space on the deck was tight so she held her ground. She could stand up to Verro and bullies like Hibblig without a qualm, but two girls in braids with an endless supply of questions were daunting. Queen Signý saved Fercha from having to answer, however.

"Sigrun. Rannveigr," said the queen in a regal, or perhaps maternal voice.

In this context, thought Fercha, *the two were much the same.*

"Sit down and let Fercha *show* you the answers to your questions," said Queen Signý.

"Thank you, Your Majesty," said Fercha. "I *can* build such a gate." She saw smiles on the faces of the Roma and King Bjarni and even detected traces of amusement in the body language of the three hooded Bifurland wizards. She turned her head to Mafuta. "Did you get everything I asked for?" Fercha asked.

"I did," said the older Roma wizard. "We had to buy up every foot of rope in Nova Eboracum to do it and cannibalize a few torsion catapults, but we've got enough for both ends of the gate."

"Excellent," said Fercha. "Take care with the splices."

"Of course," said Mafuta.

"We found enough waterproof glue in ships stores to check off that item," added King Bjarni.

"With luck, the glue won't need to be waterproof, but it can't hurt if it is," said Fercha. "What about *your* wizards?"

"We will do our part," said the hooded Bifurland wizard on the right. The amber-robed wizard's voice was pitched so it was hard to tell if the speaker was a man or a woman. "Other wizards from divisions of the fleet will be here soon to assist. We're quite eager to learn your technique for constructing marine gates."

I'll bet you are, thought Fercha. Bifurland ships had a history of showing up unexpectedly to raid other kingdoms' ports.

"And at your end?" Fercha asked Mafuta.

"Twenty wizards are on ships in Nova Eboracum harbor awaiting instructions," Mafuta replied.

Fercha saw Quintillius smiling at the thought of *his* wizards learning how to make large gates through water as well, though the Roma had always been more of a land than a sea power. *Perhaps it was unwise to share the techniques for making large gates more widely,* thought Fercha. *It will change the nature of war in Orluin for generations to come. Still, if Ealdamon could learn how to do it, so could others.* She straightened her shoulders and got on with the process.

"King Bjarni has graciously found space on his longships for my legions," said Quintillius, noting Fercha's glance. "It will get us home faster than marching back to our original gate."

"We Bifurlanders pride ourselves on our hospitality," said King

Bjarni. Queen Signý stifled a laugh. Fercha suspected some sort of side deal had been struck between Quin and Bjarni.

"First, we need to set up a system to dip the rope in glue, coat it with powdered magestone dust, and dry it," said Fercha. "You can handle that for yards of rope at a time."

Mafuta opened a communications-ring link to her colleagues to the north and relayed instructions while the three hooded Bifurland wizards raised their hands near their mouths and spoke quietly. King Bjarni, with help from Quintillius, instructed Bifurland warriors and Roma legionnaires aboard the flagship to organize the rope, the pots of glue, and stations for wizards with heat spells for drying. A few minutes later, two dozen Bifurland wizards on flying disks descended to occupy every bit of open space on the flagship that wasn't already claimed for coating rope. *These* wizards weren't wearing deep hoods like the ones attending Bjarni and Signý. They'd come from other longships in the Bifurland fleet and were dressed in the same sort of diversely creative ensembles that typified free wizards in Dâron.

I wonder if the only crown wizards in Bifurland are the ones wearing deep hoods, mused Fercha. *That would fit with what she knew of the Far Northerners' temperament.*

Fercha consulted with King Bjarni and Queen Signý and soon the flagship shifted to the west side of the Brenavon a hundred yards south of the thinning ice sheet and anchored. A second long-ship, not much smaller than the flagship, took up a corresponding position close to the east bank and did the same. The river was wide enough for three of the narrow ships in the Bifurland fleet to pass between the anchored vessels. Half an hour later, hundreds of yards of rope coated with powdered magestones lay coiled on the deck. Mafuta nodded, indicating the wizards in Nova Eboracum were finished coating their rope as well.

"I need your best wizards working solidified sound," Fercha instructed. Two dozen Bifurland wizards came forward, but half of them stepped back when one of the hooded wizards waved an arm. Mafuta increased the diameter of her communications spell so the Roma wizards in Nova Eboracum harbor could follow. Fercha asked a warrior and a legionnaire to pull a few yards of coated rope from the coil and hold it in front of her. She generated a thin blue tube of solidified sound around the length of rope and demonstrated the steps needed to create the tube for the other wizards. Then she stepped back and watched as the Bifurland wizards made a continuous yellow tube around their rope at this end while the Roma wizards made a purple tube around theirs in the distant harbor.

When the rope was protected with solidified sound from end to end, Fercha had King Bjarni find a skilled sailor to splice the ends together with heavy thread so they formed a continuous loop. She waited to ensure the Roma had spliced their rope, then showed how to join the ends of the tubes of solidified sound as well, so every inch of the rope was protected.

It's a good thing rope is circular, thought Fercha. *Her father had told her about accidentally putting a twist in a ribbon he'd used to make an experimental gate. Everything he tried to send through it came right back to where it started instead of going to his desired destination.*

Mafuta nodded to let Fercha know the Roma wizards had completed their huge loop of rope. Now it was time to create the gate. Fercha explained what was necessary. Warrior sailors and legionnaires began tying ballast stones to a length of rope wide enough to cross the river between the anchored ships. Fercha gave Mafuta the number of feet required, and she had her team in Nova Eboracum harbor duplicate that measurement.

Two wizards each lifted up segments and deployed them on and above the riverbed between the flagship and its companion vessel, forming a rounded rectangle of rope that was tall enough vertically to allow the tops of the longships' masts to pass beneath. After assurances everything was ready at both ends, Fercha reached out to her new magestone. It responded promptly.

The huge marine gate snapped into place, extending from the river bottom to the corners held aloft by pairs of wizards. The end of the gate in Nova Eboracum harbor was within the required precision necessary for a connection and soon Fercha and her companions could see the fortress walls of the Roma capital across a broad stretch of open water.

"Send them through," she said.

King Bjarni gave the order and the ships of the Bifurland fleet rowed through the marine gate from the Brenavon to the mouth of the Abbenoth and the harbor, oars dipping smoothly in and out of the water. Fercha watched them glide past, hastening like sea steeds over the swan road, to borrow a description from a Bifurland ballad known across Orluin. The entire fleet passed through surprisingly quickly, leaving only the flagship and its counterpart on the east bank still in Dâron. The diminishing sheet of ice on the Brenavon was still visible upstream to either side of the gate.

"Well done!" said King Bjarni.

"And quite impressive," said the queen.

"I want to *fly* through it," said Sigrun.

"And me!" added Rannveigr.

The two girls moved to the prow, climbed atop their small gold dragons, and launched themselves through the gate.

Quintillius laughed.

"What?" asked King Bjarni.

"He's just imagining when his son Primus will be old enough to try something like that," said Mafuta. The older wizard bent down and came up holding a large jug. "This accomplishment deserves a toast," she said. "I brought sorghum beer!"

"I'll match you with Bjarniston's best mead, though we'll have to be quick about it," said the king. "Fetch mugs for our guests," he commanded, speaking to no one in particular. A dozen hands provided the items requested, including a large sealed crockery pitcher. Mafuta began filling mugs first.

Fercha had a mug of sorghum beer shoved into her left hand and a cup of mead placed in her right. The beer had a sour taste that was nicely balanced by the mead and she drained mug and cup in a few swallows, leaving her lightheaded. She couldn't remember when—or if—she'd had breakfast. The drinking vessels in both her hands were quickly refilled and drained while sailors and legionnaires cheered. Fercha wasn't sure, but they might have been filled a third time. It was a pleasure to be appreciated.

"We'll need two wizards to hold the upper corners of the gate open," said Mafuta. "I need to go with Quintillius to Nova Eboracum."

"Of course," said Fercha. "I'll stay and take one corner."

An amber-robed and deep-hooded Bifurland wizard whispered to Queen Signý.

"Our wizards will need to come with us through the gate, too," said the queen.

"I'll do it," said Felix, the tall young Roma wizard and Mafuta's former apprentice. "I can fly back through the gate the army used."

"Don't dawdle in Dâron," Mafuta teased.

Felix shook his head and grimaced, unwilling to dignify Mafuta's alliterative comment with more of an answer.

"Take this as a thank you," said King Bjarni. He put a sealed pitcher of mead at Fercha's feet.

Not to be outdone, Quintillius added a jug of sorghum beer. "This is for you, not *him*," he said, pointing at Felix.

"Shafe traffels," said Fercha.

She put her flying disk on the deck. Somehow the pitcher and jug, along with the mug and cup, ended up on her disk. She waved, awkwardly, as she ascended and took the corner of the rope from the pair of Bifurland wizards. Fercha took a deep breath and held as steady as she could while Felix relieved the other pair of wizards. She watched as the flagship's companion ship crossed the gate boundary and sailed into Nova Eboracum harbor. She could feel her head starting to spin like the beginnings of a whirlpool.

Fercha heard a loud crack behind her. She turned on her flying disk and saw an ice floe forty feet wide and as big across as the Brenavon float downstream toward the rope and the flagship. If the ice struck the rope while her Bifurland and Roma friends were in mid-transit, the ship would be cut in half and both segments would surely sink. Her mind felt filled with fog as she tried to decide what to do. By force of will, she pulled herself together and called to Felix.

"Sh'top the ice!" Fercha shouted.

The young Roma wizard followed her eyes and saw what was about to happen. Without dropping his end of the rope, Felix simultaneously launched a dozen large spheres of solidified sound at the free-floating ice sheet. The force of the spheres' momentum slowed the sheet's motion downstream for a few seconds.

Smart, thought Fercha. *If the Roma had tried to brace himself and use a rod of solidified sound to hold back the ice, it would have pushed his flying disk and the rope out of position.* She created a huge hand of solidified sound behind the Bifurland flagship and shoved. A fraction of a second later, the flagship followed the rest of the fleet through the wide marine gate, its curved and intricately carved stern making the transition from river to harbor far faster than expected.

Felix whistled in amazement as the ice sheet flowed through the gate from the north and disrupted its connection to Nova Eboracum. "Is it safe to drop the rope?" he asked.

Fercha wasn't sure if he'd asked the question a few times before she finally heard it. She shook her head and thought of something, not understanding the gate was gone.

"I can make a construct of sholidified sound to hold up your end," she called across the river to Felix. "You can go through from here if you'd like."

"I don't think so," said Felix, puzzled by Fercha's lack of perception and accurately guessing the reason for her lapse. He brought his end of the rope over to where Fercha hovered and took the corner of the rope she was holding from her. He flew west and dropped the rope—even the part with ballast stones tied to it—on the bank. Then he returned to Fercha.

"Let's get you someplace safe where you can rest," said Felix. "Shall we go back to the Dormant Dragon?"

"No," said Fercha. *I can handle mead, but sorghum beer is stronger than I thought,* part of her brain remarked. "Take me home—to my townhouse."

"Where's that?" asked Felix.

"Brendinash," said Fercha. She was starting to sway on her flying disk. *Don't want Verro at the inn to shee me like thish.*

Felix brought his flying disk closer to Fercha's until their edges overlapped. He put his arm around the older wizard's shoulders to support her and keep her flight path steady. It wouldn't be the first time he'd helped a drunken wizard get home safely. Together, the two mages flew through the bright afternoon sun toward Dâron's capital.

Chapter 11

Wizard and Princess

Princess Gwýnnett's long nails pressed into Hibblig's tight stomach muscles through his robes as they flew north away from the Dormant Dragon.

"You took your time rescuing me," said the princess, in a tone that reminded Hibblig of his tutor in rhetoric and grammar when he was a child. The tutor had been one of Hibblig's least favorite instructors and had been sent packing when ten-year-old Hibblig complained to his parents of the woman's incompetence. He'd always thought her voice sounded like chalk scraping on slate. That was ancient history, however. He put the memory aside and focused on his passenger.

"My apologies, Your Highness," said Hibblig, bowing slightly—though Gwýnnett would only be able to feel the bow, not see it. "It took a few hours to recruit allies and confirm your location. We came as fast as we could."

"Do better next time," commanded Gwýnnett. She paused, then spoke in an even harsher tone. "And there'd better not *be* a next time."

"No, Your Highness," said Hibblig. He leaned back to balance his flying disk and smiled, enjoying the feel of Gwýnnett's body pressed against his.

"What's your plan?" asked Princess Gwýnnett. "Where are we headed?"

"I thought we'd go to a hunting lodge my family owns in the mountains southwest of Tyford and lay low until things sort out," said Hibblig. "I can monitor events in Brendinas through loyal members of our faction, so we can return when it's to our best advantage."

"Fool," Gwýnnett hissed in his ear. "Take me to Brendinas. I don't hold any cards at the moment now that I've lost my king—both my kings, now that I think about it."

Hibblig changed course, heading northeast, rather than north-west. The pair of wizards flanking him followed suit.

"How do you intend to improve your hand?" he asked.

"By collecting a queen," Gwýnnett answered. She laughed, low in her throat.

Hibblig smiled. "I like the way you think, Your Highness."

"We'll use the secret entrance to the palace near the docks," said Gwýnnett. "You know the one."

"Of course," said Hibblig. "Would you like to stop at my city house first to freshen up before we go to the palace?"

"That might be best," said Gwýnnett. "I have a few nice gowns there and a change of clothes would be appreciated, especially if I'll need to overawe the guards."

"My thought exactly," said Hibblig.

"I *know* what you were thinking, and it has more to do with getting me out of *this* gown than getting me into another one."

"Do you blame me?" asked Hibblig.

"Of course not," said Gwýnnett. Her nails pressed into Hibblig's stomach a bit harder and the wizard added more energy to his flying disk, increasing their speed.

Queen Carys won't be as easy to control as Hibblig, thought Gwýnnett. She soon saw the walls of Brendinas flash by below them and was pleased when they landed on the flat, crenelated roof of the tower integrated into one corner of Hibblig's home in the city. He also had a country house on the land held by his sister, a countess with an estate up the Brenavon, though she'd never seen it. Assignations in the city were much easier to arrange.

An hour later, Gwýnnett and Hibblig were ready to return to the royal palace. Gwýnnett considered that there were advantages to keeping company with a wizard who could instantly warm all the hot water she needed. *Plus, the man had* other *uses,* she mused.

They'd agreed to take Hibblig's closed carriage from his home to the docks. There would be less chance for Gwýnnett to be recognized that way. She wore a dark hooded cloak Hibblig had appropriated from one of his servants over a sky-blue satin gown.

The gown's neckline was square-cut but low and outlined with hundreds of tiny pearls. It wasn't one of her favorites—she kept it at Hibblig's after all—but it *was* impressive and would help her intimidate the queen's guards, she expected. Most of the kingdom's wizards were with the army and that blasted Astrí wouldn't be there to guard the queen, so Gwýnnett didn't anticipate many problems.

Hibblig dismissed the other two mages who'd helped him with Gwýnnett's rescue. He told the princess they didn't need more wizards to execute her plan and insisted on bringing two of his personal retainers on their mission instead. Both were skilled swordsmen, he'd said, and had once been with the palace guard.

Gwýnnett saw they wore Dâron-blue palace livery under voluminous black capes. From the look of them, she doubted they'd ever been guardsmen. They seemed more like bravos Hibblig had recruited in a tavern near their destination at the docks. One had a long thin blade strapped to his side. He was small and rat-faced, with deft fingers that seemed like they'd be better at picking pockets, throwing dice, or holding cards than swordplay. The other was built like a castle wall—about Hibblig's height but with even more mass and muscle. He didn't have a neck from what Gwýnnett could see and carried a heavy broadsword. The sword was so massive it looked like it could chop through a solid oak door in only a few cuts. *Let's hope it doesn't come to that,* thought Gwýnnett. She immediately forgot the names of Hibblig's retainers and resolved to call the pair Rat and Block.

The far-too-dirty streets of Brendinas weren't bustling that afternoon. Everyone had heard the good news about the wisent stampede and the subsequent defeat of Tamloch's army, but so many people from the city had traveled south to visit the battlefield that the capital seemed empty instead of exuberant. Rat scanned the road from a seat next to the carriage driver while Block sat high in the back, intimidating anyone close at hand by his very presence. Gwýnnett and Hibblig sat across from each other inside. The carriage wheels squeaked and wobbled like a thousand drunken mice. *Probably because of Block's weight,* she thought, one corner of her mouth turning up.

Hibblig saw her smile. "Thinking of me?" he asked.

"Of course," said Gwýnnett, putting a touch of honey in her voice. *He was* so *easy to manipulate!* Then she switched to vinegar and leaned close to the wizard. "Try to think with your big head, not your small one, Hibblig." He scowled but she continued. "I mean it. This will require your full attention to be successful."

Hibblig lowered his eyes and nodded.

"Don't fail me!" Gwýnnett said, in a tight, intense tone. "We need to kidnap and hold the queen—then convince Dârio that if he doesn't obey me her life is forfeit." The princess sat back and straightened her skirt. She smiled like a poacher who'd just taken a deer from a noble's estate. "He needs to learn that his mother knows best."

"Yes, Your Highness," said Hibblig, lifting his eyes. "That's quite true about Dârio—and you can count on me. For anything."

A leer accompanied the wizard's last two words. Gwýnnett managed to avoid rolling her eyes. She had potions to deal with Hibblig if he ever became a liability. Gwýnnett stretched her arms inside the compartment and admired the heavy bands on her fingers. Two had large stones in silver settings—an emerald and a sapphire—each with a hidden compartment. One was a gold signet ring, for marking documents. Finely ground sleeping powder was stored beneath the carved seal. The last was her favorite, a flexible circle of watered steel holding a flat polished oval of black onyx that flipped up to reveal a hollow spike like a serpent's tooth. She knew each ring's special purpose and felt more herself with them in place. It was a good thing she'd stored some of her rings at Hibblig's city house. They might prove quite useful.

The squeak of the carriage wheels stopped and Gwýnnett pulled her curtain back an inch to see that they'd reached the docks by the palace. Rat had kicked the steps down, so Hibblig descended and turned to help Gwýnnett down. She almost stumbled when the carriage jerked upward. *Block must have jumped off,* she realized. She hated appearing anything but completely in control but held back a tongue-lashing for the big swordsman.

"This way," said Gwýnnett, pointing toward a wide door in the outer wall of the palace banded with strips of black iron. Tufts of grass had grown up in a thin layer of soil blown against the door by the wind. *We won't need Block's sword to open this one,* thought Gwýnnett. She led the four of them to the door and removed an amulet from her neck. Gwýnnett had taken the amulet from her husband Dâri's body before he'd been buried. It was rumored to have been made for the Crown Prince by Master Mage Ealdamon himself.

Pressing the amulet to the lock was enough to open the door. Block entered first, followed by Hibblig, Gwýnnett, and Rat. Hibblig held up his hand and said, *"Llachar!"* A glowing ball appeared above the wizard's head, revealing their surroundings. Just past the level vestibule where they were standing, a broad wooden ramp led down at a shallow angle into darkness. They could see eye-bolts, ropes, and pulleys on the walls to the left and right. Thin lengths of wood extended across the ramp at six-foot intervals.

"Must be for loadin' barrels, don'tcha think?" asked Block. "Are there tuns of ale at the end of the ramp, I wonder? I expect I could drink a tun of ale, don't you?"

"I expect you could, my friend," said Rat, "just not at one sitting. Maybe in a week or two."

"It would be fun to try though, don'tcha think?" asked Block.

"The storerooms for the palace kitchens are below," said Gwýnnett. "This entrance was closed a dozen years ago after the kitchens were expanded. It's only used now by servants looking for a quiet place to practice various diversions."

Hibblig gave Gwýnnett a knowing smile. She ignored him.

"I hope we don't find any diverted servants," said Block. He chuckled and tugged on Rat's arm. "I like bein' diverted, ya'know."

"I do," said Rat. "Send the glowball down the ramp, please, and we'll scout ahead."

"I'll do better than that," said Hibblig. With a word and a gesture, he summoned another sphere of light and set it a foot above Rat's head. "Be quick about it," Hibblig ordered. "We don't want to worry about running into someone bringing the queen honeycakes while we're in her apartments." Rat tilted his head to indicate he understood and trotted down the ramp with Block close at his heels.

"Now that we're alone," said Hibblig, "why don't we indulge in our own diversion?"

Gwýnnett pointed down the ramp. "Start walking, or I'll roll you down the ramp like a barrel."

"Yes, Your Highness," said Hibblig. "I live to serve."

They reached the base of the ramp without incident, rejoined the others, and found themselves in a room full of barrels that smelled like an odd amalgam of yeast, wine, pickles, and dust. Rows of racked bottles were against the wall on either side of a broad door. Rat slid a bottle from its slot, removed its cork with his teeth, and took a swallow.

"Bah!" he said. "This swill is cooking wine, not a drinkable vintage."

"They wouldn't keep the good stuff by the door," said Hibblig.

"I'll drink it," said Block. He grabbed the bottle from Rat's hands and nearly drained it. "Not bad," he said, wiping his mouth with the back of his hand. Block swallowed again, then belched.

"You couldn't tell good wine from day-old dried plum juice," said Rat.

"Stop arguing or I'll have Hibblig seal you in a cask of ale," grumbled Gwýnnett.

"What a way to go," said Block, getting in the last word.

Gwýnnett shook her head in disgust, put her finger to her lips to signal the others to be quiet, and led them out of the cellars. The princess took them along empty corridors and up narrow deserted staircases until the four of them stood by a plain wooden door.

"This is the servants' entrance to the queen's suite," whispered Gwýnnett. "There may be guards inside and there will *certainly* be guards near the queen herself—I just don't know how many."

"Let me listen," said Hibblig. He made a small gesture by his ear and spoke a phrase under his breath, then leaned the side of his head against the door. Gwýnnett was growing impatient when Hibblig held up one finger. "There's just one guard on the other side," whispered the wizard. He nodded to Block and spoke softly. "You take him—and don't let him spread the alarm."

Block waited for Gwýnnett to use her amulet to open the servants' door. Moving more lightly on his feet than Gwýnnett imagined was possible, the big man stepped inside. Through the partially opened door the others heard a sound like two hams smacking a melon, followed by the muffled thud of a body hitting the floor.

The door opened all the way, revealing a grinning Block. The big bravo bent down, picked up the door-guard's unconscious form, and attached the guard's body to the wall by hanging his mail shirt on a coat hook. They were in a narrow hallway with a dark blue curtain flocked with silver stars covering the opposite end.

"So far, so good," said Hibblig. He put the tips of his fingers to his forehead and listened, straining to hear more, then spoke softly. "There are four guards, and a less-steady heartbeat that must belong to Queen Carys."

Rat and Block drew their blades and crossed to the curtain. Hibblig and Gwýnnett stood close behind the pair. Using the point of his slender sword, Rat opened one side of the curtain and stepped through. Block was less subtle. He grabbed the curtain on his side of the opening in one of his meaty hands and tugged. It came free from its mounting and puddled on the stone floor of the hall. Beyond, Hibblig and Gwýnnett could see Queen Carys seated in her usual comfortable chair, flanked by four guards—two on her left and two on her right.

"Come in, Gwýnnett, Hibblig," said the queen. "I've been expecting you. Sit down, dears. Have some tea."

Chapter 12

Princess and Queen

Nyssia smiled when the queen invited Princess Gwýnnett and Hibblig to sit down for tea. She was standing with an older guard to the queen's right. Her fiancé Gruffyd—another new guards-man—was on the queen's left matched with a more-seasoned royal protector armed with sword and halberd. The princess and her wizard were the queen's problem, so Nyssia focused on the two armed bravos entering with them. Her hand moved to the hilt of her sword and she mentally marked the smaller rat-faced man as her preferred opponent. *Let Gruffyd take the big one,* she thought. *They're more of a size.*

Gwýnnett and Hibblig didn't move. They still seemed shocked by the queen's invitation. The two bravos separated so they could counter attacks from both pairs of guards if necessary. As she'd been told to expect, the queen asked Nyssia for assistance.

"Please help our guests find their seats, dear," said the queen. "Your father must be so pleased you're following in his footsteps."

"He is, Your Majesty," said Nyssia. "Thank you for asking." She stepped forward and indicated that Hibblig should take the well-padded blue-leather chair on the right, facing Queen Carys from the opposite side of a low table. An elegant teapot and a single cup rested on the table. Glancing for more, she saw a second empty cup on the flat arm of the queen's chair. *Where was the third?* Nyssia wondered.

Afternoon sunlight streamed through a tall window behind the queen. *The light will shine in the eyes of anyone sitting across from her and give her an advantage,* Nyssia realized. She'd only been guarding Queen Carys for a few shifts but learned something new from her on each one. She looked at the queen for a moment, admiring the way the sun's rays turned her white hair gold, like Nyssia's own. Nyssia hoped *she'd* have the same sort of self-contained *presence* when *she* was the old queen's age. She pulled her mind back to her duties.

"Mind her rings, dear," said the queen. "It's best to stay out of her reach."

"Yes, Ma'am," said Nyssia. She directed Gwýnnett to the matching chair on the left beside Hibblig. It had a small side table on *its* left with the third empty teacup. Nyssia smiled to herself. She understood the queen's intent. The delicate cups were separately positioned to reduce the chance of the princess putting some sort of potion in the dowager queen's tea.

"Will you pour, please?" asked Queen Carys. "There are mugs and a jug of cider from Duke Háiddon's estate on the sideboard for our other guests."

Nyssia let her smile show this time at the two bravos' reaction. Their heads turned, looking for the sideboard, the jug, and the mugs. *It would have been a perfect time for Gruffyd and the other guards to attack the bravos,* she considered. *They certainly were distracted, but it was the queen's play.*

Trying not to feel too much at risk as she filled Princess Gwýnnett's teacup, Nyssia saw Queen Carys motion that Gruffyd should serve the bravos. She focused on staying calm and took deep, even breaths. *It wouldn't do to spill hot tea on Gwýnnett or Hibblig,* she mused. *I hope Gruffyd can keep* his *temper under control serving the bravos.* She crossed to fill Hibblig's cup, then the queen's.

"Leave the pot here," said Queen Carys, pointing to the wide flat arm of her chair behind her teacup. "We don't want to tempt the princess into doing anything *else* foolish."

"Enough of this nonsense," said Gwýnnett. "Isn't it time for you to get off the stage and join your husband?"

"My," said Queen Carys. "What an elegant way to wish me dead. I knew you were a clever girl from the first day you came to court."

"You never knew I existed when I first came to court," Gwýnnett protested. "I was young and hid behind my mother's skirts."

"The cooks told me you'd gone to the kitchens and were asking them about spices," said Carys.

"Mother sent me there to have them prepare her breakfast to her precise specifications," said Gwýnnett.

"Your mother sent you to the kitchens to get you out of the way while she was dallying with her lover, Duke Carriath. But you knew that, even then," said the queen. "She was the one who taught you to seek every advantage."

"And I did," said Gwýnnett. "So did you."

"Gwýnnie," said Hibblig, leaning forward. "Is now the best time for this discussion?"

"Shut up," said Gwýnnett without turning her head. "I'll deal with you later." Hibblig sat back and closed his open mouth.

"Gwýnnie," said the queen as if pronouncing judgment. Nyssia saw Princess Gwýnnett wince.

The princess stared poisoned daggers at the queen. "Don't ever say that again."

"I won't," said Queen Carys. "Unlike you, I'm *not* needlessly cruel. It's not just a matter of temperament—I'm not allowed to be. I'm *Good Queen Carys,* you know." Her eyes caught and held Gwýnnett's. "That doesn't mean I can't be hard when it's necessary for the good of the kingdom. My mistake was not making it clear to my grandson just how much of a fool he would be to marry you."

"He was already quite a fool *before* I married him," said Gwýnnett, smiling. Carys smiled back.

"He was at that, wasn't he?" said the queen.

Nyssia spared a moment to check on Gruffyd. Her betrothed was refilling the bravos' large mugs with more hard cider. *The applejack from Duke Háiddon's estate was almost as good as Applegarth's Finest,* she considered. She'd had her first taste of *that* delightful drink on the day when she'd met Gruffyd's childhood friend Merry and her tall companion, Eynon, back in the Rhuthro valley. *Everything is still going according to plan,* she thought. *So far, at least.*

"How did you know we were coming?" asked Gwýnnett.

"You tell me," said Carys. "You're a clever woman."

"Someone from the Dormant Dragon told you I'd escaped," said Gwýnnett. "Doethan. Or Fercha or Dârio."

"That's not it," said the queen. "I hadn't heard from any of them, though I'd expected you to escape. You're resourceful as well as clever."

"Thank you," said Gwýnnett tentatively. "Were we spotted entering the palace?" she asked.

"Spotted, no. Detected, yes. You didn't expect me to leave the old loading ramp *completely* unsecured, did you?" asked Queen Carys.

"So you knew *someone* had entered, but didn't know who it was or where they were headed," said Gwýnnett. "You must have known ahead of time that *I* was coming, but how?"

"You're being too devious for your own good, dear," said Carys. "Think of a simpler answer."

"Oh," said Gwýnnett after a few moments of reflection. "You have spies watching Hibblig's city house."

"Correct," said Queen Carys. "Older, non-magical methods of surveillance can still be quite effective."

"I'll remember," said Gwýnnett. She glanced at the signet ring on her right hand and thought of the sleeping powder it contained.

"I wouldn't do that if I were you," said the queen. "I'm not Túathal to fall for your tricks."

"Speaking of Túathal..." began Gwýnnett.

"Your future *husband*," continued Carys, raising one eyebrow.

"That remains to be seen," said Gwýnnett. "Do you have any word about him? Does he live?"

"Yes, but no thanks to *you*," said Carys. "You should have been sure to marry him before you tried to kill him. We could have been dowager queens together if you'd been better at poisoning him afterward."

"I can't think of anything I'd enjoy less," said Gwýnnett.

"You're slipping, dear," said the queen. "That would have been so much more cutting if you'd phrased it in terms of a compliment."

"And *you're* slipping, Carys," said Gwýnnett. "You're forgetting that *I* have a wizard with me."

"Am I?" asked the queen.

Gwýnnett sat quietly for a moment. She looked at her tea but didn't touch her cup. "No," she said. "That's not something you'd forget. Is Astrí hiding behind your chair, waiting to throw up a shield of solidified sound if Hibblig tosses a fireball in your direction?"

Nyssia stiffened. Just listening to this verbal fencing match was more stressful than five hours working out with rapiers in her father's salon. She consciously relaxed her shoulders, trusting the queen. When she turned her head to catch Gruffyd, she saw the two bravos were quite relaxed themselves. Gruffyd kept filling their mugs with hard cider.

Hibblig sat up when he heard his name, but Gwýnnett glared at him until he sank back into his well-padded broad-backed chair.

Chairs with broad backs are popular because they're comfortable for wizards with their flying disks strapped on, realized Nyssia. That's *something else I've learned serving the queen!*

"Care to test my defenses and see?" asked Carys.

Gwýnnett didn't like the way the queen's smile resembled a cat's expression when playing with a mouse. At least that's how it seemed to Nyssia and she could see both women's faces. She wasn't surprised when Gwýnnett—the mouse—surrendered.

"I think not," said Gwýnnett, nodding her head and moving her hand in a motion like tipping her king to acknowledge defeat in *shah mat.* "What next?"

"You'll be held in your own quarters under house arrest until Dârio returns and can decide what to do with you long term," said Queen Carys. "Or maybe you will be Dârianûd's problem, if he takes the throne of Dâron."

"Dârianûd?" asked Gwýnnett.

"That's right," said Queen Carys. "I'd heard you were still recovering from a sleeping potion for *that* bit of news. Astrí once went by another name—Princess Seren. She's my daughter. Ealdamon taught her wizardry."

"So she's out of the line of succession," said Gwýnnett.

"Correct," said Carys. "As is *her* daughter—Fercha."

"Oh," said Gwýnnett. Her face looked like it had been slapped by the flat of a broadsword.

"Fercha and Verro were secretly married—and *their* son, Dârianûd, is *not* a wizard..."

"...and the rightful king of Dâron, not my Dârio," Gwýnnett completed. She moved a hand to her neck. "Fercha is married to *Verro?* That makes their son second in line to Tamloch as well."

"Also correct," said Carys. "You'll have plenty of time to contemplate all the other missing holes in your knowledge when you go to your quarters. Put your rings on the table, please."

Gwýnnett slowly removed her rings and placed them by her teacup.

"Time to go, dear," said Carys.

The older guard who'd stood behind Nyssia escorted Princess Gwýnnett out the main door of the queen's suite. She heard several footsteps walking down the corridor outside.

"Call in more guards, please," Queen Carys instructed. "You'll need help to cart off the two swordsmen. You may *need* a cart for the big one."

Nyssia laughed when she saw both bravos asleep on the floor. The scent of hard cider was so strong she could smell it from here. It took six guards to carry the big one out of the queen's suite, while the small one was tossed over a seventh guard's shoulder like a sack of meal. Nyssia winked at Gruffyd and the two of them resumed their posts on either side of the queen.

"Now," said Queen Carys, staring at Hibblig. "What am I going to do about *you?*" The big wizard was sitting on the edge of his chair.

"Release me to serve my kingdom with the other members of the Conclave?" asked Hibblig hopefully.

Carys tilted her head. "Try again," she said, more amused than angry.

"How about *this!*" said Hibblig. He tossed a sphere of solidified sound onto the table in front of him. It exploded in a blast of light and sound, turning the teapot into dozens of fragments and sending once-hot tea in all directions. A yard-wide jet-black circle opened in the floor in front of Hibblig's chair and the big wizard jumped through it, disappearing along with the interface of his emergency gate a moment later.

Nyssia and the other guards interposed their bodies to intercept most of the flying fragments, but the queen still collected a few scratches and a damp dress.

"That was exciting," said the queen, drying herself off with a napkin.

"It certainly was," said Nyssia. "You were bluffing, weren't you? You didn't have a wizard in reserve."

"That's right," said the queen. "And it worked, at least for Gwýnnett. Astrí's gone off who knows where with Damon and I can't begrudge the two of them a chance to spend time together after so many years."

Nyssia smiled. So did Gruffyd.

"You both did quite well with your assigned tasks," said Queen Carys. "I'll see that you're both formally commended."

"Thank you, Your Majesty," said Nyssia. "May I ask a question?"

"Of course, child. Ask away," said the queen.

"Did you drug the cider? Or the tea?" she asked.

"Of course not," said Carys. "The cider is potent enough on its own without adding a sleeping draught and serving tea was just a way to keep Gwýnnett off balance."

"Because *she* would have poisoned it," said Nyssia.

"Precisely," said the queen. "Now why don't the two of you go down the hall to the see how the poor young man guarding *that* entrance is doing. I didn't intend for him to be hurt."

"Of course, Your Majesty," said Nyssia.

"Our pleasure, Ma'am," added Gruffyd.

Carys got in the last word. "On your way back, could you please rehang the dark blue curtain with the flocked silver stars? That big swordsman pulled it down and I'll be much happier when everything is back as it should be."

Chapter 13

Eynon's Cottage

Eynon's parents were still outside doing chores. Braith had been impressed they could talk to another wizard on the other side of the kingdom but was distressed by Merry's reaction to what she'd seen and heard through the interface. Her curiosity and interest in Nûd ensured she would stay near at hand and pay close attention.

Merry scowled when the contact severed. She watched in evident frustration as Eynon shrank Doethan's communications ring and put it back on his finger. For her, a scowl wasn't an uncommon expression, but she thought it was the first time she'd ever seen a scowl on Eynon's face. One of the reasons she loved him was because he always seemed to stay cheerful in the face of adversity. *It's probably because most of the time he doesn't know any better,* Merry considered. Then she took a second look at Eynon's hard expression and reconsidered.

"We're in trouble now," said Eynon. "If Túathal finds Viridáxés..."

"Or vice versa," said Nûd.

"We'd have the most ruthless man west of the Ocean commanding the most powerful force in Orluin," said Merry.

"Not to forget having Dârio's mother back on the loose," Nûd reminded. "Maybe she can link up with Túathal, poison him again, and do it right this time."

Braith gave Nûd a sharp look. "What kind of person are you to wish anyone poisoned?" she asked.

Nûd lowered his eyes and his shoulders slumped. "Sorry," he said.

"Túathal must not be a very nice man for you to wish him dead," Braith replied. She put her hand on Nûd's forearm. He gently removed it.

"Not from everything Damon's told me about him," said Nûd. "He's the last person I'd want commanding Viridáxés."

"Are you sure Túathal's bad reputation isn't just how Dâron's nobles want us to see him?" asked Eynon. "Dârio doesn't have a very good reputation either, but *he's* a good man. Maybe Túathal is considered a wise, just king back in Tamloch."

Merry surprised them all by grabbing Eynon's upper arms and shaking him. Using strength gained from archery practice and guiding boats down the Rhuthro, she pulled Eynon's face close to hers.

"Are you blind?" she asked with quiet intensity. She shook Eynon again. Her voice increased in volume until she was shouting. "Did you forget he had a knife to my brother's throat?"

Merry's face was flushed and her magestone pulsed in angry flashes of cold, blue light. She saw Eynon's shocked impression, released him, took a step back, and sighed.

"Forgive me," she said. Fire drained out of her, replaced by worry.

"There's nothing to forgive," said Eynon. "I have to learn that not everyone deserves the benefit of the doubt. The wider world isn't like the Coombe."

"It certainly isn't," said Merry. She balled her hands into fists and slammed them on the nearby table, making a pair of loud thumps. "I just feel so frustrated not being able to help my brother."

"Or not knowing what's happening back at the inn," said Eynon. He opened his arms and Merry stepped into his embrace. She hugged his chest and tried to hold back tears while Eynon held her. Nûd and Braith observed uncomfortably.

"Maybe I'd better contact Damon," said Nûd. "Viridáxés seems like a Damon-sized problem."

"Wait a moment," advised Braith. "My brother and Merry should have their say in the matter and they need a bit more time."

"What do *you* think we should do?" Nûd asked Braith while they waited.

Chee chose that moment to leap from the rafters above to Nûd's right shoulder, which tipped the big man off balance so he bumped into Braith. Nûd frowned at Chee. Flashing his teeth in something like a smile, the raconette hopped to the tabletop and wrapped his long arms around his own back, imitating Eynon and Merry. He puckered his thin lips in a close approximation of a kiss and tilted his small head. Nûd and Braith laughed. Their laughter led to Eynon and Merry spotting Chee's pose on the table. Soon *they* were laughing. It was nervous laughter—given the threat from Viridáxés—but cathartic nonetheless.

"I think we should lock Chee in a cage and throw away the key," said Braith. She winked at Chee and the little beast did three somersaults down the dining room table. His antics served to distract the humans. Braith tossed Chee a small apple from a basket near the sink. It disappeared into his cheek pouch, stems, seeds and all.

Merry gave Eynon an especially tight hug and took two steps back. "I think I'm back in control of myself," she said.

"Good," said Braith.

"*Very* good," said Nûd.

"Well, now that I've had some sense shaken into me, I realized something important," said Eynon.

"What's that?" asked Merry.

"We have to warn everyone in the Coombe about Viridáxés," Eynon replied. "There were already observers from Wherrel watching him emerge and word travels fast."

"You don't think every stonecutter taking a look in the quarry will turn around as soon as they spot a giant dragon?" asked Merry.

"Think about it," said Braith. "Eynon's not unusual for the Coombe. People here won't see Viridáxés and think they should stay away in case he might eat them. They might camp out to watch him sleep for all I know."

"One of our cousins might bring a cart to sell beer and honey cakes to the gawkers," said Eynon.

"I think I know which one you mean," said Braith. She grinned at Eynon and Nûd admired the way her eyes danced. "I'd like to see the dragon too, you know. Will you take me with you when you fly back to the quarry."

"I don't know about that," said Eynon.

"Of course," said Nûd.

Merry watched Nûd and Eynon exchange glances like quarter-staff blows. A moment later she smiled as she saw Braith use a big-eyed expression to silently plead with her big brother.

"All right," said Eynon reluctantly. "You can come."

"Yay!" said Braith. "I'll ride on Rocky with *you*," she informed Nûd. The big man rolled his eyes.

"You can ride with me or with Merry," said Eynon. "We still need to get the word out to people across the Coombe." He heard a pair of footsteps and the door to the cottage creak open. His parents were back.

"Get the word out about what?" asked Daffyd as he wiped his boots on the mat.

"About staying away from Viridáxés," Eynon replied.

"Don't worry about that," said Glenys. "We've taken care of it." She put a covered wooden pail pail down by the sink. Chee sat up on the table and stared at the pail.

"What do you mean?" asked Eynon.

"We told everyone in the village about the dragon," said Daffyd.

"Volunteers are heading for Wherrel now to keep watch on Viridáxés," added Glenys. "They'll ensure the stonecutters stay out of the quarry. We'll use the villages' news chain to pass the word when he wakes."

"Nothing is faster than the news chain," said Braith. "Not even wizards' rings."

Nûd and Merry laughed. Eynon was already well aware of how fast news traveled in the Coombe. When he was younger, his mother always knew about any trouble he'd gotten into before he made it home.

"Other volunteers are heading to Brynhill and the nearby villages to warn people to stay indoors," said Daffyd.

"If that doesn't prompt half the young people to walk to Wherrel," joked Eynon. Despite himself, he yawned.

"You don't think I told them it was a *dragon*, do you?" asked Eynon's father.

"I didn't think you did," said Nûd. Eynon thought he was trying to get on Daffyd's good side, but his words lost some of their effectiveness when Nûd was caught by a loud yawn of his own. Merry put her hand over her mouth to hide a similar signal she needed some rest.

Glenys pointed to the pail. "I've brought you some milk," she said. "It's still warm from the cow. If you each drink a cup, you should be able to catch a quick nap, even with the sun not far past noon."

"What about Túathal?" asked Eynon.

"Whoever Túathal is, he can be someone else's problem for an hour," said Daffyd. "All three of you can barely keep your eyelids up."

Glenys brought five fired-clay mugs to the sink and filled them with milk from the pail. Braith took three mugs—one for herself, one for Nûd, and the third for Chee. Glenys handed mugs to Eynon and Merry. She shook her head when Braith invited Nûd to rest on her bed.

"I don't think so," said Glenys in a tone only a parent could match. "Take Nûd to Glynneth's cottage so he can get some rest." She handed Braith a stack of blankets with a pillow on top and smiled at Nûd. "Tell Glynneth we really appreciate her hospitality— and come right back to do your chores." Braith waited for Nûd to open the cottage door, then laughed as Chee hopped on Nûd's shoulder and begged her for a treat.

"Maybe Glynneth will give you a sweet cake," said Braith.

Chee was nodding vigorously as they left.

Eynon and Merry sat at the table without speaking. They drank their milk in long, slow swallows.

Daffyd joined Glenys at the sink to prepare root vegetables and a few leafy greens for what would turn out to be a very early dinner. Ten minutes later he looked over his shoulder, then nudged his wife. Both of them turned around and smiled. Eynon and Merry's heads were on the table, flanked by clay mugs. The two young wizards were holding hands, sleeping soundly.

Chapter 14

Eynon and Glenys

Eynon woke to the sound of meat sizzling in a cast iron skillet. He slowly lifted his head and sniffed. His mother was cooking venison steaks in bacon grease. He saw her sitting by the fireplace on a squared stone from the quarry at Wherrel. She was watching the skillet where it rested on a low metal tripod above hot coals. The family's cauldron hung from a metal arm farther back in the fireplace above a pair of seasoned pine logs that crackled and threw off occasional sparks. As if sensing Eynon's eyes on her, Glenys turned and smiled at him.

"I'm glad you're awake," she said. "The others are outside."

"Oh," said Eynon, still not fully conscious. "How long was I asleep?"

"Not long enough," said his mother. "Perhaps an hour. There's still plenty of light left in the day. You slept through Chee's chittering. He was going to climb up your back and sit on your head, but your friend Nûd stopped him."

"I'll have to thank him for that," said Eynon. "I guess I needed the rest."

"You did," said Glenys. "You need to take better care of yourself."

"I know, mother," said Eynon, smiling. "I just had so much to do..."

"Saving the kingdom," teased Glenys. "Nûd and Merry told me about the wisents and the gold for the Bifurlanders and freezing the Brenavon. You could have knocked me over with a dandelion puff when I heard. To think that *my* son is now a great and powerful wizard..."

"I still have a lot to learn," said Eynon. He got up from the table, walked over to his mother, and hugged her shoulders. "And I'm still the same person who left here a few weeks ago on my wander year with your cheese in my pack."

"Maybe you are," said Glenys. "And maybe you're not." She stared at Eynon's red magestone in its circular gold setting, then turned away and focused her attention on the skillet.

"Is there anything I can do to help with dinner?" Eynon asked, eying the steaks as moisture in the bacon grease popped. "It feels like we just had lunch an hour ago."

"We did—and don't worry, I have everything in hand," Glenys responded. "Braith will set the table. You can go out and fetch her in a few minutes.

"I'd be glad to," said Eynon. "Why are we eating so early? And where did we get fresh venison? We usually cull deer in the fall, not the spring. How did you get the village council's approval to take a stag?"

"As for dinner, I want to feed you and your friends *now,* while I have the chance," said Glenys. "With a dragon nearby, there's no telling what might happen to pull you all away without warning. I want to make sure you at least leave with full stomachs."

Eynon smiled at his mother. That was exactly the way she would think. He raised his eyebrows, silently asking for an answer to his second question.

"Daffyd and I found an eight-point buck outside our back door when we returned from fetching water," said Glenys. "Nûd told us to consider it a gift from Rocky. Is that the name of another one of your new friends?"

"In a way," said Eynon. "Rocky is my wyvern—though he's quite fond of Nûd, too."

"Is he the beast who left a steaming pile of dung as big as a shepherd's hut in the square a few hours ago?"

"Yes, unfortunately," said Eynon. "I'm sorry. I'll clean it up."

"No need for that," said Glenys. "Braith told the neighbors that wyvern dung makes everything grow twice as fast as cow manure. Half the people in Haywall were back in the square with wheelbarrows and shovels a few minutes after you left."

"She always was clever," said Eynon.

"She takes after her brother," teased Glenys. Using a thick wool pad to grip the skillet's handle, she moved the venison steaks and tripod away from the hottest coals.

Eynon shrugged his shoulders and turned up his palms.

"Was that wyvern here yesterday, too?" asked Glenys.

"Yes," said Eynon. "He dropped us off, then I sent him away to the eastern mountains, so he wouldn't disturb the cows."

"You always were considerate as well as clever," said Glenys. She looked away from the cooking steaks for a moment and rubbed her chin. "That explains why your cousin Bûgail was complaining about losing one of her ewes yesterday morning." His mother gave Eynon a stern look. "You'll have to make it up to her," she said.

"I will," said Eynon. "Once I figure out what to do about a green dragon bigger than the milking barn."

"Don't be too long figuring it out," said Glenys. "We have crops to plant soon and don't want to be looking over our shoulders all the time to see if a dragon is planning to eat us."

"I can understand how that would be distracting," teased Eynon. "What's in the cauldron?" He leaned in to inhale some of the steam rising from the big pot. "Turnips?" he asked.

"And carrots and parsnips," said Glenys. "Your father chopped them up just the way you like them and stewed them in beer with leeks and wild onions."

"Sounds delicious," said Eynon. He spotted four large loaves of bread resting on a shelf on the far side of the fire and waved toward them. "Those look wonderful, too."

"They're for breakfast tomorrow as well as dinner," said Glenys, "so don't think you can claim half a loaf for yourself tonight." She pretended to frown, then gave Eynon a worried smile. "Do *you* think the dragon will try to eat us?" she asked.

"I wish I could say *of course not,* but I'm not sure *what* Viridáxés might do. I hope to get him away from the Coombe as soon as I can."

"Please do," said Glenys. "He's bigger than the milking barn, you say? And green?"

"He's bigger than three milking barns," said Eynon, "and greener than spring leaves."

"That reminds me," said Glenys. "Your father also made a salad with fresh lettuce, sliced morels, and vinegar sauce."

"I'm honored," said Eynon.

"Don't get a swelled head, O Great and Powerful Wizard," said Eynon's mother with a grin. "Dinner wouldn't be nearly as fancy if you hadn't brought friends with you."

Eynon bent down and kissed his mother's forehead. It was warm from sitting close to the fire.

"Speaking of my friends," said Eynon. "What are they doing outside? If you sent them to wash up before dinner it shouldn't have taken this long."

"They're giving your father a hand with patching the roof," said Glenys. "He thought Merry and her flying disk would make it a lot easier to fill in the thatch near the ridge line. Nûd is with Merry on her disk doing the patching."

"Is Chee with them?" asked Eynon.

"Oh yes," said Glenys. "He's *helping,* though I don't think your father would agree. The little scamp decided to take a nap in one of the holes to be patched and wouldn't move until Merry tempted him out with an apple."

"They should have covered him with thatching straw instead," said Eynon.

Glenys smiled. "The neighbors have been asking Nûd when the wyvern is coming back," she said. "Especially the ones who weren't able to collect a share of the earlier deposit of wyvern dung."

Eynon laughed. "What's Braith doing? Supervising?"

"No," said Glenys. "Last I looked, she was sitting on your father's shoulders adding more thatching to the eaves. I think Glynneth's goats might be hopping up there and eating the straw around the edges when we're not home."

Eynon licked his lips, remembering the delicious sweet cakes the woman in the cottage next door liked to make. When they were little, he and Braith always contrived to play outside Glynneth's door when they could smell the small cakes baking. Most of the time, they were given half a dozen—one each to eat now, and the rest to take home. As Eynon saw it, putting up with Glynneth's goats' depredations was a small price to pay for a chance to nibble on her sweet cakes.

"How is our good neighbor's health?" asked Eynon. Glynneth walked with a cane now, but that didn't seem to affect the quality or frequency of her baking.

"She's doing as well as can be expected for someone who's seen four score years," said Glenys, "except when it's raining or about to. Then her rheumatism flares and she prefers to spend her time sitting by the fire."

"I'm glad she's still getting around," said Eynon. He watched as his mother moved the skillet completely off the coals. She handed Eynon a willow basket from a corner of the table.

"Drop this off with Glynneth, then tell everyone supper's ready," said Glenys. "And now it really *is* time to wash up—and put on your best festival clothes as soon as you return. We're expecting visitors right after."

Eynon looked at his mother quizzically, but she didn't answer. She simply waved toward the cottage's back door. Eynon moved in that direction and left the modest structure, wondering all the while who might be coming.

Chapter 15

The Village Council

Eynon stepped out of his cottage carrying the willow-basket and saw a crowd had gathered. It seemed like half of Haywall was standing on the grass or paving slates, watching Merry and Nûd as they hovered near the roof line, making final repairs to the thatching. Chee was at ground level, dancing and turning somersaults to amuse a gaggle of young children. Eynon was pleased to see they were laughing and clapping, enjoying Chee's antics. He waved, and several children waved back. Their parents, and many of the village's oldest residents watched from farther back. Several held shovels and a few brought wheelbarrows.

I hope Rocky keeps his distance, thought Eynon. *Braith is likely to figure out that she can sell wyvern dung, not just dispose of it quickly.*

There were a few young people in their teens looking on as well. Most were too young to leave on their wander years, though a few were older than Eynon and had returned, with or without spouses. Nûd received a lot of attention from that group. He was tall, dark, and at least somewhat handsome, after all. Some of the same young women who had teased Eynon when he was growing up were sighing every time Nûd flexed his muscles to insert more straw in a sparse spot on the roof. The younger girls—Braith's friends—were whispering to each other and giggling. Eynon wasn't as fond of the looks the young men near his age were giving Merry. Like Nûd, she was a newcomer to Haywall, and therefore shared his novel appeal.

"How are the repairs going, darling," Eynon called to Merry.

"Fine, sweetheart," said Nûd with a grin.

Eynon stuck his tongue out at Nûd and the big man laughed, tipping the flying disk a few degrees.

"We're almost done," said Merry, bring her disk back level. "Is it time for dinner?"

"Uh huh," said Eynon. "My mother says there's just enough time to wash up and put on good clothes. She's expecting company after dinner."

"But I don't have anything nice to wear," said Merry.

At that moment Braith, still on her father's shoulders, came around the corner of the cottage. She leaned up and stuck her last bit of thatching into the eaves.

"Don't worry, I'll loan you something," said Braith.

"Are you finished?" asked Daffyd.

"All done," said Braith. "You can put me down."

Two of the older boys looking on helped Eynon's sister slide off her elevated position on Daffyd's neck. Eynon knew she was perfectly capable of getting down by herself but was glad to see Braith had admirers closer to her own age. Then he reconsidered. He knew both boys, and neither one had brains enough for more than milking cows and raking hay. His sister deserved a partner who was every bit as clever as she was—in a few years.

Eynon's father teased his daughter. "You're not the same feather of a girl you were when you first rode on my shoulders," he said.

"I'm not five anymore, father," Braith replied. "It's been almost ten years since then."

"Don't remind me," said Daffyd. "I'll get the bucket and water from the well. You can get a towel and some soap from your mother."

Braith grinned, glanced up to see if Nûd was watching her—he wasn't—and ran inside their cottage.

"What's in the basket?" asked Merry as she and Nûd descended to a spot of unoccupied grass.

"Stewed vegetables and venison for Glynneth," said Eynon. "To thank her for giving Nûd a place to sleep."

"Don't stand around here talking then," said Merry. "Deliver the basket before what's in it gets cold."

"Yes, dear," said Eynon.

Merry flipped the slightly-dished edge of her flying disk up so it jumped into her hand and gave it to Nûd. Then she took the basket from Eynon and hung it from Nûd's free hand. Before

Eynon realized what was happening, she hugged him and gave him an enthusiastic kiss that made him light-headed and short of breath. When the kiss ended, there were cheers and whistles from old and young spectators alike. Eynon could feel his heart race when he reclaimed the basket. He smiled at Merry and headed for Glynneth's cottage, enjoying the jealous looks from the other young men as he walked. All the onlookers gave him plenty of room, though some stared in wonder at his red magestone. Nûd held Merry's flying disk in front of him like a shield and led the way back to Eynon's parents' cottage. Chee waved goodbye to the children and followed.

* * * * *

The sun was still several hands above the western horizon. It was only mid-afternoon when they gathered around the table for an early dinner.

"The venison is delicious," said Merry, nodding toward Eynon's mother. "What did you season it with?"

"Salt, cider vinegar, and dried teaberries," said Glenys. "The vinegar helps make it tender."

"I thought I tasted a hint of mint," said Merry. "My mother doesn't use teaberries for cooking. She just ferments the leaves and brews tea from them. I thought teaberries were only for tea."

"Yet another reason for the people in the Coombe and the folk of the Rhuthro valley to meet more often," said Eynon. "We could share recipes." He was sitting on a bench next to Merry at his family's dinner table, across from Braith and Nûd. His parents sat on chairs at the head and foot.

"You'll be too busy doing mage things to worry about recipes," said Braith.

Eynon admired his sister while she spoke. She'd changed into her festival finery before dinner. Now she wore a white blouse, a long black skirt, and an elaborately embroidered red vest. Eynon wore a similar ensemble, with pants instead of a skirt. It was custom in the Coombe to embroider your own vest, and Eynon admired how much his sister's stitching had improved in the past year.

The embroidery on his father's vest was as much better than Eynon's as Eynon's was better than his sister's. Daffyd had a fine eye and a knack for stitching wildflowers. His mother's vest was covered in knotwork and stylized versions of birds and small animals.

Merry wore one of his mother's older festival outfits with the waistband of the skirt rolled. Her red vest had embroidered spring and fall leaves. Nûd wore black pants and a white shirt handed down to Eynon from a slightly larger uncle. His vest—covered with geometric shapes in six colors of thread—wasn't quite big enough to close.

Braith nudged Nûd and caught his eye, then glanced at her mother. Nûd swallowed a thick slice of parsnip and turned to Glenys.

"The entire meal is wonderful," he said. "I can see where Eynon learned his skill in the kitchen."

"You're very kind," said Glenys.

"Not really," said Braith. "Nûd told me he's a terrible cook and any meal he doesn't prepare himself is excellent, by default."

Nûd shot Braith a stern look. "I told you that in confidence," he said, "though it's true."

"If you have a chance to stay for a few days, I'd be glad to give you cooking lessons," said Daffyd.

"That would be appreciated—if we're here for a few days," Nûd answered.

"I suspect you'll have reason to come back to the Coombe from time to time, even if you can't stay long now," said Daffyd. He smiled at Braith and was entertained as his daughter made a face at him. Eynon shook his head.

Nûd thought it best to change the subject. "What *are* teaberries?" he asked.

Before Daffyd could launch into a ten-minute explanation of where teaberries could be found and how best to prepare them, there was an authoritative knock on the cottage door. Glenys rose from her chair, crossed the room, and opened it. Six people— three men and three women, all in festival clothes—were waiting outside.

"Come in, come in," said Glenys, motioning the newcomers inside. A few minutes later, introductions were made, chairs and benches were repositioned, and all twelve of them were seated around a braided rug that Eynon's father had made several years ago. Eynon now understood why Glynneth had sent him home with two dozen sweet cakes this time. Before sitting down, Daffyd had circulated a platter filled with cakes and everyone present had taken one. Glynneth's sweet cakes were well known in the Coombe and Nûd and Merry had heard Eynon praise them, so they were glad to try the honey-rich confections. Eynon gave Chee half of his and the raconette climbed into the rafters to eat and observe.

"We're pleased to have the village council visit our home," said Glenys.

Eynon knew both his parents had served on the council in the past, and two of the members present were second, or maybe third cousins. It was hard to keep such things straight in the Coombe. One of the women was originally from Caercadel, the baronial seat in the south, and one of the men had been born in Liamston near the Coombe's northeastern border. Both had resettled in Haywall after their wander years. Eynon thought it was disconcerting when the head of the village council, a white-haired woman old enough to be his grandmother, spoke directly to him.

"What are you going to do about the dragon?" she asked.

"I don't know," said Eynon.

"That's not good enough," said the head of the council. "I've known you since you were smaller than a goose. Your parents say you're a wizard now. They told us you saved the kingdom in a battle near the capital and even froze the Brenavon." She inhaled and seemed to grow larger in proportion to the air she took in, seeming more like six-foot-two than five-foot-two. "You've got a *red* magestone. I can see it. You've *got* to do something."

"I'll do my best," said Eynon, "but Viridáxés is a *very* big dragon. Big dragons tend to do what they want."

The council member from Liamston was shocked. "It has a *name?*"

The council member from Caercadel jumped in. "It's intelligent?"

"Yes, and yes," said Merry. Eynon could see her cheeks getting red.

"If it attacks Haywall it will make our cows udders dry up from fear," said one council member.

"If it doesn't *eat* our cows," complained another.

"Or *us,*" said a third.

"This just won't *do,*" said the head of the council. "You have to get the dragon to leave the Coombe."

"Technically, Viridáxés isn't *in* the Coombe," said Braith. "The quarry is just west of the mountains."

Daffyd and Glenys stared at their daughter. Her comment didn't help the current situation.

Eynon rubbed his chin, trying to decide what to say. Then he spoke. "Do you remember the ice storm from five years ago?" he asked. "The one that coated every house and barn and road in an inch of ice?"

The council members all nodded.

"Would you ask a wizard to stop the storm or have it pass over the Coombe?"

The members of the village council looked to the council's head. She looked at Eynon.

"You're saying this dragon is like an ice storm?"

"Worse, actually," said Eynon. "And better."

"Why worse?" asked Eynon's mother.

"Because Viridáxés could be much more destructive, if he decides to be," said Merry. She stared at Nûd and slowly everyone else stared at the big man, too.

"Why better?" asked the head of the council, trying to understand why there might be some reason for optimism.

"Because we may be able to reason with Viridáxés," Eynon replied, "and he seems inclined to follow instructions from those of royal blood."

"What?" asked Nûd. He shrugged. "Do I look like royalty?"

Merry and Eynon nodded. Everyone else looked puzzled.

"All right," said Nûd. "I'll try to talk Viridáxés into leaving the Coombe."

"Excellent!" said the head of the village council, looking like a great weight had been lifted from her shoulders. "You'll have to head for the quarry right away. We have reports that the monster is waking up."

"How can you tell?" asked Nûd.

"It opens one eye, like a cat," said the head of the council. "And there's a rumbling sound coming from deep in its chest."

"I think that's his breathing," said Merry. "Dragons have big lungs."

"I think they're right," said Nûd. He rubbed behind his right ear. "Viridáxés is waking. I can sense it somehow."

"When did you get word about this?" asked Eynon.

"A few minutes ago," said a council member. "It was relayed at top priority along the news network."

"Time to go," said Eynon. He grabbed his pack and a small sack filled with sweet cakes. Nûd handed Merry and Eynon their flying disks. They were ready to leave for the quarry when a tremendous pounding rattled the door of the cottage. Braith opened the portal and saw Rocky's huge head poking inside.

"Just in time," said Nûd.

"I'm coming with you," declared Braith.

"No you're *not*," said Daffyd and Glenys and Eynon simultaneously.

Her parents each held one of her arms. Braith shouted protests as Eynon, Nûd and Merry pushed past Rocky and went outside.

Despite the recent equinox, Eynon was sure it was going to be a very long day.

"Wait!" came his mother's voice from inside the cottage. "You've got to change your clothes!"

Chapter 16

The Green Magestone Quarry

After a short delay to follow Eynon's mother's instructions and switch to their traveling clothes, Eynon, Merry, and Nûd, plus Rocky and Chee were flying west toward the quarry. Before leaving Haywall, they'd agreed to stay silent so they wouldn't wake the dragon if by chance he wasn't already awake. Merry had given Chee a small cup of applejack while they were still on the ground. The raconette had swallowed it enthusiastically and promptly fallen asleep, guaranteeing he wouldn't be chittering. Eynon had carefully strapped Chee to Rocky's back so he'd be safe.

Eynon took the lead, since he knew the relevant landmarks to guide them. It didn't take them long to reach Wherrel, the village near the quarry. Instead of approaching from the east, through the gap leading back to the Coombe, Eynon circled north, coming in from the same vector Verro and the wizards from Tamloch had used on their raid to steal green magestones. A hundred-foot cliff of green-gray stone marked the quarry's northern border. Behind the tall cliff was a field covered in new grass and blooming mountain laurel. It gently sloped down away from the cliff down to a collection of trees not quite large enough to be called a wood. Eynon knew the hill was a favorite spot for young people from Wherrel to visit on picnics. Families avoided the area because it was too easy for a wayward child to fall over the cliff.

Eynon, Merry, and Nûd—on Rocky—landed a few dozen paces from the edge of the cliff so the three of them could inch forward and determine if Viridáxés was still sleeping. They crawled toward the cliff and noticed a greenish glow radiating from inside the quarry. When they'd progressed enough to peer down, they froze. Viridáxés was no longer asleep. The great dragon sat on the quarry floor and stretched until his roundshield-sized eyes were at the same level as their own. The greenish glow came from Viridáxés' eyes and escaped from his mouth when he yawned. Eynon was awed by Viridáxés' teeth. They were bigger than broadswords.

"You're back," said the dragon.

Eynon could feel the stones of the cliff-face vibrate beneath him as they resonated with Viridáxés' words.

"We were informed Your Magnificence was waking," said Eynon, still in his prone position.

"We came at once," said Merry.

"Have *you* nothing to say, Prince of Tamloch?" asked Viridáxés, fixing his glowing gaze on Nûd.

Nûd stood up and pulled his shoulders back.

"Do not presume to tell a prince when he should or should not speak," Nûd declared. "My friends and I came to see if you were rested, not to be ordered about."

Eynon and Merry exchanged concerned glances and got to their feet behind Nûd. *I hope he knows what he's doing,* thought Eynon.

"Yes, Your Highness. Of course, Your Highness," said Viridáxés. "I am a servant of Tamloch. Forgive my impertinence." The immense dragon dipped his head and shrank back, pulling his long neck in on itself for a moment, before returning to his previous position.

Eynon exhaled and heard Merry release a held breath from where she stood beside him. *Nûd's gambit had worked.*

"Tell me, good and glorious servant, are you rested?" asked Nûd. "Are your energies restored?"

"They are, Your Highness," said Viridáxés. "Will you take me to the king? I can sense him, far to the east—and the crown prince as well. I want to serve and smash the Roma, if they've come to Orluin."

Nûd frowned and Viridáxés dipped his head again.

"Have the Roma crossed the Ocean?" the dragon asked contritely.

"Yes," said Nûd, "but much has changed since you were placed in this quarry. Orluin is a lot different now."

Viridáxés' eyes glowed brighter and a stronger green light escaped from his throat.

"Perchance, will you tell me how things stand today?" asked the dragon. "Surely this is an age of greatness. Are there tales of heroic kings and glorious battles you can tell? Or stories of valiant mages and wizards' duels you can share? I love stories!"

For a heartbeat, Eynon thought Viridáxés resembled a puppy begging for a treat.

Nûd turned to look at Eynon and Merry. He nodded at them and they nodded back. Eynon wasn't sure what Nûd planned, but he was prepared to follow his friend's lead.

"We'd be glad to," said Nûd, pleased by the opportunity to distract the dragon. "Each of us will tell you a story about the world as it is today. Then *you* will tell us a story about Orluin at the time of the First Ships." He paused to see Viridáxés' reaction. The huge dragon was nodding, so Nûd continued. "When the stories have been told, we can all fly east to find the king and his heir."

"Three new stories would be a treasure worth hoarding," said Viridáxés. "If they don't take *too* long..."

The dragon sounded like he wanted to say more.

"And...?" asked Nûd.

"Might I have something to eat before we leave? I haven't had a cow since before I was buried—and I don't think you'd approve of me eating one of the villagers keeping watch."

"We certainly would *not!*" insisted Merry.

Eynon looked down at Viridáxés' vast bulk stretching the length of the quarry. *I wonder if even my biggest fireball would stop him?* he mused.

Nûd laughed and Viridáxés lowered his head.

"Have I offended Your Highness?" asked the dragon.

"By no means," said Nûd. "But consider. If you weren't much bigger than a wyvern when you were planted in the quarry, a single cow would be a sizable meal."

Viridáxés tilted his colossal head and nodded.

Nûd went on. "Now," he said, "a single cow would be no more than a tiny morsel. You'd need an entire herd of cows to fill your belly."

Viridáxés opened his enormous mouth wide. Eynon heard the same deep rumble he'd taken to be amusement earlier.

"Very true, Your Highness," said the dragon. "Yet even a morsel would be a meal when breaking a fast of two thousand years."

"Agreed," said Nûd. He turned to Eynon. "Do you think we can convince Rocky to fetch us a few elk for our big friend?"

"We can try," said Eynon.

Rocky pushed his blocky head into Eynon's back and snorted. His meaning was clear.

"When am *I* going to get a familiar?" protested Merry under her breath.

"What are elk?" asked Viridáxés.

"Big deer," said Nûd.

"Good," said Viridáxés. "I like venison—and their antlers are crunchy."

"You'll be expensive to feed if you'll require a herd of cows to eat every day," noted Eynon.

"I don't *need* to eat," said Viridáxés. "At least if I return to this quarry every month or so to soak up more energy. But I *like* to eat every now and then—and threatening to consume a few farmers is good for a dragon's fearsome reputation."

"Do *not* eat any farmers," Nûd commanded. "It will reflect badly on the crown of Tamloch."

"Yes, Your Highness," said Viridáxés, looking downcast. Then the dragon's eyes glowed brighter. "What about really old ones who can't work any longer?"

"No eating farmers, old *or* young," said Nûd.

"Nobles?" asked Viridáxés tentatively.

"You may not eat *any* humans," said Nûd, "no matter what their station."

"And no cows, either," said Eynon. "Cows belong to people and they get upset when you eat them."

"The people or the cows?" asked Viridáxés.

"Both," said Eynon sternly.

In the distance, Eynon saw the tip of Viridáxés' tail flip petulantly. He pitied the dragon for a few seconds and sympathized. It was unpleasant to be told what one could and couldn't eat. Still, there were limits.

Rocky unfurled his wings. Chee, disturbed by the wyvern's movement, sat up and reached the end of the straps holding him in place.

"Chee-ee-ee," he said plaintively, moving his small head in woozy circles.

Eynon released the raconette, picked him up, and cradled him in his arms while Merry searched for water and willow bark in her pack. After a nod of his big wedge-shaped head, Rocky launched himself into the sky to search for elk.

"Thank you, Your Highness and friends," said Viridáxés. "Which one of you is going to go first?"

"I will," said Eynon, "but you'll have to wait for a few minutes. The three of us need to talk first to make sure we aren't all planning to tell the same story. We'll also want to start a fire. It's a bit chilly for sitting and telling stories, even with afternoon sun."

"I can help with your fire," said Viridáxés. The green glow from his throat intensified.

"That's quite all right," said Merry. "We don't want to be incinerated by accident if your flame spreads farther than you anticipated."

"Hmmm," said Viridáxés. "It might at that. Best to avoid the possibility. I remember when a peddler got too near a cow I'd planned to roast for dinner and..."

"You can stop right there," said Nûd. "Well-behaved dragons should know better than to discuss such things in front of humans. Contemplating peddlers being turned to ash by stray flames can be disconcerting and ruin a person's appetite."

"Sorry, Your Highness," said Viridáxés. His huge head tilted again, in a way Eynon was learning meant the giant dragon was remembering something.

"It was more charcoal than ash, actually," said Viridáxés. "And it didn't ruin *my* appetite—quite the opposite. Plus, the cow was delicious."

"You should go to the far end of the quarry," said Nûd, changing the subject. "Give us privacy to build our fire and talk. I'll call for you when Eynon is ready to start his tale."

"When will the wyvern arrive with my elk?" asked Viridáxés. "Talking about roast cows is making me hungry."

"Go," said Nûd, pointing to the south.

Viridáxés turned—nearly brushing the eastern wall of the quarry—and moved away from the high cliff. Merry cast a privacy sphere around the three of them, plus Chee. The raconette was chewing on willow bark and sitting precariously on Eynon's left shoulder. Eynon spoke first.

"I was worried Viridáxés was going to eat you when you scolded him," he said to Nûd. "I'm impressed that he obeyed you."

"I'm glad it worked," said Nûd. "I'm trying hard not to let all those *Your Highnesses* go to my head."

"Of course not, Your Majesty," said Merry.

Nûd threw up his hands. "Stop that! You know I don't want to be king of Dâron."

"Being a prince of Tamloch means we're not candidates for Viridáxés' breakfast," said Eynon. "You need to keep answering to Your Highness until we can figure out what to do about Tamloch's extra-large-sized new *servant*."

"I don't think it would be a good idea to say anything about us being from Dâron either," added Merry. "Viridáxés seems to think we're all from Tamloch—and I don't want him learning we aren't."

"It's understandable," said Nûd. "This land *was* part of Tamloch at the time of the First Ships. Dâron got the land east of the mountains and south, while Tamloch had their lands in the north *and* all the mountains, until the Clan Landers claimed their strongholds. There have been a lot of adjustments to the borders in two thousand years."

"How did you know this part of Dâron was once Tamloch?" asked Merry.

"History books in the library at Melyncárreg," Nûd replied.

"We'll have to adjust our stories to make sure we don't give away the fact that we're from Dâron," said Eynon.

"Would it really matter?" asked Merry. "Viridáxés told us Tamloch and Dâron were allied at the time of the First Ships. The Roma were their primary fear."

"I hope you're right," said Nûd. "What story do you plan to tell, Eynon?"

"Something that will paint the Roma as less of an enemy," Eynon replied. "I *will* have to tell Viridáxés about Occidens Province, though. I hope that doesn't upset him."

"It can't be helped," said Nûd. "While Eynon is telling his tale, Merry can maintain a privacy sphere while I contact Damon—or Fercha—to get their advice."

Eynon removed a plain gold ring and handed it to Nûd. "Take this one, too, and try to reach Doethan again. Maybe he won't be quite so busy now."

"I can try," said Nûd. He slid Eynon's ring over a finger.

"I'll figure out my story while Eynon is telling his," said Merry. "In the meantime, I'll fly down to the trees at the base of the hill and collect some firewood."

"I'll come with you," said Eynon.

"That means I get to stay here to reassure Viridáxés we haven't abandoned him," said Nûd.

"Just another part of your royal responsibilities," said Merry. She grinned and Nûd rolled his eyes.

"Be quick about gathering firewood," he said. "We don't want to strain Viridáxés' patience. I don't think we'd like it if he was angry."

"I'll second that," said Eynon. He moved Chee from his shoulder to Nûd's. "You don't want to be nearby if I have to use my axe, little friend," said Eynon.

Chee nodded weakly and waved as Merry and Eynon climbed on their flying disks and floated down the back of the hill toward the trees.

Chapter 17

Eynon's Tale

A fire was crackling pleasantly in a small circle of rocks on top of the hill. Eynon had kindled it with his red magestone and its flames cast a cheery glow much different from the dragon's glowing green eyes. Viridáxés' head rested on top of the cliff, not far from the fire. His gaze was focused on Eynon with an intensity Eynon found unnerving. *Dragons do have that effect on people in books,* Eynon remembered.

All three humans were seated on rocks that must have been placed on top of the cliff for the benefit of the young people having picnics and courting there. Chee was asleep in Eynon's lap. Nûd was to his left and Merry to his right. He squeezed her hand and began his story, remembering how he'd heard one of his cousins—really more of an honorary great-aunt—tell it around a midsummer festival campfire half a decade ago.

"A long time ago," began Eynon, using one of the standard storytelling formulas. *Once upon a time* would have been more appropriate for an imaginary story, Eynon considered, but this one was true—or mostly true. According to his mother, his honorary great-aunt had a tendency to exaggerate.

"How long ago?" asked Viridáxés. "Two thousand years? Maybe I will know some of the people you'll be talking about."

"This was twenty-five years ago, not two thousand," said Eynon. "It's my great-aunt Kelayna's story. She was a soldier."

"Good," said Viridáxés. "I like stories about soldiers." The green circles of the dragon's eyes spun around his night-dark pupils.

"Twenty-five years ago," said Eynon, trying to get back on track, "the armies of Tamloch and Dâron united to fight the Eagle People."

"The Roma are *here?*" asked Viridáxés. "In Orluin? *Now?* I've awakened just in time."

The dragon began to lift his head and spread his wings.

"Stop," Nûd commanded. "I told you things are different now than they were when you were placed in the quarry. The Roma arrived and claimed the valley of the Abbenoth fifteen hundred years ago, so there's no particular urgency to do anything about it. They're quite well-established and their presence as a common enemy and a buffer between Tamloch and Dâron has done more good than harm over the centuries."

"I find *that* hard to believe," protested Viridáxés. "If they'd only awakened me when the Roma ships first came to our shores..." His head settled back down on top of the cliff but Eynon could clearly see the wedge-shaped point of the dragon's tail slash across the sky.

"It's true, however," said Nûd.

"But my mission," complained Viridáxés.

"Are you going to let Eynon tell his story or not?" interjected Merry. "Perhaps you'd like to tell *your* story first so *we* can interrupt *you?*"

"I apologize," said Viridáxés, raising his head just enough to nod it solemnly at the three humans. "In my eagerness to learn more, I was impolite."

"See that it doesn't happen again," said Nûd.

"Yes, Your Highness," said Viridáxés. The dragon's head settled back in its previous position on top of the cliff. "Please continue, young wizard."

"Thank you," said Eynon. "Do you know of the islands near the mouth of the Abbenoth?" he asked.

"Of course," said Viridáxés. "There are several. One had very good places for ships to tie up. It was a long, narrow north-south island with a stone inn at the southern tip. Wizards and traders from Tamloch and Dâron used to meet there." The dragon's voice faded for a moment, then he spoke as softly as a being his size *could* speak. "I slept in its courtyard. A man with a wooden leg owned the inn, I remember. I stayed there on my way to the quarry."

"Very good," said Eynon. "The island is known as *Insula Montes,* for its hills. The site of the inn you stayed at is now a major city, Nova Eboracum, the capital of Occidens Province."

"The Roma have an entire *province* now," grumbled Viridáxés. The dragon may have thought he was talking to himself, but the humans heard it plainly.

Eynon smiled inside. *They could probably hear Viridáxés' protests all the way to Wherrel,* he considered.

"The governor of Occidens Province—not Quintillius, the current governor, but two administrators before him—foolishly tried to expand into territory belonging to both Tamloch *and* Dâron. His name was Cornelius Gracchus Germanicus and he misjudged the two kingdoms' resolve. Dâron's army fought through Roma territory to the cliffs on the west bank of the Abbenoth."

"Good!" said Viridáxés. "I hunted wild wisents in the forest atop those cliffs. The rock faces were almost like palisades."

"As you say," said Eynon. "I've never been to Nova Eboracum myself. I'm sharing my great-aunt's tale."

"Pardon my interruption," said Viridáxés.

Eynon nodded. "Tamloch's army had marched down to the western end of *Insula Longa,* the big island shaped like a fish..." he continued.

"I know it," said Viridáxés. "It had good oyster beds two thousand years ago. Does it still?"

"I have no idea," said Eynon.

Merry waggled her finger at Viridáxés, chastising him for his continuing interruptions. The dragon blew out air from his wagon-wheel-sized nostrils and settled.

"As I was saying, the army of Tamloch was opposite Nova Eboracum across a narrow river to the east."

"We called it the Thoirabhainn," said Viridáxés.

"What does *that* mean?" asked Merry.

"The East River," said the dragon.

Merry's mouth formed an O-shape while Nûd and Eynon grinned.

"Ealdamon, Dâron's Master Mage, was a very powerful wizard," said Eynon. He intentionally didn't mention that he was Ealdamon's apprentice. "Germanicus thought his fortress, at the southern tip of Insula Montes, was impregnable—guarded by high walls and the rivers—but Ealdamon proved the Roma governor wrong."

"What did he do?" asked Viridáxés. "Destroy the Roma stronghold with fire? That's what *I* would have done."

"No doubt," said Nûd. Eynon's friend spread his arms wide to indicate Viridáxés' magnificence. The dragon revealed more of its impressive teeth.

"The Master Mage of Dâron took a different approach," said Eynon. "He froze the rivers—both the Abbenoth and the river to the east. It's really one body of water south of Insula Montes."

"Brilliant," said Viridáxés. "That way, both armies could advance on Nova Eboracum and besiege the fortress."

"Exactly," said Eynon. "There was a tremendous battle before the gates of the Roma citadel."

"Did your great-aunt Kelayna lead the attack?" asked Viridáxés.

"Hardly," said Eynon. "She was part of the Coombe's levy and an ordinary foot soldier with boiled leather armor. The crown princes and their knights from both kingdoms were in the van."

"Oh," said Viridáxés.

"Don't worry," said Eynon. "Her story *does* get exciting."

"Eventually," said Merry, poking a friendly elbow in Eynon's ribs.

Chee, disturbed by Merry's motion, woke up and rolled off Eynon. He considered his options, shifted a bit to the right, climbed into Nûd's lap, and resumed napping.

"Kelayna had a hand-me-down steel sword on her belt and a round shield made from wood reinforced with iron strips," said Eynon. "Like almost everyone else in the levy she also carried a longbow over one shoulder and a tall spear strapped over the other."

"That much hasn't changed in two thousand years," remarked Viridáxés.

"Sword smithing has improved," said Nûd. "A modern blade can slice right through an ancient one, according to what I've read."

"Even the sharpest blade will not be able to cut through *my* scales," said Viridáxés.

"As you say," said Nûd.

"As *I* was saying," noted Eynon, "Kelayna was part of the Coombe's levy. Dâron's commanders put her unit in the rear, as a reserve."

"Dâron?" asked Viridáxés. "I thought this land belonged to Tamloch. It did when I was placed in this quarry."

"There have been quite a few border adjustments over the centuries," said Merry.

"As you say," said Viridáxés. "And those blasted Roma must have had a lot to do with it."

"I don't think you're wrong," said Nûd, "but it's not fair to blame the Roma for all of it."

Viridáxés snorted. "Even the youngest dragon could see that Tamloch and Dâron would always fight like brothers. A real surprise would be if they didn't."

"True enough," said Merry. She nudged Eynon in the ribs again, but gently this time.

"Anyway," said Eynon, "my great-aunt was in the rear and still out on the frozen bridge of sorts Ealdamon had created across the Abbenoth. As she recounted what happened, she had stepped near the edge of the ice to see how thick it was…"

"Not the wisest decision, I expect," rumbled Viridáxés.

"Correct," said Eynon. "She was two dozen steps away from the rest of her unit when a great stone tossed from the walls of the Roma citadel smashed into the ice behind her…"

"And let me guess," said Merry. "She floated off toward the Ocean on a sheet of ice?"

"Did you hear my great-aunt tell the story?" asked Eynon.

"No," said Merry.

"Then let me tell it," said Eynon.

"Of course," said Merry. "Then what happened?"

"My great-aunt Kelayna floated off toward the Ocean on a sheet of ice," said Eynon.

Viridáxés mouth opened a few feet and Eynon heard the special noise from deep in the dragon's belly down in the quarry. Viridáxés was laughing, and so were Eynon and Nûd. Chee looked up, decided whatever was being discussed wasn't worth his attention, and went back to sleep.

"I deserved that," said Merry.

"Great-aunt Kelayna *didn't* deserve what happened to her however," said Eynon. "The ice was caught in a southerly current and
carried farther and farther away. The other members of her unit
were summoned forward to join the attack on the Roma fortress
and Kelayna's dire situation was overlooked. I expect many of her
friends mourned for her, thinking she'd been crushed by the huge
stone tossed by the Roma's catapults."

"Understandable," said Viridáxés. The dragon nosed his head a
few feet closer to Eynon.

"The ice sheet wasn't very stable," said Eynon. "My great-aunt
had to flatten herself in the middle of the sheet to prevent it from
turning over, but that wasn't the worst of it."

The dragon's nearer eye opened wider in an unspoken *do go on*.

"The worst thing was that it was a warm current," said Eynon.
"The sheet of ice was shrinking rapidly."

"What did Kelayna do?" asked Viridáxés.

"Could she swim?" Merry inquired.

Nûd moved his head slowly from side to side, impressed by the
way his friend's story had captured Viridáxés' interest.

"Kelayna *could* swim, a little, but she was out of sight of land by
this point," said Eynon. "Swimming wouldn't do her much good.
The sheet of ice wasn't much bigger than a pair of cottage doors
now, and still shrinking. Hours passed, with no help in sight. My
great-aunt said she grew so tired, she fell asleep, but she woke up a
few minutes later when something slammed into the bottom of the
ice and tossed the sheet high in the air. Kelayna said she used her
dagger to hang on when the ice sheet tipped."

"What was it?" asked Merry.

"One of the black and white wolves of the Ocean," said Eynon.
"She said they were big and always hungry."

"How did Kelayna escape?" asked Viridáxés.

"She got to her knees and stabbed the sea wolf with her spear,"
said Eynon. "The beast pulled Kelayna even *farther* out into the
Ocean before the spear was tugged out of her hands."

Eynon paused and took a swallow of cider from his leather bottle.

He waited a moment, giving the suspense a few seconds to build.

"The ice sheet, at least what was left of it, moved from a warm current to a cold one. There was a thick fog rising from the Ocean where the two flowing masses of water met." Eynon looked up at the dragon. Viridáxés was closely following his words. "My great-aunt started to sing," said Eynon. "She's not a good singer, but she projects well."

"Did one of the mer-folk hear her and rescue her?" asked Merry. "A selkie seal who could change into a handsome man?"

"You've been listening to too many stories," said Eynon. "No, she was rescued by a Roma fisherman and his son. They thought she was a wounded dolphin and rowed to her through the fog to see if they could help the poor beast."

"I'll bet *they* were surprised," said Nûd.

"No more than my great-aunt Kelayna," said Eynon. "They fed her hot soup and took her back to port with them. They gave her clean clothes and a place to sleep in their cottage on the south shore of Insula Longa. She helped them with the nets on a few more fishing trips, too. The fisherman—his name, appropriately, was Piscator— was a student of Athican myths and legends. He'd named his little boat the *Argo,* but some children in his village had carved a capital *C* in front of the name to tease him. He thought it was a better name and didn't change it back."

Eynon moved his shoulders in a circle to loosen them. He covered his mouth and yawned. Merry squeezed his hand. Soon he'd be able to listen to *her* story. Eynon cleared his throat.

"The son's name was Petrus. He was close to Kelayna in age and didn't have to join Roma's legions, because fishermen had a critical role helping to feed soldiers. When they were alone and his father couldn't hear, he told Kelayna he was sick of nets, sick of fish and especially sick of sailing the Ocean. He still turned green when the waves grew high. His ambition was to find a plot of land that didn't move up and down and farm it."

"If I saw a Roma fishing boat, I'd sink it," declared Viridáxés.

"You'll do no such thing," said Nûd. "How many times do I have to tell you that things are different today? Don't you see the point of Eynon's story—that the Roma can be friends as well as enemies?"

"They saved Kelayna, but that doesn't make them our friends," said Viridáxés. "Roma keep slaves. They probably saved her to enslave her."

"It didn't work out that way," said Eynon. "My great-aunt came back from the war with a husband. For many of the men and women in the Coombe, service as a soldier is much the same as a wander year."

"Wander year?" asked the great green dragon.

"A custom where young people travel away from home for a year and a day, just wandering about, starting on their sixteenth birthdays," said Merry.

"Curious," said Viridáxés. "I can see how that would help prevent inbreeding."

"I always knew dragons were wise," said Eynon.

Viridáxés' eyes glowed a brighter green.

Eynon nodded to Viridáxés.

"Would you like to hear a story about my great-uncle Peter?" Eynon asked. He grinned at the dragon.

"No," said Viridáxés. "I would not, especially if he's a Roma. I still want to smash down the walls of Nova Eboracum and drive every last one of those blasted invaders back into the Ocean."

Nûd stiffened, about to rebuke the dragon, but stopped.

"Hold your commands, Your Highness," said Viridáxés. "I will do as you say—for now. But we will soon go east to see if the crown prince and the king of Tamloch agree with you. My mission is, was, and always has been to destroy the Roma. I won't vary from that course unless I'm commanded to do so by the king himself."

Nûd glanced away from Viridáxés. He caught Eynon and Merry's eyes.

"It's unfortunate not *all* dragons are wise," said Nûd. "Are you done with stories now?" he asked Viridáxés.

"I am *not*," said the dragon. "Though I hope her tale is more exciting than the other wizard's."

"It is," said Merry.

"Then get on with it," said Viridáxés.

Chapter 18

Eynon and Viridáxés

Merry stood up and stretched. "I'll share my tale as soon as I've had a chance to head down to the trees and return," she said.

"Do you need more firewood?" asked Viridáxés. "You seem to have plenty."

"More firewood would be helpful," said Merry. "But humans have other reasons for such visits. Nûd, will you come with me to keep watch?"

"Oh," said Viridáxés, "*That's* why you're going to the woods together. While I appreciate your desire to father an heir, Your Highness, is now truly the best time?"

Nûd turned red, or maybe it was just reflected light from the fire. He cradled Chee, stood up, and transferred the sleeping raconette back to Eynon's lap.

Merry laughed softly. "Viridáxés, you misunderstand. Nûd and I are friends. Eynon and I are lovers. I need to head down the hill to see to more immediate physical requirements."

Viridáxés didn't speak for a few seconds as he processed Merry's statements. Then the deep rumbling that signified the dragon's laughter echoed up from the quarry.

"So much for a dragon's reputation for wisdom," he chuckled. "Seek the relief you need. I will amuse myself talking further with your young man who has such imaginative relatives." Viridáxés snorted. "Towed by a sea wolf on a sheet of ice..." he said, allowing his words to trail off.

Merry patted Eynon's shoulder, then headed downhill with Nûd trailing behind.

Eynon stroked Chee's soft fur and looked up at Viridáxés. "I agree that the part about the sea wolf sounds far-fetched," said Eynon, "but the rest is at least plausible, especially if you know my great-uncle Peter."

"Enough about your relatives, young wizard," said the dragon. "I want to know how you came by a *red* magestone. None of the wizards from two thousand years ago had red magestones."

With several embellishments and no mention that his mentor was the master mage of Dâron, Eynon told Viridáxés the story of how he found his red magestone in the center of a polychromatic hot spring in Melyncárreg, including the challenge of fighting off more than a dozen basilisks.

"Hah!" said Viridáxés. "Basilisks have no effect on dragons. We already have a special relationship with stone in general and magestones in particular. Had I been with you, the basilisks would have hurried back into their mud pots in terror."

"No doubt," said Eynon. "As it was, I was glad to survive." Eynon shifted his body on his rock, taking care not to disturb Chee.

"Tell me, human," said Viridáxés. "Are there any other dragons on this side of the Ocean?"

"There have been rumors of dragons the size of houses in deep caves or remote forests," said Eynon, "but the only dragons I've ever seen other than Your Magnificence have been small gold dragons belonging to the Bifurlanders. They're not much bigger than horses."

"The Bifurlanders, or the gold dragons?" asked Viridáxés. "What *is* a Bifurlander, by the way? I don't recognize the word."

If Eynon hadn't been holding Chee, he would have slapped his forehead. He hadn't planned to add yet another complication to Viridáxés' picture of the modern world.

"Bifurlanders are northlanders," said Eynon. "From the colder territories beyond the Roma's empire across the Ocean. They came to Orluin a thousand years ago and settled north of Tamloch on land where wheat wouldn't grow. They trap and fish and keep milk cows. They also raise barley for beer and oats for porridge."

"*More* invaders," grunted Viridáxés. "More interlopers to drive from Orluin."

"Bifurlanders raid from time to time," said Eynon, "but no more than Tamloch and Dâron war with each other—at least from what I've read. It's complicated."

"I will make it less complicated," said Viridáxés. "The Roma *and* the Bifurlanders will need to learn to swim once I set fire to their farms, towns and cities."

"I'm confused," said Eynon.

"About what?" asked Viridáxés with a hint of a growl.

"You're two thousand years old, right?"

"Give or take a decade that's correct—from what you've told me."

"In stories, the oldest and largest dragons are also supposed to be the wisest, but you seem to be filled with anger and ready to lash out at perceived enemies before you understand all the details," said Eynon. "That doesn't seem wise."

"Hmmm," said Viridáxés. "You have a point. Perhaps it's because I've been asleep for two millennia instead of being awake and learning all that time. I have the size and power that come with age but retain the impetuosity of the young dragon I was when I was placed in the quarry."

"That may be it," said Eynon. "It's been easy for me to keep an open mind, since I knew so little to start with. For a dragon already beginning to gain wisdom, it must be much harder not to be a slave to your preconceptions."

"What?" asked Viridáxés. "My preconceptions?" The dragon stared down at Eynon. "I see where you're heading," he said. "But you're the one who's wrong. You weren't there when the Roma drove us from our homelands and forced us to take the First Ships across the Ocean. The empire is evil—it seeks to turn free folk into slaves and make everyone into identical soldiers marching in their legions."

"That may be," said Eynon, shrugging his shoulders, but not with enough vigor to interfere with Chee's nap. "I haven't met any Roma except my great-uncle Peter."

"Once you do, you'll see I'm right," said Viridáxés.

* * * * *

Merry and Nûd stood close together as they walked downslope to the line of trees. Her hands were hidden from the dragon by her body. She rubbed a spot on her finger corresponding to where Nûd had communications rings on his. Nûd nodded and Merry kept her lips tightly closed. The two remained silent until they entered the woods.

"What were you trying to tell me?" whispered Nûd, trying to confirm what he'd already guessed.

"Shhhh!" said Merry. She pulled Nûd farther back into the trees and cast a spherical privacy spell around them. Thinking back, Merry realized Fercha must have taught that spell to her in case she had to work as a spy for the Old Queen's faction.

"Can we talk now?" asked Nûd.

"Yes," said Merry. "Viridáxés can't hear us with a privacy sphere in place. Which of your rings will you try first? Who will you try to contact?"

"I'm not sure," said Nûd. "I thought I'd try them all in turn and see who answers. Eynon loaned me Doethan's ring. Maybe he is free to talk now—though after last time, it might be better to wait."

"Maybe you can reach Fercha," said Merry. "She'll know what to do."

"I'd rather not," said Nûd. His face scrunched up like he'd just eaten an unripe persimmon.

"Don't let the fact that she's your mother get in the way of asking her for help," said Merry. "We *really* need help—unless you think *you* can control Viridáxés?"

"I'm not sure I can control what comes out of my own mouth from minute to minute," said Nûd, "but I will try to contact her."

"What about Damon?" asked Merry.

"I'll try him, too," Nûd replied, "but Eynon told us he was exhausted from trying to freeze the Brenavon this morning. I don't want to bother him unless I have to."

"It may come to that," said Merry. "Being tired may affect Damon's power, but not his wisdom."

"Get moving," said Nûd. "You need to head up the hill to tell *your* story to Viridáxés. We don't want him eating Eynon out of boredom while he waits for you."

Merry smiled. "That's one thing I'm *not* worried about," she said. "Eynon would be quite a challenge to swallow."

"I expect Dâron's Conclave of Wizards will feel the same way when they meet him," teased Nûd. "How long will the privacy sphere last?"

"Another half an hour or so," said Merry. "I'll try to make my story last at least that long."

"What story do you plan to tell?" asked Nûd.

"Not *what* story, *whose* story," said Merry. "I'm going to entertain Viridáxés with a tale about an old friend from Tyford."

"I wish I could be there to hear it," said Nûd.

"Get us help quickly, and maybe you can," said Merry with a grin. She stepped through the interface of the privacy sphere and started back up the hill.

Inside the sphere, Nûd expanded a communications ring. "Hello, Mother," he said. "I need your help at the quarry near Wherrel."

Fercha answered, sounding far from her usual coherent and competent self. "Jusht a minute," she replied. "Why ish my bedroom shpinning?"

The communication ring's interface suddenly went black. It contracted to a small gold circle and Nûd dropped it to the ground in surprise. *Not one of my best ideas,* he thought.

Chapter 19

Merry's Tale

Eynon shrugged, giving Viridáxés' comment about the Roma being evil a non-verbal *if you say so*. He was saved from further discussion of the topic by Merry's noisy arrival at the top of the cliff. She was humming a song Eynon had heard before. Its words described two lovers, separated when their families moved apart, exchanging letters to keep their love strong until they could be reunited. Eynon was surprised Merry knew the tune. He'd thought it had been written in the Coombe. Eynon shook his head when he realized a lot of what he'd thought had originated in the Coombe had probably come from outside in the Rhuthro valley and beyond. In that moment of insight, he understood just how little he knew about his own history and resolved to do something about it—as soon as they figured out what to do with Viridáxés.

"Did I miss any sparkling conversation?" asked Merry.

"Not really," said Eynon. He was having trouble keeping his eyes open and didn't rise when Merry appeared because Chee was still sleeping on his lap. She sat next to Eynon and squeezed his arm.

"Sparkling, no," said Viridáxés. "Your lover is far too innocent for his own good."

"Which is one of the things I like most about him," said Merry. "Did some particular context bring that to mind, O Mighty Dragon?"

"He thinks the Roma aren't evil," replied Viridáxés, as if Eynon's believed the sun would rise in the west the next morning.

"They aren't all evil," said Merry. "No more than everyone in Dâron or Tamloch is evil—or every dragon."

"Hrrrrumph," snorted Viridáxés, emitting small clouds of steam from his nostrils. He focused his glowing green eyes on Merry. "I know what I know," said the dragon. "And I *also* know it is time for you to tell *your* story."

"Very well," said Merry. "This is the tale of a hero and a mighty warrior who fought against the Roma."

"I expect I'll like it then," said Viridáxés. "Was he tall and strong? Did he have a magic sword?"

"Not that tall," said Merry, "but he was strong. He was a cooper's son from a small village north of Tyford on the Moravon. His family also ran a ferry across the river, so his arms were powerful from guiding the ferry against the current and his eye was skillful at selecting and bending wood for barrel staves."

"Coopers are a lot like shipwrights," said Viridáxés. "They must have a feel for their materials and a talent for shaping wood to their will."

"Very true," said Merry, "but the hero of my story had dreams beyond building barrels and transporting farmers from shore to shore."

"He wanted to be a warrior!" Viridáxés exclaimed.

"Close," said Merry. "He wanted to be a soldier and serve in the king's guard."

"Which king?" asked Viridáxés.

"The king of Dâron," said Merry. "Dâroth the Twenty-fourth."

"Oh," said Viridáxés. It was obvious he was hoping for the king of Tamloch, but Dâron was at least an ally against the Roma, according to the dragon's out-of-date perspective.

"The cooper's son," began Merry.

"What was his name?" interrupted Viridáxés.

"The cooper's son," Merry restated, "was a good-natured young man. He was known to everyone in his village and the regular passengers on his ferry as Taffy. He had a big nose but was not unhandsome according to several of the young women in the village and ones from across the river who contrived to take the ferry more times than they otherwise might need to."

"Go on," said Viridáxés.

"At fifteen, Taffy was proud of his mustache, even though it looked like a fuzzy black caterpillar had crawled under his nose, according to his oldest sister," said Merry. "She was fourteen and would be filling in for Taffy running the ferry while he traveled on his wander year."

Eynon and Viridáxés were both listening closely now. Eynon nodded to encourage Merry to continue.

"Taffy's parents wanted him to come home and be a cooper, like his father. There was enough business for more than one cooper in their village, but Taffy wanted adventure," said Merry. "He built a small boat from lumber that wasn't suitable for barrel-making and set out down the Moravon, the Great River, headed for Tyford."

"What is Tyford?" asked Viridáxés. "You mentioned it before."

"It's the second-largest city in Dâron these days," said Merry. "It's on the east bank of the Moravon and has a toll bridge across the river. The bridge is so long it takes more than half-an-hour to walk across."

"Oh yes, I remember Tyford now. It was much smaller then. The great river was known as the Mórabhainn in Tamloch," said the dragon.

"Not that much different from Moravon," noted Eynon.

"Whether you call it by its name in Tamloch or Dâron, it's still a big river," said Merry. "Taffy pushed out into the current in a boat that looked more like half a barrel than a proper vessel, though it did have oars and a pointed prow. The river's flow was swift and Taffy reached Tyford just before nightfall. He pulled up to a pier at an inn and talked the innkeeper into giving him dinner and a bed, since he was on his wander year and wore the holly."

Viridáxés stared down at Eynon. "*You* wear holly in your cap."

"That's because I'm on my wander year," said Eynon.

"I'm on my wander year, too," said Merry. "Though I think I might have missed celebrating my birthday."

"Then we'll have to throw a belated party," said Eynon with a smile. He grinned at his lover. "If you're right about missing it."

"Things *have* been rather hectic lately," said Merry. "I may have lost track of the exact date."

"Can we get back to the story," said Viridáxés. It was more an order than a request. Then, as if remembering his manners, the great dragon added, "Please?"

"Of course," said Merry. "Taffy soon learned that there were only three ways for a poor young man in Tyford to become a soldier.

First, he could join the city's peacekeepers where he'd get very little training, even less pay, and spend most of his time breaking up disputes between merchants and their customers or helping drunks find their way home from taverns."

Eynon nodded, though he didn't have any direct knowledge of what Merry was talking about. *It can't hurt to have the dragon think I do,* he considered.

"Second, he could earn a place in the royal guard by showing promise. That way, the crown's instructors would teach him the arts of combat," Merry continued.

"And third?" asked Viridáxés.

"Third, Taffy could save up money to have an armsmaster give him private lessons. That would also help improve his chances of being accepted into the royal guard, since he would require less training. There's also the matter that Royal guards earn four or five times what a village cooper makes."

"I see," said the dragon. "I think I know what choice he made."

"The wise one, of course," said Merry. "He started by earning money helping the innkeeper keep order in the common room. He also collected coins for crafting and repairing barrels for the innkeeper and her customers."

"Then he hired an armsmaster to train him?" asked Viridáxés.

"It wasn't that simple," said Merry. "Taffy had to prove he'd be a worthy student. There are more students than available slots with the best armsmasters."

"He must have done well," said Viridáxés. "You said he was a hero."

Merry stared at the dragon.

"You tell it the way you will," he said. "I will be silent and listen."

Eynon and Merry both laughed at that. Chee even opened one eye before going back to sleep.

"Continue and ignore my interruptions," said Viridáxés.

"Taffy had money saved to pay for lessons," said Merry, "but he couldn't afford a soldier's kit of sword and shield and armor. He was told to appear before the armsmaster ready to fight, so he came wearing gear that looked like a fitted barrel, including what could have been a tall bucket with eye slits for a helm and a thick club filling in for a sword."

Viridáxés showed his upper teeth in what passed for a smile among dragons.

"As you might guess, the armsmaster's other students thought Taffy looked ridiculous. Their fathers were wealthy, so they all had steel swords, well-made shields, and coats of plates crafted from iron or steel."

"Taffy the Barrel Knight," said Viridáxés.

"Far from a knight at that point," said Merry. "The armsmaster sent her best student against Taffy. He tried to chop Taffy's club in half with his sword, but Taffy turned his club just so. He flipped the student's sword out of his hands and over his head."

"Good for Taffy!" Eynon exclaimed. He thought he knew who Merry was talking about.

"His attacker recovered and rushed Taffy, holding his shield ahead of him like a battering ram. He hoped to knock Taffy over with the force of his charge, but that didn't work either," said Merry. "Taffy held his ground, the barrel armor flexed and the student ended up flat on his back with Taffy's club in the middle of his stomach. All the other students were cheering Taffy, since the attacking student was often arrogant and pushed the other students around."

"Did Taffy earn his way onto the royal guard?" asked Viridáxés.

"What do *you* think?" asked Merry.

"He must have," said the dragon. "He joined the guard and fought valiantly against the Roma."

"You are wise to know how my story unfolds before I've finished it," said Merry.

"It's obvious," said Viridáxés. "Tell me of the battle."

"Eynon has told you much of it in his great-aunt's tale," said Merry. "The combined armies of Tamloch and Dâron besieged Nova Eboracum. The commander of the Roma garrison came forth and killed the crown princes of both kingdoms, but their sons avenged them with help from their royal guards."

"Like Taffy," said Viridáxés.

"And my father," said Merry, "though he doesn't talk about it. They say he helped save the life of the new crown prince of Dâron."

"And Taffy?" asked Viridáxés.

"He saved my father's life a few seconds earlier—allowing my father to save the new crown prince. Taffy learned how to use a sword, but he still carried his original club on his back, though he reinforced it with steel strips. He saw a mounted Roma *eques* with a tall-plumed helm was about to skewer my da with a spear, but Taffy threw his club. It hit the Roma knight in the helm and knocked him off his horse."

"Impressive!" said Eynon.

"Cheeeee..." said Chee softly. The raconette was beginning to wake up.

"My father received a noble title and lands," said Merry. "He's now the baron of the Upper Rhuthro."

"A well-deserved honor, I'm sure," said Viridáxés. "How was Taffy rewarded?"

"He wasn't," said Merry. She shook her head sadly. "My father gave him enough money to buy the inn where Taffy had first worked in Tyford. The innkeeper was ready to retire and was glad to sell."

"I see," said Viridáxés. "Some things haven't changed in two thousand years."

"You mean life isn't fair?" asked Merry. "Taffy seems happy as an innkeeper. After the fight at the gates of Nova Eboracum, he said he'd had his fill of battle."

"No," said Viridáxés. "What's unfair is that I wasn't there to crush the Roma's gates to dust. We can fly there immediately and remedy that oversight."

"You should wait until you consult with the crown prince of Tamloch," said Merry.

"Or the king," said Viridáxés. "He will know what to do."

"You still have Nûd's story to hear," said Merry.

"Where *is* that second heir?" asked Viridáxés. "Surely it can't take *that* long to see to necessary functions?"

"Here he comes," said Eynon. He stood and waved to his friend walking up the hill. Nûd's tall frame was easy to see.

Chee climbed on Eynon's shoulder and stared in a different direction. Then *he* started to wave.

Eynon followed Chee's eyes and generated lenses to help him see at a distance. Rocky was arriving from the northwest with two elk carcasses in his claws.

"Excellent!" said Viridáxés. "The next story can wait. I'm *hungry!*"

Chapter 20

Thieves from the Sky

Instead of gulping the elk carcasses Rocky had brought in a single bite, Viridáxés nibbled the pair of big bucks like Eynon might savor morsels of aged cheese. The dragon sat on his back legs, so he could be high enough to observe the humans on top of the hill in preparation for hearing Nûd's story while keeping his front claws free to hold an elk. Viridáxés started with the first elk's antlers, making a crunching sound like Eynon did when he ate twice-baked breadsticks. It was far enough into spring that the elks' antlers were new growth, not old.

"Go ahead and start your story," said Viridáxés. "I will listen as I snack."

"Whatever," said Nûd as he shifted from side to side on his cold stone seat.

Eynon wasn't sure why his friend was being short with the dragon until a certain look in Nûd's face made Eynon realize Nûd wasn't being curt—he was trying to stall. From reading Nûd's expression it seemed obvious he didn't know what story to tell. Before Eynon could jump in to cover for Nûd, chaos erupted.

Two gryffons swooped out of the afternoon sky. Each took an elk carcass in its talons and sped off toward the east. Summoning distance-vision lenses, Eynon could see the pair of gryffons join two more of their kind who helped them carry their stolen meal away at an even faster speed.

Viridáxés bellowed in anger. The sound bounced off the walls of the quarry causing shelves of rock to come lose and crash down, imitating a rumbling peal of thunder. The great green dragon launched his immense body into the air and gave chase. Wind from the downstrokes of his wings blew out the campfire and sent sparks exploding out around Eynon, Nûd and Merry. Chee was knocked from Eynon's lap and chittered unhappily on the ground. Rocky looked ready to pursue the gryffons himself for stealing his gifts.

Merry and Eynon stepped onto their flying disks while Nûd, joined by Chee, climbed on Rocky. They all flew east to follow Viridáxés and the gryffons. The dragon continued to trumpet his extreme displeasure as he closed the distance between himself and the gryffons, who dropped altitude quickly in hopes Viridáxés would overshoot them.

The dragon proved more maneuverable in flight than the gryffons expected, however. Viridáxés' twisted his long neck, stopped bellowing for a few seconds, and released a huge, eye-searing gout of green flames toward the lion-eagles below. Unfortunately, the gryffons scattered and the dragonfire struck a forest of pines and hardwoods on top of the mountains on the east side of the Coombe, setting the trees alight.

Merry created a cone of solidified sound to magnify her voice and shouted to Nûd.

"Follow Viridáxés," she said. "Eynon and I will deal with the fire."

Nûd—and Chee—waved to acknowledge her advice and Rocky sped east, trailing after the gryffons and dragon.

"I'll take the right side, you take the left," shouted Merry.

Eynon nodded and took stock of the blazing mountainside below. It was the same land he'd crossed on the first day of his wander year when he'd traversed that mountain before discovering Fercha's artifact. He could already see animals running downslope trying to escape the fire, included a doe and her fawn and a singed and smoke-tinged brown bear.

None of his familiar magic would do for putting out a fire. One of his fireballs might blast the localized fire away but would probably make the situation worse. Eynon inhaled slowly, looked inward, and drew on the expertise of his blue magestone to try something he'd never done before. With a gesture, he generated a congruency connecting to the lake back in Melyncárreg. Water streamed out of a hole in the sky and fell like a narrow waterfall, dousing a few trees and sending up a thin pillar of steam.

To his right, Eynon saw Merry was taking a different approach. She was creating dozens of small bubbles of solidified sound around clumps of trees then expanding them vapidly to suck all the air away from the fires, snuffing them out. Eynon decided to try a similar approach using solidified sound that leveraged the water he'd already linked to. He built a wide shallow pan of transparent solidified sound and perforated it so the descending water covered a much broader area, like a spring shower.

Merry turned to face Eynon and turned up her palms in an expression that Eynon realized was her way of telling him he was being an idiot. Eynon slapped his forehead and used both his magestones to open dozens of congruencies to the lake back in Melyncárreg. Rain now fell like a heavy thunderstorm and soon the entire mountainside was steaming and no flames remained. Eynon canceled his spells. To his right, Merry's side was no longer burning as well—her trees weren't even steaming. They moved their flying disks side by side.

"Nicely done," said Eynon.

"You too," said Merry. "After you realized what you could do."

"I'm still learning," Eynon protested.

"So am I," said Merry. She smiled at Eynon and he smiled back.

"I think those gryffons were the ones who were trying to eat me back in Melyncárreg," he said. "A momma gryffon and three gryffonlets."

"Three *big* gryffonlets," said Merry. "They seemed fully grown to me."

"Pretty much," said Eynon. "How did they get *here* I wonder?"

"They must have come through the gate from Melyncárreg with the wisents," Merry replied.

"That wasn't part of my plan," said Eynon.

"It couldn't be helped," said Merry. "The best-laid plans sometimes go awry—like our attempt to distract Viridáxés."

"True enough," said Eynon.

"Now we have to find an angry dragon," said Merry.

A tremendous blast of bright green flames flashed in the sky off to the east.

"I don't think that's going to be much of a problem," said Eynon.

Merry leaned over and gave Eynon a peck on the cheek.

"Any ideas on how to help us fly faster?" she asked.

"One or two, maybe," Eynon replied. He surrounded the two of them in a streamlined teardrop of solidified sound and channeled the energy of his red magestone into powering the flight of both their flying disks. They jumped forward at double their normal flying speed, chasing bright bursts of green fire.

Chapter 21

Back to the Dormant Dragon

Dârio stood frozen for a few seconds, unable to believe his eyes as he watched Verro's hands tighten around Túathal's throat. To Dârio's eye, Verro's expression seemed like the release of decades of pent-up anger and frustration between the brothers. The young king of Dâron watched as the knife slipped from the king of Tamloch's fingers to rest as a glint of hard steel on the bed's soft quilt. Túathal's knees buckled and his body fell, now supported only by Verro's grip on his windpipe.

Salder stood impassively, cradling Uirsé in his arms and observing the scene. When Túathal's face began to turn blue, one corner of his mouth turned up in a hint of a smile.

From the far side of the room, Doethan reacted by shoving Dârio toward the bed.

"Stop him before he kills Túathal!" Doethan commanded, ignoring the lèse-majesté. "He'll never forgive himself."

Dârio lunged for the bed and landed on the far side of it with all his weight, causing the straw mattress to sag and bounce, disrupting Verro's grip.

"I'll forgive myself, don't worry," said Verro through clenched teeth. "I've watched my brother's twisted rule for decades and felt him transform me into something more like him than myself. It's best if he dies. The girl said so."

Deciding *not* to try to break Verro's grip, Dârio threw his weight against the struggling brothers and knocked them both out of bed and onto the floor. Túathal landed on his back, striking his head on the floorboards. Verro landed on top of him, but he'd released his stranglehold and was carried sideways to land on *his* back beside Túathal. It was clear Verro's limbs weren't fully recovered from the basilisk-gaze venom. He flexed his fingers and lifted his head but made no other move to shift his position. Túathal's face was still blue. He wasn't breathing.

Doethan crossed the room and stood next to Salder, who still held Uirsé.

"Move Verro so I can work," he ordered Dârio.

The young king, now habituated to doing what Doethan told him, carefully slid Verro's legs, then upper torso, a few feet farther from the bed. Doethan knelt in the newly cleared space, bent down to Túathal, and began breathing air into the king of Tamloch's lungs. After a few breaths, he sat up and generated two spheres of solidified sound about twice the size of his head. The spheres rhythmically expanded and contracted. Doethan put one to work replacing his efforts forcing air into Túathal while the other pressed hard against the king of Tamloch's chest, encouraging his heart to beat.

"Your second sphere won't work," said Verro from his position nearby on the floor.

"Why not?" asked Doethan, most of his attention focused on his patient.

"Because my brother doesn't *have* a heart," said Verro. "Just a black block of ice where one should be."

Doethan extended a tube of solidified sound toward Túathal's chest and listened at one end.

"It may be a block of black ice, but it's beating again," said Doethan.

"Blast," said Verro, lifting his head. "Letting him live is a mistake, I can feel it. I could tell you stories about his petty cruelties, like what he did to the puppy our parents gave me when I was seven. My brother decided it would be funny if..."

"I don't want to hear it," said Salder. "I saw his true temperament displayed close at hand for two years and it made me sick. He took pleasure in humiliating everyone around him—even you, Verro."

"That's why you shouldn't have stopped me," said Verro. His head fell back down on the floor.

Salder frowned, then shifted to position Uirsé on the bed where she could rest until the sleeping potion Túathal had given her wore off.

Túathal began to cough and gasp as he drew in air. His face was contorted in pain but was no longer blue.

That's my father, thought Dârio. *How is it that I'm not a monster, too?*

"Thank goodness you're not like him," Salder told Dârio, as if reading Dârio's mind.

"How do you know I'm not?" asked Dârio. "Don't you believe all the court gossip about me? I'm irresponsible and capricious and a poor excuse for a king, don't you know."

"When you live in the capital of Tamloch and hear stories like that about Dâron's monarch, you learn to discount them," said Salder. "Besides, I worked as a spy for Queen Carys—and Ealdamon, for that matter. They wouldn't support someone who was bad for the kingdom. And my father knows Duke Háiddon. The duke speaks well of you."

"Duke Háiddon ought to," said Dârio. "He was more of a father to me than my own sire—or the man I thought was my father." Dârio shook his head. "You say you saw examples of Túathal's cruelty?"

"Every day," said Salder. "He seemed to enjoy hurting others. He would send innocent servant girls into jail cells filled with prisoners just to see what would happen."

"I can only imagine," said Dârio.

Túathal was looking stronger. Doethan watched him stretch his legs and arms and spoke to Salder.

"Go downstairs and fetch some rope, please," he said. "We need to bind Túathal, so he doesn't cause *more* trouble."

"Of course," said Salder. He checked Uirsé's pulse and smiled. It was strong. Then he left the room, moving quickly.

Dârio helped Verro sit up. The tall wizard was regaining more muscle control by the minute.

"Thank you, nephew," said Verro. "Since you wouldn't let me kill him, we're going to need to do something about Túathal sooner, rather than later. Exile either in the south or the north, at your pleasure. It will be more difficult to hold him securely if Princess Gwýnnett and the wizards in her faction can find him. Perhaps a hidden cavern somewhere would be better?"

"Where he's exiled won't matter," said Dârio. "The important thing now is for me to take the throne of Tamloch and institute a new, more benevolent rule as Túathal's successor."

"You'll find plenty of nobles in Tamloch ready to support you," said Verro. "Especially after Túathal made such a mess of his invasion of Dâron. Most of them will be hoping you'll be easier to manipulate than your father."

"It won't take me long to prove them wrong," said Dârio, "but I wonder how long it will take *them* to adapt to a ruler who tries to treat nobles and common folk fairly and respectfully."

"If that's your goal, you'll have all the help I can give you," said Verro. Tamloch's master mage held tightly to Dârio's arm and got to his feet, then sat in one of a pair of straight-backed wooden chairs by the tall windows.

"Both of you will need to get north to the battlefield soon," said Doethan. "We will be losing light in a few hours and Verro needs to introduce you as Túathal's heir to the captured leaders of Tamloch's army. There's also the small matter of helping to save Nova Eboracum from the Tamloch fleet."

Túathal was curled up on the floor with his knees against his chest, breathing regularly. He seemed to be sleeping. Dârio didn't trust him. *Hibblig could come sailing through the windows on his flying disk to take Túathal away, too,* he thought.

The old tomcat prowled over to Túathal from his previous spot at the foot of the bed, regarded the king of Tamloch, and hissed. He then shifted to twist around Dârio's ankles before crossing to Verro and jumping into the tall wizard's lap. Verro stroked his fur with one hand and rubbed the old tom under his chin with the other. The contented cat settled into the folds of Verro's green robes, purred, and went to sleep. Tamloch's master mage wouldn't be standing up anytime soon.

Salder returned with two short lengths of hemp rope. He tossed them to Dârio and moved to check on Uirsé, who was starting to stir. Her eyes were open, and she smiled up at Salder.

"Hello, my love," she said, kissing him gently as he bent down to measure her pulse. Uirsé pulled back quickly once she remembered how angry with Salder she still was. Salder stood up and stepped away, his face downcast.

"Don't hate him, Uirsé," said Verro. "He saved countless lives—in Tamloch *and* Dâron—and likely saved the kingdom from even worse troubles caused by my brother."

"I didn't like the way Túathal treated you," said Uirsé. "Or anyone else, for that matter. There was always something disturbing about the way he looked at you."

"My brother is a disturbing man in many ways," said Verro.

"I almost killed him myself a dozen times," said Salder. "He treated me and everyone else around him like small animals he could torture."

"I would have had to stop you," sighed Uirsé. "He's still my king."

"But an unworthy one," said Verro. "I can see that now. I apologize for assigning you to Túathal. I knew it would be difficult but trusted your inherent decency. I hoped it would help you avoid corruption by association."

"There wasn't a day that passed that I didn't want to ask you to be reassigned," said Uirsé. She motioned to Salder. "Help me sit up, please."

Salder stepped to the bed and leaned down. Uirsé put her arms around his neck so he could shift her upper torso to lean back against the headboard. She gave him an extra squeeze and Salder could feel her anger toward him thaw a few degrees. He wisely said nothing.

"I can feel my legs again," said Uirsé. "I want to try to walk over to sit next to Verro."

Salder watched as Uirsé swung her legs around until her feet touched the floor. He gave Uirsé his arm so she could lean on him as she took small, tentative steps over to Verro and sat in the chair beside him. Her soft brown hair glowed with bright highlights from the afternoon sun through the tall windows. She was at least a foot shorter than her mentor in wizardry. She smiled at Verro and received a smile in return.

"You've had quite a day," he said.

"And it's not over yet," Uirsé replied.

Salder stood beside her—close, but not *too* close. All three watched as Dârio finished tying the last knot in the rope around Túathal's ankles. The king of Tamloch, in his sumptuous green and gold robes, still seemed to be sleeping.

"Help me get him on the bed," said Dârio to Salder. "Keep an eye on the window for more flying disks," he told Doethan.

Túathal was unceremoniously placed on the bed by Salder and Dârio. The young king slid a pillow under his father's head and stepped back. "Time to go?" he asked Verro.

"Yes," said Verro. "I can certainly fly us back to the battlefield."

"Do you need me with you?" asked Uirsé.

"No, you and Doethan should stay here and guard Túathal," said Verro. "I'll be back once we've figured out what to do with my brother."

"I'm staying with Uirsé," said Salder.

"Of course you are," said Verro. "Give my brother more sleeping potion and keep him asleep until I return. He'll be much less trouble that way."

Uirsé nodded. She had more sleeping potion in the apothecary's small leather bag.

"Go," said Doethan. "Become the king of Tamloch and stop Tamloch's fleet."

Dârio looked at Verro. The tall wizard stood up, dislodging the tomcat, and walked to the bed to retrieve his flying disk from where Uirsé and Dârio had placed it. He glanced down at Túathal and shook his head, then nodded to Dârio.

"Please keep us posted if anything unusual happens," said Verro to Salder, Uirsé and Doethan.

"We will," replied Doethan. "I think our standards for what counts as unusual have gone up quite a bit today."

Everyone smiled. Dârio climbed on the flying disk behind Verro and the two of them flew out the tall windows.

Chapter 22

With the Dâron Army

"Where are you holding Duke Néillen and the other Tamloch nobles?" asked Dârio after Verro had flown them to the Dâron army's encampment just south of the battlefield.

"Next to our officers' mess tent, Your Majesty," replied Duke Háiddon.

The duke was Dâron's Earl Marshal and Dârio's mentor. He was also Jenet's father, a fact which Dârio appreciated every bit as much as the duke's many *official* contributions to the kingdom. Dârio listened while simultaneously scanning faces nearby, hoping to see Jenet. *She should stand out like a rose in a patch of ivy,* thought Dârio. *I miss her counsel and her comfort.* He started to chastise himself for letting a portion of his mind focus on Jenet's wisdom and beauty instead of the matter at hand but decided to forgive himself—perhaps a bit too quickly—using the excuse that he was eighteen. Thoughts of Jenet occupied a substantial portion of his mind when they were apart, and most of it when they were together.

"We built a makeshift stockade there and figured it would be easier to feed them—and guard them—if we didn't have to carry their meals too far," Duke Háiddon continued.

"Good planning," said Dârio. He hadn't seen Jenet, so he focused on her father, which he should have been doing all along. "The prisoners have been treated well?"

"Of course, Sire," said Duke Háiddon. A twinkle in the duke's eye made Dârio smile. Háiddon had been the one to instruct Dârio in the conventions of war as well as weaponry. Now that he was paying attention, Dârio noticed Duke Háiddon was looking warily at Verro, standing a few steps behind Dârio.

"Don't worry about Verro," said Dârio. "He's on *our* side now."

"And what side is that?" asked Duke Háiddon. "Dâron's or Tamloch's?"

Dârio raised an eyebrow at the duke's comment, then realized how complicated his new status as Túathal's heir made his relationship with his mentor.

Verro smiled at Duke Háiddon and Dârio. "Go ahead and talk," said Tamloch's master mage. "I'll stay close by if you want my counsel."

Dârio nodded. He'd need Verro's help soon when he addressed the captured leaders of Tamloch's routed army.

Dârio and Duke Háiddon were standing in front of the duke's pavilion, so Dârio indicated they should step inside its blue-and-white-striped canvas walls to find privacy. Duke Háiddon waved to a blue-robed crown wizard nearby, a young man of middling height who looked like he'd never missed a meal—one of Inthíra's former apprentices, if Dârio remembered correctly. The wizard followed Dârio and the duke into the pavilion.

"A privacy sphere, if you please," said Duke Háiddon.

"Certainly, Your Grace," said the young man. "What duration?"

Duke Háiddon looked to Dârio for guidance.

"A quarter-hour should be enough for now," said Dârio. "We could talk for a week, but circumstances won't allow us that much time for discussion."

The young wizard nodded.

"Please see that Verro is welcomed," added Dârio. "Find him a place to sit and ensure he has something to eat and drink."

"I'll see to it immediately," said the stocky young wizard. He cast the privacy-sphere spell, generating a translucent globe of solidified sound, and left with a bow.

Dârio hesitated, so Duke Háiddon spoke first.

"Who *are* you, Your Majesty?" he asked. "Are you the king of Dâron or the king of Tamloch or both?"

"That's complicated," Dârio answered. "And if *you* think it's confusing, so will Tamloch's nobles."

"That's *one* of my worries," said the duke.

"I know things were chaotic on the battlefield this morning. The abbreviated version is that King Túathal planted a cuckoo's egg in the Dâron line of succession," said Dârio. "By rights I'm the heir to Tamloch, not the king of Dâron.

"And the tall young man who looks a lot like you..."

"Nûd," said Dârio. "My first cousin."

"Nûd then," said Duke Háiddon. *"He's* the true king of Dâron?"

"Fercha is Nûd's mother—and Princess Seren's daughter," said Dârio. "That makes *him* Dâron's king, not me."

"Verro is Nûd's father?"

"According to Fercha, and she should know," said Dârio.

"That explains why you look so much like Verro *and* Nûd," said the duke.

"Right," said Dârio. "Our fathers are brothers."

"Now that I understand things better, I'm not sure what I should *do* about it," said Duke Háiddon. "As Dâron's Earl Marshal, is it my duty to find Nûd and support *him* as the true king, or to keep helping you confirm *your* position as king of Tamloch."

"Considering that I'm not sure Nûd even *wants* the job, I'd recommend helping me—at least for now," said Dârio. "I don't think it's going to be all that difficult to get Tamloch's nobles to accept *my* claim to the throne over my father's."

"Oh?" said the duke, lifting an eyebrow.

"Think about it," said Dârio. "Túathal is a hard-handed king who rules by fear. His nobles stay in line because they don't know when his squads of enforcers or a cadre of his trained wizards might appear at their castles and drag them off to Túathal's dungeons."

Duke Háiddon nodded, acknowledging the truth of Dârio's statement.

"I'm eighteen with a reputation for drinking too much, chasing women, and being under my mother's thumb," Dârio continued. "Of course they'll welcome me as their new king. They'll think I'll be easy to manipulate."

The duke stroked his chin. "You're probably right," he said. "How can I assist in the process?"

"By helping me convince your counterpart from Tamloch, Duke Néillen, to accept me as king," said Dârio.

"You don't think he's loyal to Túathal?" asked the duke.

"Would you be?" asked Dârio.

"Point taken," said Duke Néillen. "What about Nûd?"

"If he wants the throne of Dâron, he can have it. It's his by right and I'll expect you to serve him as you've served me."

"Of course, Your Majesty," said the duke.

"It's going to be hard," said Dârio.

"What? Convincing the Tamloch nobles?" asked the duke.

"No," said Dârio. "Learning to wear Tamloch green instead of Dâron blue. At least green robes will match my eyes."

Duke Háiddon chuckled. "There is that," he said. "Let's go find Duke Néillen."

After a five-minute walk through a maze of pavilions dodging guy ropes and tent pegs, Dârio and Duke Háiddon reached the stockade where Duke Néillen and the other Tamloch nobles were being held. Two guards holding pikes were at the entrance to the makeshift holding pen for captured officers. They nodded and greeted the king and duke.

"Your Majesty," said the first, a woman wearing a coat of plates. A single braid of brown hair stretched down the center of her back.

"Your Grace," said the second, a bald soldier in well-worn mail missing his left earlobe. Clotted blood marked the edge where the lobe had been torn off.

"What happened to you?" Dârio asked him.

"Battle injury," said the man.

"He tried to pull a mother possum off a branch and she bit him," said the first guard. She didn't bother to hide a laugh at her fellow guard's expense.

"Serves you right," said Duke Háiddon, winking at the first guard. "Please bring out Duke Néillen. The king wants to talk to him."

"Immediately, Your Grace," said the first guard. She unbarred the stockade's wooden gate and stepped inside, emerging with Duke Néillen half a minute later. Tamloch's earl marshal frowned when he saw the king and his opposite number waiting outside.

"Time to start the executions?" asked Duke Néillen. "Am I the first in line for the noose or the block?" The prisoner's hands were bound with thick ropes.

"No," said Dârio. "I am *not* Túathal." He shook his head in disgust.

"Come with us," said Duke Háiddon. "We need to talk privately."

The duke took the prisoner's arm and pulled him toward the battlefield where the turf was torn up and turned by tens of thousands of wisents' hooves. "Watch your step," said Duke Háiddon when Duke Néillen stumbled on the uneven ground. After moving fifty feet away from the stockade the king and dukes stopped. Duke Néillen's head shifted left and right uneasily. Dârio saw several links on a thick chain tattooed around Duke Néillen's neck pulsing.

"Shall I summon a wizard for a privacy sphere?" asked Duke Háiddon.

"Don't bother," said Dârio. "We're far enough away from the stockade to talk and I don't care who hears what I have to say to Duke Néillen."

"Because you're going to execute me?" asked the prisoner.

"Because I'm *not,*" said Dârio. "You can relax. Your neck will continue to connect your head and body for the foreseeable future."

Duke Néillen raised his bound hands and wiped his forehead. He watched Dârio's face warily and seemed disconcerted when Dârio smiled at the duke and removed the ropes around his wrists.

"What do you want?" asked Duke Néillen.

"Your support," said Dârio. "You heard King Túathal acknowledge me as his son. I need you to back my claim to the throne with the other Tamloch nobles."

"I'd be glad to," said Duke Néillen, "but won't Túathal object to being displaced?"

"After the defeat he suffered this morning, he's not in a position to do much about any objections," said Duke Háiddon.

"Túathal is still alive then?" asked Néillen. "The princess didn't kill him with her potion?"

"Not for lack of trying," said Dârio. "Túathal *is* alive, but he's being kept sedated until we can figure out where to exile him."

"Couldn't happen to a nicer fellow," said Duke Néillen, making it clear from his tone that his words and his feelings were diametrically opposed.

"You'll help me, then?" asked Dârio. "You'll support me as the new king of Tamloch?"

"What's in it for me?" asked Duke Néillen.

"Hah!" said Duke Háiddon.

"Who put stinging ants in *your* bedroll?" asked Duke Néillen. "A man has to look out for himself, since no one else will. We weren't all *born* to ducal rank."

"Spoken as a true mercenary," Duke Háiddon replied. King Dârio touched his arm and Dâron's Earl Marshal forced his lips tightly together.

"You can keep your lands, so long as you pledge me your fealty and don't take up arms against me," said Dârio. "You may retain your role as Earl Marshal of Tamloch for now as well, at least until I'm firmly on my throne. We'll see after that."

Duke Néillen rubbed his chin. "That's more generous than I expected," he said. "Take care. The other nobles may think you're weak if you show the same mercy to them. Túathal would not have."

"I'll say this again—I am *not* Túathal," said Dârio. "We need to convince the other nobles that they'd be better off serving me than my father. I don't expect that to be *too* difficult."

"Saying they'll serve you and truly doing so are two different propositions," said Duke Néillen.

"Having Dâron troops occupying Riyas may encourage more sincere cooperation," said Duke Háiddon.

"If they can beat the Tamloch navy back to the capital," said Duke Néillen. The corner of his mouth turned up for a fraction of a second.

"The Tamloch navy is headed for Nova Eboracum, not Riyas," said Duke Háiddon. "They're in for a big surprise when they get there."

"Or not," said Duke Néillen.

"What do you *know?*" asked Dârio. "Has the Tamloch fleet changed its plans?"

Duke Néillen spoke with a low, intense tone. "I can't say for sure, but I know Grand Admiral Sónnel. Once he learns Túathal is dead and he's the king's only remaining heir, he'll turn the fleet around and take the throne for the good of the kingdom."

"What about Túathal claiming Dârio as his son?" asked Duke Háiddon. "Would that make a difference for Sónnel?"

"I expect it would," said Néillen. "If you're Túathal's son and Verro confirms it, the Grand Admiral would support you."

"That's good news," said Dârio.

"Maybe," said Néillen "Sónnel won't make a play for Tamloch's crown, but others might."

"Pretenders always appear. It's in all the histories," said Duke Háiddon.

"You have me there," said Dârio. "Do we have a way to get word to Quintillius and King Bjarni with the Bifurland fleet to warn them Sónnel will be changing course for Riyas?"

"You'd know better than I, Sire," said Duke Háiddon. "Dealing with wizards is your department."

Dârio nodded. "Astrí left with Damon for who knows where," he said, counting off options on his fingers. "Grandmother relied on Astrí for connecting with her network in Nova Eboracum. Fercha was *with* the fleet, helping to create the gate. I'll start with her."

Duke Háiddon pulled Duke Néillen farther out onto the battlefield to give Dârio privacy. "While he's doing that, we should talk," said Duke Háiddon. "Tell me about the garrisons and fortifications around Riyas."

Fercha's communications ring expanded and the three familiar chimes sounded. Dârio waited for Fercha to acknowledge his attempt to contact her. And waited. Finally, after the interface in the center of the ring started to circle, then spiral, it turned into an image of Fercha, looking none too happy.

"What ish it?" she asked. Fercha rubbed her eyes.

Was she drunk? wondered Dârio. *How did* that *happen? Did I wake her?*

"You need to tell Quintillius and King Bjarni that Grand Admiral Sónnel probably *isn't* attacking Nova Eboracum after all. Odds are good he's turned his ships around to return to Riyas and claim the throne of Tamloch for himself."

"No way," said Fercha, her voice a bit unclear, even on two syllables.

"It's true," said Dârio.

"No," said Fercha. "I mean there's no way for me to reach them. I can't reach the Bifurlanders *or* the Roma directly. I don't have rings for any of them."

"Blast!" said Dârio. He balled his free hand into a fist and smacked it against his thigh.

"Don't deshpair," slurred Fercha. "I think I know a way."

"Thank you," said Dârio. "You're my favorite aunt."

"An' now you know I'm not jusht an honorary one," said Fercha. "I really *am* your aunt."

"I guess you are," said Dârio.

"Don't worry, nephew," said Fercha. "Keep looking up!"

She closed the connection abruptly. Dârio was caught by surprise as the communications ring collapsed. He scratched his head, puzzled his aunt's parting words. Then he saw a line of blue fire shoot up from the direction of Brendinas. It moved back and forth rapidly, painting the sky.

Dârio looked up and saw the phrase *Tamloch fleet headed for Riyas* inscribed in letters a fifty feet tall on the surface of the clouds high above the capital. They were easy to read, even in the afternoon sunlight. Given his confidence the Roma had agents in Brendinas, the fiery letters were a sure, albeit splashy way of getting word to Quintillius with the Bifurland fleet through Laetícia's spy network.

Dârio shook his head and walked across the battlefield to join the dukes.

"Come along, gentlemen," he said. "We have to convince the *rest* of the captured Tamloch nobles I'm their king."

Chapter 23

Nûd and Viridáxés

Nûd, Chee and Rocky stayed close on Viridáxés' tail as the dragon chased the gryffons—and his stolen elk-steak snacks. Rocky's velocity impressed Nûd, since he'd never experienced the wyvern moving at his equivalent of an equine full gallop. The wyvern's wings were beating so rapidly they seemed to blur. Nûd wished Eynon was closer so he could make him transparent goggles from solidified sound to help cope with the wind striking his eyes at high speed.

As he thought about it, Nûd realized that what surprised him wasn't how fast Rocky or the gryffons could fly—it was how *slow* Viridáxés flew for a creature of his great size. Each beat of the huge dragon's bat-like wings jumped him forward, but Viridáxés was *not* particularly graceful in the air. It seemed odd to consider an animal that could fly in such terms, but to Nûd's eye, the dragon seemed to *lumber* through the sky.

Graceful or not, Viridáxés was swiftly gaining on the four gryffons, who were slowed by carrying their shared burdens. Nûd looked down and saw a modest castle to his right and the glimmer of a narrow ribbon of water below. *It's probably the Rhuthro and the Earl's Keep,* thought Nûd. *My mother's tower should be downriver to the left.*

As if reading his mind, the four gryffons wheeled in that direction, gaining some distance as Viridáxés made an awkward turn to adjust to the gryffons' new vector. Nûd realized that he'd been wrong. The dragon wasn't a clumsy and an inelegant flier—he was simply unused to his new vast size. Every turn and adjustment Viridáxés made came more easily and improved his coordination.

If I'd been asleep for two thousand years, it would take me quite a while to adjust too, I expect, thought Nûd.

The dragon's wings were beating more efficiently now and he was rapidly overtaking the four gryffons. Nûd, Rocky and Chee were

slightly above and behind Viridáxés when they heard the crackling
sound from inside the dragon's body that indicated he was about to
breath fire. The gryffons must have learned to recognize that sound
as well. Before Viridáxés could release a flaming stream of burning
gas the gryffons separated, two going left, two going right.

I'm surprised they didn't do that several miles back, thought Nûd.
It's the sensible solution when pursued by an angry dragon.

The tactic didn't do the gryffons much good, however. The end
of a blast of fire set the lion's tails of two gryffons alight like the
dried ends of marshapple stalks hit by sparks from a bolt of lightning. They dropped their elk carcass in the middle of the Rhuthro
where it sank for a moment before bobbing back up and floating
on its way downriver toward Tyford. The second pair of gryffons
nearly lost their tails completely when Viridáxés' jaws snapped shut
inches behind them. The threat of more fire streaming from the
dragon's mouth encouraged the second pair of gryffons to drop
their elk carcass in the river, too.

Viridáxés roared in triumph and slammed his massive body
down into the center of the river, sending huge waves splashing up
and over the river's banks and tossing hundreds of unlucky fish—
including some large sturgeons—up on shore. The dragon's body
wasn't so wide he filled the river's channel, but nearly so. He had
landed a hundred yards upstream from Fercha's tower, which still
stood tall, unaffected by the flood on its firm stone base.

Rocky circled above the Blue Spiral Tower for a few seconds until
Nûd encouraged the wyvern to land inside the crenelations at its
top. Chee was perched high on Rocky's neck, his big eyes wide.
Nûd stood on Rocky's broad back and looked upriver at Viridáxés.
The gigantic dragon held the two elk carcasses in one set of front
claws while he plucked flopping sturgeons from a flat spot on the
western bank with the other. Viridáxés tossed each hundred-pound
fish into the air, opened his wide mouth, and slid them down his
huge gullet like a wizard eating snails at a banquet. Nûd had attended
and helped serve several feasts for select members of the Dâron
Conclave of Wizards over the years and knew their dining habits.

Some of the wizards had worse table manners than the dragon, Nûd realized.

Viridáxés, having cleared the west bank of sturgeon, was leisurely working his way downstream toward Fercha's tower. He'd spotted Nûd and Rocky and Chee atop it. Water sloshed ahead of the dragon and lapped ineffectually at the tower's foundation.

"That was a merry chase," said the dragon after he'd lifted his head until it was even with the top of the tower. "It felt good to stretch my wings and go after those furred and feathered thieves. Gryffons used to be the worst sort of bother in Tamloch before I was secreted away in the quarry."

"I don't think there are many of them east of the mountains these days," said Nûd, "though they can be a nuisance farther away from civilization."

"Dragons used to attack pride-flocks to encourage them to stay away from human settlements," said Viridáxés. "Half a dozen gryffons could be a challenge for a single smaller dragon, so we'd hunt them in wings of three or four and watch their feathers fly when we'd come down on their nests from above."

The dragon took a dainty bite from an elk carcass, removing its head with a quick snap of sharp teeth. Viridáxés' throat was so vast that there was no visual signal to mark the head passing down it. After witnessing Viridáxés' behavior, Chee slid down Rocky's neck and situated himself on Nûd's shoulder, making uncertain *chee-chee-chee* sounds. Rocky regarded Viridáxés stolidly, demonstrating he was by no means in awe of the dragon's great size.

"That must have been something to see," said Nûd, stroking Chee to reassure him. "Out west we tolerate gryffons. They help keep the basilisk population in check."

"Basilisks?" asked Viridáxés. "I didn't realize there *were* basilisks on this side of The Ocean until Eynon informed me." The dragon took another bite from the first elk carcass. "Did you know that people once thought dragons hatched from basilisk eggs?" He sniffed. "How ridiculous!"

"Why would they think such a thing, aside from the obvious similarity of having scales?" asked Nûd.

"Some book of the ancients from farther east than Athica claimed that, *'the fruit of the basilisk shall be a fiery flying serpent,'* and people mistook that as truth, which is absurd. Dragons are wise, while basilisks are as dumb as rocks," said Viridáxés.

Nûd wasn't so sure about basilisks' lack of intelligence. He'd seen the way they'd hunted him when he was in Melyncárreg trying to gather magestone fragments, but he didn't think it would reflect well on his own wisdom to mention that to the dragon.

"Where *do* dragons come from?" Nûd asked.

"Haven't your parents told you?" asked the dragon in reply. "They're found under cabbage leaves in gardens."

Nûd laughed and Chee made a jovial *chi-CHEE*. Rocky snorted and Viridáxés made the particular sort of rumble in his chest that Nûd interpreted to be laughter.

"We come from eggs, of course, prince of Tamloch," said Viridáxés. "My mother laid my egg in a cavern below the mountain at the Giant's Crossing on the Green Isle, or so I was told. I wasn't in a position to observe it happen at the time."

The Viridáxés' chest rumbled in its characteristic laugh again. Nûd wasn't sure how to deal with a dragon who joked. It seemed undignified, somehow. He stood frozen on Rocky's back for a moment while Viridáxés continued.

"Several clutches of eggs were carried across the Ocean so the line of dragons might continue in new lands—and so we could help our people stand against the Roma, should they decide to invade."

Nûd nodded. "Dragons can't fly across the Ocean?"

Viridáxés' eyes spun in contemplation. "I don't think so," he said, "though perhaps *I* could. I expect I'm the largest dragon who's ever lived."

"You certainly are big," Nûd blurted.

Viridáxés tilted his head down toward Nûd. The chuffing sound coming from his chest was more affront than amusement.

"You're not just big," said Nûd. "You're immense. Tremendous. Magnificent. The most glorious dragon ever to grace the world."

Viridáxés' eyes glowed brighter from Nûd's praise.

That's more like it, Nûd considered. Somehow it was easier to deal with Viridáxés being vain than funny.

The dragon ate the rest of the first elk and smacked his long forked tongue in satisfaction.

Eynon and Merry chose that moment to land next to Nûd, Chee and Rocky on top of Fercha's tower, opposite Viridáxés.

"We put out the fires you set," said Merry. "That was very inconsiderate of you."

"Stealing my snack was very inconsiderate of those gryffons," said Viridáxés. "Blame them, not me."

"You are a wise dragon," said Merry. "They are just animals."

"No matter," said Viridáxés. "You dealt with the fires—I dealt with the gryffons."

"Did you kill...?" began Eynon.

"They escaped," said Nûd.

Eynon released a long breath and looked pleased. Then he used his enhanced lenses to look behind Viridáxés.

"Do you realize you're damming the river?" he asked.

Viridáxés had settled his haunches down into the water when he'd lifted his head to the top of the tower. The river was backing up behind him and flooding the forested land on either bank. The dragon twisted his neck and looked over his shoulder.

"So I am," said Viridáxés. "I haven't had a bath since I wasn't much larger than that wyvern of yours, and it feels good, but I can appreciate it's wrong of me to damage good timber."

"And disrupt commerce," added Merry.

"I didn't see many traders about on the river," said the dragon. He made his amused rumbling sound again and lifted his bulk from the riverbed before stepping over to reposition himself a bit to his right on a broad flat stretch of stony shore just upriver from Fercha's tower. A tall wave of water, released by the movement, swept downstream.

I hope farmers along the river below us have their boats securely tied, thought Nûd.

"That's better," said Viridáxés. He extended his head back to put him on eye level with Eynon, Nûd and Merry. Chee considered jumping to Eynon's shoulder but decided to remain with Nûd so he didn't draw any special attention to himself. The dragon positioned the second elk carcass, ready to nibble on *its* head, but he stopped before he could do so.

A tall woman with short red hair wearing blue robes flipped open the trap door at the top of the tower and joined them.

"Who are you and what are you doing at my tower?" she asked Viridáxés.

Fercha had arrived.

Chapter 24

Fercha and Viridáxés

Eynon watched Fercha stare down a dragon so large he could consume her and the rest of them on top of Fercha's tower in a single bite. Her human-sized eyes locked with Viridáxés' huge green orbs and the line of their gaze crackled with intensity. Eynon was amazed when the dragon looked away first.

"I repeat," said Fercha. "Who are ya and whadda ya doin' at my tower?"

Eynon was surprised to hear Fercha slightly slurring her words. *Has she been drinking,* he wondered.

"My name is Viridáxés," said the dragon, who didn't seem to notice anything odd about Fercha's speech. "I came across the Ocean as an egg aboard the First Ships and seek the king of Tamloch."

"You think you'll find him *here?*" asked Fercha, shaking her head. "You've been misinformed. He's at an inn south of Brendinas."

Nûd put both hands over his face in frustration. His mother had just told Viridáxés the one thing they'd been trying hard *not* to tell him.

"Of course," said Merry, "Túathal may be back in Riyas now, for all we know."

"No, he's not," said Fercha. "He was at the Dormant Dragon not long ago, recovering from being poisoned."

Nûd was frantically signaling to Fercha to be more circumspect in what she said, but it wasn't working.

I wonder how much she's had to drink? thought Eynon. He sniffed and smelled something sweet like honey or maybe fumes from hard cider or mead wafting from Fercha's direction.

"Princess Gwýnnett nearly killed him with one of her potions, but it looks like he'll survive," Fercha continued.

"Poisoned!" rumbled Viridáxés. "My king has been poisoned? Who is this *Princess Gwýnnett* person?"

"The mother of the king of Dâron," said Fercha.

"Foul acts indeed, that a princess of Dàron should seek the death of a Tamloch royal," said Viridáxés. His eyes were spinning and flashing angry green sparks. "When the First Ships landed, there was trust between the two kingdoms, not treachery."

"That didn't last," said Fercha. "Both kingdoms have been fighting each other for millennia."

"I thought humans would outgrow such foolishness with a fresh start in the lands of the west," intoned Viridáxés in his deep, rumbling voice. "My mission is to defend Tamloch from invasion by the Eagle People, and now I hear the Roma have been in Orluin for centuries. I *must* find the king of Tamloch soon, so together we can drive the Roma back into the Ocean!"

Fercha finally noticed the expressions on Eynon, Nûd and Merry's faces. The dragon's words also made her realize she had been wrong to give Viridáxés details about Túathal's location.

"I'm not sure where Túathal is now," she said. "He may have been moved from the inn and taken somewhere he could get better care. I can find out his current location if I use my magic to contact my friends."

"Then do so immediately," said Viridáxés. He could sense Fercha was temporizing and his tone had grown more demanding.

"The artifacts I need to connect with my friends are in my tower," said Fercha. "And I'll need assistance from these young people. Help yourself to river sturgeons and deer in the nearby forests to occupy yourself while you wait."

"Very well," said Viridáxés. "I shall."

Eynon smiled inside but didn't show it. It didn't take much to convince Viridáxés to snack.

"Don't start any fires this time," he told the big dragon, wagging his finger.

"I will not," said Viridáxés. "Unless those blasted gryffons return—and then I make no promises."

"I doubt they'd be foolish enough to come back," said Merry.

Eynon didn't say anything. He'd just noticed a brown bear dragging one of the sturgeons the dragon had tossed on the bank into the woods. For the bear's sake, he hoped Viridáxés didn't spot him. Unfortunately, Viridáxés turned his focus on Eynon. Colossal claws reached down and lifted Eynon from the top of the tower by the flying disk strapped to his back. The dragon pulled Eynon close to his glowing green eye, carrying him past dozens of sharp teeth as long as the young wizard was tall. While Eynon dangled, Viridáxés instructed Fercha.

"Be quick about finding my king," said the dragon superciliously. "Any hint of dawdling will annoy me." Viridáxés opened his toothy snout and brought Eynon close enough to smell something far worse than the sulphur in the air at Melyncárreg. "I can't be responsible for my actions if you annoy me."

Eynon prepared to trigger a protective sphere of solidified sound if Viridáxés tried to eat him. He was surprised to see the dragon shift from seeming to be cowed by Fercha to trying to intimidate her. *It must be that Viridáxés initially reacts as if he were the size he was when he was first put in the quarry,* thought Eynon. *Then he realizes how big he really is and decides to throw his weight around.* Eynon filed away what he'd learned for future reference. *There's got to be a way to use Viridáxés' initial tendency to react as if he's still small to our advantage,* he considered.

Fercha responded as she would to any bully.

"Mind your manners, you overgrown batsnake!" she shouted. "And put Eynon down. I need him to help learn the king of Tamloch's current location. That *is* what you want to know, isn't it?"

"It is," said Viridáxés, glaring at Fercha.

The dragon flicked his claw skyward and sent Eynon spinning up into dark clouds and moonlight. Dizzy, but determined, Eynon gained control of his flying disk, pulling it from his back and holding it over his head as he fell. He maneuvered his way down to the top of the tower in a broad, descending swoop, touching down next to Merry. Her eyes were wide, and she was holding her own flying disk, ready to shoot up and rescue Eynon should it have been necessary. Eynon hugged her.

"I'm glad you're safe," she whispered.

Chee jumped down from Nûd's shoulder, clambered along Rocky's back, and launched himself at Eynon and Merry from the wyvern's hindquarters. He landed on Eynon's head and rapidly slid down between Eynon's body and Merry's. They laughed and the raconette gave Eynon a hug with four limbs and a tail.

"Thanks, little fellow," said Eynon. "I'm still in one piece, don't worry."

"Chi-*chee*," scolded his small familiar.

"Chi-chee," said Eynon matter-of-factly.

Merry gave them both a hug and Chee soon climbed from between the two young wizards to assume his usual position on Eynon's shoulder. They all stared at Nûd when he stood tall on Rocky's back and addressed the dragon.

"Viridáxés, servant of Tamloch," said Nûd in a tone of command that matched his mother's. "If *I* ever take the throne in Tamloch, you can be sure that *my* master mage won't fail to ensure your courtesy."

The dragon stared across at Nûd, the end of his snout a bit lower than it was a moment earlier. Then Viridáxés lifted his head haughtily, as if to say, "I'd like to see you do *that!*"

Nûd glanced at Eynon over his shoulder, then continued.

"Don't assume you're too big to be punished. Magic has changed since you were buried. Even this small human, a new wizard with less than two weeks of training, has enough power to blast your scales from your body and send you back to your magestone crypt."

"Hah!" boomed Viridáxés loud enough to reach from one side of the river valley to the other.

"Eynon," said Nûd. "Fly as high as you can, then launch a fireball the size of the one you sent up from the ship on the Brenavon yesterday. Not one of your largest, just one to impress this arrogant worm."

"As you command, my liege," said Eynon. He bowed, passed Chee to Merry, boarded his flying disk, and headed aloft. He had an idea to try that would test the capabilities of his red magestone.

Nûd caught Merry's eye, then Fercha's. He hoped they understood he wanted them at the ready to catch Eynon if his fireball knocked him off his flying disk. Merry nodded at Fercha and she returned the gesture. They both generated lenses to see at a distance and followed Eynon's path as he gained altitude. Merry held her breath, waiting for what would come next. She hoped she wouldn't need to pluck her lover out of the air as he fell.

For the space of three heartbeats nothing happened. Merry exhaled, then drew in a small lungful of air as ten thin fiery ribbons of flame seemed to extend from Eynon's outspread fingers, shooting as high above Eynon as he had flown above the top of the tower. They made high-pitched screaming sounds like the whistling arrows used by trick archers who traveled about demonstrating their shooting skills across Dâron.

Above, Eynon watched the strands of fire leave his hands, then created a thick double-walled sphere of solidified sound around himself. His blue magestone suggested sucking air from between the two spheres. Eynon wasn't sure why, but he trusted the blue magestone and expected Fercha to educate him about it later.

Nûd climbed off Rocky's back and tugged on the wyvern's neck, encouraging him to flatten against the roof of the tower, crowding Fercha and Merry in the process. Chee decided to leave Merry's arms and hide under Rocky.

Viridáxés sat back on his haunches and stretched his neck, following Eynon's movements. When the ribbons of flame flew out from Eynon's fingertips, the immense dragon's head shifted left and right, trying to track all of them at once.

Tiny pin-pricks of red showed at the end of each ribbon of flame, like needles drawing blood on foolish tailors' digits when they forgot their thimbles. Merry and Nûd closed their eyes and looked down, knowing what was likely to come next. Fercha swayed and slid into a crumpled boneless ball next to her son. Merry knelt to help her.

Viridáxés stared up skeptically, expecting to be underwhelmed.

After the time it would take to recite a short epigram, the pin-pricks expanded into a circle of ten tremendous balls of fire, brighter than the sun at noon on Midsummer's Day. Viridáxés closed his wagon-wheel-sized eyes and saw only fiery reflections. He bellowed in pain and confusion, temporarily blind. Then the shock wave hit, knocking the dragon's head down into the Rhuthro's channel and sending a splash up half as high as Fercha's tower. Viridáxés was stunned, the tip of his great snout barely above water.

Merry waited a few seconds for the fireballs' intensity to diminish, then looked up with darkened lenses of solidified sound, searching for Eynon in his double-walled bubble. Her face contorted in fear and panic when she couldn't see him.

Fercha, now back on her feet, touched Merry's arm and pointed down at the river below the tower, a dozen feet in front of the great green dragon's nearly submerged head.

A bubble of solidified sound was entering the water at high speed, sending a second fountain of water skyward. The bubble disappeared under the surface, like a rock tossed from a cliff. A long breath later it came back up and bobbed around, like an apple tossed in a tub to be washed.

Eynon dispelled his bubble and shifted upstream to hover in front of one of the dragon's wildly spinning eyes. Nûd mounted Rocky and descended to hover on the other side of Viridáxés. The dragon opened both of his eyes slowly, river water still flowing around his body and snout.

"Nicely done, for a novice wizard," Nûd shouted to Eynon.

Eynon bowed, even though Nûd couldn't see him on the other side of the dragon's huge head.

"Would you like me to try for a *big* fireball or two this time?" Eynon asked.

"There's no need for that," said Nûd. He borrowed a phrase from Fercha. "I think this overgrown batsnake will be more polite in the future."

Viridáxés closed his eyes for an interval, then reopened them and spoke with exaggerated care. "You can be assured of that, Son of Tamloch."

The immense dragon slowly pulled his bulk from the water and collapsed at the base of Fercha's tower. He stared at Eynon momentarily, then shifted his gaze to regard Nûd with increased respect.

Eynon saw his friend sitting confidently on Rocky's back and looking at him with more respect as well. *Dâron could do worse than to have a king who truly knows what it means to serve others.*

Chapter 25

In Fercha's Tower

"Are you *drunk*, Mother?" asked Nûd when the four of them, plus Chee, had climbed down into Fercha's tower.

"Maybe," said Fercha.

Merry helped her mentor into a chair next to a worktable. Fercha put her elbows on the table's surface and moved her head slowly from side to side as if testing to confirm it was still attached to her spine. She released a sound that was somewhere between a note of surprise and a moan. Chee jumped from Nûd's shoulder and sat on the table not far from Fercha with his tail curved around him. His big eyes looked at Fercha sympathetically.

"That sorghum beer was a lot stronger than I thought," said Fercha.

"What's sorghum?" asked Eynon, ever the farmer's son.

Fercha blinked twice but didn't answer.

"It's an Afarik plant," said Nûd, "quite popular in the southern provinces of the Roma's empire across the Ocean. I read about it in the library back in Melyncárreg. You can press a sweet syrup from its stalks and brew a potent liquor."

"Very potent," said Fercha, holding her head. "I shouldn't have had that third mug of beer—especially on an empty stomach."

"You got *this* drunk on three mugs of beer?" asked Merry.

"And three cups of mead," said Fercha.

"Oh," said Merry. Her single syllable made it clear Merry was disappointed by her mentor's intemperance.

"Don't judge me," said Fercha softly. "It wasn't my idea. Blame Mafuta and Quintillius and King Bjarni. I'd just helped the Bifurland fleet and Quin's legions gate through from the Brenavon to Nova Eboracum harbor."

"Oh," Merry repeated, this time with more appreciation.

"Let me fix you something to eat," said Eynon. "Where's the kitchen in this tower?" he asked Merry.

"I'll get the food," said Merry. "I know where everything is. You can come with me and carry up a jug of well water. That will help, too."

"You're right, it should," said Eynon. "Lead the way." *Drinking lots of water was a much-favored hangover cure in the Coombe,* he considered.

Eynon and Merry departed, making their way down a spiral staircase, their steps sending echoes off the curved stone walls.

"Your gate through water must have been successful, or there wouldn't have been a reason to celebrate," said Nûd. "I take it all went well with the transition?"

"It did," said Fercha. "I wasn't sure it would, since I'd never tried it before."

"Good for you," said Nûd. "I'm sure Quintillius is pleased the Tamloch fleet will be neutralized before they attack his capital."

"He seemed happy enough," said Fercha, still testing each of her words on her tongue to be sure they wouldn't cause her pain when she spoke them.

Chee moved closer to Fercha and gently stroked her forearm with his paws. Fercha pulled the raconette into her chest and cradled him like a newborn, then gave Nûd an odd look. Her eyes seemed to gaze into some infinite distance, though the walls of the tower were close by.

Nûd tilted his head in an unspoken question.

"I'm just remembering when you were a baby," she said, rocking Chee. "You were a such a *sweet* child."

"And then I grew up," said Nûd.

"That's not what I meant," said Fercha.

"You left me with grandmother," Nûd protested. "Then she left me with *Damon.*"

"It was for your own good," said Fercha.

"You can keep telling yourself that," said Nûd. "It was a lonely life."

"If Túathal had known you existed, you'd be dead by now."

"He'd kill his own nephew and the next person in line for the throne of Tamloch after Dârio?"

"If you'd gotten in his way he'd have killed you as easily as he would step on a roach."

"You could have fostered me somewhere," said Nûd. "I could have lived in Tyford or Brendinas under a different name and had a normal life. You didn't have to leave me in Melyncárreg."

"You're the true king of Dâron," said Fercha. "And you look just like Dârio—*and* Verro. People would notice."

"I could have changed my appearance with a beard or long hair."

"It wouldn't be enough," said Fercha. "Who you are shines through."

"In your opinion," said Nûd.

"I *am* your mother," said Fercha.

"And according to you, *I* am your king," said Nûd.

They both remained quiet for several moments. The only sounds in the room were low *chee chees* coming from Chee, still rocking in Fercha's arms. The raconette's big eyes were turned on Nûd.

"Have you decided to *be* my king?" asked Fercha in a voice as soft as a lullaby.

Silence returned for a dozen heartbeats, then Nûd replied.

"I'm still thinking."

Fercha rocked Chee, cooing at the raconette who replied with *chees* in the same rhythm and pitch. Nûd looked down.

"Dragons change everything," he said.

"So they do," said Fercha. "So they do."

The next segment of silence was interrupted by Eynon and Merry returning. Their conversation preceded them up the stairs.

"I would have been glad to make bacon," said Eynon. "My cousin says eating bacon is a sure cure for hangovers."

"The steward at Upper Rhuthro Keep says eating raw eels is far superior," said Merry. "And he's had more direct experience."

"There aren't many raw eels in the Coombe—and you haven't met my cousin," teased Eynon.

"Hah!" said Merry, grinning at Eynon. "I made Fercha fine white manchet toast with honey. Plain food will soothe her stomach."

"That's better than what the steward of the castle at Caercadel recommends," said Eynon.

"And what's that?" asked Nûd as the pair reached the top of the stairs.

"Pickled sheep's eyeballs," said Eynon, hiding a smile.

Fercha's face turned green. Chee jumped and scampered across the table to grab a cup of water from Eynon and take it to her. Fercha drank it down and held the cup out to Chee for a refill. Eynon poured, Chee delivered, and Fercha swallowed. Color began to return to her cheeks.

"Have some toast," said Merry. "You can dip it in honey if you like."

She put a warm plate in front of Fercha. Chee showed restraint by not immediately stealing a slice. Fercha bit off a mouthful of toast, then another. She dipped the bread in honey before her next bite, closing her eyes and sighing.

"That was exactly what I needed, Merry. Thank you."

"You're welcome."

"We're glad to help," said Eynon. "What were you and Nûd talking about while we were gone?"

"Memories," said Fercha.

"And dragons," added Nûd.

"Speaking of dragons..." Eynon began.

"...what are we going to do about Viridáxés?" finished Merry.

"Take him east to find the king of Tamloch," said Nûd. "As we promised."

"Is that wise?" asked Merry. "Do you really want a giant dragon answering to Túathal?"

"By the time we return Túathal may be deposed and Dârio the new king of Tamloch," said Fercha.

"We can hope," said Eynon.

"I can take two gates from here to Brendinas to the Dormant Dragon to learn how things stand with Túathal," said Fercha. "If there are any problems, I can contact you by communications ring while you're en route and let you know."

"That sounds sensible," said Merry. "Does that work for you, Nûd?"

"It does," he replied. "Good idea, Mother. Are you sure you're feeling well enough to manage it?"

Fercha turned to look at her son. She raised an eyebrow and one corner of her mouth turned up.

"I think so," she said. "The food helped and so did the short nap I got at my townhouse. I still feel like a herd of wisents ran over me..." Fercha smiled at Eynon and Merry. "But I'll survive."

"That sounds like a story for another day," said Nûd. "Thank you."

"For what?" asked Fercha.

"For demonstrating that you can be foolish and human, too," Nûd replied. "Somehow it makes it easier to live with my own shortcomings."

Fercha regarded her son and smiled. "That almost makes getting drunk worthwhile," she said.

With deliberate attention to her movements, Fercha rose from the table and carefully crossed the space between them to stand in front of Nûd. She put her arms around her son and gave him a long hug. Nûd leaned in and hugged her back. On top of the table, Chee wrapped his arms around his torso, imitating Nûd and Fercha. Merry and Eynon glanced away to give mother and son a private moment.

Fercha broke the hug and shifted to hold Nûd at arm's length. They smiled at each other and to Eynon's eye, something seemed to thaw in Nûd's expression.

"Safe travels, Mother," he said.

"And you—and your friends," Fercha replied. "No time like the present." She picked up her flying disk, pulled her shoulders back, and walked to a tall mirror in a wooden frame attached to a movable stand. She glanced over at Nûd again and smiled, then recited a few words to trigger the gate before stepping through the mirror's reflective surface. Merry and Eynon held hands, grinning at Nûd. Nûd looked at them and shrugged.

"What?" he asked, but he never got an answer.

WHAM!

The walls shook from a tremendous blow. Suspecting the cause, Nûd climbed to the top of the tower, followed by Eynon and Merry. Chee skipped up the steps to the roof ahead of them, stuffing toasted bread in his cheek pouches and licking honey from his fingers.

"I'm coming, I'm coming, you big lummox!" shouted Nûd. "Keep your scales on!"

WHAM!

Another heavy impact rattled the tower. Eynon, Merry and Nûd had to hold tight to the stair rail to keep from falling over. Nûd took the last few steps two at a time and reached the roof before the others. He moved to the side closest to Viridáxés and saw the dragon was primed to smack his massive head against the tower a third time.

"Stop that this instant, you pusillanimous worm!" Nûd shouted.

Eynon and Merry reached the platform at the top of the tower and watched Nûd chastise Viridáxés like a man might yell at a dog who'd snatched a whole chicken from a dinner table. They stared at each other, their expressions wary and worried.

"What does pusillanimous mean?" Eynon whispered.

"Timid," said Merry. "Or cowardly."

"Probably not the best thing to say to an angry dragon," Eynon offered.

"Wait and see," said Merry.

Viridáxés' great head rose above the Blue Spiral Tower's battlements and regarded them unhappily. Chee decided to leap on Eynon's back and held on tight to Eynon's hair with sticky fingers.

"When do we leave to find the king?" asked the dragon.

"Now," said Nûd. "We were just planning to tell you, impatient one."

"Hrrumph," said Viridáxés. "Where is the older wizard?"

"She took a gate to the east to confirm where the king of Tamloch is now," said Nûd. "She will advise me in flight."

"Then let's get on with it," said the dragon. "There are only a few more hours of daylight left."

Rocky chose that moment to return to the top of the tower. He must have left before the first head slam. The imperturbable black wyvern hovered in front of Viridáxés' snout for a few wing beats as if to make it clear the dragon didn't intimidate him. Nûd climbed on Rocky's back while Merry and Eynon, with Chee, stepped onto their flying disks.

Viridáxés launched his gigantic body into the air, water cascading from his tail that had been dangling in the river.

"Try to keep up," he bellowed, ready to zoom off.

"Aren't you forgetting something?" asked Nûd.

"What's that?" asked Viridáxés.

"You don't know where you're going," said Nûd.

"Oh," said the dragon. His wing position slowly shifted from imminent flight mode to hovering.

Nûd, on Rocky, rose and headed east. Merry and Eynon joined him on their flying disks, keeping pace with the wyvern. Eynon looked over his shoulder, feeling Chee's sticky paws pull his hair as he turned. He wasn't at all pleased by the expression on Viridáxés' toothy visage as the great green dragon trailed behind.

Chapter 26

Seeking the King

"Are we there yet?" asked Viridáxés, his deep voice carrying across the distance as they flew through the afternoon sky.

From Rocky's back, Nûd looked up at Merry and Eynon on their flying disks, now a little above and behind him. Merry caught the meaning of his glance and created a cone of solidified sound that would amplify Nûd's voice. Dragons were reputed to have good hearing, but there *was* a lot of noise from rushing wind, given how fast they were traveling.

"Not yet," Nûd told Viridáxés. "We just passed Tyford."

"I knew that river had to be the Moravon," said the dragon. "It seemed a lot bigger when I flew over it on the way to be buried in the quarry."

"*You're* a lot bigger now," said Merry.

"True," said Viridáxés. He rotated his head for a moment to admire his huge body before bringing it forward again. "I *am* magnificent, aren't I?"

"You're the biggest dragon *I've* ever seen," said Eynon, feeding Viridáxés' ego.

Merry held back a smile. Other than the small gold dragons belonging to the fierce and fun-loving young Bifurlanders, Viridáxés was the *only* dragon Eynon had ever seen as far as *she* knew. Merry made a note to ask Eynon if he'd intended to stroke Viridáxés' pride or was simply stating a fact. With Eynon, she could never be sure.

"How far is it to our destination?" asked Viridáxés, taking another approach to determine when they'd arrive at wherever it was they were going.

"Less than a hundred miles," said Nûd.

"How much is that in leagues?" asked the dragon.

"Not quite thirty," answered Nûd.

Eynon smiled. *It made sense that a dragon buried in a quarry for two thousand years would prefer the older measurement,* he realized. *So did the elders in the Coombe, for that matter. Things didn't change very quickly there.*

Merry noticed Eynon's faraway look and touched her ears. She triggered a listening spell—the one she'd taught Eynon when they were traveling down the Rhuthro delivering cider. Merry had to wave a few times to get Eynon's attention, but when he did she pointed to her ears again. Eynon caught her meaning and cast the listening spell on himself.

"What were you thinking?" she asked. Merry spoke softly so Viridáxés couldn't tell what she was saying. Thanks to the listening spell, Eynon had no such problem.

"About how backward things are in the Coombe," he replied.

"Don't you mean how *traditional* things are?" asked Merry. "That's what my father used to say about the people west of the Rhuthro valley. They wanted to preserve the old traditions?" She didn't share the fact that her *da* had also called the Coombe-folk old fashioned.

"It's much the same thing either way," said Eynon. "If not for wander years, none of the people I know would have ever left the Coombe."

"Thank goodness for wander years, then," said Merry. She smiled at Eynon affectionately and suddenly it seemed to him like the afternoon sky was twice as bright. Merry angled her flying disk closer to Eynon's so she could squeeze his hand. It was sticky—probably from the honey Chee had unintentionally smeared in Eynon's hair. She made a face at the raconette. Chee made one back at her.

The question *When will I get a familiar?* played in her brain for the thousandth time. *Maybe her familiar would be a dog, like Doethan's big hound Rowsch, or a bird like Fercha's owl?* Merry thought about the gryffons who had recently stolen food from Viridáxés and an absurd image popped into her head. She imagined a creature with the wings, front claws and head of an owl joined to some sort of canine's hindquarters. *Wouldn't* that *be something!* Sadly, owl-dogs didn't exist, as far as Merry knew.

Eynon tightened his grip on Merry's hand. "Sorry about the honey," he said. "I guess we'll have to stick together."

"You can count on that," said Merry reflexively. It was clear her mind was still elsewhere.

"What are *you* thinking about?" asked Eynon.

"Familiars," said Merry. "You have two and I don't have any."

"I don't know if Rocky is really my familiar or if he just appreciated the taste of my magic and adopted me," said Eynon. "He seems rather fond of Nûd, too. Chee may only be staying with me because I keep him well fed."

"You don't need to say things like that just to make me feel better," said Merry. She squeezed Eynon's hand to let him know she was pleased by his attempt no matter what she'd said.

Eynon started to chuckle.

"What's so funny?" asked Merry.

"He could have been your familiar." Eynon shifted his head quickly to indicate Viridáxés keeping pace behind them.

Merry's eyes went wide. She brought her free hand up to cover her mouth so her *"Oh!"* of surprise wouldn't escape. She glanced over her shoulder at the dragon and Eynon felt a shudder run through her body that made the hand he was holding tremble.

"Can you imagine?" asked Merry. *"Me,* with a dragon the size of Viridáxés as a familiar? How would I feed such a creature?"

"Just tell it to rest in a magestone quarry whenever it's hungry," teased Eynon. "Or send it to Melyncárreg to eat wisents and commune with the *cuddio tân.*"

"The what?" asked Merry.

"The *cuddio tân.* They're the deep fires under Melyncárreg that produce the geysers, hot pools, mud pots, and sulphur smell."

"Those *do* sound of interest to a dragon," said Merry. "What's a geyser?"

"A hot water jet. Didn't I tell you about them?"

"No," said Merry, "though we *have* been a bit busy lately. Maybe you can give me a tour of Melyncárreg when things quiet down as part of my wander year."

"I expect we'll be grandparents by the time things quiet down," said Eynon, "given the way things have been going for the past few days."

"Eynon's not going anywhere soon," Nûd interjected. He held up a small charm shaped like an ear and smiled.

"I didn't know you could put listening spells into charms," said Eynon.

"There's a lot you don't..." began Merry, but she cut herself off. There was a lot about magic *she* didn't know, either. "Why isn't Eynon going anywhere soon?"

"Because if I let them make me king of Dâron, he'll be my master mage."

"What about Damon?" asked Eynon. "He's the Master Mage of Dâron."

"Didn't he tell you?" asked Nûd. "He wants you to take the job, so he can spend time catching up with Princess Seren—I mean the Queen's wizard, Astrí."

"But I'm brand new at learning magic," protested Eynon. "I hardly know anything about wizardry."

"From what he told me, neither did Damon when he took the job," said Nûd. "It's a matter of power and potential, not depth of knowledge."

"You've got plenty of power, that's for sure!" noted Merry.

"Are you talking about *me?*" asked Viridáxés.

"Yes, Your Wondrousness," said Nûd. "We're discussing your incredible power and strength. Your wing beats breed whirlwinds, your roar is like ten thousand lions."

Merry didn't think Nûd was in the least bit sincere. She worried he might be laying on compliments thicker than a sloppy bricklayer slathered on mortar, but Viridáxés didn't recognize Nûd's feigned fawning.

"*Thank you,* son of Tamloch," said Viridáxés. "You're wise to recognize true greatness when you see it."

There was little Nûd, Eynon or Merry could say to that. Chee still kept a honey-coated hold on Eynon's hair. Eynon could hear the raconette snoring softly as fine farmland sped by beneath them.

At least someone is getting some sleep, thought Eynon.

"Are we there yet?" Viridáxés asked again a few minutes later. The big dragon reminded Eynon of one of his impatient younger cousins traveling with him from Haywall to Caercadel to deliver livestock to the baron. Those four words were on his cousin's lips every five hundred steps.

Eynon was surprised by the course Nûd was taking. They'd angled far more toward the south when they'd left Tyford and were decreasing their altitude steadily. Now Eynon understood why. Nûd didn't want Viridáxés to see the battlefield—or the herd of wisents. That would take a lot of explaining that none of them wanted to provide.

"That's our destination," shouted Nûd. "The big building with a blue-slate roof and courtyard."

"It looks like an inn," said Viridáxés, flying slower to match Rocky, Merry and Eynon.

"It is," said Nûd.

At Nûd's command, Rocky circled instead of immediately landing. Viridáxés hovered one of his body-lengths above them. Eynon saw Nûd open one of his communications rings—talking to Fercha, he assumed. Nûd closed his ring and had Rocky rise to be closer to Viridáxés. Merry and Eynon, with Chee, maintained their original height above the Dormant Dragon.

"I've been informed that the king of Tamloch isn't here," said Nûd, "but he is close by, a mile or two north of the inn."

Viridáxés' eyes flashed, and his long snout opened, revealing bright green flames, barely contained, deep within.

"You're lying!" bellowed the great green dragon. "The king of Tamloch is inside the inn. I can sense him—and I will *find* him!"

Viridáxés wrapped his wings against his immense body and fell like half a mountain toward the inn. Eynon and Merry had to move quickly to get out of his way. Chee, now awake, clutched Eynon's hair so hard it seemed like clumps of it would come out by the roots. At the last possible second, Viridáxés opened his wings wide to slow his fall and landed in the courtyard, cracking hundreds of paving slates.

Like a cat trying to fit in a bowl far too small for him, most of the dragon's body spilled over the low stone walls defining the courtyard or extended tens of yards to the south, away from the inn. His tail was arched up, its barbed point twitching in anger and agitation.

"BRING FORTH THE KING!" roared Viridáxés. "I KNOW HE'S THERE! SHOW HIM TO ME OR I WILL TEAR OFF YOUR ROOF AND FIND HIM MYSELF!"

A tall leaded-glass window on the second floor overlooking the courtyard opened and a young wizard with long brown hair spoke to Viridáxés. If the dragon frightened the wizard, she didn't show it. Behind her, Merry could see her brother standing protectively.

"Salder," she whispered.

"Túathal isn't here," said Uirsé. "He went north, just moments ago."

"MY KING!" bellowed Viridáxés.

The ground shook as the dragon pushed off and headed into the air, the tips of his rear claws scraping blue slates from the roof of the inn. Nûd, on Rocky's back, circled down to talk to Eynon and Merry.

"Fercha has Túathal," he said. "He's still unconscious. She's taking him north to the battlefield. Dârio is there and she's hoping to convince Viridáxés that *Dârio* is king of Tamloch, not Túathal."

Good luck with that, thought Merry.

"She also said you needed to talk to Doethan," said Nûd. "Stay here for now and find him. As next in line for the throne of Tamloch, I need to go north immediately and lend weight to Dârio's claim."

"Good luck," said Eynon, echoing Merry's unspoken words and making it sound more like a question.

Nûd and Rocky flew off, following Viridáxés. Uirsé stepped out of the inn's front door into the damaged courtyard with Salder a pace behind her. When Merry saw her brother, she ran to him and gave him a hug.

"I'm glad you're safe," she said.

"You too," said Salder. He held his sister at arm's length. "Merry, this is Uirsé, the woman I love—if she'll still have me. Uirsé, this is my sister Merry."

"Pleased to meet you," said the two women in unison. Then they laughed. Salder looked uneasy as the two exchanged glances that warned him he'd soon be a topic for private discussion. He wasn't yet back on firm ground with Uirsé, so he wasn't sure how he felt about the stories his sister might tell about his behavior as a child.

"Fercha said we're supposed to talk to Doethan," said Eynon. He addressed Uirsé and Salder. "Do you have any idea where we might find him?"

Doethan, holding hands with two young girls, chose that moment to walk out on the courtyard. The girls were talking nonstop about the dragon. They paused to be polite when Doethan spoke.

"Did someone mention my name?" he asked.

"Doethan!" shouted Merry. She ran to her first mentor in wizardry and gave *him* a hug as exuberant as the one she'd given her brother. The two girls had to drop Doethan's hands to make room for Merry.

"We know why you're supposed to talk to him," said one girl.

"Uh huh," said the other. "It's about what we found last night."

Plenna and Mercha, thought Eynon. *The cook and innkeeper's children.*

"What did you find last night?" he asked.

Doethan opened his mouth to speak but lost his chance.

"We don't want to *tell* you," said Plenna.

"We want to *show* you!" said Mercha.

Plenna grabbed Eynon's hand and Mercha took Merry's.

"Can we ride on your flying disks?" asked both girls in unison.

Eynon and Merry looked at Doethan, trying to figure out what to do. Coegi, the inn's talented cook, and Gwest, her partner the innkeeper appeared at the front door.

"Get along then," said Coegi. "We have a lot of sharp slates to clean up and it will be best if you and the children aren't underfoot."

"Don't go too high," said Gwest.

"We won't," the girls declared.

"Where are we headed?" asked Eynon.

"West, to the blue magestone quarry," said Doethan. "It's not far."

Salder climbed on Uirsé's flying disk behind her and put his hands around her waist. She didn't move them to her hips, which Salder took as a sign their relationship was continuing to thaw. Plenna climbed on next to Eynon and Mercha joined Merry. Chee was jittery, overwhelmed by Viridáxés' anger. He sought a calm refuge away from the girls' attentions and sat in the center of Doethan's flying disk, licking his fingers. All four wizards rose two feet in the air and followed as Doethan led them off the courtyard.

"Wait," said Eynon. He turned his flying disk around so he faced Coegi and Gwest who were trying to use brooms to brush heavy slate fragments off to one side. Eynon waved the cook and innkeeper out of the courtyard and created a plane of solidified sound. He moved the plane across the courtyard until all the fragments were gathered in a long line against one of the low walls.

Merry clapped her hands. "I can help, too. Where do you want us to put the broken slates?"

"Behind the kitchen, if you please, good wizard," said Gwest. "I can use them for roof repairs in the future."

"Excellent," said Merry. She made a box of solidified sound with one open side. Eynon adjusted his plane so it swept the slate fragments inside Merry's construct and Merry transported the box over the roof of the inn. She circled back to ensure the fragments were released by the kitchen, then returned to join the rest of the party.

Eynon whispered to Merry. "You're good at repairing thatched roofs—we'll have to try our hand helping with slate roofs later."

"When things calm down," teased Merry.

"Right," said Eynon. "In a few years then, maybe."

"Maybe," said Merry. "Doethan's moving again."

"So he is," said Eynon.

Plenna was tugging at Eynon's leggings.

"Eynon," she said, "We want to show you the blue triangle we found."

"Blue triangle?" asked Eynon, remembering what they'd found in the green magestone quarry near Wherrel.

"Do you think...?" asked Merry.

"It *must* be your new familiar," said Eynon.

Merry didn't say what she wanted to say in reply, afraid Plenna and Mercha might repeat it. Instead, she tossed a small sphere of solidified sound at the back of Eynon's head. It hit with the force of a similarly-sized apple. Eynon turned and grinned at Merry, unaware that the sphere was still stuck to his hair by the remains of Chee's honey.

Eynon and Merry both shared the same thought. They hoped they wouldn't soon have *another* big scaly, fire-breathing problem on their hands.

Chapter 27

Exit, Pursued by Dragon

Fercha flew north from the inn as if her life depended on it, which it probably did. Túathal's limp body was curled around her feet on her flying disk as she leaned forward into the wind, urging her disk onward. She could hear Viridáxés' protests from not far enough behind her. *They could probably hear him all the way to Brendinas,* Fercha considered. She'd just flown out the same tall leaded-glass windows Hibblig had taken Gwýnnett through earlier. Fercha knew she had only seconds before the displeased dragon began to pursue her and resolved to put as much distance as possible between herself and the inn before he did.

Must go faster, thought Fercha. She redoubled her speed, instinctively casting a streamlined bubble of solidified sound around herself and Túathal. From the sound of things, Viridáxés was in the air now. His vast flapping wings blasted the air like a constant peel of thunder. Over their boom, she could hear the dragon's loud and angry bellowing. *"My king! My king!"*

Thank goodness he can't risk sending a jet of fire my way because I'm carrying Túathal, she realized.

The distance between the inn and the battlefield was covered quickly. *Where was Dârio? Perhaps he could convince Viridáxés he was the legitimate king of Tamloch?* Fercha laughed. She'd *married* Verro, but the same wasn't the case with Túathal and Gwýnnett, not that Tamloch's royal family ever cared much about the legitimacy of its heirs. For that matter, Gwýnnett was already married to the crown prince of Dâron when Dârio was conceived.

Stop thinking about genealogies and concentrate on staying alive, Fercha told herself. She generated a pair of distance-vision-enhancing lenses and spotted Dârio standing on top of a barrel talking to more than forty prisoners held inside a simple wooden stockade next to a pavilion with cooking cauldrons steaming outside it. Fercha dove for a clear space in front of the barrel and saw Verro, Duke Háiddon and several guards standing near her nephew. Genealogies popped back into her mind uninvited, but she pushed them aside.

Her landing was far from elegant. Fercha's flying disk hit the soft ground in front of the barrel without losing all of its considerable momentum. It came in at an angle and stuck in the turf, quivering like a new-shot bolt from a crossbow. Fercha somersaulted half a flip forward, ending up with her tailbone smacking against the near side of the barrel Dârio stood on. Túathal's unconscious body rolled until his chest reached the top of Fercha's head, then stopped.

The men and women—captured Tamloch nobles, Fercha assumed—stepped back, not sure what to make of her arrival. One of the prisoners realized Fercha's passenger was Túathal and moved to kneel beside his king. The man wasn't known to Fercha, but from his extensive tattoos she thought he must be Duke Néillen. He untied Túathal and started speaking to him in a voice too soft for Fercha to hear.

Verro stepped forward and extended his hand to help Fercha rise. They were about to hug when Viridáxés appeared above them and the screaming started.

The ground shook like a tremendous earthquake when the huge dragon landed on the battlefield just beyond the stockade. Viridáxés' legs pushed deep into the ground like a child's fingers inserted in a sand pile. His body formed a long, not-so-shallow oval of depressed earth, the shiny green of his scales contrasting with the darker green of the field's fresh grass. Viridáxés' great tail was curved high above his back, slashing back and forth like a skilled swordmaster cutting the air with his blade. The dragon stretched his long neck down toward the stockade, stopping only when the sharp teeth at the front of his long snout were less than the length of a lance above Dârio's head.

The noble Tamloch officers in the stockade had gone strangely silent, their screams extinguished by the reality of Viridáxés' fearsome head. The dragon opened his tooth-filled mouth and snapped it shut, twice, drawing in air like a blacksmith's bellows each time. Then he lowered his nostrils until they were directly over Dârio and sniffed.

"I am Viridáxés," said the dragon in a powerful voice. Then, uncertainly, he spoke to Dârio. "My king?"

"Claim the throne of Tamloch," whispered Fercha from her position standing below Dârio, who was still atop the barrel. "Do it *now!*"

"*I* am the king of Tamloch!" shouted Dârio. He unsheathed his sword and held it aloft, looking quite impressive save for the dragon who made them all seem small.

Viridáxés sniffed again, turned his head so his eyes could peer down more easily, and finally noticed Túathal on the ground next to Fercha. The dragon's head moved even lower for a closer inspection. After inhaling deeply, the dragon moved his head back up and curved his neck to address Dârio.

"*He* smells like the king of Tamloch," said Viridáxés, indicating Túathal with a foreclaw, "and so do *you*. How can this be?"

"Simple, O Might One," said Dârio. "The man on the ground is my father. I defeated him in battle on this very field. He placed his hands between mine and pledged me his fealty just a few hours ago—therefore *I* am the king of Tamloch."

"You're wearing blue," said Viridáxés matter-of-factly. "How can you be king of Tamloch?"

Fercha stepped forward, stood tall, and addressed the dragon. "You still haven't learned wisdom have you, you overgrown garden snake?" Fercha shouted, using a truncated cone of solidified sound to make her voice boom. "Dârio is king of Dâron *and* Tamloch, that's why he's wearing blue."

"But..." began Viridáxés.

"But nothing," Fercha continued. "Dârio's father—the unconscious man in green robes below me—acknowledged him as his heir this morning after his army was routed on the field."

"My wife's words are true," said Verro. "I speak as a Son of Tamloch. Túathal is my brother. Dârio is my nephew. I heard Túathal name Dârio, his son, as his heir and pledge him his fealty. Dârio is king now."

"Why can't he speak for himself?" asked Viridáxés.

"I *can* speak for myself," insisted Dârio.

"Not you, your father," said Viridáxés. "You're confusing me!" Something rumbled deep in the dragon's chest. It didn't sound like laughter. "Wake Túathal up. Let's hear what he has to say for himself." Viridáxés' thick brow ridges lowered. "It's confusing having *two* kings of Tamloch, one of whom also happens to be king of Dâron. That's certainly not how I expected to find things when I woke up after two thousand years."

"Clearly, you have a lot more to learn," said Fercha, trying to keep Viridáxés unbalanced. She glanced down and confirmed that Túathal was still comatose, his head supported by Duke Néillen.

"Perhaps," said Viridáxés, putting the tip of a claw to the end of his snout. "What say you, noble warriors of Tamloch? Which man is your king?"

The prisoners muttered among themselves, then some shouted *Dârio*, others *Túathal*. Dârio gracefully dismounted from his barrel and spoke softly to Fercha and Verro.

"I talked quite a few of them over to my side earlier," he said. "They're not all that fond of Túathal and as expected, believe I'd be much easier to manipulate."

"Hah!" said Fercha, not caring who heard.

"You were winning them over," said Verro, frowning at Viridáxés. "Half of them, anyway."

"I'm guessing the other half would be just as glad to see the dragon eat *me* instead of him," said Dârio, pointing down at Túathal with an outstretched hand.

Duke Háiddon stepped out from behind the barrel Dârio had stood on. He glared at the noble Tamloch prisoners. A few more of them changed their shouts to *Dârio*.

A moment later, Duke Néillen carefully lowered Túathal's head to the grass and stood.

"Why don't you do what the dragon says and ask Túathal who *he* thinks is the rightful king of Tamloch?" asked Duke Néillen.

"Who would have thought *he* would stay loyal to Túathal?" muttered Duke Háiddon loud enough for Dârio, Fercha and Verro to hear. Dârio shook his head and sighed. *Giant dragons changed everything.*

"Let Túathal rise and speak for himself," said Viridáxés. "Stand and have your say," he commanded.

"Alas, Your Magnificence, my king cannot stand," said Duke Néillen. "He was poisoned by a princess from Dâron."

"You told me something about that earlier," said Viridáxés, turning one of his huge green eyes on Fercha.

"I did," said Fercha. "And it's true, but the poison has been neutralized. We're keeping him asleep until we can determine where to exile him."

"This. Will. Not. Do," said Viridáxés, emphasizing each word with care. His gigantic eyes spun furiously. To Fercha it seemed more like confusion than anger.

"It's for Túathal's own good," Fercha insisted.

"Step away from the king," said Viridáxés by way of answer. Dârio, Fercha and Verro moved to stand beside Duke Háiddon. "You too," Viridáxés demanded, indicating Duke Néillen with a tip of a claw. Túathal's earl marshal joined a trio of captured Tamloch nobles wearing green-enameled breastplates. His eyes tracked the dragon's movements.

Viridáxés leaned in until his nostrils were almost touching Túathal's body. Like a small child lightly blowing on a dandelion puff, a warm verdant mist emerged from deep in the dragon's lungs and gently surrounded Túathal's unconscious form. Strands of green fog wove around Túathal and lifted him up, cradling him like a babe and imbuing him with restorative energy before setting him upright and leaving him standing, arrogant and alert, between the barrel and the Tamloch nobles.

Túathal stared at Viridáxés. He sensed the change in his tactical position immediately. "Do you serve the king of Tamloch?" he asked the dragon.

"I do," said Viridáxés.

"*I* am the king of Tamloch," Túathal asserted. "My impatient son can wait his turn."

"Very good, Your Majesty," said Viridáxés. "What is your will?"

"Free my nobles and take us all to Riyas immediately," said Túathal.

Before Fercha could react, one of Viridáxés' claws snapped down on her flying disk, flipping it up against her torso and knocking her to the ground. Clods of dirt caught by her disk earlier rained down on her, blocking her mouth and nose. When Viridáxés pulled his claw tip up, it intentionally collided with Verro, sending Tamloch's master mage down on top of Fercha. By the time the two wizards sorted themselves out, it was too late. Fercha stared at the sky with clenched fists, frustrated to see Túathal, Duke Néillen, and the formerly captured Tamloch nobles on Viridáxés' broad back, flying northeast toward Tamloch's capital. Verro put his arms around Fercha.

Dârio, Duke Háiddon and the barrel were knocked over by the wind from the dragon's tremendous wings. The young king set the barrel upright and levered its top off with his sword. It was full to the brim with sweet water. Duke Háiddon found four abandoned mugs that had been assigned to the noble prisoners and passed them out. Still tasting dirt, Fercha needed cool water more than the king or the duke. The duke filled her mug first.

"I'm sorry, Your Majesty," she said after a long swallow. "There was nothing I could do to stop Túathal—or Viridáxés."

"I failed as well," said Verro. "My apologies."

"A temporary setback," said Dârio. "I'm just glad you're both safe."

Verro nodded and pointed to the sky, his eyes following a shrinking green speck headed northeast. "At least the dragon's course doesn't suggest he's set on attacking Brendinas."

"Yet," said Dârio.

Duke Háiddon offered Verro more water.

"My apologies, Your Grace. I must decline," said Verro. "I'm quite full and not the least bit thirsty. Before coming with you to the stockade, that young wizard who made your privacy sphere assigned three servants to ply me with food and drink for half an hour. He kept me company and ate more than half of everything provided."

Duke Háiddon smiled at that, despite the current dire circumstances. "So long as *you* had enough," he said, draining the contents of his own mug like a thirsty soldier tossing back strong beer.

"Are all our plans in tatters because I was taken by surprise at the inn?" asked Fercha. "Have we lost all hope of putting you on the throne of Tamloch now?"

"Not necessarily," Dârio answered. "I still need your help."

"With what?" asked Fercha. "Name it, and it's done."

"I need you to inspect the wide gate that brought Túathal's army through from Riyas to this battlefield and ensure it's still safe and functioning properly," said Dârio.

"With pleasure," said Fercha.

Dârio grinned at the others conspiratorially. "It will take Túathal until morning to fly overland. With a wide gate direct to Riyas, the entire Dâron army could arrive there in a few hours."

"Interesting," said Duke Háiddon. "Grand Admiral Sónnel should arrive in Riyas harbor with Tamloch's fleet by first light tomorrow."

"And if my message in the clouds worked, which I'm sure it did," said Fercha, "The Bifurland longships and the Roma legionnaires aboard them..."

"...should be right behind Grand Admiral Sónnel," completed Dârio. "We need to get our army there first and prepare for their arrival."

"Aren't you forgetting Viridáxés?" asked Duke Háiddon. "How do we counter a giant green dragon?"

"Good question," said Dârio. He turned to Fercha. "Any idea where we can find Eynon?"

"Yes," replied Fercha. "I have a *very* good idea where to find him. He was outside the Dormant Dragon a few minutes ago. I'll fly down and fetch him. Perhaps a slice of one of Coegi's delicious pies will help get the taste of topsoil out of my mouth."

"Excellent," said Dârio. "Send him here when you find him and hurry back yourself—after a slice of pie—to help inspect the wide gate to Riyas."

"As my king and nephew commands," said Fercha. She smacked her flying disk with her boot to dislodge a few remaining clods stuck to the edge, then climbed aboard. Fercha hovered a few feet off the ground and looked toward Verro.

"I'll come with you," said Verro. "In case you encounter *another* giant dragon."

"What are the odds of that?" teased Fercha. She smiled at Verro.

Together the two tall wizards, one in blue, one in green, flew south hand in hand.

Chapter 28

The Blue Magestone Quarry

Eynon was surprised to see how different one quarry was from another. He'd thought the quarry he knew just west of Wherrel was the model for what such things were. Finding another example of one that was so different made him rethink his definition of what made a quarry, well, a quarry. They'd just passed through the narrow entrance to *this* quarry and Eynon was struck by the exposed rock faces' blue tinge—like the slates on the inn's roof—and the long, deep-blue lake that ran down its center. The quarry in the Coombe was bowl-shaped. This one was more angular, but still broad from side to side. The lake was wider than he could throw a stone across, at least not without using magic. It was shaped more like a teardrop, with the wide rounded end to the north, where they'd just entered. Eynon could see the walls of the quarry narrow far to the south where the lake seemed to taper away to a point.

"Take us higher," said Plenna, tugging on Eynon's leggings. "Being this close to the ground is for babies." Eynon saw the fierceness in the girl's eyes and knew she'd make a fine soldier when she was older.

Mercha, the younger girl, squeezed Merry's hand. "Momma Gwest said we shouldn't go too high!" she insisted.

"I want to go higher, so I can spot the blue triangle," said Plenna.

Eynon rose, lifting his flying disk from two feet above the ground to ten. Merry did the same and put a comforting hand on Mercha's shoulder. They were floating above a flat stretch of broken ground strewn with boulders between the lake and the cliffs at the northern end of the quarry. Doethan, a dozen feet behind Eynon and Merry, was distracted by Chee twining between his legs nervously. Uirsé and Salder brought up the rear of the small flying procession, wrapped up in a private discussion.

"Are you the reason there are so many wisents around, trampling farmers' fields?" Plenna asked Eynon.

"Momma Coegi said wizards sent a herd of wisents against the green soldiers," said Mercha. "Wisents are good to eat," she added as an afterthought. "Momma Coegi says so."

"They probably taste like cows," said Plenna.

"They *are* cows," said Mercha.

"Cattle, maybe," said Merry, "but they're not the same as the milk cows you have in the barn or the usual breeds raised for beef in Dâron."

"Momma Coegi makes good beef pies," Mercha informed them.

"I expect she'd make excellent wisent pies, too," said Eynon. "What exactly are we looking for again?"

"You're looking for a blue sphere of solidified sound," said Doethan, who had just hovered up to join them. "I put a protective sphere around the triangle last night so that anyone visiting the quarry wouldn't disturb it."

"You mean so *we* wouldn't disturb it," protested Plenna. "We're the only ones who visit the quarry these days, except when someone in the village needs more slate to repair their roof."

"You're too young to be so wise," replied Doethan. Plenna bowed at the older wizard and flashed him a big smile.

"I'm wise, too," said Mercha. "Wise enough to look ahead and see your big blue magic ball."

Doethan, Eynon and Merry all responded with the same word. "Where?"

"Fifty paces from here on the right," said Mercha. "Fifty grown-up paces," she clarified. "It would take more of mine."

"You're not only wise, you're observant," said Merry, ruffling Mercha's hair affectionately.

"Maybe you all should *observe* that the ball is twitching," said Plenna.

"Twitching?" asked Doethan. "Balls of solidified sound shouldn't move on their own."

Eynon and Merry exchanged a quick, concerned glance.

"Do you think…?" asked Eynon.

"We *are* in a magestone quarry," said Merry. "Do you think it's safe for the children to be with us?" she asked Eynon softly.

"It's a little late for that," said Eynon whispered.

"The quarry is safe if we don't go near the lake," said Mercha, who'd overheard everything.

"And stay away from the rock faces," said Plenna.

"Sometimes stones fall off," noted Mercha.

"And we have to watch out for batsnakes," added Plenna.

"Momma Coegi and Momma Gwest don't really like us going to the quarry by ourselves at all," said Mercha. The little girl looked up at Merry and squeezed her hand.

"Everyone," said Merry, raising her voice. "Be prepared to fly up in a hurry in case anything strange happens."

Eynon could see that Salder and Uirsé weren't paying much attention to their surroundings. The two seemed totally focused on an intense conversation they were sharing. Uirsé's flying disk was no longer following the others and had drifted to the south, over the lake. *At least Uirsé is letting Merry's brother put his arm around her shoulder,* thought Eynon. He didn't want to disturb the two of them, especially if they were getting along better now, so he generated a small sphere of solidified sound and used it to gently begin to nudge Salder and Uirsé back toward the rest of the group. From what he could tell, Uirsé and Salder didn't notice his redirection.

A minute later, Eynon, Merry, Doethan and their respective passengers floated above the twitching blue sphere. Eynon thought it was rocking back and forth like an egg about to hatch. *That might be exactly what it's doing,* he considered. Then he remembered Viridáxés had already hatched and was a wyvern-sized dragon when one of the mages from the time of the First Ships had arranged for him to be buried. He rubbed his chin then his eyes went wide.

"What?" asked Merry.

"Viridáxés wasn't *buried* in the green magestone quarry," replied Eynon. "He was planted—so he could grow."

Merry shook her head. "I thought you understood that," she said. "You should. You grew up on a farm after all."

"True enough," said Eynon, "but I wasn't thinking about it properly. It's strange to think a dragon is like a turnip."

"Who is Vir-i-dáx-és?" asked Mercha.

"The dragon, silly," said Plenna. "The one who landed in our courtyard."

"Oh," said Mercha, her eyes dancing. *"That* dragon."

Eynon was glad the two girls weren't both on the same flying disk, because he expected they might start tickling each other. That's what he would have done to Braith in similar circumstances.

"Could you drop your sphere so we can get a better look at what's under it?" Merry asked Doethan.

"Certainly," said the older wizard. He waved a palm and the blue globe of solidified sound popped like a soap bubble.

Eynon and Merry exchanged another glance. The twitching triangle looked like a twin of the tip of Viridáxés' tail, save for color. "Let's gain some altitude," he said, matching actions to words and rising up higher than the top of Fercha's tower. Merry and Doethan promptly joined him at that height, but Salder and Uirsé hadn't followed. Eynon shifted his guiding sphere of solidified sound from the edge to the bottom of Uirsé's flying disk, lifting the reconciling lovers up with the rest of them.

Plenna stared at the leathery twitching triangle below, but her younger sister couldn't help but look around, her eyes now as big in proportion to her head as Chee's oversized orbs were to his. Mercha had never been so high up in her life, her head swiveling to see as much as she could see from horizon to horizon. Merry watched the little girl take in the view and slowly rotated her flying disk to help her. Except for a slight wind, everything was quiet. Eynon and Merry hoped it wasn't the calm before the hurricane. The calm only lasted another minute.

"There's Rocky!" Mercha shouted. She was pointing off to the north, toward the battlefield.

Plenna, Eynon, Merry, Doethan and Chee all turned their heads to follow Mercha's outstretched arm. Rocky, with Nûd on his back, had spotted them and was winging his way toward their location at speed. Nûd waved as he approached and soon Rocky was hovering next to the others. Eynon noticed water dripping from Nûd's boots. It trailed down the wyvern's sides.

"How did things go with Dârio?" asked Eynon. "Did Viridáxés accept him as the rightful king of Tamloch?"

They could read the frustration in Nûd's face before he spoke.

"I wish I knew," he said. "I wasn't there to see what happened."

"Why not?" asked Merry.

"Ask Rocky," Nûd replied. "He's the one who decided to stop for an early dinner and skip supporting Dârio."

Eynon gave Rocky a disapproving look, but the wyvern was unperturbed. "What happened?" he asked.

"Rocky spotted a stray wisent drinking from a brook not far from here and pounced on it, breaking the beast's neck," said Nûd. "His dive almost broke *my* neck, but I rolled off just in time, narrowly avoiding a fresh wisent patty in the process. When I stood up, Rocky was ignoring me and eating the wisent."

"Did it taste like cow?" asked Mercha.

"You'll have to ask Rocky," answered Nûd.

The wyvern nodded to Mercha, causing Eynon—and Merry and Doethan and Nûd—to reevaluate just how intelligent Rocky was.

"We hadn't traveled that far north, so I started walking back to the inn," Nûd continued. "It would have been smarter to go east and take the road, but I thought I could save time by going more directly overland. Rocky must not have been *that* hungry. He came back and picked me up a few minutes ago."

"That explains your wet boots," remarked Doethan. "There are lots of small streams and rivulets feeding into the Brenavon nearby." Doethan paused to catch Rocky's eye. "Keep still, please," he said to the wyvern. "I'm going to dry off Nûd's boots." Rocky nodded again, to Doethan this time, and adjusted his wing beats to keep his passenger as stable as possible. Doethan made a few passes with his hands and spoke a few quiet words.

Nûd laughed. "That tickled," he said. "But it worked. My boots are dry, and my feet are warm for a change."

"I do my part to serve my king," said Doethan.

Nûd sighed. "If that's what it takes to get warm feet..." he said, his voice trailing off.

"Something's happening!" shouted Plenna. Nûd's arrival seemed to speed up whatever was occurring on the ground. Plenna pointed below. The girl had taken a proprietary interest in the blue triangle. Even Rocky's arrival couldn't distract her from it for long. Everyone's eyes looked at the blue triangle—except Salder and Uirsé's. Theirs remained locked on each other.

Cracking sounds like tree limbs breaking ascended from the quarry. Eynon watched the triangle begin to break free from its matrix of stone. To the south, he saw tall waves form on the deep blue lake and was glad he'd encouraged them all to gain altitude. Ten-foot waves swept northward from the lake, drenching the rocky plain near the triangle. Then the ground began to split, and the cracking sounds grew louder until it seemed like an entire forest of limbs was breaking off simultaneously. The waves of sound rose up like the waves of water on the lake.

"It's like ice cracking on the Rhuthro in the spring!" shouted Merry. She had to raise her voice to be heard.

Plenna put her arms around Eynon's waist and pressed her head against his body when she realized her blue triangle was the tip of a great tail. *Even future warriors can be afraid,* thought Eynon. *I think I know what's coming and can't say I'm not scared.*

Lake water was sloshing up and down the steep sides of the quarry now. A broad scaly hump of blue appeared in the lake's center and rose higher as they watched. It was the exact shade of dark blue as the heraldic charge on the kingdom of Dâron's banners, but it sparkled. *From magestone powder?* wondered Eynon. With a ripping noise more like tearing fabric than layers of snapping stone, the entire tail broke free and whipped skyward. Eynon was glad he'd moved high enough to be above the tail as it flicked left and right, celebrating its liberation. Then the massive hindquarters lifted, raising the tail-tip's reach still higher. Eynon tilted his chin up and the wizards' flying disks rose another fifty feet.

Farther down the lake, the water frothed and roiled. Vast, bat-like wings unfurled and flapped in the sun to dry. The children looked in rapt attention as a giant wedge-shaped head, dripping with water, escaped from rocks permeated with magestones' magical energy. Stretching out its long neck, the gigantic creature's eyes noted the observers. It shifted its mass to face them.

"I think it's bigger than Viridáxés," whispered Eynon.

"I agree, and I think she's female," replied Merry.

"How can you tell?" asked Eynon.

"Think about it," said Merry. "Why would the men and women from the time of the First Ships plant two *male* dragons?"

"How do we know they only planted two?" Eynon asked in return.

"You have a point," said Merry.

The scaly head stretched up to its maximum extension and looked curiously at the assemblage flying overhead. Even Salder and Uirsé were paying attention now. They followed the others' flying disks down as Eynon guided them to float at the newly-emerged creature's eye level.

"You are correct, young wizard, I *am* female," said the great blue dragon in a low, mellifluous voice like Applegarth's Finest cider laced with honey. "My name is Zûrafiérix."

Chee waved both front paws at the dragon and performed a pair of impressive backflips on Doethan's flying disk.

"Pleased to meet you," said Merry, followed by similar polite greetings from Eynon, Doethan, Salder and Uirsé. Even the children said hello. Mercha's words of welcome were soft, but clear.

"I'm glad to meet you, Zûr-a-fi-ér-ix," said the girl, taking particular care to repeat the dragon's name correctly.

The dragon nodded to each of them. A sound something like a *basso* purr came from her chest as she did. The patterns inside her huge blue eyes spun in pleasant, pleasing spirals. The dragon's eyes blinked and expanded when she saw Nûd hovering beside the others. She moved her immense wedge-shaped head in front of Nûd and dipped it respectfully.

"Son of Dâron," said Zûrafiérix. "My king. Is it time?"

Chapter 29

King and Dragon

Here we go again, thought Eynon.

Nûd was more confident dealing with Zûrafiérix than he had been with Viridáxés initially.

"The time for attacking the Roma was fifteen centuries ago, when they first arrived," Nûd announced. "That's when they founded a province along the Abbenoth. Now they're firmly established in Orluin."

"Really?" asked Zûrafiérix. Her large eyes spun thoughtfully. She scanned the others and saw them nod—even Chee and the children. "It seems I've overslept—and am far larger than I expected to be."

"You *are* quite big," said Merry.

"Very big," said Mercha, who poked her head out from behind Merry to comment.

"The Roma's Occidens Province does more good than harm on this side of the Ocean," Nûd continued. "Their presence as a buffer between Dâron and Tamloch has historically reduced conflict between the two kingdoms, and today they're Dâron's allies, along with the Bifurlanders, against Tamloch."

"Bifurlanders?" asked Zûrafiérix. The dragon tilted her head quizzically.

"A kingdom north of Tamloch, established by settlers from lands north of the Roma's empire across the Ocean," said Eynon. "They are skilled warriors and sailors who travel in longships with broad square sails."

"I'm not familiar with them," said the dragon. "It seems I have a lot to learn. Clearly, a great deal has changed since I was planted here." Zûrafiérix waved a wingtip to take in her surroundings. Broken rock from her release was everywhere and the lake's old boundaries were now less neatly defined. "If my goal is no longer to push the Roma into the Ocean," said Zûrafiérix, "I will need your guidance in determining how I can best serve the kingdom."

"I'm pleased that you're being so sensible about your change in mission," said Nûd. "Viridáxés still wants to smash the Roma, despite our alliance with them."

"Viridáxés is a foolish hothead," said Zûrafiérix. She made a sigh like steam coming from a teakettle the size of Eynon's family's cottage. "He always was. It's quite unfortunate."

"Unfortunate?" asked Merry.

"Yes," said Zûrafiérix. "For me, since he's to be my mate."

"Oh!" said Merry. "I'm so sorry. You have no choice in the matter?"

"Not if I want to lay a clutch and continue our species," said Zûrafiérix. "The Athicans called us *draco megálo,* great dragons, to distinguish us from the lesser breeds."

"You certainly are great, at least in size," said Doethan. "I've never heard of or read about dragons anywhere near the size of you and Viridáxés."

"Ah, that is the defining characteristic of *draco megálo,*" said Zûrafiérix. "Every year we get larger and larger. Magical energy from magestones accelerates the process. How long was I asleep? It must have been quite a while for me to be *this* size."

"Two thousand years," said Nûd, "give or take a decade."

"That long?" mused Zûrafiérix. She rubbed the point of a claw along the end of her snout. "I *do* have a lot to learn."

"Great Zûrafiérix, ma'am?" asked Plenna.

"Yes, child?" the dragon responded. "You don't need to call me *great.* I don't require constant compliments to know my own value."

"Why is it unfortunate that you have to mate with Viridáxés?"

Eynon covered his mouth so Zûrafiérix wouldn't see him smile. *Out of the mouths of babes,* he thought.

"Is it because he doesn't think before he acts?" asked Mercha. "Momma Coegi and Momma Gwest aren't happy with me when *I'm* thoughtless—and Vir-i-dáx-és did break our courtyard."

"That's a large part of it," Zûrafiérix told Mercha. "But give me a century to work on him and I'll help Viridáxés lose his arrogance and find wisdom."

"Unfortunately," said Merry, "we don't have a century."

They heard a whistling sound and turned to see Fercha arriving at high speed. Her flying disk stopped abruptly when she saw Zûrafiérix.

Fercha's eyes went wide. She shook her head and threw her arms wide. "A *blue* dragon? Of *course* there's a blue dragon. That solves Dârio's problem."

"Who is Dârio?" asked Zûrafiérix. "For that matter, who are you?"

"Esteemed dragon, protector of Dâron," said Nûd, "this talented wizard is Fercha—my mother. Fercha, meet Zûrafiérix."

"Pleased to meet you, great Zûrafiérix," said Fercha.

"You don't need to call me great," said the dragon. "I'm not the emperor of the Roma to require *Magnus* before my name. For that matter, since you're my king's mother, *you* can call me Zûra."

"I'm honored, Zûra," said Fercha with a smile. She pulled her arms in and hugged herself.

"Could you please answer my question," said Zûrafiérix.

"What?" said Fercha. She paused and squinted for a moment, trying to remember what the dragon has asked. "Oh. Sorry. Dârio is the king of Dâron."

"I thought *you* were the king of Dâron," said Zûrafiérix, moving her head close to Nûd.

"I am," said Nûd.

"He is," said Eynon, Merry, Doethan and Fercha in chorus.

"That's right," said Salder a beat later.

"Uh huh," said Plenna and Mercha, nodding their heads.

Chee nodded his head in imitation.

"Does Dâron have *two* kings?" asked Zûrafiérix.

"Yes," said Eynon.

"No," said Fercha.

"Sort of," said Merry.

"I'm the Old King's granddaughter," said Fercha. "Nûd is my son and the true heir to Dâron's throne."

Zûrafiérix sniffed. "As my senses inform me," said the dragon. "Tell me the rest."

"Dârio's mother, Princess Gwýnnett, was married to the Old King's grandson, but he didn't get Gwýnnett pregnant, King Túathal of Tamloch did," Fercha explained. "That means Dârio, the young man everyone *thought* was king of Dâron, is really the heir to Tamloch."

"I can't say I approve of King Túathal's behavior," said Zûrafiérix. "And I don't even know the man."

"He's a terrible person," volunteered Uirsé. "He doesn't care a bit for the welfare of his people, just his own power and privilege."

"So Túathal is Dârio's problem?" asked the dragon.

"Túathal allied with Viridáxés is Dârio's problem," said Fercha. "The two of them are a problem for everyone in Orluin who's not Túathal or Viridáxés."

"I see," said Zûrafiérix. "Or at least I'm beginning to." She looked to Nûd for guidance. "What next, My Liege?"

Nûd glanced at Fercha. "My mother knows the most about the present situation."

"I was sent to fetch Eynon to Dârio," said Fercha. "It would be a pleasant surprise for my nephew if his cousin came along, arriving on your back."

Rocky coughed three times, sounding like a large black crow was cawing deep in his throat. A moment later, he ejected a smooth stone from his mouth like a cat tossing a hairball. They all watched it fall to land in the lake below with an audible *plop.*

"I get the message," said Nûd, patting the wyvern's neck. "I think I'll stay on Rocky's back." He nodded to Zûrafiérix. "No offense intended."

"None taken," said the dragon, revealing rows of sword-like teeth as she gave the draconic equivalent of a smile.

Eynon wondered if Rocky had intentionally stopped to snack on the lone wisent. *Could the wyvern have sensed Zûrafiérix beneath the quarry and Nûd's connection to her?*

Zûrafiérix took a moment to stretch her very impressive wings and soak up the late afternoon sun's waning heat, then focused her attention on Fercha. "You're Dârio's aunt?" she asked. The enormous scaled head turned back to Nûd. "And you're his cousin?" The dragon's head moved slowly back and forth while a rumbling purr Nûd interpreted as laughter came from deep inside her massive chest. "One would naturally follow from the other," said Zûrafiérix.

"My husband, Nûd's father, is Verro—King Túathal's brother and master mage of Tamloch," said Fercha. "He flew south with me from the battlefield but stopped to speak to a party of Tamloch wizards who'd been sharing a barrel of ale in the village's fish-drying shed."

The dragon's brow ridges rose.

"He's hovering right behind me, isn't he?" said Fercha. She rotated her flying disk and opened her arms to hug Verro instead of herself. Then she took his hand and introduced him to the dragon. "This, as you've no doubt gathered, is my husband Verro," said Fercha. "Verro, meet Zûrafiérix."

"It is a great pleasure to make your acquaintance, Zûrafiérix," said Verro.

"And mine in return," said the dragon. "I don't mind *great* used in *that* context."

"Something stinks!" said Mercha, holding her nose.

"I know where *he's* been," said Plenna, making the same gesture.

"How were your wizards?" asked Fercha. "Hung over?"

"Sadly, yes," said Verro. "And that apothecary I'd sent to help sober them up was drunk as well. He said it was the only way to avoid the stink in the drying shed."

Zûrafiérix sniffed Verro. "I understand his point, Master Mage. You may want to consider a bath in the near future."

"I doubt he'll have time for that," said Doethan. "Give me a moment and I'll take care of it. Merry, could you fetch me half a sphere as tall as Eynon full of lake water? You know what to do with it."

Fercha knew what Doethan planned as well. She dropped Verro's hand and moved three spear-lengths away from her husband, then watched proudly as her apprentice raised a transparent sphere of solidified sound filled with water from the lake below. Seconds later, the sphere floated above Verro's head.

Tamloch's master mage sighed. "If you must," he said. Fercha grinned at him.

"You too," Doethan told Fercha. "You hugged him. I don't want to be smelling dried fish on *your* robes, either."

"Shared misery is lessened," said Verro, beckoning to Fercha.

"So *you* say," she replied. Her flying disk slowly returned to its former position next to Verro's. The two wizards embraced again and at Doethan's signal, Merry released the cold lake water, drenching them both. Fercha and Verro shouted from the sudden chill and started to shiver. Doethan spoke the words of his drying spell and gestured at them, moving his hands as if flicking water off his fingertips. Seconds later, Fercha and Verro's robes were dry and the two were smiling.

"Thank you," said Fercha. "And thanks for the extra heat at the end to counter the cold."

"Glad to assist," said Doethan.

"I could have done it myself," said Verro, giving Doethan a mock frown.

"Where would the fun be in that?" asked Doethan. "How is your sister?"

"Rúth is well," said Verro. He inspected Doethan from his balding head to the solid boots on his feet. "Perhaps there will be a chance for the two of you if relations between Tamloch and Dâron improve once all this mess is over."

"Perhaps," said Doethan, not looking all that hopeful.

Zûrafiérix shook her immense head. "Now I'm *sure* there's a lot for me to learn," she said. "Royal houses and their connections have always been complicated. I could tell you stories from the time of the First Ships about Princess Dâret and the seven sea captains..."

"Perhaps another time," said Fercha. "We need to join Dârio back on the battlefield."

"I forgot," said Verro, looking over at the girls on Eynon and Merry's disks. "Your mothers said it's time for you to come home and do your chores before you have supper."

Eynon grinned at Merry. He held up three fingers, then lowered them one by one.

Perfectly on cue, Plenna and Mercha protested in high soprano unison. "*Awww!* Do we *have* to?"

"I'll take the children back," volunteered Uirsé. "Salder and I still have a lot to talk about." Salder held Uirsé's waist while she shifted to take on a pair of small passengers.

"I would like to meet the children's mothers," said Zûrafiérix. "Do I understand correctly they run an inn? There was a hostelry near the quarry when I was planted. Its name was the Blue Roof Inn."

"Now it's the Dormant Dragon," said Plenna.

Mercha stared at Zûrafiérix. "Maybe we'll have to change the name," she said.

Chee waved goodbye to Salder, Uirsé and the girls as Uirsé's flying disk descended toward the inn. The raconette judged the distances and jumped from Doethan's flying disk to Eynon's as easily as he would have leapt from one branch to another in the forests along the Rhuthro.

"Welcome back, my friend," said Eynon, rubbing Chee under his chin. "Why does Dârio want to see *me?*" he asked Fercha.

"It's best if he explains things," said Fercha. "Frankly, it's less of an issue now that Zûrafiérix is in the picture."

"Oh," said Eynon, not quite sure how he felt about that.

"Let's get moving," said Merry. She started north toward the battlefield with Eynon, Doethan, Fercha, Verro, Nûd—on Rocky's back, and Zûrafiérix close behind.

Chapter 30

Back to the Battlefield

"Your Majesty," said Duke Háiddon, who was standing outside the royal pavilion near the battlefield. He lifted his chin and pointed to the south. "Look! Up in the sky!"

Dârio put one hand above his eyes to shield them from the afternoon sun and followed the duke's arm. Half a moment later he shook his head and sighed. "*Two* of them?" he said. "As if one dragon wasn't enough trouble."

"It could be worse," said Duke Háiddon.

"How?" asked Dârio.

"Three dragons?" suggested the duke.

Dârio shook his head again and moved his palm from shading his eyes to holding his forehead. "I wonder why *shah mat* boards don't include dragons as pieces," he said.

Duke Háiddon continued staring to the south and answered without turning. "Was that a rhetorical question, or do you really want to know?"

"It *was* a rhetorical question," said Dârio, "but if you have an answer, I'd love to hear it."

"The reason there aren't dragons as pieces on a *shah mat* board," said the duke, "is because dragons tend to knock all the pieces in the game off the board."

"I'll keep that in mind," said Dârio.

"There are wizards on flying disks with the dragon," Duke Háiddon reported.

"We *did* ask Fercha to bring Eynon north," said Dârio. "Perhaps he's brought his friends?"

"There's also a wyvern," added the duke.

"Of course there is," said Dârio. "That means the newly revealed true king of Dâron will be here soon. Maybe I can make all this *his* problem?"

"You're still the king of Dâron until all this is sorted out," said Duke Háiddon.

"Given that King Túathal is now allied with a dragon bigger than a wing of the royal palace, the matter of me taking the throne of Tamloch suddenly has a lower priority," said Dârio. He filled his lungs and squared his shoulders, preparing to deal with the new arrivals. Without warning, his mouth opened wide as arms encircled his waist and squeezed, forcing air out of his lungs in an explosive burst. "Oof!" he said.

"That wasn't kind," said Duke Háiddon, turning his head and smiling at his dark-haired daughter. "The king has a lot on his mind and you're distracting him."

"Why do you think I did it?" Jenet replied. She smiled back at her father and kissed Dârio gently when he spun around and took her in his arms. She disengaged herself after the kiss and stepped back. "I heard you talking about *shah mat*—and dragons. Father used to say I behaved like a dragon when I was small and would knock all the pieces off the board when I was losing."

"So that's where you got the idea," said Dârio, nodding to Duke Háiddon.

"My daughter was a delightful little dragon," said the duke.

"I was four," said Jenet. She made a face at her father. He didn't see it—his attentions were focused on the sky—but Dârio did and stifled a laugh. Jenet kissed him again, on his cheek this time, and spoke louder to ensure her father's attention. "What's your plan for dealing with *that* dragon?" she asked, referring to the great bat-winged creature growing larger above them.

"I'm not sure," said Dârio. "Dragons tend to set their own agendas."

"True enough," said Jenet.

"Our pre-dragon plan to send Dâron's army through the wide gate to Riyas is still going well, at least," said Duke Háiddon. "They'll be ready to march through as soon as Fercha confirms the gate is working properly. Quintillius instructed his legionnaires who couldn't fit on King Bjarni's ships to join us."

"You don't have them bringing up the rear, do you?" asked Jenet.

"Who taught you strategy?" replied Duke Háiddon.

"You did," said Jenet, making an amused face her father could see this time. "And you taught me well. That's why I can take both of you at *shah mat,* three games out of five."

"The legionnaires will be marching in the middle of our troops," said the duke. "I don't want them in a position to attack our rear if they determine it's to their advantage."

"I'm less worried about our allies and more worried about Tamloch, Túathal, and Grand Admiral Sónnel," said Dârio. "We have to prioritize our problems."

"Some problems prioritize themselves," said Jenet, glancing upward.

The afternoon *had* been quiet, except for Viridáxés' appearance earlier, but now soldiers in every corner of the encampment began to shout, their cries echoing like honks from a hundred flocks of noisy geese. They'd seen the dragon.

"Time to head to the battlefield," said Duke Háiddon.

"To the place where Viridáxés landed?" asked Dârio.

"That would be wise," said the duke. "A dragon that size won't fit inside the royal pavilion."

"Hah!" said Dârio. "You're a better earl marshal than court jester."

"Thank you, Your Majesty," said Duke Háiddon with a grin. "Now get moving." The duke moved his left arm in a broad sweep that ended with his outstretched fingers point north.

"I'm coming along," said Jenet. She took Dârio's hand and tugged him in the direction her father had indicated, threading a narrow path between tent ropes.

Duke Háiddon watched his daughter and Dârio together for a few seconds and smiled to himself, thinking the two were well-matched. He nodded to a squad of royal guards who'd been standing twenty paces away to give the king privacy, then set off after Jenet and Dârio. The guards trailed behind him like so many well-armed ducklings and the duke, an experienced military commander, restrained himself from saying, "Quack!"

* * * * *

Soldiers carrying pikes, swords, crossbows, and other weapons lined the edges of the battlefield wearing their sky-blue and dark-blue kingdom of Dâron surcoats. None of them wanted to miss seeing *this* dragon. Mounted knights rode along the ranks, keeping order and ensuring the soldiers gave the king and duke plenty of space for welcoming the new arrivals.

Fercha landed first, touching down in front of Dârio with much more grace than the hasty landing she'd made earlier when pursued by Viridáxés. Verro landed a moment later, followed by Eynon with Chee, Merry, and Doethan. Rocky decided to show off. The wyvern tilted his wings at an angle and twisted down in a tight spiral like a falling maple seed's spinning *samara*.

"I brought Eynon as you commanded," said Fercha, smiling at Dârio. Verro stepped close to her and put his arm around her waist, causing Fercha to redirect her smile at him.

Eynon bowed and Dârio acknowledged the young wizard with a nod. "I'm pleased you brought a few of his friends as well," said Dârio, welcoming all of them by opening his arms wide. He tilted his head to observe the dragon circling high overhead. "Including what I hope will be a very *big* friend."

"I share your hope and believe it's justified," said Fercha. "Zûrafiérix wanted your assurance that none of Dâron's archers would shoot at her when she landed."

"Zûrafiérix," said Dârio, chewing on the dragon's name and deciding he liked its taste. "Please let her know any soldier with a longbow or crossbow taking a shot at her will be sent to guard our borders with the Southern Clan Landers," he said. "Let her know that's *not* a pleasant duty."

"She's heard you, I'm sure," said Fercha. "Dragons have excellent hearing—at least this one does."

Dârio waved to the dragon as Nûd made his way over to join the rest of the group, weaving slightly.

"Rocky's little trick made me dizzy," he said. He waggled a chastising finger at the wyvern. Chee, on Eynon's shoulder, imitated Nûd's gesture. Rocky yawned and cleaned a bit of wisent sinew from between his front teeth with the tip of his right wing. He only held the others' attention for the space of a breath before all eyes lifted to follow the dragon.

Zûrafiérix slowly descended toward the battlefield, her graceful movements a distinct contrast to Viridáxés' heavy-bodied fall to the muddy ground. Watching soldiers were impressed by her size, true enough, but also by her control. The blue dragon's landing was far less crude than her green counterpart's. Instead of furling her wings and dropping to the field from fifty feet up as Viridáxés had, Zûrafiérix kept her wings spread wide and hovered until she was inches above the grass. The ground didn't shake when she touched down, and she didn't leave a depression resembling the basin of a shallow lake where her body struck dirt. The lower curves of her massive frame didn't even crush the vegetation previously bent by the wisents' stampede. Zûrafiérix tucked in one wing, then the other as excited murmurs raced along the line of soldiers faster than a cavalry charge. Several put their hands on the blue dragons appliqued or painted on their surcoats, awed by the symbol of Dâron appearing before them, alive in scale and flesh.

"Please join us," said Nûd, smiling and waving up to Zûrafiérix. The blue dragon shifted her neck down until her huge head was next to Nûd. "Zûrafiérix," he said, "I'd like to introduce you to King Dârio, Duke Háiddon, the kingdom earl marshal, and..."

"I'm Jenet," said the dark-haired girl holding Dârio's hand. "Very pleased to meet you, Zûra!"

The dragon made the rumbling purr sound that indicated she was laughing. "I think I like you, Jen, if I may indulge in the same familiarity."

"Of course," said Jenet. She dropped Dârio's hand and stepped forward fearlessly to touch the end of the dragon's long and toothy snout, but Zûrafiérix smoothly pulled away. "Too familiar?" asked Jenet.

"Without asking permission first, yes," said Zûrafiérix. "Dragons have their dignity."

"May I?" asked Jenet.

"You may," said Zûrafiérix, lowering her head back into reach.

"You're warm, not cold and slimy, like a salamander," said Jenet.

The rumbling purr deep inside the dragon turned into an angry echo of thunder.

"Do you always insult your guests?" asked the dragon.

"I'm sorry!" said Jenet. "I didn't mean to insult you." She backed away and returned to Dârio's side, squeezing his hand so hard her knuckles turned white.

"Viridáxés would have eaten you for mentioning him in the same breath as a tiny lizard," said Zûrafiérix. She opened her mouth and closed it quickly, sharp teeth snapping. Jenet held her ground and didn't flinch. "But *I* am not Viridáxés," said the blue dragon. Zûrafiérix brought her head close to Jenet and turned it so one of her tremendous eyes was only a few feet from the dark-haired young woman. "Do you know *why* dragons are warm, not cold?"

"Yes, Zûra," Jenet replied. "You have congruencies inside you. Dragons are magical creatures."

"Very good," said Zûrafiérix. "You're not as ignorant as I thought," noted the dragon as she pulled her head back next to Nûd.

"Now who's being insulting," said Jenet.

"Forgive *me,*" said Zûrafiérix. "I am but an egg and was thoughtless."

Duke Háiddon cleared his throat. "If you and my daughter don't mind, we have more important things to do than debate what is and isn't an insult to human or dragon kind. We have an invasion to plan."

"Tamloch is the enemy, correct? Not the Roma?" Zûrafiérix asked Nûd. "That will take time to get used to."

"The Roma are our allies, as I'd told you," said Nûd.

"We're going to need your help countering Viridáxés," added Dârio.

"Hmmm..." said Zûrafiérix. "It takes a dragon to match a dragon— that's what the captains of the First Ships and their wizards used to say." Zûrafiérix shifted her front legs forward and arched her back, like a big cat stretching. "Viridáxés and I used to wrestle before we were planted, but neither of us had an advantage over the other." She turned her head to regard her body. "I wonder what it would be like to wrestle him now that I'm so much larger?"

"Viridáxés is quite large as well," said Merry.

"Of course he is," said Zûrafiérix. "I could see his size from his imprint on the field while I was circling above. Please know that I won't harm Viridáxés—he's to be my mate, after all. But I'll do what I can."

Nûd spoke softly, but with authority. "The biggest thing you can do to help is ensure Viridáxés doesn't harm Dâron's soldiers. We can handle the rest."

"I can do that," said Zûrafiérix. "I'll play on Viri's ego."

"I expect that's even bigger than he is," said Eynon, causing a wave of laughter to circle the group.

Nûd faced Dârio, Jenet, and Duke Háiddon. "You're the military strategists," he said. "Where do you want Zûrafiérix and me to go?"

Rocky, on the other side of Nûd, gentle tapped Nûd's back with a wing tip. "Zûrafiérix, *Rocky,* and me," he corrected.

"You should follow Túathal and Viridáxés to Riyas," said Duke Háiddon, looking at Dârio for confirmation. The king and Jenet nodded.

"The wide gate back to Riyas the army will be using is big, but not big enough for you," said Dârio. "Is there a way you can stay in touch with us so we can coordinate?"

"I can give you my communications ring that's paired with one of Nûd's," said Fercha.

"No need," said Doethan. He reached into his pouch and pulled out two plain gold rings. "I always keep a few spare sets on hand."

"Excellent," said Dârio. He took one and tossed the other to Nûd, thinking how much his cousin looked like Verro.

"I assume you still want me to confirm the integrity of the wide gate to Riyas," said Fercha.

"If you would," said Dârio.

"I'll meet you in Riyas," said Verro, giving Fercha a gentle hug. "You know where."

"I do," said Fercha, thinking fondly of nights spent in Verro's suite in the Tamloch royal palace.

"What about us?" asked Merry. "How can *we* help?"

"You did summon me after all," said Eynon.

"I thought you'd be needed to neutralize Viridáxés," said Dârio.

"But now you aren't," said Zûrafiérix, revealing her own sense of self-importance.

"I have an idea," said Jenet. All eyes turned to her. "You have to remember the way you win in *shah mat.*"

Eynon tilted his head in an unspoken question.

"What if we…" Jenet began. Everyone listened attentively as she explained.

"Brilliant," said Duke Háiddon when his daughter had finished describing her plan.

"Thank you," said Jenet. "Now we need Inthíra—she has great technique with complex shapes. She's in camp somewhere."

"I'll track her down," said her father. "She'll be where she can help the most."

Jenet nodded. "We also need detailed maps of Tamloch's capital."

"Once I gate to the royal palace I can get them easily," said Verro. "I'll bring them to Eynon and Merry, so they can practice."

"And I can coordinate our communications," said Doethan.

"It's too bad we have no way to reach Quintillius or King Bjarni without using sky writing," said Dârio.

"I do have a gate from Brendinas to Nova Eboracum, though," said Fercha. "Doethan and I used it when we went back to give Laetícia the alliance agreement you signed, Your Majesty."

Dârio nodded and moved his hand in a *go on* gesture.

"Doethan can gate to the Roma provincial capital and give Laetícia a communications ring," said Fercha. "I'm sure *she* can reach Quintillius."

"Good thinking," said Dârio.

"But…" said Doethan.

"What?" snapped Fercha.

"I don't have a token to get into the palace," Doethan replied. He shifted nervously from foot to foot. "What if the guards…" he began.

"You're a powerful wizard—you'll think of something," said Fercha. "And don't get distracted by *qua-qua*."

Chapter 31

In the Southern Clan Lands

"It's not my fault," said Fox. The former Mastlander and his brothers, Oaf, Dolt, and Fool—as Eynon called them—stood with their backs to an outcrop of granite. A dozen southern Clan Lands' wizards in motley robes stood in an arc around them, ready to pass judgment. Their magestones were mostly shades of brown and gray—smoky quartz, tigereye, agate and jasper. Two wore blue stones. None of them looked happy. Twenty yards to the west, rescuers were several hours into extracting tartan-clad warriors from piles of talus, straining to dig their comrades free like dogs scrabbling for long-buried bones.

A mage of medium height with a dust-coated face and a polished gray marble magestone pointed at Fox and frowned. "Yuir th' wun t' palaver wit' th' green-robed wizzerd," he said. "Yuir th' wun to take th' blame!"

"We all agreed to do as Verro asked in return for the pick of the loot from Dâron's army," said Fox.

"An' how did tha' work out for us, y'fool?" asked a second mage. He shook his staff at Fox and his brothers.

"How was I to know a single wizard had enough power to bring down half the mountain?" Fox protested. "No one could have expected that!"

"Ain't he th' laddie cut off yer brothers' toze?" asked a second wizard. "Ye shoudda kenned he'd be a danger."

Fox's face filled with panic as he realized he didn't have an answer that would help save his skin. He was aided temporarily when one of the Clan Lands wizards with a blue magestone threw him a metaphorical rope. "The best laid schemes o' mice an' men gang aft a-gley," said the wizard. He had a full ginger beard just touched by frost and his robes were better made than the others.

"That be a fine turn o' phrase, Ceanneig," said an older wizard with a horseshoe of white hair standing nearby. "Ye hae the soul o' a poet."

"Share a bottle o' fortified winter wine wi' me Padruig and you'll hear more verses," said Ceanneig.

"Did ye write that one yerself?" asked Padruig.

"Read it in a book," said Ceanneig. He looked at Fox and his brothers and sniffed. "Now let's see wha' we should do wi' these four."

Several wizards shouted to make eunuchs of them, using more earthy language. Another suggested using their necks to test the sharpness of a headsman's axe, while a wizard bigger than Oaf with overdeveloped shoulder muscles bulging under his robes offered to whip them until his arms grew tired.

Fox's brothers crowded closer to him, hoping he'd be able to talk them out of trouble this time as he had many times in the past. As the oldest brother, they considered it his responsibility. Fox looked left and right, but other than a smile from Ceanneig, everyone else around the arc of wizards was frowning.

"Wait!" Fox exclaimed. "You hate the northerners—we hate the northerners. You hate the wizard with the red magestone, my brothers and I *despise* him. Instead of talking about blame, why aren't we talking about revenge?"

Fox could tell from the mutters from the wizards that the idea appealed to them. Revenge and payback for slights, real or imagined, were cherished southern Clan Lands' traditions.

"What d' ye hae in mind?" asked the wizard with the dust-coated face who'd spoken first. "The blasted blue-tabards be too far away for us t' do more than nibble on the edges of their kingdom."

"That's why we gave Verro's plan a chance," said the second mage with the staff.

"I think I know a way into the royal palace in Brendinas if we can fly there," said Fox. "One of the neighbor lads from when we were back on the Rhuthro is a royal guardsman. He's dumb as a stump. I think I can trick him into helping us get inside on the quiet. Then we can make King Dârio hurt like he hurt us—and collect some treasure while we're at it."

"It will be days o' flyin' for us to get there," said Padruig.

"An' wha' about th' young mage wi' the red stone?" asked the wizard with the staff. "Wha' if he blasts us?"

"Then we'll have to blast him first," said Fox.

"I'm for that!" said the wizard with the dust-coated face. "But how d' we get t' Brendinas quickly?"

"There may be a way," said Ceanneig. "Let m' have a private conversation wi' th' laddie and see if he truly knows a way into th' palace." He tossed his flying disk on the ground, mounted, and beckoned to Fox. "Come on," said Ceanneig. "You're going to try breathing clouds."

Fox reluctantly joined Ceanneig and up they went.

* * * * *

The two of them weren't actually *in* a cloud—they were above the clouds and had an excellent view of the sun just a few fingers past its zenith. Things were tight on the flying disk, but they could face each other to talk without risk of falling.

"Tell me straight, do you have a way into the palace or not?" asked Ceanneig without a trace of southern Clan Lands accent.

"What?" asked Fox. He was both nervous and confused, which wasn't a pleasant combination.

"My name is Kennig. My father is a baron with estates just north-west of the capital. I killed a rival for a lover with a lightning bolt and exiled myself to the southern Clan Lands before I could be imprisoned twelve years ago."

Fox tried to take all this new information in. "You're a Dâron wizard?"

"I was," said Kennig. "A rising member of the Conclave before I did something blasted stupid."

"I can understand *that,*" said Fox.

"Were you lying when you said you could get into the palace?" asked Kennig.

"Exaggerating a bit, but not lying," said Fox. "I really do know a guardsman. If he thinks we're holding one of his sisters captive, he'll let us into the palace."

"Distasteful, but that should work," said Kennig.

"How do we get to Brendinas in less than three days of flying?" asked Fox.

"Do you know about emergency gates?" asked Kennig.

"No," said Fox, looking puzzled.

"Wizards make them in advance, so they can escape if they get into something they can't handle," said Kennig. "Emergency gates usually lead somewhere hidden and private."

"How does that help us?" asked Fox. Even after the debacle at the wide gate Verro's wizards had constructed, he wasn't sure about the concept.

"*My* emergency gate comes out near my home," said Kennig. "It connects to a hidden cave. My cousin and I are the only ones who know about it."

"Who's your cousin?" asked Fox.

"It's not important," said Kennig. "Staging our raid is." He rubbed his chin, then spoke. "Eight of us should be enough—myself and three more wizards for brains and magic, you and your brothers for muscle. I think I can hold my emergency gate open long enough for us all to get through."

"Sounds like a plan," said Fox. "My odds of staying out of Dâron Castle's dungeons go up with wizards along."

"Be ready to act quickly," said Kennig. "The best way to attack wizards is to take them by surprise."

"We'll hold up our end," said Fox. He pulled out his sword in a smooth, practiced motion and slashed the air before returning it to his sheath.

"Good," said Kennig. "When we get there, see if you can find that wizard with the red magestone, too. I'd love to give him a taste of what he gave us."

"So would I," said Fox.

"To revenge," said Kennig.

"Revenge," said Fox, holding up a fist. He hoped it would be sweet and promised himself he'd be looking for Merry, not just Eynon. Fox rubbed his hands together and smiled an unsettling smile like a small boy about to pull the wings off a fly.

Chapter 32

Dragonback

Túathal was growing tired of the cold wind blowing in his face. He wished he was still on good terms with his brother. Verro could have generated a protective barrier of solidified sound around him with a wave of his hand. It was amazing what wizards could do with solidified sound, a magical non-substance that could be shaped into almost anything. Unfortunately, without Verro, or even that little mouse of a wizard Uirsé who was so easy to terrorize, he was prey for the biting air. After interviewing the other nobles with him on dragonback to learn everything they knew of what had happened since he was poisoned, Túathal insisted they sit in front of him and serve as a wind break. His comfort mattered far more than theirs, after all.

At least the great green dragon was making good time on the way to Riyas. The sun was still a finger's breadth above the western horizon and Túathal could see the wide blue ribbon of the Abbenoth river fast-approaching below. Viridáxés was on schedule to arrive in Tamloch's capital well before dawn. Túathal smiled when he considered the reaction of his subjects to their king swooping out of the clouds on dragonback. Their screams would be music to his ears, especially after what had happened to the main Tamloch army in Dâron.

Viridáxés would overawe any would-be rivals considering a play for the throne. Duke Néillen, the kingdom earl marshal, was ambitious, but not overly so. He'd be glad to return to his role as Túathal's primary military commander. Grand Admiral Sónnel was a potential candidate, especially given his position in the line of succession and his role commanding Tamloch's navy, but one look at Viridáxés would convince Sónnel not to try. The dragon could destroy Sónnel's entire fleet before a single ship could fire a ballista bolt or launch a rock from a deck-mounted catapult. Sónnel wouldn't challenge him.

Túathal closed his eyes and smiled, considering how Viridáxés' arrival increased the odds he could convince Dârio to switch his allegiance from Dâron to Tamloch, especially now that Verro's son with Fercha turned out to be the true king of Dâron, leaving Dârio without a royal title in the southern kingdom. From what he'd heard from the other nobles riding with him on Viridáxés, Dârianûd was young, inexperienced, and quite likely easy for Túathal to manipulate. He'd control both kingdoms yet!

He wished he was wearing gloves. His hands were nearly frozen, and it felt like they were buzzing. *Was it frostbite? No! One of his rings was announcing an incoming communication!* Túathal tightened his legs around the protruding scale in front of him and expanded the ring without taking time to identify which of the more than a dozen rings had been signaling him. Three small chimes sounded as it opened.

"Who is it?" he snapped, before the image at the center of the thin gold circle sharpened. Then he remembered. He'd given the mate to this ring to a man who could feed him information about what went on in Dâron's Conclave.

"Ummm, Hibblig, Your Majesty. Princess Gwýnnett's senior wizard," said Hibblig, sounding like a child asking for an undeserved honey cake before dinner.

"Why would I possibly want to talk to a fool who serves a bigger fool?" asked Túathal. "Especially when your mistress tried to kill me?"

"How did you know we were sleeping together?" asked Hibblig, his eyes wide.

"I didn't, you idiot, but I do now," said Túathal, filing the information away for possible use as blackmail. "I meant you served her, not that you swived her."

"Of course, Your Majesty," said Hibblig. The big man tugged at his chin without seeming to notice he was doing so. "It's just that the princess tried to kidnap Queen Carys and..."

"The old harridan put Gwýnnett firmly in her place, I assume," Túathal completed.

"Carys has royal guards holding the princess prisoner in her own suite in the palace," said Hibblig. "I barely escaped before I could be captured as well."

"Luck more than skill, I expect," said Túathal.

"Your Majesty?" said Hibblig, too much on edge to realize he'd been insulted.

"Never mind," said Túathal. "What do you want *me* to do about it?"

"You once valued Princess Gwýnnett as an ally," said Hibblig. "She told me you were going to marry her and make her queen of a united realm of Tamloch and Dâron, though I'd still be her partner in other things because you preferred men to women."

"Stop blathering," said Túathal. "Next to none of that's relevant any longer."

"I heard about your dragon," said Hibblig, "and wanted to beg sanctuary with you in Tamloch. It won't be safe for me here when what I've done comes to Dârio's attention."

"So that's how it is, is it?" said Túathal. "You want to save your own skin?"

"I'm a powerful wizard, Your Majesty," said Hibblig. "I could be useful to you."

"I'll think on that," said Túathal.

"I could also deliver Princess Gwýnnett to you," added Hibblig. "She had value to you in the past and as Dârio's mother, she might again."

"That *would* strengthen your case to gain my protection," said Túathal.

"Wouldn't you *enjoy* having the woman who poisoned you and nearly killed you under your control?" asked Hibblig.

"Hah!" said Túathal. One corner of his mouth turned up as he contemplated what he might do to teach Gwýnnett the folly of her earlier actions. Hibblig smiled back through the ring's interface.

"Have we reached an agreement?" asked the wizard. "Princess Gwýnnett for your protection and sanctuary in Riyas?"

"I can see that you and your mistress are woven from the same thread," said Túathal. "If you can get Gwýnnett out of the palace under the nose of Queen Carys, contact me again and you can meet me in Riyas."

"Thank you, Your Majesty," said Hibblig. The big wizard was smiling broadly and he'd stopped tugging his chin. "Expect to hear from me not long after sundown."

"Whenever," said Túathal. "I won't be back in Riyas myself until morning." He'd remembered other people he needed to contact and was ready for *this* conversation to be over.

"Are you on *dragonback?*" asked Hibblig, noticing Túathal's surroundings for the first time.

"No," said the king of Tamloch. "I've got a hundred overly-muscled dancing boys stripped to the waist waving fans at my face while sitting on a scaly green carpet."

"But it *looks* like you're..." began Hibblig.

Túathal cut the connection before the wizard could further demonstrate his foolishness. He held both his hands outstretched in front of him and considered the other rings he wore. *This one,* he thought, removing one from his left hand. *Grand Admiral Sónnel needed to be reminded who was king of Tamloch and commanded the might of Viridáxés.*

Chapter 33

Aboard the Búa Mór

Grand Admiral Sónnel grumbled softly, but loud enough that his second in command, Captain Maírné, could hear him from a few feet away. "Blasted Túathal only gave us three wizards for the entire fleet," Sónnel muttered. "With a dozen we could have raised enough wind to be back in Riyas harbor twice as fast." Sónnel adjusted his green felt hat. "Fire and lightning, what a mess! The army routed by a herd of cows—and now it's up to the navy to set things right." He smacked his fist into his palm. "I'd love to wrap the man in anchor chains and toss him over the side, dead *or* alive."

"Careful," said Maírné. "It's not kind to speak ill of the dead—and not wise to criticize the king if he still lives. I'll understand, but Túathal's spies won't—and they're everywhere."

"Lucky for me you know every one of them," said Sónnel, turning his one remaining eye on Maírné. "We're alone here on the fore-deck, so I'm not worried. I appreciate your caution, and your indulgence in listening to me storm on with my complaints like a tattered jib rattling in a gale. I'm sorry you have to hear them, but you're the only one aboard I know I can trust."

"Believe me, I share your frustration," said Maírné, who also served as captain of the *Búa Mór,* the fleet's flagship. "We were supposed to attack an understrength Roma garrison at Nova Eboracum and return to port with our holds full of treasure. Now we're sailing full-out back to Riyas as fast as the wind can drive us to prevent some minor baron declaring himself king."

"Instead of putting me on the throne?" asked Sónnel.

Maírné chuckled. "I'd be pleased to have you as king instead of a random baron," he said. "And overjoyed if you replaced Túathal. Nine out of ten nobles in the kingdom would welcome that change."

"And the tenth owes his rank to Túathal's favor," said Sónnel. He stared off the port bow at the shore that was still part of Occidens

Province, regretting how much harder it was for him to judge the distance from the *Búa Mór* to the seals barking on the distant rocks. He turned his eye to Maírné. "Not that I wouldn't make you a duke if I had the chance, old friend."

"I would welcome any opportunity to serve," said Maírné, tipping *his* green felt cap.

"I'm sure you would," said Sónnel. "Did you hear the rumor about Túathal's heir?"

"Half the fleet's probably heard he claimed the pup who rules in Brendinas for that honor," said Maírné.

"Túathal is playing a long game," Sónnel replied. "And he's got balls the size of blackseed melons to have planted his heir in Princess Gwýnnett."

"I heard she was the one who poisoned him," said Maírné.

"Maybe," said Sónnel. "That would fit with Gwýnnett's reputation. Alternatively, there's a chance a sack of Túathal's own vile essence grew too full inside him and burst open."

"I doubt it," said Maírné.

"Right," said Sónnel. "He doesn't hold his vileness in, he sprays it on everyone around him."

Captain Maírné mimed wiping his sleeve. So did Grand Admiral Sónnel. Both men grimaced and shook their heads. Maírné looked at the reddening sky to the west. The seas, for now, were calm.

"What does your arm tell you about tomorrow's weather?" asked Maírné.

Admiral Sónnel's right arm had almost been severed by a warrior's battleaxe ten years earlier during a large-scale Bifurland raid on Bhaile Pónaire, a major Tamloch city north of Fishhook Cape. The arm would have been lost if not for two flasks of healing potion and the efforts of a particularly skilled hedge wizard then assigned to Sónnel's command. The arm was fully functional, but it ached when bad weather was coming. The admiral stretched it then bent it at the elbow. "It feels fine," he said, after rubbing the arm and giving it a final visual inspection. "We won't have to deal with rain overnight or in the morning."

"That's good news," said Maírné. "Especially since we won't know what to expect when we enter Riyas harbor."

"The forts on Red Island may be able to signal us and pass along *some* information," said Sónnel. "And I might send one of our wizards ahead to scout things out before we dock. Which one is most trustworthy?"

"None of them," said Maírné. "They're all loyal to Verro."

"Then we'll just choose one at random," said Sónnel. "Word has it that Verro's *own* loyalties are now in question."

"You mean the stories about the tall wizard with short red hair?" asked Maírné.

"That, and the fact that Verro's son is the true king of Dâron," said Sónnel. "A wizard on the battlefield passed that bit of gossip on to one of the wizards with the fleet."

"I'm glad *I'm* not related to royalty," said Maírné.

"I'm only Túathal's third cousin," said Sónnel. "His great-grandfather was my great-grandfather's brother."

"You're still next in line if Túathal dies without an heir, aren't you?" asked Maírné. "That *is* why we're sailing back to Riyas?"

"It is," said Sónnel. The grand admiral sighed. "I'm glad my wife and I only have daughters. I'd hate to have one of my sons have to carry the weight of the crown."

"Most would jump at the chance," said Maírné. "And you still have time to father sons."

"My wife is too old for more children."

"Then find a willing woman who's not your wife," said Maírné. "That's what Túathal did."

"I'm not Túathal," said Sónnel.

"Thank goodness for *that,*" said Maírné. He grinned at his friend.

Instead of smiling back, Sónnel's face tightened and his eyebrows tried to pull together over his nose.

"What is it?" asked Maírné.

"One of my communications rings is buzzing."

"Then *who* is it?"

"Túathal, I think," said Sónnel. He removed the ring from his hand and pulled it open as three chimes sounded. "Yes, Your Majesty?"

"Grand Admiral Sónnel," said Túathal, sounding displeased, which wasn't unusual. There was something odd about his voice, like he was trying to speak in a high wind. When the image on the other side of the interface came into focus, Sónnel understood why. Túathal was on the back of some enormous green-scaled beast. "Report!" barked the king. "What is the status and disposition of the fleet?"

Captain Maírné moved to a spot on an angle where he could see the images in the center of the thin gold hoop but not be seen by Túathal.

"We're headed back to Riyas in good order," said Sónnel. "All ships are in excellent repair and we're in the sound between Insula Longa and lands held by Occidens Province. At our current speed, we expect to arrive at the docks in Riyas just after dawn tomorrow."

"Those were not my orders, Grand Admiral," said Túathal, his tone even more unhappy. "You were to take and sack Nova Eboracum while its garrisons were understrength."

"I'm sorry, Your Majesty. After what happened on the battlefield in Dâron and word that you'd been poisoned and were dying, I exercised my own initiative and decided to return the fleet to the capital in order to secure the throne from all potential usurpers until Your Majesty's status could be confirmed."

"From *all* potential usurpers, Grand Admiral?" asked Túathal. "Do you consider yourself among them?"

"We've discussed this, Sire," said Sónnel. "I'm much happier walking a deck than I would be sitting a throne, I'm sure."

"That's why you've been trusted with command of the fleet, Grand Admiral," said Túathal. "I appreciate your initiative in changing course and heading home. Your ships and troops will be needed in Riyas."

"I'm glad you support my decision," said Sónnel.

"You may have noticed the balance of power has changed," said Túathal. He shifted the ring's interface so Sónnel could take in more scaly back and long tail.

"I see *something* huge," said Sónnel, "but I'm not sure my mind can comprehend what my eyes are seeing."

"You'll meet Viridáxés in the morning," said Túathal. "He's a dragon larger than a dozen of the biggest ships in your fleet combined. On top of that he breathes fire and is nearly unstoppable. No one can stand before me and my dragon—not Dâron, not Bifurland, not the Clan Lands, not the Roma—and especially not *you,* cousin. Do we understand each other?"

"Completely, Your Majesty," said Sónnel. "You can depend on me to be your loyal servant."

"Good," said Túathal. "You'll want to send a wizard back towards Nova Eboracum. I've heard rumors that the Bifurland fleet is there now and following your wakes."

"That's impossible," said Sónnel. "Every report put the longships on the Brenavon just south of Brendinas, blocked by a blasted sheet of ice. It would take them days to sail or row to the mouth of the river then reach Nova Eboracum."

"Do I need to *order* you to send a wizard?" asked Túathal. His eyes stared cold and hard into Sónnel's through the ring's interface.

"No, Sire. I'll send a wizard to scout behind the fleet as soon as you end our discussion."

"Excellent," said Túathal. "My regards to you as well, Captain Maírné."

"Thank you, Your Majesty," said Maírné after he stepped into direct sight of the interface.

"Remember, Captain, my eyes and ears are everywhere," warned Túathal. The king's face looked like a hungry gryffon contemplating Sónnel and Maírné as its first and second courses for dinner. "Good sailing," said the king.

The interface in Sónnel's hands went black and the circle of gold contracted back into a ring. He put it back on his finger. The admiral and his fleet captain locked eyes for a moment before lowering their heads and shaking them.

"Now can you tell why I'm not thrilled to be Túathal's third cousin?" asked Sónnel.

"I can," said Maírné. "I'm going to draw a basin of water to wash the feel of that man off me—after I send a wizard to scout for an impossible fleet of Bifurland longships."

"Thank you, old friend," said Sónnel. "I'm washing up *and* changing my uniform. I've sweated through this one."

"Good idea," said Maírné. "I'll do the same."

"Túathal has a dragon. A *big* dragon larger than a dozen ships," mused Sónnel. He put his hand on his old friend's arm before Maírné could leave. "Maybe an impossible fleet of longships is possible after all."

Chapter 34

Nova Eboracum

The streets of Nova Eboracum were every bit as crowded and bustling as Doethan remembered. He'd become fond of the slower pace of life in his tower along the Rhuthro and would be glad to restrict his trips to a big city like Brendinas to quarterly meetings of the Dâron Conclave once things settled down again, if they ever did. Nova Eboracum was even bigger than Brendinas—the Roma had an affinity for urban life—and his path to the governor's palace was filled with noises and smells that assaulted his senses. Doethan was glad Rowsch, his large hound familiar, wasn't along. His dog might be even more overwhelmed than he was.

"Dough rings! Dough rings!" shouted a man carrying a long wooden pole that held circles of fresh-baked dough covered in seeds. *From the northeastern part of the Empire,* thought Doethan, remembering something he'd read in Robin Oddfellow's *Peregrinations.* The rings smelled delicious—Doethan couldn't resist fresh bread—so he stopped the vendor and asked for one. *I am on a mission to deliver rings after all,* Doethan considered. *There's been so much excitement and I haven't had anything to eat since a slice of egg pie back at the inn.*

"Is one enough for you, good wizard?" asked the vendor, a pleasant-faced man in off-white robes wearing a purple sash. Doethan smiled to see the vendor's hair had receded nearly as far as his own. "If you buy two, you get one free," said the vendor, sensing Doethan's interest.

"Three then," said Doethan, "if you have something I can carry the other two in."

"Of course," said the vendor as he removed three of the rings from his pole and put two of them in a small net bag with long handles that he looped over a forearm. "Butter or soft cheese?" asked the vendor, holding the third dough ring tantalizingly close to Doethan's nose.

"Soft cheese," Doethan replied, thinking this must be some odd Nova Eboracum custom. *When with the Roma, do as the Roma do,* he thought. The epigram reminded him of Ealdamon. He hoped his old friend and Astrí were enjoying themselves, wherever they had gone.

The vendor expertly bisected the dough ring horizontally with a knife taken from a sheath at his belt. Then he turned so Doethan could see two heavy pottery crocks in a web of supporting leather straps attached behind the knife. In a practiced motion, the vendor supported his pole of rings with an elbow and spread soft cheese on the hot ring. He closed the two halves of the ring back together and passed it to Doethan. Soft white cheese oozed out the sides of the ring in sharp contrast to the well-baked dark dough and poppy seeds. Doethan took a bite while the vendor closed the cheese crock and cleaned his knife.

"This is amazingly good," said Doethan. He wiped excess soft cheese from his lips, then licked his fingers.

"Aren't you glad you decided to get three?" asked the vendor, still holding the other two.

"Yes," said Doethan, nodding and taking another bite.

"You're a visitor here, aren't you?" asked the vendor.

Doethan nodded again, unwilling to swallow what he was chewing too soon. He wanted to savor the exotic Roma flavors.

"If you're looking for a place to stay, my sister runs an inn not far from here," said the vendor. "My brother-in-law cooks for the inn's taverna at street level. They rent me space for my cauldrons and ovens in the back in return for bread and dough rings for the taverna."

"Why does a baker need cauldrons?" asked Doethan once his mouth was available for speaking again.

"I boil the dough rings, good wizard," said the vendor. "That's what makes their crusts so chewy."

"Fascinating," said Doethan. "I'll have to stop by and watch the process when I'm not so pressed for time."

"They're made twice a day," said the vendor. "I'm up before dawn for the morning batches and my daughter does the afternoon ones.

These are her handiwork." The vendor held up the stick for Doethan to admire. "Are you sure I can't interest you in a dozen? The sooner I sell these, the sooner I'm done for the day."

Doethan had another bite of dough ring and soft cheese in his mouth, but he spoke around it. "I'll take a dusshen."

The vendor smiled. Doethan was clearly not the first customer who had fallen for his patter.

Doethan swallowed. "How much are they?" he asked. "And do you take coins from Dâron?"

"Of course," said the vendor. "At a discount, unfortunately."

Reaching into his belt-pouch, Doethan pulled out a pair of bright copper pennies marked with the head of King Dârio.

"You'll need more than that, good wizard," the vendor protested. "You couldn't buy *one* dough ring with two Dâron pennies."

"In a moment, these will be *special* pennies," said Doethan, lowering his head to stare at his palm. He concentrated on the coins and bound them to tiny congruencies tied to the far north.

"What did you just do?" asked the vendor.

"Here," said Doethan, passing the coins to the vendor.

"They're cold," said the vendor. "Really cold!" He shifted the coins from one hand to the other.

"Put one of these in the lid of your butter crock and the other with your soft cheese," said Doethan. "They'll stay cold all day and all night."

"*Thank you,* good wizard," said the vendor. "Thanks a thousand times over! I am in your debt. Our wizards charge so much for such spells a poor merchant can't afford them."

"Could I have my dozen dough rings, please?" asked Doethan.

"Of course, of course," said the vendor. He put his new cold cash in his coin pouch and produced a larger net bag from a collection of them that had been tied to the lower end of his purple sash. He filled the bag with twelve dough rings and handed it and the smaller bag with two rings to Doethan. The vendor was talking to himself softly and seemed to be almost in a daze. "If I commission a crock with two compartments, I can use it for both butter *and* cheese and then have the other coin free to chill *wine,*" Doethan overheard. "The taverna will have customers standing in line to enter!"

"Thank you for the dough rings," said Doethan as he secured both net bags to his belt. He turned to leave and had gotten half a dozen paces farther toward the palace when the vendor caught up to him.

"Good wizard," said the vendor. "I forgot to ask. How long will the spell last?"

"Last?" asked Doethan. "The spell will last as long as I live, unless the coins' copper is melted down or some other such foolishness. They should serve you and your family for many years to come."

"You're a most excellent wizard!" said the vendor. "May you live to be five hundred."

"That seems a bit excessive," said Doethan. He fended off a hug with an upraised hand and watched the vendor rush off down the street, his feet barely touching the cobblestones.

* * * * *

Doethan double-checked the contents of his belt-pouch to see if any light-fingered street entrepreneur had tried to steal from him. He would have been an easy mark for thieves and pickpockets while distracted by the vendor. Everything seemed to be in its place, however. Perhaps Nova Eboracum wasn't any more dangerous than Brendinas when it came to street crime. As a wizard he was seldom bothered in Dâron's capital. It took a particularly brazen thief to try to steal from a wizard. Just then he felt a tug at his belt. His hand shot down and grabbed a bony wrist belonging to a child of indeterminate age and gender.

"Trying to steal my dough rings, are you?" asked Doethan. He tightened the handles of the large bag around his belt and examined his captive. The face was dirty, but the hair was relatively clean, Doethan noted.

"Don't hurt me, sir," said the child. "Your grip is too tight."

"Your legs are too fast for me to catch you, if I let you go," said Doethan. "Are you hungry."

"Yes," said the urchin, looking down.

I don't see any lice, thought Doethan, inspecting the child's scalp from above. He hobbled the child's feet with a cord of solidified sound around his ankles. He made the hobble bright blue so his captive would see it and not try to run. Doethan opened the large net bag and removed a dough ring. "Here," he said. "Have something to eat."

"Thank you, your wizardness," said the child. Two bites of dough ring disappeared in two heartbeats.

"What's your name?" asked Doethan. He smiled when he remembered Eynon had shown the same level of innocent formality.

"Oc-tá-vi," said the child between bites.

Ah, thought Doethan. *A boy. Maybe—he still wasn't sure.* "Named after Octavian, the second emperor?" he asked.

"Named 'cause o' me seven older brothers and sisters," said the lad—or lass. "I'm the eighth."

"I'm sure your mother loves you every bit as much as she does her other children," said Doethan.

"Can't," said the child. "She's dead—and besides, she sold me."

Doethan felt uncomfortable confronting one of the least admirable aspects of Roma society. Captives could be held as slaves for twenty years, children sold as slaves for ten. Any adult Roma man or woman could trade their free status for a term of slavery in exchange for a payment from their owner when the contract commenced and every year thereafter until the slave chose to be free again on a subsequent anniversary. Some never did. Being a thrall in Bifurland was worse in some ways and better in others. Now was not the time to challenge Roma custom, Doethan decided. He wouldn't ask if the child was a runaway, especially since he thought he knew the answer. He'd simply feed the dirty-faced child and be on his way.

"Sorry about your mother, Octávi," said Doethan. "Enjoy the dough ring." He dispelled the construct binding the would-be thief's ankles and began to move away.

"Távi," said the child. "Everyone calls me Távi."

Doethan saw Távi slip through the other pedestrians to join what looked like a pack of similar urchins across the street in a shadowy space between two tall apartment buildings. He generated distance lenses from solidified sound and watched. Távi broke the remaining dough ring into three pieces and shared them with the three smallest pack members. Doethan held up another dough ring and waved Távi back to him. Távi took the ring from his hand and started to turn back to his pack. "Wait!" said Doethan. He took another shiny penny stamped with King Dârio's likeness from his belt-pouch and flipped it to Távi. The child snatched it out of the air and looked at it quizzically.

"Alms for the poor?" asked Távi. "You must be poor yourself if this is all you can give. I thought all wizards were rich." Távi held up the penny and nodded to Doethan. "No choices for beggars, they say—not that we're beggars. Me and mine make our own way in the world."

Doethan smiled at Távi. "I'm sure you do," he said. "If you and your friends can make your own way to the shop where the dough-ring vendor does his baking, you'll get more than a pair of dough rings." Távi stared at Doethan, clearly more used to kicks than kindness. "Give the dough-ring baker the coin you're holding," Doethan instructed, "and tell him I'll enchant it for him on my way home if he sees that you and your friends get a hot meal tonight."

Távi nodded. "If your word is true, me and mine will owe you one," said the child. A moment later Távi was back with the other children, all moving so fast they might have stepped through a gate.

Doethan reminded himself to find the baker's shop when he'd given a communications ring to Laetícia—if the guards would allow him *into* the governor's palace and the province's spymaster would permit him to *leave*.

* * * * *

Passers-by in Nova Eboracum were still avoiding the paving stones closest to the entrance to the governor's palace. *Nothing has changed in a day or two to make the guards' unsheathed swords less intimidating,* thought Doethan. He summoned his courage and approached the nearest guard, glad it wasn't Stultio, the tall young man who'd been such a bother the last time he'd tried to gain entry.

"I need to see Laetícia," said Doethan. "I don't have a token, but I do have a very important message from King Dârio."

This guard—as young as Stultio but not as tall—smiled at Doethan. "Just a moment," she said. "I'll need to consult with…"

At that moment, the senior guard who'd been at the palace entrance when Doethan had been there with Fercha stepped up. "Doethan," she said. "It's a pleasure to see you again. Laetícia told us to expect *someone* from Dâron. I'm glad it's you. My name is Antica—we haven't been formally introduced."

"And *I'm* glad you're still in charge here, Antica," said Doethan. "It makes things a lot easier. My congratulations on the professionalism of the guard who greeted me." He waved at the first guard.

"Propitia is on her best behavior, aren't you?" said Antica. She smiled at Propitia, who kept her face neutral and didn't smile back. "All the guards are now. Stultio has four more days of punishment to work off and the other guards don't want to give me any reason for them to face a similar fate. Do you have any idea how long it takes to run ten times around the city walls in full kit?"

"I can't say that I do," said Doethan.

"Just as well," said Antica. "It's probably a military secret."

"How did Laetícia know someone was coming from Dâron?" asked Doethan.

"I don't know, really," said Antica, who motioned Doethan to follow her into the governor's palace. "She said something crazy about reading the writing on the clouds."

"Ah," said Doethan. He had to lengthen his stride to keep up with Antica and was amused by the way the plates on her *lorica segmentata* body armor *chinged* like bells as she walked.

"You can probably see Stultio running from the windows in Laetícia's tower," said Antica. "I think he has another lap to go before sundown."

"I'll watch for him if I have the chance," said Doethan.

* * * * *

Laetícia's study proved to be eight stories up. *Her tower almost scrapes the sky,* thought Doethan as he followed the upward flow of the tower's central stairwell. He shook his head, his mind and his knees far from thrilled with the idea of such a climb.

"She sent word you can use your flying disk," said Antica. "Take the landing on the top on the left. The guards there will show you in."

"Thank you," said Doethan. "I appreciate your help." He stepped on his flying disk, rose to the specified landing, and with her guards' permission, entered Laetícia's study.

"Doethan! How thoughtful!" exclaimed Occidens Province's spymaster. "You brought dough rings!"

Chapter 35
Doethan and Laetícia

"More wine?" asked Laetícia. The two of them sat across from each other at a beautiful ivory-inlaid table made from a dark wood Doethan didn't recognize. The dough rings, a bowl of soft cheese, a sharp knife, and a pair of flat knives rested on the table between them. Laetícia occupied a high padded stool identical to Doethan's seat, demonstrating her perfect posture. She held a thick green glass bottle above Doethan's goblet.

"Just a sip or three," said Doethan. "I can handle wine, but I understand that sorghum beer you Roma drink hits like the butt-end of a spear to the faceplate."

"It helps if you grow up drinking it," said Laetícia. "I can get a mug of it for you if you'd like to taste it for yourself." She shifted her head and smiled. The beads on her braids made a distracting susurrus, like rain on a slate roof.

It's almost hypnotic, thought Doethan. "Some other time," he said. Doethan accepted more of the fruity red wine—far more than three sips—then reduced the height of the liquid in his goblet by two fingers. He didn't tell Laetícia she had a dab of soft cheese on the corner of her mouth. She was tall, though not by any means as tall as her husband Quintillius, the governor and military leader of Occidens Province. Laetícia wore lavender wizard's robes covered in subtle geometric patterns of sparkling thread and her deep-purple magestone glowed on a gold plate resting just below her throat. With her bright, intelligent eyes and ebony skin she looked more like a queen than a spymaster. *She might as well be a queen, from everything I've heard,* thought Doethan.

"I'm so glad you brought dough rings," said Laetícia. "I like them quite a lot, and so do the children, but the palace cooks don't often serve them, since they need to be boiled as well as baked. Did you know that?"

"I learned it recently," said Doethan. "They certainly have a unique taste and consistency. They're chewy, without being tough."

"A concise and accurate description," said Laetícia.

"How many children do you have?" asked Doethan, sincerely interested *and* trying to get through the obligatory small talk as quickly as possible.

"Three," said Laetícia. "Primus, Seconda, and Tertia—a boy and two girls."

"Interesting," said Doethan, trying not to show his surprise.

"What?" asked Laetícia. "You don't approve of their names?"

"It's not that," said Doethan. "It's just that I expected parents like you and Quintillius to be more creative in your choice of names than calling your offspring First, Second, and Third."

Laetícia laughed and shook her head in mirth. Her beads clacked like hail on a slate roof, not rain. "Thank you!" she said. "I haven't laughed like that since Seconda tried to put our cat in a toga."

"I hope I haven't offended," said Doethan.

"By no means," said Laetícia. She artfully refilled his goblet while she recovered. "It's customary for Roma parents to give their children nicknames—use names for everyday inside the family. Primus is Quintillius Marius Occidentalis."

"That makes more sense then," said Doethan. "I'm glad I brought enough dough rings for your little Roma numerals to enjoy as well."

Laetícia took a deep breath and worked to return her face to its usual neutral expression. The corners of her mouth kept rising, so she distracted Doethan with trivia. "Do you know what we call the vendors who *make* dough rings?" she asked.

"Bakers?" asked Doethan.

Laetícia smiled, then caught herself. "No," she said, deadpan. "They're named for the way they carry their wares on long wooden rods."

"Do you call them *Sticks* then?" asked Doethan, playing along.

"Close," Laetícia answered. "We call them *Poles*."

"And the province they come from must then be Pole Land," added Doethan.

"That's far too whimsical a name for imperial Roma administrators," said Laetícia. "It's North Sarmatia."

"A pity," said Doethan, tilting his goblet toward Laetícia to show his appreciation for the information she'd shared, no matter how irrelevant it was to the current situation.

"I suppose you didn't make the trip from Brendinas to Nova Eboracum to sample our local delicacies," said Laetícia, motioning toward the tabletop.

"Dough rings are far from delicate," teased Doethan, "but you're right. King Dârio sent me."

"Would that be the Dârio who's king of Dâron or the one who hopes to rule in Tamloch?"

"Both, sort of," said Doethan. "Things are still in flux at the moment."

"I suppose they are," said Laetícia.

"You probably already know that Dârio plans to lead the Dâron army through a wide gate to Riyas to head off Túathal."

"I do," said Laetícia. "It's a shame."

"What's a shame?" asked Doethan.

"That Túathal isn't dead," said Laetícia. "Everything would be so much easier if Princess Gwýnnett hadn't been incompetent."

"If she was competent, we'd have a different set of problems," said Doethan.

"True enough," said Laetícia. "Now tell me the *big* news."

"From your emphasis, I expect you've already been informed," said Doethan.

"Yes, but I find it hard to believe a green dragon as large as a baronial keep now serves Túathal," said Laetícia.

"What's harder to believe? The size of the dragon or the fact that it does Túathal's bidding?" asked Doethan.

"More the former than the latter," said Laetícia. "Túathal has a talent for commanding obedience from subordinates."

"Other than by holding their families hostage?" asked Doethan.

"Don't forget noble titles and bribes," said Laetícia. She shook her head again, but so slowly that the beads in her braids were silent. Laetícia held Doethan's eyes before she spoke again.

"What are we doing to do about Túathal's dragon? Wizards can deal with smaller dragons, but the size of this one is unprecedented."

"King Dârio has a plan," said Doethan.

"Forgive me if the thought of a plan from an eighteen-year-old king who's barely worn his crown for two years doesn't fill me with optimism." Laetícia rubbed her chin and stared at the tabletop as if it was a *shah mat* board. "Especially when he may not be a king at all—not of Dâron *or* of Tamloch."

"Is it wise to discount a plan before you've heard it?" asked Doethan.

"No," said Laetícia, "but is it wise to send an army or a fleet against a dragon as big as mountain?"

"Viridáxés isn't *that* big, unless you mean a relatively small mountain," said Doethan.

"A dragon like that could destroy Nova Eboracum in an afternoon," said Laetícia. "All it would have to do is land on our walls and they'd fall."

"He also breathes fire," said Doethan.

"Oh joy," said Laetícia, looking the opposite of how she'd seemed when she was laughing. "Maybe our siege engines could hold it off? A ballista bolt through the heart might discourage the thing."

"Viridáxés is intelligent—and clever," said Doethan. "If commanded to raze Nova Eboracum, he'd find a way."

"Then what should we do?" asked Laetícia. "It's hard to take in anything that monstrous being intelligent, even if it *is* a dragon." She stared back at the tabletop as if the dough rings were *shah mat* pieces and there weren't any viable moves.

"I told you," said Doethan. "Dârio has a plan. He also has a *very* powerful wizard."

"The young man who froze the river?" asked Laetícia. "The one with the red magestone?"

"Correct," said Doethan. He reached into his belt-pouch and pulled out a plain gold ring, placing it in the center of the table. "Dârio asked me to give this to you so he could coordinate more effectively with Quintillius and King Bjarni." He indicated the rings on Laetícia's hands with his own. "I assume you have a way to contact the governor general."

Laetícia's look said *you know very well I do.* "You want me to take this—" she pointed to the ring on the table "—and relay messages, like a common soldier?"

"Like a well-informed spymaster," said Doethan.

"I have a better idea," said Laetícia. She removed one of the plain gold bands from her own hand. "Take this," she said, offering it to Doethan. "It's the ring the children use when they want to hear bedtime stories from their father."

"I couldn't," said Doethan, moving his hand away from the offered ring. "Family is important."

"They can use my ring," said Laetícia. "I'd rather increase the odds that my Quin will come home safely than serve my own convenience."

"On those terms then, I *will* take it," said Doethan. He put the ring on the little finger of his left hand. Leaning forward, he pushed the ring he'd put on the table earlier toward Laetícia, like moving a queen across a *shah mat* board. "Take this one linked to Dârio, please," said Doethan. "It will be helpful for the two of you to stay in touch directly as well."

"It doesn't include a listening spell, so you can hear my conversations with others when I'm wearing it, does it?"

"You're a talented wizard—check it for yourself and see," said Doethan. Laetícia focused on the ring, then raised her eyes.

"It is what it appears to be—a traditional communications ring," she said. She put the ring on the finger where the one she'd given Doethan had been.

"Thank you for your generous hospitality," said Doethan. "I hope that improved communications will help us coordinate more effectively against Túathal and his new overly large associate."

"That's my hope as well," she said, smiling.

"Good," said Doethan. He stood up and so did Laetícia. "One more thing," Doethan added. "If there are any Roma wizards available who can work *ad hoc* gates, King Dârio would greatly appreciate details on the disposition of any Tamloch forces in Riyas and the location and speed of the Tamloch fleet." Doethan could count the number of wizards in Orluin able to spontaneously jump from one point to another without building a physical gate on one hand with fingers left over. Damon was one of them, Verro another. Rumor had it that Laetícia could, too. Her appearance over the battle at the quarry the previous morning and her consequent gating back to the skies above Nova Eboracum with Fercha and Doethan proved she had that talent.

"Why not Damon?" asked Laetícia. "Or Verro? My sources tell me he no longer supports his brother."

"They're correct in that," said Doethan. "I'm only sorry it took so long for Verro to see Túathal's true nature. As to your questions, Damon is away, working on a special project, and Verro has another role to play in King Dârio's plan." Doethan felt a bit guilty not giving Jenet credit but thought Laetícia might give the plan more weight if she believed it came from an eighteen-year-old king instead of the earl marshal's seventeen-year-old daughter. *I'm probably underestimating Laetícia,* he admitted.

"I'll see if I can find any Roma wizards interested in the job," said Laetícia. A glint in her eye helped Doethan think she'd handle the requested reconnaissance personally.

Doethan realized Laetícia was the closest thing the Roma on this side of the Ocean had to a master mage. *Would that be* domina magi *in the Roma tongue?* he wondered. *Did the ability to create ad hoc gates stem from being a master mage, or was he reversing the arrow of causality? What did that mean for Eynon if Damon's hope to pass his title on to his former apprentice came to pass? And were there other wizards with the same skill who didn't advertise the fact? What about the southern Clan Landers? Did* they *have a master mage?*

"Doethan?" said Laetícia. It seemed she might have said his name twice before, but he hadn't noticed.

"Sorry," he said. "I have a lot on my mind." *I have to remember to stop at the baker's shop on my way back to Brendinas,* he reminded himself.

"We all do," said Laetícia. "I'll make sure Dârio gets the intelligence he needs."

"Thank you," said Doethan. He crossed to the door to Laetícia's study and nodded to the guards outside, then turned back. "There's something else," he said.

"What?" asked Laetícia. Her purple magestone pulsed, clearly trying to anticipate her guest's next words.

"There's also a great *blue* dragon," said Doethan.

He pulled the study door shut behind him, stood on his flying disk, and descended the central stairwell of Laetícia's tower to begin his return to Brendinas.

* * * * *

Laetícia leaned over the railing of her spiral staircase and shouted "STOP!" at Doethan's descending form. "Come back here this instant!" she demanded, adding *"Please,"* as a polite afterthought. Doethan fixed the need to get more dough rings firmly in his mind then ascended back to the landing outside Laetícia's study. His host was standing by the door. "Come inside," she said. "We need to keep talking." The beads on Laetícia's long braided hair clacked as she watched Doethan reenter her study and closed the door firmly behind him.

"Sorry to spring the existence of a blue dragon on you like that," said Doethan. He walked to the table, sliced a dough ring in half with a sharp plane of solidified sound, and used a flat narrow construct to spread the bisected dough ring with soft white cheese. *This would go well with smoked fish,* he considered as he bit into it and chewed.

Laetícia took the other half of the dough ring and coated it with soft cheese too. When she'd swallowed her first bite, Laetícia wagged a finger at Doethan. "I understand the value of making an impressive exit, but I must know more about this *blue* dragon."

"Of course," said Doethan. "Right after you provide Dârio with the dispositions of Tamloch's remaining troops and the location of their fleet," said Doethan.

"Duke Háiddon already has what you've asked for," said Laetícia. "I sent him detailed reports an hour ago."

"Oh," said Doethan. "Your messenger must have been headed to Brendinas while I was on my way to Nova Eboracum."

"I expect so," said Laetícia. "The timing fits." One corner of her mouth turned up.

"In that case, you might as well take the children's ring back," said Doethan. "I expect I'll be here for quite a while." He returned Laetícia's ring to her and settled into a comfortable chair, licking soft cheese from his fingers. "Let me tell you about Zûrafiérix…"

Chapter 36

Constructs on the Battlefield

Eynon and Merry both hugged Nûd before he and Rocky left with Zûrafiérix. Chee jumped from Eynon's shoulder to Nûd's and hugged the big man's neck with all four limbs and his prehensile tail. The raconette held on for so long, Eynon and Merry had to unwind and detach him. Eynon stepped to Rocky and rubbed the wyvern's snout. It looked like a much smaller version of a dragon's. "Take good care of Nûd," Eynon instructed. "And yourself."

Rocky bobbed his head and lowered his body to make it easier for Nûd to board. Zûrafiérix added her parting comments.

"I'll take good care of the true king of Dâron, don't worry," said the dragon. She opened her jaws wide and closed them slowly. "Then I will neutralize Viridáxés. Túathal will be *your* problem."

"We appreciate any help you can give us," said Dârio.

Zûrafiérix nodded her huge head. "Riyas is still where it was two thousand years ago, correct? At the northern end of Fadacaolo Bay?"

"That's right," said Verro. "Look for two tall hills, nearly identical, on the west bank of the Ádhabhainn. The walls of Riyas enclose the hill and plain below that are close to the river. The kingdom army's marshalling field is below the one farther west."

"I'll find it," said Zûrafiérix. She turned her head and caught Nûd's eye. "My king will guide me," said the dragon. Then she glanced at Rocky. "Try to keep up," Zûrafiérix told the wyvern as she unfurled her wings and rose gently, careful not to blast the fragile humans with gusts of wind from her downstrokes. Rocky launched himself into the air and headed northeast at the speed of a bolt shot from a siege engine.

"Does Nûd know the way to Riyas?" asked Jenet.

"He ought to," said Eynon. "I'm sure he's pored over every map in the map room back in Melyncárreg."

"What and where is Melyncárreg?" asked Jenet.

"That's a long story..." began Eynon.

"It's a school for wizards and scholars, far to the west, where the wisents came from," said Merry.

"Oh," said Jenet. "Thank you."

Fercha waved to them, boarded her flying disk, and flew north-west toward the wide gate to Riyas. Verro stepped on his disk, ascended twenty yards, and disappeared through an *ad hoc* gate that looked like a shimmering black circle. Doethan had left a few minutes earlier, grumbling under his breath and not looking too happy about his mission.

"I'm going to walk the camp to ensure the troops are ready to march through the gate once Fercha says its safe," said Dârio.

"I told you they were," said Duke Háiddon, "but please walk the camp. It will be good for morale for your soldiers to see their king."

"Or Tamloch's heir," teased Dârio.

"Don't make things more complicated than they need to be," said the duke. "Soldiers fight for comrades, king, and kingdom, in that order. They just won a bloodless victory—let them know that *we* have a dragon to counter Túathal's and they'll take you all the way to the throne room in Riyas."

"Yes, Your Grace," said Dârio. "I remember your daily *king lessons* fondly."

"Then put them to good use and start walking," said Duke Háiddon. He waved to the royal guardsmen. "Stay close," he told their squad's captain, "and watch the skies as well. There are still Tamloch wizards unaccounted for."

"I'll keep Dârio company and make sure he stays out of trouble," said Jenet, taking Dârio's hand.

"Right," said her father. He rolled his eyes, making sure Jenet saw him.

"I can help him raise morale, anyway," said Jenet.

She took Dârio's hand and the two of them walked west along the line of soldiers mustering to go through the gate. The couple were accompanied by the squad of royal guards marching along in single file ten paces behind them.

Dutiful ducklings, thought the duke. *Dangerous ducklings who'd die for Dârio, if it comes to that,* Duke Háiddon considered. *I should probably get a squad of guards for myself. I'm as much of a target for Túathal and Tamloch as the king.* He set his shoulders and made a mental note to address the issue later, then headed for the camp to find Inthíra.

Eynon and Merry found themselves the only two left on the battlefield, save for a grazing wisent who was wandering painfully close to one of the deep holes left by Viridáxés' left hind leg. With a small sphere of solidified sound, Eynon gently urged the wayward wisent to change course and move away from danger. Chee curled up in the space between Eynon's shoulders and the top edge of his flying disk and began to snore softly. That made Merry laugh, though she did so quietly, not wanting to wake the sleeping raconette. Merry kissed Eynon gently on the lips and he kissed her back the same way.

"What should we be doing now?" Eynon asked Merry. "Should we fly to Brendinas? Stay here until Verro gets back with the drawings? Wait for Inthíra? Or none of the above?"

"I think we need to start practicing," said Merry. "Jenet's plan depends on our wizardry creating something believable."

"Out here on the battlefield where everyone can see?" asked Eynon. "Is that wise?"

"Most of the soldiers are mustering west of here, getting ready to gate to Riyas," said Merry. "Now that Zûrafiérix has flown off, there's nothing to hold observers' attention."

"Maybe," said Eynon, his voice uncertain.

"You can try something small," said Merry. "Cover the hole that wisent almost fell into."

The imprint of Viridáxés' left hind leg wasn't exactly small. It would have made a good pond for feeding stock back in the Coombe if it were filled with water, but Eynon gave it a try. He used a tiny portion of the power of his red magestone to generate a brown circle of solidified sound above the hole, expanding it until it was just a bit larger in diameter than the hole itself. Then he lowered the thin disk until it touched the surface and covered the cylindrical depression.

"Like that?" asked Eynon.

"Exactly like that," said Merry. "It's a great start. Now add grass."

"What?" asked Eynon. "How do I do that?"

"I don't know," said Merry. "You're the genius with solidified sound. Use your imagination."

"Grass," thought Eynon, enjoying Merry's compliment. *He was a farm boy,* he thought. *He knew a lot about grass. Grass grows from seeds.* Eynon held the circle of solidified sound steady and imagined a minuscule sphere of solidified sound as a tiny seed sown on top of the circle. He used some of the knowledge stored in his blue magestone, the one that had belonged to Fercha, to transform the sphere into a shoot and then a stalk that rose a foot above the upper surface of the circle.

"Wow!" said Merry. "That's amazing—but it doesn't need to be that tall. Make it match the grass around it—and it should be green, not blue."

"Oops!" said Eynon. "I missed that." He focused, guiding his magestones, and the stalk changed color from deep heraldic blue to the green of spring grass. A moment later, it shrank until it matched the height of the surrounding vegetation.

"Wonderful," said Merry. "Now make more—lots more."

"Yes, dear lady," Eynon replied. His blue magestone knew how to replicate processes. He created another *seed* and let it *grow* into a blade of grass the proper height and color. Then he had his red magestone, supported by his blue one, make ten thousand of the tiny *seeds* in the air above the circle. Falling on the circle triggered them and soon the hole Viridáxés' left hind leg had left disappeared, replaced by Eynon's creation.

Merry clapped her hands. "That's it!" she said. "Now *I* want to try something."

Eynon watched his friend and lover concentrate. She stared at a spot in the middle of the circle Eynon had generated and lifted her hands, shooting out rods of tight light with her fingers. Her digits danced until Eynon could tell what she had formed. It looked like a wisent made from tight-light beams. "I can see through your cow," he said.

"I'm trying to make a *bull* wisent, not a cow," Merry replied. "I've got the shape right, but how do I make the hide and the shaggy fur around his head."

Eynon thought for a moment and remembered his geometry lessons from the retired engineer who'd served in the Old King's army. "Try polygons," he said. "Use rectangles and squares and triangles—*lots* of triangles."

Merry frowned and her face tightened. She stared at her construct, adding polygons in dusty brown until slowly her wisent began to look more real. "What about the horns?" she asked.

"Conic sections," Eynon replied.

"Of course," said Merry. "I should have thought of that." Seconds later, the wisent she'd constructed sported a pair of upturned cone-shaped horns above round black eyes.

"Still looks like a cow, not a bull," said Eynon. "And the sides are too smooth."

"I know," said Merry. "I'm trying to figure out how to generate hair."

"You could do it the same way I made the grass," said Eynon. "Just change the color and texture."

"Tell me," said Merry. Eynon explained and Merry caught on quickly. Her magestone understood his trick about duplicating constructs. Ten heartbeats later, a *wisent* made from tight light and solidified sound bent his thick-furred head to graze on Eynon's magically generated *grass*.

"There's only one thing missing," said Eynon.

"What's that?" asked Merry, shooting an accusatory glance at her friend.

Behind her, the newly-made wisent snorted and grunted.

"Oh," said Merry. "I'll add that to my recipe."

Using the same technique that had made his water-distilling system back in Melyncárreg stable until dispelled, Eynon stabilized the construct covering the hole in the battlefield. He made the circle solid enough to support the weight of soldiers marching as well, in case any units from the eastern edge of Dâron's army passed this way. He hadn't intended to create a pit trap, after all.

"Fercha showed me that trick," said Merry. She made her wisent stable as well.

"An impressive piece of work, dear lady," said Eynon. He took her hand and kissed it, now that her full attention was no longer needed by her construct.

"Wouldn't it be funny if soldiers tried to herd it over to one of the mess tents to be served up for dinner?" asked Merry. "I don't know if it looks enough like a real wisent for that to happen."

"Don't sell yourself short," said Eynon. He motioned toward her construct and both of them laughed. The wisent Eynon had saved earlier was now grazing contentedly next to Merry's wisent.

"I've heard that wisents have notoriously bad eyesight," said Eynon.

"I wonder if the same is true for dragons?" asked Merry.

"I can't say," said Inthíra, "but you'll want to add a few more movements to your wisent, Merry. Observers will get suspicious if it stays in the same spot too long."

Eynon and Merry jumped. Behind them stood a comfortable-looking wizard with short curly brown hair wearing a solid sky-blue robe. She was a few years younger than Doethan to Eynon's eye and she was smiling.

"How long have *you* been here?" asked Merry.

"Long enough to be impressed with you both," said Inthíra. "Few wizards can work such subtleties with tight light and solidified sound."

"Thank you," said Eynon.

Inthíra nodded. "You'll want to blend the edges of your circle into the surrounding ground cover more carefully." She pointed and Eynon's eyes followed. "Can you see the sharp division where your circle ends, and the actual vegetation begins?"

"Yes, good wizard," said Eynon. "I'll fix it now. I didn't even think of it." He made the necessary adjustments and restablized his constructs.

"To make absolutely sure it's perfect, you'll want to observe it from above, too," said Inthíra. "That increases your odds of fooling wizards, not just wisents."

Eynon laughed and Merry smiled. "I'll remember that," said Eynon.

"Constructs of light and sound have been part of the most powerful wizards' repertoire since the first mages in Athica," said Inthíra. "The Roma wizards use them for spectacles to awe their slaves and citizens. Here in Dâron we tend to save them for enhancing our spy networks and misdirecting opposing armies."

"By letting them think we have more soldiers than we do?" asked Merry.

"And disguising the soldiers we *do* have as something else," said Inthíra. "Both are effective tactics—made more so if they're a surprise. We try to keep such abilities secret."

"I wonder if Jenet read about magical misdirection in books on military history?" mused Eynon. "Her father is the kingdom earl marshal, after all."

"I don't think that's what Inthíra is trying to say," said Merry. She touched Eynon's arm and raised one eyebrow.

"Huh?" said Eynon. He thought for a moment, then it came to him. "Oh," he said. "Maybe we should be practicing somewhere less public?"

"An excellent idea," said Inthíra.

"Do you have somewhere in mind?" asked Merry.

"I do," Inthíra answered. "It's in Brendinas. Do you want to fly directly to the capital or take the gate from the Dormant Dragon?"

"Can we fly all the way?" asked Eynon. "I've never seen the land between here and the Brendinas."

"Neither have I," added Merry.

"Certainly," said Inthíra.

The three of them stepped on their flying disks and prepared to rise. Suddenly, a translucent blue dome of solidified sound thirty feet high appeared around them. Inthíra, on her flying disk, waved down from near the apex of the dome. It seemed like she'd just materialized there without crossing the intervening distance.

"How did...?" Eynon began. "Did you gate...?" He looked to his left and confirmed Inthíra was still standing beside him, balancing on her flying disk. Then he got it.

"Brilliant," said Merry. "Which one is you, and which one is the construct?"

Chapter 37

In the Great Hall

"We're going to practice in the Great Hall?" asked Merry, her voice rising from mellow alto to high soprano.

"Dârio's not using it," said Inthíra.

"I don't expect Nûd will be needing it anytime soon either," added Eynon.

"What about Queen Carys?" Merry protested.

"She suggested it," said Inthíra. "I told her we needed complete privacy and a lot of space."

"That's why there are guards posted at all the entrances?" asked Eynon.

"Precisely," said Inthíra.

The Great Hall was, to Eynon's eyes, *great*. There were four pairs of double doors spaced out along each long wall and matching pairs in the center of each narrow end. They were painted a deep Dâron blue and ornamented with reflective bits of polished quartz and marble mimicking sparkling diamonds and lustrous pearls.

The hall's ceiling was high and supported by massive oak beams fit together in impressive arches. Most of it was painted light blue and the timbers supporting the ceiling were varnished with a stain so translucent it made the vaulting members look like thin clouds against an azure sky. Shields bearing heraldic devices ringed the hall a few feet above eye level where each timbered arch was anchored to the hall's long walls.

The only ones Eynon was sure he recognized were Applegarth's wavy blue line between two red apples on a white background and Dâron's dark blue dragon with one claw raised on a light-blue field. He'd have to ask Merry to explain which families were represented by the other shields later.

Chee had jumped from Eynon's shoulder when they'd first entered and was climbing around the beams like a squirrel exploring a new stand of trees. Eynon hoped Chee's claws wouldn't damage the woodwork. He turned his head left and right and saw balconies at either end of the hall. There were doors leading behind each one. *For musicians?* Eynon wondered. *Or maybe one end connected to the king's royal chambers? He hoped they were guarded.* Merry tugged at his arm.

"Pay attention," she whispered. "Inthíra is going to teach us how to shape solidified sound so it looks like Riyas."

"Not exactly," said Inthíra, "or not *yet*. We don't have the plans for Riyas and won't until Verro gets back." She smiled at Eynon and Merry. "We're going to build a scale model of Brendinas instead."

"I have a cousin from Liamston who built a scale model of the baron's castle in Caercadel down at the south end of the Coombe," said Eynon. "He carved individual stones from blocks of wood, painted them gray, and stuck them together with glue made from milk that looks like mortar."

"That's nice," said Merry, "but not particularly relevant." She rolled her eyes at Eynon and he frowned at her but didn't mean it.

"My cousin is planning to build a model of Rhuthro Keep next," said Eynon, "but he hasn't had a chance to get there to make sketches."

"You can tell me about your relatives and their hobbies later," said Merry. "I want to learn what Inthíra has to teach us."

"Eynon's cousin is a good example of one approach for constructing buildings and landscapes from solidified sound," said Inthíra, "so it's not completely irrelevant, just not the approach I'll show you today. Instead of building up from component parts, I'll demonstrate how to give constructs the outward seeming of the original *without* having to assemble them stone by stone."

"There's a wooden wall in my father's castle that's painted to look like it's made from granite blocks," said Merry. "Is that what you mean?"

"Yes," said Inthíra, "but on an even larger scale. We're going to create a huge illusion—a simulation of an entire city—on top of the marshalling field just west of Riyas. It doesn't have to be perfect. It just has to be good enough to fool a dragon. We'll generate fog as well, so fine details won't be necessary."

"I'm not sure, but I think dragons have excellent night vision," said Eynon. "Will that matter?"

"Fog isn't the same as darkness," said Merry. "It's not as easy to see through."

"That's right," said Inthíra. "We're going to need lots of simulated people, too—Dâron soldiers and Tamloch citizens of all ages, including children."

"If we want to discredit Túathal," said Merry.

"That *is* the point, as I understand it," said Inthíra. "At least according to Duke Háiddon."

Someone knocked on the double doors at the end of the Great Hall closest to them.

"Help me open it, please," said Inthíra. "It must be the delivery I've been expecting."

Eynon and Merry unbarred the broad doors from the inside and pulled them open. Guards wheeled something forward that would have dwarfed a room smaller than the Great Hall. It was tall and thin and covered with enough fabric to be a giant's handkerchief. The guards moved it into the hall on a pair of squeaky-wheeled dollies, then bowed to the wizards and left without speaking.

Eynon stared at the covered object like he was trying to see through the fabric. "What is it?" he asked.

"Use your head," said Merry, teasing him with the same tone she'd used with him on their first day on the river. Her subtext, clearly, was *you fool*.

"Think it through," said Inthíra, more gently. "You should be able to figure it out from what I've told you."

Eynon rubbed his chin for a few moments before a smile lit up his face. "Verro's not back with the plans for Riyas, so this must be the plans for Brendinas."

"Close," said Inthíra. She motioned to Merry and Eynon. "Help me take the cover off."

Eynon grabbed one end of the fabric draped over the tall, thin object on the dollies while Merry held the other. They stepped on their flying disks and rose high enough to remove the fabric, revealing a giant painting—a long cityscape with the massive fortifications and towers of old Dâron Castle on the heights looking down on the walls and streets of the capital. It looked like it had been painted by someone flying high above Brendinas. Every street, park, and house was captured with meticulous brush strokes. It seemed so real Eynon felt like he could fly into the painting and hover above the city.

"That will be much easier to work with than maps or street plans drawn with pen and ink," said Merry. "Where did it come from?"

"The Council chambers," said Inthíra. "It's on one long wall, along with a smaller picture of Tyford. There's a large map of Orluin painted on the opposite wall. All three were made late in the Old King's reign."

"So this one isn't too far out of date?" asked Eynon, indicating the picture of Brendinas.

"It's five years old, but close enough," said Inthíra. "Don't let the best be the enemy of the good."

"Ealdamon's *Epigrams,*" said Eynon and Merry simultaneously. They both laughed. So did Inthíra.

Eynon saw Chee climbing high in the beams above him, not far from the near balcony. The raconette saw him look and waved. Eynon waved back.

"Is your familiar enjoying himself?" asked Inthíra when she realized Chee's location.

"He seems to be," said Eynon. "Raconettes are naturally curious."

"So am I!" Merry interjected. "Can we start our lessons?"

"Of course," said Inthíra. "Take a *good* look at the painting, Fix it firmly in your mind's eye." She waited a few seconds. "Got it?" Inthíra asked. Eynon and Merry nodded. "Good," said the older wizard.

Inthíra indicated that Eynon should stand to her left and Merry to her right. Both young wizards put their flying disks and packs on the floor under the balcony. Inthíra motioned for them to turn around and face out into the Great Hall instead of looking at the painting.

"Start by making a thin sheet of solidified sound," Inthíra instructed.

"How big?" asked Eynon.

"Make it a square about half the width of the hall, so Merry can do the same," said Inthíra. "You can change the size later."

"Yes ma'am," said Eynon, making Merry smile inside, appreciating his good manners. "My geometry teacher back in the Coombe called this a plane."

"I'm pleased you have a basic understanding of geometry," said Inthíra. "It will make explaining shape magic simpler."

"Does it matter what color I make my sheet?" asked Merry.

"We can worry about color later," said Inthíra. "But if you want to get a head start, make it the predominant color of the city as best you remember from the painting." Merry's head began to turn. "No cheating," said Inthíra. "Use what you remember and hold that in your mind, not the painting itself."

"Yes ma'am," said Merry. She giggled, realizing that Eynon's politeness was catching. Her plane turned the gray of the limestone and granite used to construct the city's walls and buildings. She looked to her left and saw that Eynon's plane had changed color to match hers a heartbeat later.

"What are the most important details in the painting?" asked Inthíra.

"Dâron Castle on top of the hill," said Eynon. "It's like a big watchdog guarding the city."

"Very good," said Inthíra. "What else?"

"The city walls," said Merry. "And the royal palace and gardens." Inthíra nodded. "And the river," added Merry in a rush.

"We'll come back to the river—making solidified sound look like water is challenging and unnecessary at this point," said Inthíra. "We'll focus on the other important details first. Imagine your planes are fine linen bedsheets you're going to drape over a model of the city made by someone like Eynon's cousin. Let the hill and Dâron Castle and the city walls and the palace poke up from underneath."

"I can do that," said Eynon. One end of his sheet rose and took on the form of the citadel above Brendinas, while a three-dimensional outline of the city walls took shape at the other. Eynon's breathing slowed and his focus intensified as he added more and more buildings, filling in larger ones first, then smaller. None of them had much detail, but he'd captured the overall shape of the city.

Merry didn't replicate Dâron Castle and its heights. She started by pushing the city walls up and capturing details. Her walls looked like the walls in the painting, with each massive stone delineated and the correct number of crenelations between towers. Merry's tongue pressed against her lower teeth and the muscles on her neck tensed as she added buildings in full detail, one by one. She'd finished the royal palace and a row of townhouses when Inthíra spoke.

"That's enough for this stage," said the older wizard. "Hold your constructs stable—you know how to do that, don't you?"

"Yes ma'am," said Eynon. Merry nodded.

"Look at each other's renderings and tell me what you see," said Inthíra. "You can learn a lot from each other."

"Eynon has scope," said Merry. "He's constructed the entire city." Inthíra nodded and encouraged Merry to continue. "I have the fine details—stones, windows, light and shadow—but could only finish the walls and a few buildings."

"You're right," said Inthíra. "Both scope and details are necessary, but you don't always have the time to give them equal attention."

Merry looked at Eynon's cityscape. "Scope is more important than detail, I guess," she said.

"That's very often true," said Inthíra. "The general rule is to make sure you have sufficient scope, then add in details for the parts of the overall construct that are closest to observers. You can skip fine details on the rest."

"I get it," said Merry. "I should have included Dâron Castle in mine, since everyone expects it."

"Right," said Inthíra. "Note how Eynon's captured the subtle changes in elevation as the city rises from the river to the base of Castle Hill. You kept your sheet mostly flat."

"Farmers learn the importance of terrain and drainage," said Eynon.

"That's important for people who manage orchards too," said

Merry. "I was just paying more attention to the buildings than the lay of the land."

"The answer, good wizards, is to do both," said Inthíra. "I was impressed by your constructs. Creating complex shapes from solidified sound is a rare talent among wizards and you're both quite skilled, especially since you've only been working with magic for a short time."

"Thank you, ma'am," said Eynon. He nodded to Inthíra then stepped past her and took Merry's hand. "Why don't we try working together to model the city?"

"That's a great idea," said Merry. She lifted her construct a few feet and shifted it to the center of the Great Hall. Eynon slid his model in beneath hers and Merry's detailed version combined with Eynon's more comprehensive view.

"It's a lot better now," said Eynon.

"Absolutely," said Merry when she saw how well the two constructs fit together. "I *like* it!"

"So do I," said Eynon. "Let me add vegetation on the hillsides and fill in the greenery in the parks."

"I'll do more buildings and put tiny people and carts on the streets," said Merry.

"I'll add noise!" exclaimed Eynon. A realistic scale model of Brendinas rapidly took shape.

"We've got sight and sound," said Merry. "What about..."

"There's no need to add the smell of horse manure and slop buckets," said Inthíra. "Queen Carys would object. There hasn't been a horse in the Great Hall since the Mad King rode his charger from one end of it to the other five hundred years ago."

"I've heard that story," said Merry.

"I haven't," said Eynon. "The horseshoes must have done terrible things to these lovely wooden floors."

"The floors have been redone a dozen times since then," said Inthíra. "Boot spurs tear them up."

"I expect so," said Eynon, though he'd had very little personal experience with knights or horses.

Merry was about to tease Eynon about his extensive familiarity with knights' footwear when Chee began chittering overhead. The small creature's voice was so loud Merry thought the raconette's tail might be on fire. She looked up, along with Eynon and Inthíra. Chee was jumping on the railing of the nearest balcony, waving his arms wildly.

"What is it?" called Eynon. "What has you so upset?"

Chee waved even more frantically. Behind him, the door to the balcony was opening.

Chapter 38

The Secret Chamber

Hibblig had been smugly satisfied when he'd discovered a safe hiding place so close to Brendinas. It was on one of his uncle's estates, six or seven miles northwest of the capital, close to the course of the Cûddávon, a major tributary of the Brenavon. He and a cousin had been exploring an old springhouse set into the side of a hill. Behind the modest entrance built from granite slabs was a cool subterranean storeroom, ten feet wide by twenty deep, carved into solid rock. Abandoned for decades after his uncle had hired a wizard to build a cold room off his kitchens, the springhouse was an exciting place for children's adventures, serving as a site for buried treasure, a castle's dungeon, and an escape from adult observation.

When Hibblig reached his teens, it became a private place to visit with young women hoping for different sorts of adventures—an interest Hibblig avidly shared. He was a novice wizard by then, and his skills with magic, among other things, proved attractive to the relevant gender.

"Do you feel that?" Hibblig had asked his partner at the time, a taut woman with short ash-blonde hair and muscular legs who worked with the horses on his uncle's estate.

"Feel what?" she had asked, shifting her hips. "I felt it more a few minutes ago."

"Not *that*," said Hibblig had answered. They'd been making love on a thick fur cloak next to the back wall of the springhouse. Hibblig had felt a breeze on his back coming from a crack in the rear wall, not from the entrance. He hadn't said more at the time, but returned later, alone. There *had* been air entering through the crack. Hibblig used solidified sound to expand the crack, then removed enough stone from the wall to see what lay behind it. It was a natural cave that extended into and below the hill for hundreds of yards.

Hibblig covered over the enlarged crack with a rudimentary solidified sound patch he painted to mimic the original rear wall of the springhouse. He spent the next several holidays from his training in wizardry exploring what he'd found. Decades later, he still hadn't finished tracing the cave completely, but he did use the large chamber behind the springhouse as his emergency escape location. It was cool, dry, and appeared unused by animals. There weren't even bats on the ceiling.

He kept the large chamber stocked with spare clothing, food, and supplies in case it ever became expedient to disappear for a few days. He'd been tempted to bring women to the cave but decided against it. Beds were softer than cloaks on hard ground and he wasn't seventeen any longer. Comfort mattered.

The only other person who knew about the cave was his cousin Kennig, the one who'd shared adventures in the springhouse with Hibblig when they were both boys. He was Hibblig's favorite cousin, and since Kennig was also a wizard, they were particularly close—or had been. Sadly, they also shared hot tempers. Kennig's temper had gotten the best of him a dozen years ago. He'd blasted the second son of an earl with a lightning bolt after catching him in bed with his most recent infatuation and had made a quick escape to the southern Clan Lands before he could be apprehended and imprisoned. He was no longer a factor in anything. Hibblig would have the cave to himself while he mapped out his plan to free Gwýnnett and link up with Túathal—and his dragon.

Hibblig sat on a rock in the large chamber. He was chewing on a twice-baked biscuit the size of his fist with a density similar to the rock on which he sat. *I should replace my emergency supplies more often than once every five years,* he thought. Three brightly glowing balls floating near the top of the chamber provided illumination and allowed him to see the large wooden chest twenty feet away where he kept jugs of water, packets of jerky, and more of the stone-like biscuits.

Hibblig had already spread out his bedroll and berated himself for not providing any padding to put beneath it. *No matter,* he considered.

With luck, Gwýnnett and I will be in a featherbed in Riyas tomorrow evening. I can endure sleeping on bare limestone for one night. Then he shook his head. *Perhaps not, unfortunately. Túathal might frown on Hibblig sleeping with his queen-to-be, if Gwýnnett still was, even though Túathal himself wouldn't be interested in female companionship.*

Hibblig could understand why non-wizards unable to detect poisons or generate protective shields might think twice before sleeping with Gwýnnett. He enjoyed it well enough, though, allowing for the fact she thought she was using sex to control him. He knew she was using him. Hibblig was certainly using Gwýnnett. They were both using each other. Gwýnnett, through Túathal, could be a way for Hibblig to end up as the master mage of Tamloch, since Verro's recent betrayal now disqualified *him* for the role, even if he was Túathal's brother. Damon's brief reappearance in Dâron had temporarily put Hibblig's designs on being his home kingdom's master mage on hold, but now Damon had disappeared again, so *both* kingdoms had openings at the top of their magical hierarchies. *Wouldn't it be marvelous to be master mage of Dâron* and *Tamloch simultaneously?* he mused.

Taking pity on his teeth and his taste buds, Hibblig decided to soak his biscuit in hot water before trying to gnaw on it again. He stood up, walked over to the wooden chest, and removed two small metal pots which he filled with water from a glazed pottery jug. He tasted the water before putting the cork back in and decided on the sharp rhubarb tea rather than the milder elderberry. He removed the dark red tin, not the light purple one, from the chest along with a large ceramic mug.

Hibblig plopped the biscuit in one of the small pots with a twist of his wrist and gently shook a measure of chopped dried rhubarb stalks into the other, then used small congruencies to set both pots boiling. While the biscuit was softening—he hoped—and the chopped stalks were infusing the hot water, Hibblig leaned into the wooden chest and located a small crock of honey.

At least I don't have to worry about it going bad, he thought. *Honey lasts forever. There are tales of five-thousand-year-old honey from tombs in the southeast of Roma's empire across the Ocean still being sweet and worth eating,* he considered. Hibblig sniffed at the contents of his crock and tasted it by dipping and licking his little finger. *Still good,* he decided. *And a lot less than five thousand years old.*

I don't know how non-wizards manage, thought Hibblig as he used a construct of solidified sound shaped like his hand to pour the contents of the pot of steeping tea into his mug. A second construct, a flat disk with dozens of holes in it, trapped the dried rhubarb stalks before they could fall into his mug. A third, a thin rod of solidified sound, worked well to stir the honey at the bottom of his mug into the warm flavored liquid. *Perhaps nobles could hire wizards to create solidified sound liners for pots so they'd be easier to clean,* Hibblig considered. *No, servants are far cheaper—and scrubbing keeps them busy.*

Hibblig carried his mug of tea back to his rock and sat down again to think. He needed to plan out his approach for rescuing Princess Gwýnnett. The first order of business would be getting her guards out of the way and keeping other mages in the palace occupied.

One of his spies from Gwýnnett's faction had recently informed him via communications ring that Inthíra, along with the young wizard with the red magestone and the blasted girl who'd trapped him with a web of solidified sound earlier were busy doing *something* in the Great Hall.

Dealing with the wizards would be a real challenge, but a more conventional distraction would be useful for handling the guards. What would be best? he thought. A fire in the kitchens might be enough. Ten thousand gallons of water from the Brenavon streaming down halls of the palace might be even better. A few dozen wisents careening along the corridors near Gwýnnett's suite—to borrow an idea from that young wizard with the red magestone—might be better still. He'd almost decided on an option when he was so surprised he dropped his mug, not even hearing it shatter on the chamber's floor.

Wizards on flying disks, with passengers, were appearing in front of Hibblig. The first descended from a black circle halfway to the chamber's ceiling—the interface of an emergency gate. His disk nearly knocked Hibblig off his rock when he sped out of the way of the *next* wizard immediately behind him. This one had a passenger, too. He moved away on a different vector, but Hibblig was still frozen in place, unsure what was happening. A third wizard with a passenger fell through the circle and finally so did a fourth.

The circle closed with a loud *pop* and the wizards grounded their flying disks, allowing their passengers to step off. Three of the passengers were large muscular bearded men who smelled like they hadn't bathed in a few weeks—or months. Two carried crossbows. A smaller man with a thin goatee, a waxed mustache, and a sly, feral look *had* bathed recently. He looked like he was more intelligent than the other three passengers combined. The four of them resembled each other enough that Hibblig assumed they were brothers. He wasn't interested in brothers, however. He was interested in cousins.

Kennig had been the fourth wizard to enter Hibblig's secret chamber. He and the other three wizards were dressed in the brown robes of mages from the southern Clan Lands.

"Thank you for making tea," said Kennig. "I'll take mine with honey. Sorry for popping in unexpectedly—and bringing guests."

"Not at all," said Hibblig. "You and your friends couldn't have come at a better time."

"Oh?" said Kennig. "Do tell? *We're* here to make trouble for Dârio and put that obnoxious young wizard with the red magestone in his place."

"Seeking revenge, are you?" asked Hibblig. "I can help with that. Let me tell you what I have in mind."

Chapter 39

Diversion

Three pairs of eyes were on Chee as the balcony door opened. Eynon, Merry and Inthíra threw up hemispherical shields of solidified sound against whatever threat might present itself. Then Dârio stepped through the door and they relaxed, lowering their shields.

"How are things going?" asked the king.

Dârio's voice didn't sound right to Eynon's ear. *Maybe he'd caught a cold?* Eynon considered. *Or perhaps it was pollen? There were lots of flowering trees dotting the palace gardens.*

The king closed the door behind him and moved to the railing. He smiled and looked down at the three wizards and the magically generated scale model of Brendinas. Eynon was surprised when Chee continued to jump up and down and wave his arms, making *chee-chee-chee-CHEE* sounds instead of trying to climb on Dârio's shoulders and rub the king's shaved head. Now Dârio was looking at Chee with an expression that indicated he wanted to strangle Eynon's familiar. *That wasn't right,* thought Eynon. *Dârio had always been more amused by Chee than angered.*

"Fine, Your Majesty," said Inthíra. "Eynon and Merry are making excellent progress. They'll be ready in the morning."

"That's wonderful," said Dârio. "Glad to hear it." Chee's cries grew louder and Eynon was horrified when the king said, "Be quiet, you horrid little beast!" and pushed the raconette off the balcony's railing.

"I've got you," said Eynon as he stepped forward to catch Chee. Unfortunately, he never completed his rescue. A beam of tight light caught Eynon between his shoulder blades, slamming him to the floor. Eynon's head snapped forward and bounced, leaving him stunned and semi-conscious. He heard thumps on either side and sensed, rather than reasoned that Merry and Inthíra had been attacked as well. *And what about Chee?*

"Hurry," came a deeper, older voice from the balcony. "Take their magestones and bind them. Quickly!"

Eynon heard heavy footsteps nearby. He summoned just enough energy to open his eyelids a fraction without moving his head and saw a large black boot with a poorly sewn leather patch on its toe. He *knew* that boot. He'd been the one to cut off its owner's toe with a makeshift sword adapted from a shard from a shattered flying disk. *How did a Mastlands brother end up in the royal palace in Brendinas?* Eynon's mind was just fuzzy enough to waste precious seconds wondering why King Dârio had betrayed them before realizing the man on the balcony hadn't been Dârio.

The person wearing the boot rolled Eynon on his back and fumbled at Eynon's neck until he found the heavy gold links of the chain supporting his artifact with its red magestone. Patchboot lifted Eynon's head, removed his artifact, and let Eynon's skull fall back on the wooden floor with a solid thud and a second bounce. Then Eynon was shoved onto his stomach again, as if he were a sack of grain being turned, and bound hand and foot with rough rope.

All things considered, thought Eynon's hazy brain, *I'd rather be bouncing off rocks in the Rhuthro.* Somehow, considering the time he'd fallen overboard and been buffeted by the cold river helped Eynon's mind grow clearer. They'd taken his *red* magestone, but his blue one—Fercha's former stone—was still warm against his skin under his linen shirt.

Eynon opened his eyes a fraction and saw Merry trussed up two feet away. She caught his eye and smiled a tender smile, or at least one Eynon's battered brain had decided was tender. Eynon nodded and Merry's smile grew wider before her eyes closed. He understood why when he saw a large lump rising in the middle of her forehead. He couldn't risk turning to check on Inthíra's condition and was almost afraid to look for Chee, worried that his small companion's body might be sprawled and broken on the Great Hall's polished wooden floor.

"Nicely done," Eynon heard the deeper, older voice say. It wasn't coming from above any longer—it came from behind him. The man must be a wizard with illusion-generating talents like Inthíra. The false Dârio could have been a complete construct of solidified sound, or maybe just a mask to disguise the wizard's face and make him *look* like Dârio. *That would be a good skill to master,* Eynon considered. Part of his brain added *later,* since he had more important things to worry about. Then he reconsidered—*now* would be ideal.

"Here are their artifacts," said another voice. Eynon recognized it as belonging to the sly Mastlands brother he'd named *Fox.*

"Very good," said the deeper, older-voiced man who was clearly in charge. Eynon could hear the clink of chains and assumed his artifact— and Merry's and Inthíra's—were hanging from the man's belt.

"What do you want us to do with the Dâron wizards?" asked Fox. His tone indicated he had plenty of unpleasant suggestions to offer.

"The boy goes back with us, of course," said the man in charge. "The Clan chiefs will enjoy dealing with him in their own, unique way. I won't stay to watch—too much screaming upsets me."

"Is that why you pushed the beast off the railing, Kennig?" asked Fox.

"Yes," the man answered. "It took the annoying creature a while, but he sensed my presence on the balcony and was going to spoil our surprise before I could give you the signal to attack."

Kennig, thought Eynon, filing the name away in a not-to-be-forgotten spot in his far-too-sore head. Eynon reached into his blue magestone and drew on healing energy. Now that he knew how to interpret them, he saw that Fercha had stored quite a few spells for repairing tissues and restoring depleted resources. He simultaneously began directing subtle tendrils of transparent solidified sound to loosen the ropes binding his hands and feet and started to heal his battered skull. Spending time at the mercy of the chiefs of the southern clans didn't appeal much to Eynon, since he doubted he'd be shown any mercy whatsoever. He focused and made a copy of himself from solidified sound while disguising his own location.

"Where *is* the little tree rat?" asked Kennig.

Something that had been as tense as a torsion catapult's twisted rope inside Eynon relaxed. *Chee was alive! And these men didn't have him.* Eynon was feeling better with every moment.

"Up in the rafters," said a thick voice Eynon thought might be Oaf's. He'd never heard the man speak when he was sober, so he wasn't sure.

"Won't catch him there," said a similar voice—*Dolt,* figured Eynon. *It doesn't really matter. Those two are interchangeable.*

"Maybe I can use the beast for target practice?" broke in a new, younger voice. *Fool, the Mastlands' brother close to Merry's age,* Eynon determined, thus proving his mind *was* working better now. He heard the distinctive *click* of a crossbow being cocked.

"Wadda 'boot *treasure?*" asked another voice in a strong southern Clan Lands accent. "Where dae th' king o' th' blue-tabards keep 'is gold and gems?"

"Mebbe th' older one will know?" asked yet another of the southern Clan Landers.

"Want me to sit her up?" asked Oaf, or maybe Dolt.

"Go ahead," said Kennig. "Did any of you bring a water skin?"

"I did," said Fool. "But it's full of beer."

"Of course it is," said Kennig. "That will have to do. Squirt some in her mouth."

Eynon heard the unmistakable sound of liquid jetting, then Inthíra coughed and spluttered.

"Wha...?" she said.

Eynon sympathized. Warm beer was not what he would want soon after a head injury.

"Where does Dârio keep his valuables that *aren't* behind a dozen guarded, locked and warded doors in the treasury?" asked Kennig. "Tell us and we'll bring you along and ransom you back later. Hold out and the blood from your slit throat will stain the floorboards."

Eynon worked harder to loosen the ropes around his wrists and ankles, then decided that wasn't worth the effort and readied a pair of thin, sharp blades of transparent solidified sound to simply *cut* them when the time was right.

"Who *are* you?" asked Inthíra, sounding much more coherent than Eynon thought *he* would have been without help from his blue magestone. "Wait!" said Inthíra. "I *know* you. You're Hibblig's cousin—the one who exiled himself."

"You have a good memory, Inthíra," said Kennig. "Do you remember that I have a hot temper? I'm not a patient man. Where can we find things Dârio values?"

"The young king values every man, woman and child in the kingdom," said Inthíra.

"Don't be that way," said Kennig. "I wouldn't enjoy killing you— though I remember *you* now, too. You always *were* a stubborn one, according to my cousin."

"Hibblig's problem—one of them at least—was that he didn't take *no* for an answer," said Inthíra. "If pushing his grabby hands away with my shields counts as being stubborn, then I'll gladly accept that label."

"Fine," said Kennig. "We're not here to discuss Hibblig *or* to converse on Dârio's love for his subjects. I want to know where we can easily get our hands on valuables—things that are light enough for us to carry back south."

"You'll find plenty of gems and jewelry for the taking in Princess Gwýnnett's suite," said Inthíra.

"Those are off limits for reasons I don't care to go into," said Kennig.

"Hibblig is in Gwýnnett's faction and doesn't want you to take them," said Inthíra matter-of-factly.

"Correct," said Kennig. "Where else should we look?"

"There's a room just down the hall from the king's study," said Inthíra. "The servants keep visiting nobles' jewelry there in individual strongboxes and retrieve what's needed on request."

"Nice try," said Kennig. "But I know that's the door to Ealdamon's apartments. I have no interest in triggering *his* wards, especially since word has it he's returned."

"I had to make the attempt," said Inthíra.

"Now I have to up the stakes," said Kennig. "The clan chiefs want the boy for their own revenge, but the girl is fair game. How many fingers will she have to lose before you tell me what I want to know?"

"None," said Inthíra quickly. "I might as well tell you. There are three places that fit your criteria. The kitchen steward has the key to the chest holding the best spices. It wouldn't take much to convince him to part with it, or you can simply take the chest and open it with a battleaxe later. King Dârio won't appreciate being forced to eat bland food or the cost of replacing what was lost."

"That's more like it," said Kennig. "What's the second place?"

"The counting house at the far end of the west wing of the palace," said Inthíra. "It's only five years old and after your time. There will be lots of coins there being counted by the exchequer's clerks before they're taken to the vaults."

"Won't it be guarded?" asked Kennig.

"Of course, but with only a quarter as many guards as usual," said Inthíra. "The rest are with the army."

"How much coin are they counting on any given day?" asked Kennig.

"Enough to be worth your while," said Inthíra.

"What's the third place?" asked Kennig.

"King Dârio's royal suite," said Inthíra. "You just came from there, unless the opening door was *also* an illusion."

"Unfortunately, it was," said Kennig.

"I know a way inside," said Inthíra. "Through the servants' entrance."

"What valuables does King Dârio keep in his suite?" asked Kennig.

"Three *very* expensive *shah mat* boards, among other things," said Inthíra. "One where the pieces are made from gold and platinum, another where they're cut from sapphires and emeralds, and the last one's pieces are rare magical constructs that move on their own."

"Portable, *and* valuable," said Kennig. "Your young associate can keep her fingers."

"What about Eynon?" asked Inthíra.

"I don't have any choice about the boy," said Kennig. He called to the Mastlands brothers. "Are the smudge pots ready?"

"They're all in place," said Fox. "Do you want *us* to light them, or will you wizards handle that?"

"Don'cha worry yoir heads 'boot thae," said one of the southern Clan Lands wizards. "We cae handle a bit o' foir."

"Excellent," said Kennig. "Time to go, then. One of you grab the boy. Inthíra is coming with me. The girl can stay. Her head's close enough to the floor she *might* still be able to breath after smoke fills the hall."

"Blast!" said Fox. "We have a score to settle with her."

"Better the lad than the lass," said Kennig. "Now move!"

Eynon heard footsteps and doors opening, followed by armored bodies hitting the floor and the small *whoosh* of flames being lit. *I've got to make my move,* he thought. Eynon had been mapping out his plan while he'd been listening to Kennig and Inthíra. He called on his blue magestone for light rather than heat, shouting, "Llacha-lla-CHAR!" as loud as he could manage. A bright ball of light exploded a dozen feet above Eynon's head. He kept his eyes shut tight and cut the ropes around his hands and feet.

Eynon hoped to jump up, take stock of who was where, and deal with his opponents one by one as soon as he knew each man's location, but his feet betrayed him. They'd been denied proper circulation for too many minutes. Eynon fell to his knees and saw he'd been unwise to delay taking action. His light spell had been for naught. Inthíra, Kennig, the Mastlands brothers and the southern Clan Lands wizards were gone. They'd taken the illusion-generated copy of his body he'd made as well. Then Eynon coughed. The smudge pots their attackers had placed around the Great Hall were rapidly filling the space with thick black smoke.

Merry! thought Eynon as he put a sphere of solidified sound around his head to filter out the smoke. When he knee-walked a few feet to Merry's side he saw her smiling up at him, her head also protected by a sphere similar to his own. "How...?" he asked.

"I still have my training stone," said Merry hesitantly. She touched the center of her forehead and winced. "You wouldn't happen to have another one of Doethan's healing potions, would you?" she smiled at Eynon and he smiled back. "Where's Chee?" Merry asked.

Eynon scanned the room, but didn't see the raconette. A moment later, he heard a *hissing* sound like liquid from a water skin squirted on a fire, then realized a nearby smudge pot had gone out. He looked up and saw Chee waving at him from a support beam directly above the smudge pot. The raconette clambered down from his perch and approached Eynon and Merry with something in his hands—three magical artifacts hanging from chains.

"What a *fine* boy!" said Eynon. He took his artifact from Chee and placed it around his neck, then handed Merry's to her. Wearing his red stone made Eynon feel whole again. He put Inthíra's artifact in his pouch to return later, feeling a bit odd about having *three* magestones, even temporarily. Eynon reseated his flying disk across his back and Chee climbed up to his usual spot between Eynon's shoulders.

"We should probably get out of here," said Merry. "The smoke is getting thicker."

"I'll take care of it," said Eynon. He sent small spheres of solidified sound out to each smudge pot and cut their burning wicks off from air. Then he created a congruency connecting the center of the Great Hall to a point high in the sky where the air was thinner. The smoke quickly dissipated.

"We still need to leave," said Merry. "This is just a distraction." She rubbed her bruised forehead and winced. Eynon stepped beside her.

"I know," said Eynon. "They're going to steal valuable *shah mat* pieces from King Dârio!"

"I don't think so," said Merry. "Dârio doesn't strike me as the sort who'd keep boards like that in his quarters. They'd be safely stored away in the treasury."

"Huh," said Eynon. "Maybe."

"I think this whole southern Clan Lands raid is a distraction," said Merry. "We need to rescue Inthíra then stop what Hibblig has planned."

"Hibblig?" asked Eynon. "Kennig's cousin?"

"He's one of Princess Gwýnnett's faction's wizards," said Merry. "I watched him duel with Doethan. He's not a nice man. I'd bet *he's* behind this."

"Do you know how to get to the king's royal suite?" asked Eynon.

"I've been to his study, it can't be far from there," said Merry.

"Let's get moving, then," said Eynon. "I have something to return to Inthíra."

"Good idea," said Merry. "You don't need *three* magestones—and Eynon..."

"What?" he replied.

"At least we don't have to dispel our model of Brendinas," said Merry. "It disappeared when we were attacked."

"Good," said Eynon. "Now we can get more practice." He hugged her, put his hands on her forehead and used one of Fercha's spells from her blue magestone to heal Merry's bruised forehead. "There," he said. "That looks much better. I'm glad you're safe."

"Thank you," said Merry. "It *feels* much better. I'm glad you're safe, too." They kissed but didn't put too much into it because they had to rush off to rescue Inthíra.

As they walked to one of the side doors, Eynon turned to Merry. "I have a question," he said. Merry raised both eyebrows to encourage him. "How did the southern Clan Landers get into the Great Hall?"

"If they're good with illusions, maybe when the painting of Brendinas was brought in," Merry offered.

"That makes sense," said Eynon. "I have another question."

"Let's hear it," said Merry, smiling.

"If the balcony where Kennig was standing connects to the king's suite, why don't we just go through that door and be waiting for the southern Clan Lands' raiders when we get there?"

"Brilliant," said Merry. She put her flying disk on the floor and used it to lift Eynon and herself up to the balcony. Eynon didn't want to use his own disk because Chee was sleeping. "Do you want to open the door or should I?" asked Merry.

"After you, dear lady," said Eynon. They could hear shouts from outside the Great Hall's doors and fists banging to be let in to fight what the guards thought was a fire. Since the hall still smelled like smoke, it was easy to understand the guards' misapprehension. *Somebody is going to need to clean this place after the damage caused by the smudge pots,* thought Eynon. *I'm glad I could put them out before they made a real mess of things.*

Merry probed the lock with thin beams of tight light until it clicked.

"Couldn't one of the southern Clan Lands' wizards have done that?" asked Eynon. "Oh, right. None of them seem all that bright."

Merry nodded, rolled her eyes, and smiled at Eynon. They entered the king's suite together.

Chapter 40

Rescuing Gwýnnett

Hibblig waited until he heard shouting from the direction of the Great Hall before emerging from his observation post. He was crouched on his flying disk and pressed against the ceiling of a seldom-used stairway near Princess Gwýnnett's suite watching the four vigilant guards outside Gwýnnett's door. Hibblig didn't have his cousin's skill with solidified sound illusions, so Kennig had modified and stabilized the bottom of Hibblig's flying disk to match the gray of the stones used to build the palace. Hibblig hoped that would be sufficient camouflage in case someone on the stairs happened to glance up. So far, the servants using the stairs had been carrying trays of food or delivering letters. They'd been more focused on their own thoughts than anything above them. They also paid no attention to the sound of squeaking rats in dark corners.

Alarm bells and louder shouts made Hibblig smile. Smoke was beginning to waft out of the Great Hall and up the stairs to the floor where the suites for Princess Gwýnnett, Old Queen Carys, and King Dârio were located. *There should be more smoke,* Hibblig noted. *If those idiot brothers from the Rhuthro valley Kennig had brought along couldn't be trusted to do something as simple as set out smudge pots and light them, he'd have strong words with his cousin next time they met.*

Someone was climbing the staircase, sounding like an asthmatic cow escaping a pack of wolves. Heavy breathing and heavier footfalls from what must be a guard's boots passed beneath Hibblig's hiding place. He'd been waiting for that and risked a look over the edge of his flying disk. A senior guardsman had reached the landing and was lumbering along the hall. Hibblig watched him speak with the quartet of door guards for a few seconds, then leave with two of the four, heading to the far end of the hall where a perpendicular corridor led to stairs down to the Great Hall.

So far, everything was going according to plan. He used distance-viewing lenses made from solidified sound to identify the guards who remained. They looked very young and must be new to their positions. One was a slender woman with long blonde hair and the sophisticated look of someone raised in Brendinas. The other was a stocky, overly-muscled young man with the fresh earnest face of someone from the rural western edge of the kingdom. Both had been in the queen's chamber and contributed to his humiliation and Gwýnnett's recapture. *It will be a pleasure to put them in their place,* thought Hibblig. *Time for another, more proximate diversion.*

When the guards weren't looking in Hibblig's direction, he floated a sphere of solidified sound filled with dozens of cubes of cheese above their heads. Right behind it came a second sphere holding thirty large gray rats he'd collected from the warehouse district on his way to the palace. When both spheres were in place, Hibblig dispelled them. Cheese cubes and rats fell from the ceiling. Soon, dozens of rats were scurrying around the guards' legs, providing a more-than-adequate distraction.

Hibblig guided his camouflaged flying disk down the hall along the ceiling, confident he wouldn't be noticed. The slender woman remained at her post and was skewering rats with the point of her rapier, flipping each body off the end of her blade with confident twists of her wrist. The other guard took a different approach, using his heavy boots to kick rats hard enough they slammed into the opposite wall. It was time for another distraction. A voice that sounded like Queen Carys called from the far end of the hall where the other guards had gone.

"Help!" said the voice. "I tripped and can't get up!"

Hibblig expected both guards to help the Old Queen out of instinct, but only the young man moved toward where the voice had been coming from.

"I'll stay on the door, you help Queen Carys," said the woman after she tossed a rat uncomfortably close to Hibblig. She didn't seem to notice him, however, being too busy dealing with the last few rats.

I'll have to try another approach, thought Hibblig. *Maybe I should have skipped the rats and tried this first.* He looked over the edge of his flying disk and generated an opaque sphere of solidified sound around the remaining guard's head. If his rescue of Princess Gwýnnett went smoothly, he might dispel the sphere before she suffocated. It would be more satisfying if the woman lived to regret her defeat, but her death would also be acceptable. He descended and put his flying disk on his back, then shoved the oxygen-starved guard out of his way.

Hibblig focused his attention on the lock on Princess Gwýnnett's door. It wasn't one of the new magically augmented locks, so it didn't take him long to get it open. *The palace really needs to improve its security,* Hibblig mused. *Things would change when* he *was in charge.* He pulled the door's handle, but it didn't open. *Had Gwýnnett barred her own door for privacy?*

"Let me in," Hibblig shouted. "I'm here to rescue you!"

"Just a minute," said Gwýnnett. "I have to grab a few things."

"Lift the bar and I'll help you," said Hibblig, raising his voice and trying hard not to let it sound as exasperated as he felt.

"Lift it yourself," said Gwýnnett.

"Fine," said Hibblig. He was constructing a thin flat strip of solidified sound to lift the bar, grumbling to himself about Gwýnnett's priorities, when a rat ran across his foot, climbed his short boot, and bit the back of his leg. "Blast!" shouted Hibblig. "Fire and lightning!" His concentration failed, causing the sphere around the guard's head and the flat strip he'd been forming to fade away. To make matters worse, the second guard had returned and was standing at the far end of the hall, staring at him—or maybe the other guard.

Hibblig had hoped his sonic distraction would have lasted longer. He'd tied the imitation of the voice of Queen Carys to yet another sphere of solidified sound that he'd instructed to roll down the crossing corridor so the guards would chase it. Now the muscle-bound guard was running toward him and the guard with the rapier was gasping as she sucked in air. Soon she'd be a renewed threat.

Hibblig pounded on the door to Gwýnnett's suite. "Let me in!" he shouted. "Hurry!" He heard the second guard's hurried footsteps growing louder, then saw a rat on the tip of the first guard's rapier swing past his head, spraying blood from the rat's wounds. Hibblig turned to see that the first guard hadn't fully recovered. She was swinging her counterweighted blade wildly as she shifted her body from one side of the hall to the other, trying to make up for lost breaths. He pounded louder and faster—almost as fast as the rhythm of the second guard's approach. "Gwýnnett! Open up!"

He'd nearly given up on receiving help from inside and was readying his shields to push the guards away when the door to Gwýnnett's suite opened. His princess stood on the other side, wearing a sour expression and a dress with blue and green stripes he hadn't seen before. Hibblig stepped inside and shoved the door shut, dropping the bar back in place just before something heavy— the second guard in all likelihood—thumped against it. "I'm here to rescue you," said Hibblig.

"Looks more like I just rescued *you*," said Gwýnnett. She inspected Hibblig and sniffed. "You have drops of blood on your robes, and your leg is bleeding." The princess found a linen handkerchief in a chest of drawers to one side of the door and moistened it with water from a silver pitcher. Gwýnnett tossed the damp cloth to Hibblig. "Clean yourself up," she commanded. "What happened? Can't you plan a simple rescue without being injured?"

"Plainly, I *can* plan a rescue," said Hibblig. "I'm here, aren't I? And as for what happened to my leg, I was bitten by a rat."

"You should drink a potion for that," said Gwýnnett. "Rat bites are unpleasant."

"Oh?" said Hibblig. "I hadn't noticed."

"There's no need to take *that* tone, wizard," said Gwýnnett. "What about the drops of blood on your robes? Are they from a second injury?"

Hibblig looked down and saw what Gwýnnett was referring to—an arc of red across the sky blue and white stripes of his robes. The robes only came to mid-thigh, so he paused for a moment to admire his muscular legs before continuing. "That's not my blood," he said. Hibblig was aware of continued thumps as one or more people outside pounded on the barred door, making the heavy length of wood preventing their entrance rattle in its supports.

"Whose is it?" asked Gwýnnett, her acidic tone matching her continued sour expression.

"A random rat's."

"Two-legged or four-legged?" asked the princess.

"Four," said Hibblig.

"Ewww," said Gwýnnett. She shook her head. "Take a potion *soon,*" said the princess. "I don't want you dying of rat-bite fever."

"I didn't know you cared," Hibblig replied.

"I don't," said Gwýnnett. "But wizards *do* have their uses."

Hibblig raised an eyebrow and leered at Gwýnnett.

"Not that," said Gwýnnett. "Or not *just* that," she corrected. "I'm certainly not going to sleep with you again until your wound is fully healed."

"Easily done," said Hibblig. He removed a small stoppered flask from his belt-pouch, took out the cork and tossed down its contents. He poured the few drops left in the flask directly on his wounded calf. The rat bite immediately faded. "There," he said. "Satisfied? Ready to sleep with me now?"

"I think we have other priorities at present," said Gwýnnett. "What was your plan for getting us out of my suite, O brave rescuer?"

"I'd planned to take you through my emergency gate," said Hibblig. "It comes out in a cave northwest of the city."

"And then what?" asked Gwýnnett. "You never were good at planning more than one or two steps ahead."

"And you never offer a kind word when a cross one will do," said Hibblig. "If you must know, we have to get to Riyas to link up with Túathal."

Gwýnnett looked surprised. "Why would Túathal want anything to do with *me* after I poisoned him? And for that matter, why isn't he dead?"

"I think that young Tamloch wizard helped keep him alive," said Hibblig. "The one with short brown hair."

"Uirsé," said Gwýnnett.

"If you say so," said Hibblig. "I think Túathal will be willing to ally with you again. He understands treachery down to his bones and would have poisoned you in a heartbeat if he'd found it expedient."

"True enough," said Gwýnnett.

"Besides," said Hibblig. "The fundamental reasons you were valuable to him haven't changed—at least not much."

"Hah," said Gwýnnett. "Dârio will never trust me again. I'll never regain my former influence over him."

"You only have to slip a potion past Dârio's guard once to make him compliant," said Hibblig. "I think you're up to that challenge."

"Perhaps," said Gwýnnett. One corner of her mouth turned up. "No," she added. "Certainly."

"There's my princess," said Hibblig.

"I don't understand why you want me to renew my alliance with Túathal," said Gwýnnett. "His army is captured, and his credibility is low after his loss on the battlefield."

"Ah," said Hibblig. "That's right. You don't know about Viridáxés."

"Is he one of those ancient Athican wizards you mages study?" asked Gwýnnett.

"No," said Hibblig. "Viridáxés is a two-thousand-year-old green dragon who serves Túathal."

"Why should a single dragon make a difference? Didn't the Bifurlanders sail with a dozen gold ones?"

"Those were small *young* dragons about the size of a wisent," said Hibblig. "Apparently, dragons grow larger as they age."

"So a two-thousand-year-old dragon..." Gwýnnett began.

"Is bigger than four sections of city wall," Hibblig completed.

"That *does* change things, doesn't it?" said Gwýnnett. "A renewed alliance with Túathal is definitely recommended."

"I thought you'd feel that way," said Hibblig. The pounding on the door to Gwýnnett's suite increased its intensity.

"How are we getting to Riyas after we gate out to your cave?" asked Gwýnnett as she took a long black cloak with a deep hood from a peg by her door and donned it.

"Worst case, we'll fly there," said Hibblig. "That's what Túathal and Viridáxés are doing. I don't know how to fly fast enough to catch up to them."

"It would be easier if we could gate directly to Riyas," said Gwýnnett.

"Do *you* know where to find such a gate?" asked Hibblig. "I don't."

"Queen Carys isn't the only royal in the palace with a spy network," said Gwýnnett. "My spies tracked Túathal's spies to a tavern by the docks. I'm sure there's a gate to Riyas in the building."

"It won't do us much good if we don't know the words to open the gate," said Hibblig.

"But Túathal knows them," said Gwýnnett. She touched one of the plain gold rings on her finger. "We'll ask him."

"That may work," said Hibblig. "It will take an hour to fly from my cave back to the city."

"Why would we want to do that?" asked Gwýnnett. "The tavern is only a five-minute hop from the palace on your flying disk."

Hibblig gestured to the door, still vibrating from blows. "We're stuck in here unless we use my emergency gate."

"Or," said Gwýnnett, "we could do what I'd planned when I was ready to make my own escape."

She crossed to a low table with a mirror and collected what looked to Hibblig like a box of face powder. Then she shifted to her desk and found a large envelope, made from paper carefully folded and glued. Such things were inventions borrowed from the Roma who had raised reporting and bureaucracy to a high art. Gwýnnett dumped the box of face powder into the envelope, taking care not to breath any particles that escaped. She handed the envelope to Hibblig. "Slide the open end under the door then put your heel on the back of it so they don't pull it through," Gwýnnett ordered.

"Yes, my princess," said Hibblig. He did as he was told and smiled, wondered what Gwýnnett was up to. The pounding on the door stopped. Hibblig felt someone tugging from the other side. Gwýnnett stamped hard on the back of the envelope. He heard muffled thuds through the door.

"It should be safe to unbar the door now," said Gwýnnett, "though you might want to put spheres of solidified sound around our heads when we first step out."

"An excellent thought," said Hibblig. He surrounded their heads with large spheres that would give them several minutes of air, then unbarred the door and opened it. The two guards were sprawled on the hard stone floor with their eyes closed. "Did you kill them?" he asked.

"No," said Gwýnnett. "It was just sleeping powder. Anything more potent would have been easier to detect under my face powder."

"Remind me to stay on your good side," said Hibblig as they entered the corridor.

"You'll be fine if you do exactly what I say at all times," said Gwýnnett. She wasn't smiling.

"Don't I always, my princess?" asked Hibblig. He, on the other hand, was smiling.

"Stop that nonsense and get us out of the palace," said Gwýnnett as she carefully stepped around dead rats. "Then tell me more about Túathal's dragon!"

Chapter 41

The King's Suite

Eynon didn't know what he expected a king's bedchamber to look like, but he was sure this wasn't it. The walls were freshly painted white plaster. One held a detailed map of the kingdom with every city, town, castle and village noted by name and symbol. Beside it was a map of Orluin as far west as the mountains, with Dâron's territory in sky blue, Tamloch's in light green, Occidens province in pale red, Bifurland in a bright yellow, and the northern and southern Clan Lands marked in muddy brown. Major rivers and the Inland Seas were in deep blue and major roads were shown as dashed red lines. Eynon resolved to ask Dârio for permission to come back and see the maps again someday so he could commit them both to memory.

The king's furniture wasn't what Eynon expected either. Instead of a giant intricately carved four-poster oak bed with hanging curtains draped around it, there was a simple headboard on a mattress just big enough for two people to sleep comfortably. Chee jumped on it and made his way to the pair of pillows at the top of the bed. He curled up on one of them and pretended to sleep—at least Eynon hoped Chee was pretending. None of the rest of the furnishings were particularly regal either. A utilitarian desk covered in books and papers was against one wall near a leaded-glass window. A tall chest of drawers and a dressing table holding a pitcher and wash basin flanked a door opposite the one they'd entered. Two nightstands stood sentry to the left and right of the bed. Both held wizard lamps and books.

Eynon's gaze took in a small round table and two wooden armchairs between the desk and the bed. Sky blue cushions with Dâron's royal dragon picked out in dark blue needlepoint rested on the seat of each chair. An onyx and opal *shah mat* board was in the center of the small table. Simple dark-and-light-stained pieces—kings, queens, advisers, knights, castles, and pawns—were lined up in their initial positions waiting for play to commence.

Stepping closer, Eynon smiled when he examined the pieces in greater detail. Their forms were so basic a child might have carved them. *I wonder if Dârio whittled them himself?* thought Eynon. *And whose bright idea was it to make* those *chair cushions? It didn't show much respect to* sit *on the Dâron dragon—though he could see Dârio appreciating it as a joke. Maybe someday Nûd would sit astride Zûrafiérix,* Eynon mused. *Not that doing so would be remotely the same thing.* He started shaping a solidified-sound copy of the board and pieces. It snapped into place floating a few feet to one one side of the original.

Merry turned, saw Eynon's construct, and shook her head slowly. "Very nice, but we're not here to play *shah mat,* sweetie," she said from her position beside the door to the next chamber in the king's suite. "We're here to ambush the southern Clan Lands' wizards and those Mastlands fools…"

"And save Inthíra," added Eynon. He grinned at Merry and mouthed, "Sweetie?" back to her without speaking.

She sighed like Braith being told what to do by her mother, then smiled back. "Sorry," said Merry. "It just slipped out. Of course we're here to save Inthíra. That's the primary purpose of our ambush." She waved Eynon closer. "Help me listen. I want to see if anyone is in the next room."

Eynon cast a listening spell on himself to match Merry's and put his ear to the door a foot above where Merry listened. "I don't hear anything," he said.

"Good," said Merry. "You go through and scope things out. I'll be ready to close the far door with tight light if it opens suddenly."

With his ears tuned for any new noises on the other side, Eynon put his hand on the handle of the door from king Dârio's private sleeping quarters to the semi-private room beyond. *These rooms were where Old King Dâroth and Queen Carys lived,* thought Eynon. *They must have been a lot different back then. Wait,* Eynon realized. *The Old King died only two years ago. It wasn't ancient history.*

His musings were interrupted by Chee landing on his shoulder and slipping back into his usual spot between Eynon's back and his flying disk. "You had enough rest then, my friend?" asked Eynon softly. "If these weren't Dârio's chambers I might have joined you for a nap myself."

"Chee," said the raconette decisively, making it sound like he would have been glad to have Eynon's company—there were *two* pillows, after all.

Eynon reached up to rub Chee's fur then moved his hand down to push the door open. Its hinges squeaked like rusty mice. *So Dârio would be warned if anyone tried to enter while he slept,* Eynon realized. He moved his eyes left and right and saw that the next room was decorated in what he assumed was far more the Old King's style than Dârio's. The massive furniture Eynon had expected was there, including a table for ten with matching chairs, three carved sideboards, one of them holding bottles, and four overstuffed chairs arrayed around a faded blue and white braided rug.

Despite the fact that it had more than a dozen windows, the light was dim inside because the windows were thin slits of the sort archers might use to defend a castle. *That doesn't make sense in a palace,* thought Eynon. The walls had dark walnut wainscoting as tall as Eynon's chest and were painted sky blue above that. Artisans had laboriously added thousands of tiny dark blue dragons in a busy and dizzying pattern. Eynon was thankful there were portraits of kings and queens hanging over the dragon decorations to give his eyes a break. Few of the men and women in the portraits were smiling. *Nûd may be up there someday,* thought Eynon. *And Dârio, for that matter.*

"What's inside?" called Merry. "Can you hear the southern Clan Lands' raiding party?"

"It's all clear in here," said Eynon.

"Chee!" added Chee.

Eynon didn't watch Merry enter, he was too busy examining the massive fireplace carved from a smooth, blue-veined stone on the far wall. Merry moved to stand beside Eynon, touched the hearth, and inhaled sharply.

"It's Carreg Glas blue marble," she said. "This much of it must be worth a king's weight in gold."

"May I remind you where we are?" teased Eynon.

"Yes, I know, but..." Merry started. Her voice trailed off as she ran her finger over the head of a marble dragon sculpted to spiral around one of the hearth's pillars.

Eynon was drawn to the blue dragons painted on the walls. Close up, they looked odd to him. He touched one and jerked his hand back as if the dragon's teeth had bitten him. *They're fuzzy,* he realized. *Like a tiny flock of sheep. And they're not painted individually. They're printed on paper somehow and the paper is glued to the walls. Maybe with woodblocks?* He wanted to see the workshop where the wall paper was made—but that could wait until later.

"Take your hands off that dragon and help me listen at the next door," teased Eynon.

"This room would be so much brighter if they replaced those narrow windows," said Merry as she waved at the offending slits. "Maybe even knock down the wall to the next room to make it more open and less stuffy...?"

"You can give Nûd advice on redecorating some other time," said Eynon. "Let's get moving!"

"Sorry," said Merry as she pulled her hands away. "You're forgiven."

"What do *I* need to be forgiven for?" Eynon protested.

"For getting caught up in your own head instead of focusing on our mission," said Merry. She smiled at Eynon. "It can happen to anyone, I expect."

"Especially wizards," said Eynon.

The two shifted to stand by the door to the next room. With their bodies close together, they leaned their ears against its panels.

"Nothing," said Merry when she stood up straight. "I can't hear *anything*. What do *you* think is on the other side?"

"I don't know," said Eynon, standing up himself. "You're the one who grew up in a castle."

"It can't be Dârio's study. That's not in the same wing as the Great Hall," said Merry. "I'd bet it's a room for servants, somewhere they can wait close at hand in case the king needs anything."

"And stage meals to be served at the table in *this* room," offered Eynon.

"That makes sense," said Merry. "Where would the royal guards wait?"

"Outside in the hall," said Eynon. "Plus one or two on the balcony."

"And another pair close to each monarch," said Merry. "Why haven't we encountered more guards then?"

"Ummm..." said Eynon.

Merry shook her head and laughed at her own error. "It might have something to do with the fact that Dârio isn't in residence," she said.

"I think that's likely," said Eynon, keeping his tone level and his face expressionless.

Merry punched his arm lightly.

"Hey!" said Eynon.

"Do you think there will be guards out in the hall making sure nobody can enter the king's suite?" asked Merry.

"Unless they rushed off to help fight the faked fire in the Great Hall," said Eynon. He opened the door to the next room and walked in, holding it open for Merry to join him.

"You were right," said Merry. "It's a room for staging meals."

The walls of the outer room were plaster, like in Dârio's quarters. There were plain wooden prep tables, a sink, racks for bottles of wine, and three casks on high stands. They had rock-maple turn-screw taps labeled Beer, Cider, and Water. A few flat-backed birchwood chairs with seats woven from rushes were at the prep tables or against the walls. No servants were in evidence.

"Do you think they're with the army?" asked Eynon.

"Or they sped off to see what the excitement was about," offered Merry. "Let's listen at the next door."

This time the door was not flush with the wall. It was recessed a yard or so, but there was enough room for both of them to fit in the opening. They repeated their previous manuever with Merry and Eynon's heads a foot apart, ears pressed against the door's heavy oak panels. Eynon was glad his hearing was enhanced by wizardry—he'd never hear anything through that much wood otherwise.

"Wouldn't you think the guards outside would jingle or clank?" asked Eynon after a minute. "I'd expect their mail shirts would give them away."

"Agreed," said Merry.

Eynon tried to push open the outer door, but it wouldn't budge. "It's locked," he said.

"Which explains why the rooms in the king's suite are unguarded," said Merry. "Shift to your right a bit, please." She put an affectionate hand a foot below Eynon's belt, squeezed his cheek, and pushed him gently.

Eynon did as he was instructed and reminded himself to return the favor to Merry at the next opportunity—then thought better of it. He watched Merry bend close and use delicate tendrils of tight light to probe the door's keyhole until he heard a click-thunk. "Should I open it now?" he asked.

"Be my guest," said Merry, stepping back and stretching.

Eynon opened the outer door and confirmed that it led to a wide hall. No guards or servants were in evidence. He motioned for Merry to join him and they noted the niches three feet wide and three deep on either side of the door.

"Guard stations," said Merry.

"That gives me an idea," said Eynon. "Eight-to-two odds aren't optimal, wouldn't you agree?"

"It's hard to argue with that," said Merry.

"What if I could get Inthíra's magestone back to her?" Eynon offered. "Eight-to-*three* odds are marginally better."

"When the third on our side is Inthíra, I'd say they're substantially better," said Merry. "What's your plan?"

"These halls in the palace look a lot alike, don't they?" asked Eynon. Merry nodded. "What if we make the door to the king's suite look like a wall...?"

"And do the same with the guard stations..." said Merry.

"Where we'll be hiding," Eynon completed. "I can step out and give Inthíra her magestone when she walks by."

"You'll want some sort of distraction, so they won't attack you as soon as you show yourself," said Merry.

"I thought of that," said Eynon. "I was thinking I'd generate an illusion of a giant boulder rolling down the hall straight for the southern Clan Landers."

"That's clever," said Merry, "But not particularly believable. Why not a squad of royal guards with pikes and swords?"

"I don't think I could generate something like that and still be able to give Inthíra her magestone," said Eynon.

"No, but *I* could," said Merry. She put a hand around her artifact, closed her eyes, and concentrated. Royal guards appeared at the far end of the hall and began rushing toward them.

Eynon applauded softly. "Wonderful!" he said. "You'll want to add sound to make it fully believable."

"I know," said Merry. "I just didn't want to give anything away in case the raiding party was close by." Merry waved her hand and the faux guards faded. "Let's get in place," she said.

Eynon took the niche to the right of the door and Merry the left. He got Chee's attention and put a finger to his lips to indicate the raconette should stay quiet and hoped his familiar would understand him. Eynon disguised the door and the niches to look like the corridor walls with carefully crafted solidified-sound panels, being sure to match the colors, textures, and fine details as best he could manage. Then they waited.

It wasn't long before grunts and heavy footsteps echoed off the walls. Eynon and Merry could see through Eynon's illusions—he'd taken care to put holes disguised as imperfections in the plaster at the proper height for both of them. The raiders were coming up the hall toward their position.

"I thought you said it was on this hallway," said Fox, who was walking next to Kennig at the front of the raiding party. One of the southern Clan Lands' wizards was on the other side of Kennig. His hair was wild and shaggy.

"Shut yer trap and let Ceanneig work," said the shaggy-haired wizard. "Bad enough t' lose th' boy."

"We had him, Grúgàch," muttered Fox. "He just disappeared."

Fool walked behind Kennig, Fox and Grúgàch with his crossbow at the ready, prepared to shoot at anything or anyone threatening. Oaf and Dolt came next, holding Inthíra between them. Her hands were bound, and she didn't look happy. The remaining two southern Clan Lands' wizards were in the rear.

"CHEEEEE!" cried Chee when Inthíra was even with the niche where he and Eynon waited.

Eynon sighed and paused to give Merry time to generate *her* illusion. The raiders were disoriented, trying to figure out where the raconette's exclamation had come from. Fool was swinging his crossbow wildly, making Eynon wish he had the spare concentration to generate a shield as well as his imitation of the corridor's wall. Then what looked like a squad of royal guards charged toward the raiders from the far end of the hall, shouting challenges. Their mail shirts sounded like tiny bells.

The two wizards in the rear pulled their flying disks off their backs and ascended close to the ceiling to get the high ground. Kennig and the wizard with him in the front threw up shields to slow the guards' progress. They were both surprised when their shields had no effect. Fox went for the crossbow at *his* belt and got off a shot at the attacking guards before Fool calmed down enough to get a bolt off a moment later. Oaf and Dolt released Inthíra and drew their swords, ready and quite willing to fight.

Deciding that it would be easier to give Chee a chance to redeem himself than to add his own body to the confusion in the hallway, Eynon handed Inthíra's magestone to Chee and motioned for the raconette to deliver it to its owner. Chee smiled at Eynon, nodded, and scooted out of the right-hand guard niche with a soft *chee-chee-chee-CHEE.* Eynon watched him navigate around Oaf's legs and climb up Inthíra's robes before lowering her artifact and its blue magestone around her neck on its fine platinum chain.

When Inthíra had her magestone again, everything grew even *more* chaotic. A pack of hounds the size and temperament of wolves howled down the hall on either side of Merry's illusory guards. They were snapping at the raiders and unaffected by Oaf and Dolt's swinging blades. Inthíra cut her bonds with a sharp wedge of solidified sound, then directed two thick pillars of solidified sound up at the wizards floating near the ceiling, smashing them against it. The wizards fell, their flying disks and bodies landing on Oaf and Dolt who collapsed to the floor along with them. Kennig hopped on his flying disk. He'd realized the guards weren't real but understood that the odds had shifted against him. Fox jumped on the disk behind Kennig and Fool did the same behind the other southern Clan Lands' wizard.

Eynon stepped out of his niche and dropped his wall-illusion. He generated a giant boulder rolling toward them behind Merry's guards, but Kennig, Fox, Fool and the other wizard flew right through the guards *and* the boulder, disappearing around a distant bend in the hall. Merry left her niche, shrugged her shoulders, and canceled her illusion. Eynon did likewise.

"I told you it would be unbelievable," said Merry. Eynon nodded sheepishly.

Inthíra had removed the two southern Clan Lands' wizards' magestones and put them in her pouch. Eynon and Merry helped Inthíra bind Oaf, Dolt, and the wizards with strips cut from the wizards' robes. When they'd finished, Inthíra generated bubbles of solidified sound around the raiders' heads.

"Don't *kill* them," said Merry.

"I should, but I won't," said Inthíra. "I just want them unconscious, so they don't cause more trouble until we can get some *real* guards to deal with them." She looked at Merry. "Nice illusion, by the way."

"Thank you," said Merry.

"I made the false wall," said Eynon, earning a smile from Inthíra.

"That should be long enough," Inthíra said, dispelling the spheres around their prisoners' heads. All four lay limp in the center of the hall.

"Now what should we do?" asked Merry.

"I know what *I'm* going to do," said Inthíra. Taking careful aim, she kicked Oaf at the spot where his legs met his body, seeming to take particular delight with the sound her pointed boot made when it hit. She did the same thing to Dolt and put her hands on her hips, staring at Eynon and Merry as if daring them to criticize her actions.

"Remind me never to get you mad at *me*," said Eynon.

"They *touched* me," said Inthíra. "And I couldn't stop them. I wanted them to know there'd be consequences."

"You're more considerate than *I* would have been," said Merry. "I'd have wanted them awake when I did it."

"Remind me never to get *you* mad at me either," said Eynon.

Chapter 42

Dârio at the Gate

The soldiers waiting to enter the wide wizard gate to Riyas were pleased to see Dârio, Jenet, and their trailing train of guard-ducklings.

"Ready to kick Tamloch's ass, Dârio?" called an earthy alto voice.

"Will you lead the attack?" asked a hardened basso.

"Who's the beauty?" came a sensual soprano.

"Don't you recognize your king?" Jenet replied.

Laughter rippled up and down the ranks and a row of warriors with long pikes planted their weapons and applauded.

"That's telling her, Jenet," said a mature tenor from the row of pikes.

Dârio and Jenet kept walking, shaking hands and wishing the soldiers good luck when they passed through to the other side of the gate. Jenet saw a large contingent of men and women ahead, mustered under tall poles supporting square black banners, each bearing a large white heraldic rose with a drop of red in its center.

"The troops of the Duchess of Whitrose are coming up," whispered Jenet. "They support..."

"...my mother, I know," said Dârio. "But they're here, fighting in *my* army..."

"...and your mother isn't exactly in a position to leverage support from the duchess at present," Jenet continued.

"We *hope*," said Dârio. He waved to the Whitrose knights and levies and proceeded to walk along their lines. The usual supportive calls came from the foot soldiers, but a question of a different sort came from a baron on a chestnut stallion.

"Is it true you're *not* the king of Dâron?" he bellowed loud enough to be heard up and down the assembled troops.

"Is Túathal your real father?" asked an armored woman on a war horse beside the baron.

"How are we going to fight *dragons?*" came a young man's plaintive cry from a few rows back.

Dârio took a deep breath and was about to respond when a commanding woman in her forties with long dark wavy hair rode her mount forward. Nearby knights parted around her and nodded as she passed. The woman wore fine mail and polished steel elbows, knee cops, and gauntlets. Her horse was barded in black boiled leather painted with hundreds of white roses. She sat erect on a jousting saddle with a high back taller than her shoulders and carried a shield on her left arm bearing the same white rose design as the banners. Her mount obeyed her unspoken commands and pranced out on the battlefield, then turned so the woman could face her troops and confront Dârio.

"Who *is* the true king of Dâron?" she asked.

"My cousin, Dârianûd, Your Grace," said Dârio, shaping his voice to be heard as Jenet's father had taught him. "His grandmother is Princess Seren."

"The lost princess?" asked the Duchess. "That sounds like a children's story, not truth." An errant breeze blew her hair away from her face so Dârio could see her eyes go wide.

"She wasn't lost, Your Grace," said Dârio. "She just didn't wish to be found."

"Huh," said the duchess, now looking more angry than amazed.

Dârio could almost hear her unspoken thought: *A likely story.*

"Where is this so-called king Dârianûd? Why isn't *he* leading the army?" she asked.

Jenet spoke up, proving *she* had learned how to make her voice heard as well. "He has his own part to play," she asserted. "You'll soon see he's a worthy monarch."

"How do we know going through this gate isn't a plot you and Túathal cooked up to see us captured and imprisoned in Riyas?" asked the baron who'd spoken first.

Dârio started to laugh. So did Jenet. A moment later the squad of royal guards began to laugh as well. Ripples of laugher rolled up and down the rows of soldiers. Even the Duchess of Whitrose smiled, almost involuntarily. Dârio concentrated and got himself under control, then responded.

"Let me see if I understand your question," said Dârio. "Are you asking whether or not Túathal and I conspired to utterly defeat Tamloch's army without more than a few scratches to our forces in order to set up Dâron's army to be captured when we gate through to take Riyas?" he asked. "Have you been too close to burning hemp fields on your lands recently, Baron Nobblig?"

Renewed rounds of laugher spread out from Dârio as if he'd dropped a boulder in a pond. The baron sputtered and seemed prepared to answer, but the duchess raised her hand and stopped him. "I hope you understand," she began, but Jenet interrupted.

"I hope you understand *Your Majesty*."

"Whatever," said the duchess, pausing to glare at Jenet before turning back to Dârio. "I'll say it plainly then. If you're Túathal's son, you're not to be trusted."

"Yet you trust my mother," said Dârio, showing a hint of a smile.

"She has the best interests of the kingdom at heart," said the duchess.

"She has her own interest at heart—always," muttered Jenet loud enough for Whitrose to hear. The duchess continued as if Jenet hadn't spoken.

"It would have been better for all of Orluin if Princess Gwýnnett had *killed* Túathal," she said. "Why did you save him?"

"I didn't," said Dârio. "One of his wizards, a skillful healer, saved him—though I must admit I don't want to see poisoning kings become a custom."

More laughter—the nervous rather than the amused kind—floated up from the soldiers. The Duchess of Whitrose and Baron Nobblig seemed ready to continue their interrogation, but the young king had heard more than enough from them both.

Dârio ran toward the duchess and shifted to her left side. He stretched to grip the side of the tall saddleback and clambered up her horse's barding until he was sitting on the well-trained animal's hindquarters behind the duchess. In one continuous motion, he got to his feet and vaulted above her to balance on the saddleback's flat top, facing the troops.

Dârio smiled at the Whitrose forces, looking left and right. He opened his arms wide to acknowledge cheers for his rapid and acrobatic ascent. The troops' applause sounded like a cavalry charge. Their praise continued for a dozen heartbeats. After more smiles, Dârio lowered his arms and the men and women around him went silent.

"People of Dâron..." he began. "...I am *not* your true king. But you *are* my army. I would give my life for any one of you, but more than that, I will dedicate my life to making sure that you win victories and live to return to your homes when the battles are over." Soldiers cheered again and Dârio nodded. Jenet smiled up at him.

"We won this morning with next to no casualties—unless some of you tried to annoy stray wisents," said Dârio. That drew more laughs than cheers. "Tomorrow morning, you can help me win the support of the people of Riyas—they are *not* the enemy. They're our brothers and sisters going back to the time of the First Ships. Tamloch and Dâron began as friends. Dârianûd and I are friends and cousins. Together we can lead both kingdoms on a path to lasting peace!"

Dârio raised his hands above his head again as the troops cheered up and down the line. Their cheers went far further than his words could have carried. He couldn't see the expression on the face of the duchess but was sure it resembled something rough-carved from granite. Baron Nobblig looked thoughtful. Dârio suspected he was already trying to figure out how to manipulate Nûd to his advantage.

After the cheers faded, Dârio leaned down from his high perch and whispered to the duchess. "If you hear from my mother, tell her I'll let her live—in exile." He didn't expect or receive a reply. Dârio waved to the soldiers again and dismounted by sliding down the tall jousting saddle to stand on the horse's rump before performing a skillful back flip that brought him to the ground several feet behind the steed's long black tail. He didn't remain there long, not wanting to risk being kicked.

Jenet gave Dârio a hug and a kiss when he returned to her side, earning her shouts of approval from the ranks. She took his hand and pulled Dârio along, eager to get to the next noble's contingent of soldiers. They stopped when they heard a young man softly calling, "Your Majesty…" He was also wearing fine mail and steel, but held a shield with a long-stemmed white rose instead of just the blossom. He had his mother's dark wavy hair, but didn't share her predatory expression. Two guards rushed close. They backed off when they realized the young man's identity.

"What can the interim king of Dâron do for the Earl of Thorn Hill?" asked Dârio.

"Sorry to intrude, Your Majesty," said the young earl who was nodding nervously.

Jenet and Dârio smiled at him in an attempt to put him at ease. Dârio moved his hand in a circular gesture that meant *go on*.

"Well, Sire," said the earl. "You didn't answer my question." He paused to look left and right, then leaned in close to Dârio and Jenet.

"Which is?" asked Jenet, putting her hand on the young man's arm.

"My apologies," said the earl. "I'm the one who spoke after Baron Nobblig and his senior knight. My question is how are we going to fight *dragons?*"

Chapter 43
Nûd and Zûrafiérix

Rocky had no problem keeping pace with Zûrafiérix as the wyvern, the young man, and the dragon flew toward Riyas. To the west, the sun was setting, bathing the horizon in warm, red-orange rays. Zûrafiérix was a steady flier, flapping her huge blue bat-like wings in smooth patterns that propelled her forward. Rocky's wings beat more frequently, but that didn't translate into a bumpy ride. Young man and wyvern maintained a position ten yards to the right of the dragon's massive head.

At least dragons don't have to depend on their wings alone to keep them aloft, thought Nûd. *Energy from internal congruencies did that, if the books he'd read in the library in Melyncárreg were correct. Congruencies also helped dragons breathe fire and chilling cold and strong winds, for that matter.* A practical part of Nûd's brain added *while regulating dragons' internal temperature. That must be a challenge for something the size of Zûrafiérix—or Viridáxés.* Nûd wondered why the big beautiful blue dragon was so sure *he* was someone of significance.

"How do you know I'm the true king of Dâron?" Nûd asked.

"Is it something you doubt?" Zûrafiérix replied.

"Every day," said Nûd. "Every hour. Most minutes, too."

"You need not worry," said Zûrafiérix. "You *are* the true king of Dâron."

"Yes," said Nûd. "I understand that my grandmother was Princess Seren and my great-grandfather was the Old King, but I don't feel up to the job."

"Few kings do," said Zûrafiérix. "At least from what *I've* read."

"You read?" asked Nûd. "Somehow I never associated dragons with reading."

"How do you think we become wise?" asked Zûrafiérix, making her rumbling purr sort of laughter. "Unfortunately, I haven't read a book in two-thousand years."

"Reading will be more of a challenge for you at your current size," said Nûd.

"I hadn't considered that," said Zûrafiérix. The dragon tilted her head so her large spinning eye was fixed on Nûd. "Would you read to me?"

"It would be my pleasure," Nûd replied, "and far easier than crafting books large enough for you to handle." He grinned at Zûrafiérix and heard the rumbling purr again.

"Where could I find books?" asked the dragon. "I expect any tomes I found would be new to me."

"A reasonable expectation, given how long you were sleeping," said Nûd. "There's a street of booksellers in Tyford, and two streets in Brendinas if you want to buy some."

"What about ahead of us instead of behind?" asked Zûrafiérix. "I'm not fond of waiting. I've done so much of it already."

"Let me think," said Nûd. "My grandfather sometimes goes to Nova Eboracum for books the Roma import across the Ocean. That's on our route."

"Perhaps," said Zûrafiérix, "though I would have to work on overcoming my distaste of everything Roma."

"I've told you, the Roma are our allies now," said Nûd.

"Of course," said Zûrafiérix. "I didn't mean to imply otherwise. It's just that I'm still coming to terms with *Tamloch* being our enemy, not the Roma."

"Tamloch's not our enemy either," said Nûd. "Túathal is."

"And Viridáxés serves him," said Zûrafiérix, tilting her head down for a moment as if that thought made her sad.

"Cheer up," said Nûd. "We don't have to stop to buy books—I have one with me."

"You do?" asked Zûrafiérix. "What is it about?"

"It's a book of epigrams," Nûd replied.

"Wise sayings?" asked Zûrafiérix. "That sounds promising."

"You haven't met the author," said Nûd.

The dragon raised her near eye-ridge.

"My grandfather. Ealdamon," Nûd continued.

"Ealdamon's *Epigrams* does have a nice rhythm to it as a title,"
said Zûrafiérix. "I like its paired dactyls."

"Dactyls?" asked Nûd.

"Poetic stresses," said Zûrafiérix. "EAL-da-mon's EP-i-grams.
DUM-da-da DUM-da-dum."

"Dragons appreciate poetry?" asked Nûd.

"Some do," said Zûrafiérix. "Some even write it, as do some kings."

"I've been writing things down for years," said Nûd.

"What do you write?" asked the dragon.

"This and that," said Nûd. "Thoughts about being a servant,
thoughts about loneliness, thoughts about nature."

"Will you share what you've written?" asked Zûrafiérix.

"I'd be too embarrassed to read my journals to you," said Nûd.

"I'll trade you for some of my poems," said the dragon.

"Well, maybe," said Nûd. "But they're back in Melyncárreg."

"I've waited for two thousand years," said Zûrafiérix. "I can wait
a little longer. Read me some epigrams, if you would. I'd love to
hear them."

"Certainly," said Nûd. He reached into his jacket and removed a
thin volume bound in wisent leather. "I hope I can read you several
before sunset."

"Thank you," said Zûrafiérix. "Are there any about dragons?"

"Yes," said Nûd. "I'll try to find them. I was told my friend Eynon's
great-grandfather used to say, 'Let sleeping dragons lie.'"

"The same was said about cats two thousand years ago," said
Zûrafiérix.

"Ones with wings or ones without?" asked Nûd.

"I don't think it mattered," said Zûrafiérix.

"Cats of all sorts are still cats," said Nûd with a smile. He noticed
they were no longer flying over land but were now above a large
body of open water that stretched to the eastern horizon. It seemed
much larger than the lake at Melyncárreg. From his study of the
maps in the map room back at the Academy, he figured they must
be over the Ocean. "Are you sure you know where you're going?"
he asked.

"Unless the shape of the world has changed in two thousand years, I think I do," said Zûrafiérix. "This is the fastest way to fly to Riyas from Brendinas."

"Good," said Nûd. "It's still round, so I don't think there's anything to worry about. Remember, the Tamloch fleet and Bifurland's longships are likely on the sound between the Roma's Insula Longa and the southern coast of Tamloch." He glanced north, under the dragon's neck, and saw a long, low shore. "We should probably make contact with the Bifurlanders in case Doethan couldn't establish communications through Laetícia," he continued.

"The Roma hold both shores of the Abbenoth now?" asked Zûrafiérix. "Tamloch used to claim the east bank and Dâron the west."

"The two kingdoms used to stage constant raids across the river according to the history books," said Nûd. "Now they respect the power of the legions, and things build to large-scale conflicts only once a generation instead of four or five times a year."

"I suppose that's some sort of victory," said Zûrafiérix. Nûd saw the dragon eye the long island to their left carefully, as if sizing up what it would take to attack it.

Time for a distraction, thought Nûd. He flipped through the pages of Ealdamon's *Epigrams.* "I found one," he said. "Dragons exist to show the powerful the limits of their power."

"Hmmm," said Zûrafiérix, sounding like the lowest string on a bass viol thrumming. "I don't know if I'm fond of that one. I'd like to think my existence means more than teaching kings they're not all-powerful."

"Damon may have been in a bad mood when he wrote that one," said Nûd. "Or he could have been using it as an oblique way to criticize Túathal—possibly both. I'll look for another one."

"Damon?" asked Zûrafiérix.

"Ealdamon, my grandfather," said Nûd. "He said he preferred to be called Damon most of the time, because Ealdamon was too fancy for everyday use."

"A sign of wisdom, as I see it," said Zûrafiérix. "Friends and family shouldn't need to use long names all the time. Shorter names indicate intimacy. When we were fresh from our eggs, Viridáxés always insisted on being called by every syllable of his name, but I never minded humans calling me Zûra." The dragon's ears flicked from some inner amusement. "I tried several nicknames—Viri, Vee, Áxés, Iri—but the only one he would tolerate without getting angry was Dáx."

"Dáx does have more dignity than Viri," said Nûd. *And I like Nûd a lot more than my own birth name of Dârianûd,* he considered.

"Dáx would be so much easier to use than Viridáxés when we eventually mate," said Zûra. *"Stroke my wing sockets, Dáx,* would be so much more intimate than saying the same thing using his *full* name."

Nûd's face grew as red as Eynon's magestone at the thought of dragons mating. He took three slow breaths and tried to put aside the disturbing images his imagination was generating. "I understand— in theory—that it's much the same when humans mate," said Nûd after biting his knuckle. His brain spun when he realized that he'd need to find a queen soon if he took the throne. *How will I be sure to chose someone competent and caring, like Merry or an older version of Eynon's sister Braith instead of someone who seems like a good match on the outside but will turn out more like Princess Gwýnnett?*

"You haven't mated?" asked Zûra. "Is that usual?"

"That's a very private matter," said Nûd. "It's not a question humans typically ask each other."

"My apologies," said Zûra. "Before I slept in the quarry, back in the days of the First Ships, men and women used to *brag* about their mating partners. Has that custom changed?"

"No," said Nûd. "Bragging is still common among people with no respect for their partners—or manners."

"I have offended you," said Zûrafiérix. "That was not my intent. I will drop the subject immediately. I don't want to be known as a dragon without manners."

"Please don't worry about it," said Nûd. "You have excellent manners— far better than Viridáxés. It's just that I was raised in near-isolation, far from Brendinas, and didn't have a chance to meet any people near my own age."

"You are very kind, my king," said the dragon. "I will say no more about your lack of mating partners."

Rocky snorted and Nûd slapped the side of the wyvern's neck. "You mind *your* manners, too!" said Nûd affectionately.

"Here's another dragon-related epigram," said Nûd after a few minutes of flying in silence. "It will have to be one of the last ones until tomorrow, since the light is fading."

"I'm all ears," said Zûrafiérix. She twisted her head on her long neck and observed the great mass of her body and wings, then spoke again. "Actually, ears are only a tiny part of what I am, but I *am* listening."

"Good," said Nûd. "It is better to pluck feathers from a gryffon than steal scales from a dragon."

"That's it?" asked Zûra.

"It's what's written in the book," said Nûd. "The next one is almost the same: It is better to feed a dog than a wolf."

"They're not the same at all," said Zûra.

"Each one starts with '*It is better,*' teased Nûd.

"But their meanings are quite different," said Zûra. "One is…"

The dragon's explanation was cut off by Rocky's insistent bugling. The wyvern jerked his neck down toward the water below and Nûd's eyes followed. In the dim twilight, he could just make out two white square sails and what looked to be a large black rock.

"Looks like a ship has run aground!" shouted Nûd. "Let's see if there's anything we can do to help."

Rocky angled down and flew toward the scene. As Nûd got closer, he could see that the sails were attached to a large ship—a sort of wider, rounder double-masted vessel that reminded him of half an oversized barrel with a pointed prow and stern. He saw large ballistas like giant crossbows mounted on platforms fore and aft, and smaller ones attached on raised pedestals amidships, one next to either mast. Tamloch's kingdom banner, gold with a green quatrefoil, flew from the foremast.

"A whaling ship has gotten into trouble," said Zûrafiérix as she descended to join Nûd and Rocky.

"Clearly," said Nûd. "They must have hit that big black rock."

"Look again," said Zûra. Nûd did and noticed both the ship and the *rock* were bobbing with the waves.

"It's not a rock, is it?" asked Nûd.

"It's a whale," said Zûra. "And it may have done some damage before they killed it."

"I've read about whales but reading about them doesn't prepare you for how *big* they are," said Nûd.

"Sort of like dragons," teased Zûra.

"Very *much* like dragons," Nûd replied. He and Rocky were now close enough to the ship that they could make out individual sailors—and *they* could see Zûrafiérix. Panic over rising water levels inside the ship was replaced by panic over Zûra's appearance. Nûd swooped between the masts to reassure them the dragon wasn't a threat. He saw a man and a woman on the aft ballista tilt it up to aim at Zûra and directed Rocky to land on an open square of deck beside them.

"The dragon's here to HELP you!" Nûd shouted. "Don't shoot!" He was sure that Zûra would shrug off ordinary crossbow bolts, but a missile as big around as his leg shot from a ballista might actually harm the dragon.

The man and woman paid no attention to Nûd and turned the ballista in its rotating mount to track Zûrafiérix. Nûd caught the woman by the neck of her leather jacket and pulled her away from her weapon, but the man continued to aim at the dragon. The woman turned and landed two quick punches in Nûd's abdomen, so he stepped in, slid a foot behind her knee, and tripped her to the deck. Rocky charged the man who remained with the ballista and smashed the not-inconsiderable weight of his body into the siege engine's frame. The ballista spun thirty degrees to starboard and discharged, sending its thick quarrel toward a stray cloud far from Zûrafiérix.

"Who's your captain?" shouted Nûd.

"I am," said the man at the ballista. "Néalach's my name. Who are you?"

"You wouldn't believe me if I told you, but you can call me Nûd."

"His Majesty, the king of Dâron," announced Zûrafiérix.

"If you have a dragon, maybe you *are* a king," said Néalach. "Kings and dragons go together in the old tales."

"Worry less about the old tales and more about your ship," said the woman Nûd had tripped. She was on her feet now and looking at Néalach like she doubted his sanity. "Stop being a fool and see if the dragon can lift us out of the water before we have to *swim* back to the Isle of Vines."

"This is my first mate, Náuta," said Néalach. "She's also my wife."

"I would have never guessed," said Nûd. Captain and mate both smiled. Nûd saw they were both in their mid-thirties with skin turned dark and hair turned light by the sun. "I'll ask Zûrafiérix if she can lift your ship," he said.

"The dragon has a name?" asked Náuta.

"They do in all the stories," said Néalach. He smiled up at Zûrafiérix and waved.

Zûrafiérix circled down and hovered just above the tops of the masts. "I want to pick it up amidships," she said. "But I can't fit between the masts. Do you have any rope?"

"It talks," said Náuta.

"Dragons do in all the stories," teased Néalach. He raised his head and called to Zûrafiérix. "We wouldn't be much of a whaling ship if we didn't have plenty of rope. I'll have the crew anchor lines to the sides and make loops large enough for you to lift with."

"Thank you," said the dragon, nodding her huge head.

"She's polite, too," said Náuta. "And don't try to tell me dragons are polite in all the stories!" She jumped down from the ballista platform and ordered various crew members to get busy tying off ropes. A few minutes later, Zûrafiérix held four loops of heavy harpooning line in her claws and the ship was a few feet above the surface of the water. "Tie off and go over the side!" Náuta shouted. "Hurry up with patching and caulking. We worked hard to catch that whale. We need to get it aboard before it sinks—and now we don't have to worry about sinking ourselves!"

Nûd was amused to hear crew members replying with "Aye aye, Capt'n Náuta, sir!"

"We're really co-captains," said Néalach softly. "I'm good at finding whales, Náuta's good at catching and processing them."

"Sounds like a productive partnership," said Nûd. A moment later he received a gentle nudge from Rocky. "Just like ours, boy, just like ours."

"Are they nearly done?" asked Zûrafiérix. "I'm not having any trouble holding up the ship, but I know we need to be going."

"They're just finishing up the second coat of pitch," said Náuta. She leaned over the side to confirm. "And now they're done. You can ease her down, most excellent dragon. You have my thanks and my husband's and our crew's."

"Glad to help," said Zûrafiérix, "though you can save the compliments and call me Zûra."

"Just doing what they say to do in the stories when you're talking to dragons," said Náuta. "Néalach would give me grief if I didn't."

"Very well," said the dragon. She hovered a few feet lower until the whaler was afloat again.

"Mind the torches with the fresh pitch!" Náuta instructed the crew.

"Yes, First Mate, ma'am," said a sailor showing off her pair of gold-capped front teeth. Nûd realized Náuta was demoted to first mate when she told the crew members what they already knew. He resolved not to make the same mistake trying to tell people how to do their jobs if and when he ever took the throne.

"Would you like a share of whale meat, Zûra?" asked Néalach. "You've earned it."

"Thank you for the offer, but I don't have time to stay and dine," said Zûra. "I ate one of those smaller black and white whales with the tall top fins many years ago and thought it was tasty. I'll have to come back and hunt for something larger once I take care of my current pressing business."

"Safe travels then," said Néalach.

"If you decide to come back and want to scout out whales for us from the air, we'd be glad to have you," added Náuta. "If we're not at sea you can find us on the Isle of Vines, west of the King's preserve on Bucket Island." She gave Nûd a hug. "Sorry for punching you," Náuta offered.

"Sorry for knocking you over in return," said Nûd.

"Have a nice trip, see you in the fall," said Náuta.

Rocky trumpeted and Zûrafiérix made her deep rumbling purr.

"You've never heard that one before?" asked Nûd as he climbed on Rocky's back.

Rocky's head moved side to side, then the wyvern launched himself up above the mast tops. Together, dragon, wyvern and wyvern-rider flew northeast into the moonlit sky to find the Bifurland fleet.

Chapter 44

With the Bifurland Fleet

The sun had set more than an hour ago, leaving the terrain below them limned only by starlight and moonlight. Given that the moon was close to full however, man, wyvern and dragon could identify major landmarks. They had found Insula Longa without difficulty.

"I see a long line of lights," said Zûrafiérix.

"Settlements on the north shore of the long island?" asked Nûd when he saw them too. He was back in his usual spot with Rocky flying close to Zûra's massive head. "No," he continued. "The farms there are too far apart. It's got to be the Bifurland fleet."

"Or Tamloch's fleet," Zûra offered.

"Maybe," said Nûd. "Time for a closer inspection?"

"Agreed," said Zûrafiérix. She prepared to angle her flightpath down toward the lights.

"Zûra," said Nûd.

"Yes?" the dragon responded.

"You probably don't want to fly directly over the fleet. They don't know you're an ally and dragons of your size are unprecedented."

"Yes, Your Majesty. Of course, Your Majesty. I will restrain my impulse to overawe the Bifurlanders and sink a few of their vessels just for show," said the dragon.

"I'm sorry," said Nûd. "I didn't mean to suggest you'd do anything of the sort. I'm still trying to figure things out."

"Understood," said Zûrafiérix. "May I recommend treating your partners and friends as intelligent beings capable of acting wisely and professionally."

Rocky turned his head to look at Nûd, reinforcing Zûra's message.

"Of course," said Nûd. "You're far wiser than I am."

Rocky nodded and faced forward again. Zûrafiérix made her rumbling purr sound of amusement.

"That remains to be seen," said the dragon. She was ready to maneuver closer to the lights.

"Zûra," said Nûd.

"Yes, Your Majesty?" asked the dragon cautiously.

"I want to double-check about something."

"Do you want to confirm I know how to break out of my shell?" asked Zûrafiérix. "There's no need to worry about that. With dragons, it's instinctual."

"I understand," said Nûd. "This is more a matter of ensuring logic will win out over instinct."

"Oh?" asked the dragon.

"You know the Bifurland fleet is carrying Roma legionnaires as well as Bifurlanders?"

"Yes," said Zûra.

"And Quintillius Marius Africanus, the governor-general of Occidens Province—the emperor's representative here in Orluin?"

"Y-e-s," said Zûra, drawing out the word as if the dragon was evaluating her feelings as she spoke.

"I'm not trying to cause offense or instruct you in breaking eggshells," said Nûd, "but are you confident you'll be able to treat *these* Roma as allies rather than enemies?"

Zûrafiérix flew on quietly for a few seconds, her huge blue eyes spinning hypnotically. Nûd shifted his head to watch the ground to give Zûra time to think. After a few more wing strokes, the dragon spoke.

"No offense was taken, my friend," she said. "In fact, it shows your wisdom and compassion that you cared enough to ask."

Nûd smiled at Zûra, confident her eyes would be able to mark his expression.

"Some dragons may be solely ruled by their passions..." Zûrafiérix continued, knowing that she and Nûd both knew she was referring to Viridáxés. "...but I am not one of them. I was taught from my hatching that my mission was to protect Dâron from a future Roma invasion, but since I slept through the Roma's arrival..."

"Fifteen-hundred years ago," noted Nûd.

"As you say," said Zûra. "Now where was I?"

"Sleeping through the Roma's invasion of Orluin."

"Right," said Zûrafiérix. "Reason tells me that my larger mission is to protect Dâron. I've seen that Túathal is a greater danger to Dâron than Quintillius and his legions or these strange new people from the far north you tell me are called Bifurlanders."

Nûd nodded. "So you're not going to start sinking ships, just because they're carrying Roma?"

A rumbling purr crossed the distance from the dragon to Nûd.

"I'll try to restrain those impulses," said Zûrafiérix.

"Glad to hear it," said Nûd. "If it's not an imposition, I have one more question?"

"Yes?" asked Zûra.

Nûd cleared his throat. "How do you plan to approach the Bifurlanders' fleet *without* frightening them into attacking you?"

"Ah," said Zûrafiérix. "Let me tell you something you may not know about dragons."

* * * * *

Rocky was recognized by lookouts on the Bifurland flagship, so he didn't have to dodge crossbow bolts as he descended. Quintillius, King Bjarni, and Queen Signý were waiting as the wyvern landed on an open spot on the deck behind the mast. Sigrun and Rannveigr ran up and began to fuss over Rocky as soon as his claws hit the planking. Nûd dismounted, waved to the girls—who didn't notice—and nodded to the adults before joining them.

"I guess I could be a pile of fish guts," said Nûd, smiling at Quin and the Bifurland monarchs.

"The girls don't often have a chance to play with a wyvern," said King Bjarni.

"I hope their dragons don't get jealous," said Queen Signý.

Those little gold dragons are in for a big surprise in the near future, thought Nûd. *I doubt they'll remember to feel jealous about Rocky.*

"He enjoys the attention," said Nûd as he watched Rocky turn his jaw for more efficient rubbing.

"It's good to see you, Your Majesty," said Quintillius. "I assume you're here to discuss more than jealous dragons?"

"Yes, actually," said Nûd, "though talking about dragons *is* high on my list." He was still feeling awkward when addressed as *Your Majesty*. Zûrafiérix seemed to only use his royal title when she thought he was getting too full of himself. "As king of Dâron, I thought it was important to make sure you had the latest information."

"You've decided to accept the throne then?" asked Bjarni.

"We'd heard you weren't sure you wanted the job," said Signý in a supportive tone.

"There have been some big changes since then," said Nûd. *"Very* big changes. That's what I wanted to talk to you about."

Rocky, Sigrun and Rannveigr had moved from the open area behind the mast to a spot along the port side gunwales. The wyvern and the girls were staring into the water beside the Bifurlanders' flagship.

"Mother! Father! Come look!" shouted Sigrun.

"Aunt Signý, Uncle Bjarni, Uncle Quin—you've *got* to see this!" added Rannveigr.

Bjarni and Signý stood up and stepped to the side of the ship, standing next to their niece and daughter.

Nûd spoke to Quintillius. "I didn't know you were related to Bifurland's royal family."

"I'm an honorary uncle," said the governor-general with a smile. "Sigrun is only a few years older than my Primus. Shall we join the others and see what's managed to excite the young ladies?"

"I think I know," said Nûd.

Three of the tall Roma's paces took him to stand behind Bjarni and Signý. His height allowed Quintillius to see what had captured everyone's attention—a pair of colossal blue orbs glowing like giant luminous jellyfish a dozen feet below the surface of the sound. "What *are* they?" Quin asked. "I've been in Orluin more than a decade and I've never seen anything remotely like them."

"They're spinning," observed Queen Signý.

"I think they're embedded in something scaly, like a crocodile on one of the southern rivers back in the empire," Quintillius after a quick intake of breath.

"I can't figure out what they are," said King Bjarni.

"That's easy," said Rannveigr.

"They're *eyes!*" said Sigrun.

"A kraken!" exclaimed Bjarni.

"On this side of the Ocean?" asked Queen Signý.

"Krakens can swim," said Bjarni. Signý frowned for a moment, then smiled at her husband affectionately. Nûd observed their interaction, comparing it to Eynon's parents. He spared a few seconds to feel sorry for himself since *he* didn't really have his parents around when he was growing up. After a brief indulgence in self-pity, he pulled his shoulders back and stood next to Quin. Nûd could see past Sigrun without any problem since she was leaning over the side of the ship trying to get closer to the unusual phenomenon.

"They *are* eyes!" Sigrun repeated.

Other crew members and supernumerary legionnaires joined the noble observers at the side of the ship. The flagship's captain had to impose order and only allow half the crew and Roma to line the port side so the longship didn't tip too far in that direction. Sigrun and Rannveigr's small gold dragons bugled from their perch at the prow. Rocky made a similar sound an octave lower. Their calls echoed across the sound, joined by shouts from crew and legionnaires as the blue orbs began to rise.

Nûd watched Quintillius shift farther forward to put his hand on the arm of a legionnaire about to throw a seven-foot iron-tipped pilum at the rising eyes, preventing her from releasing her spear. *Something like that would just bounce off Zûra's scales,* thought Nûd, *but maybe her eyes were more vulnerable.* He smiled as Zûrafiérix lifted her head above the surface. Salt water dripped from it in five hundred small waterfalls. The dragon noticed Nûd standing at the rail.

"Did you tell them?" Zûrafiérix asked Nûd.

"I hadn't gotten around to it," said Nûd, smiling at the dragon. Zûra's head was now a few feet higher than the longship's deck. It was as big as the ship from prow to mast and the wet scales covering it sparkled in the moonlight. Nûd knew the bulk of Zûra's body extended back underwater several ship lengths. The dragon made a rumbling purr somewhere in her throat that sent ripples through the water.

"Zûrafiérix, meet King Bjarni and Queen Signý of Bifurland," said Nûd. "These girls are Sigrun and Rannveigr, their daughter and niece."

"It's a pleasure to meet you all," said Zûra, tilting her head to acknowledge the Bifurlanders.

"You're a *dragon?*" asked Sigrun after she'd closed her open mouth.

"We ride dragons," added Rannveigr. The small gold dragons by the prow trumpeted their existence—and respect for Zûra—to support Rannveigr's words.

"Our dragons are nowhere near as big as you are, mighty Zûrafiérix!" said Sigrun. "Do you think you could let us ride *you?*"

"Certainly," said Zûrafiérix. "I'd be glad to give you *and* your dragons and your whole family a ride some day, but not now. We have important things to do."

"That's fine," said Sigrun.

"It would be better to get a ride in daylight anyway," added Rannveigr. "Don't you think so, Aunt Signý?"

Queen Signý didn't answer. She was too busy staring.

Quintillius returned to Nûd's side. The legionnaire with the pilum stood nearby, looking chastened. Her spear wasn't quite as tall as the governor-general. Quin looked at Nûd and raised an eyebrow, reminding Nûd of his manners.

"Zûrafiérix," he said, "this is Quintillius Marius Africanus, governor of Roma's Occidens Province, and the victorious general who conquered Timbuktu for the empire."

"I am honored to meet such a magnificent dragon," said Quin. "I can only imagine the power and might that's still beneath the surface but look forward to admiring your immense form once it's fully revealed."

"Thank you," said Zûrafiérix as her rumbling purr grew louder. "Are all Roma so well-spoken?"

"A wise leader must use words as his legionnaires—and his diplomats," said Quintillius, smiling.

"She's a beautiful big snake isn't she, governor-general sir?" noted the legionnaire with the pilum.

"Even your foot soldiers have a way with words," said Zûrafiérix. "Do you think I might trouble you to scratch my right eye ridge with that spear, good woman? This salt water is making it itch."

The legionnaire looked at Quintillius for confirmation and he nodded his approval. She stowed her pilum on her back and jumped across the short distance from the ship's deck to Zûra's upper neck. While Zûrafiérix was having her eye ridge scratched, Nûd filled Bjarni, Signý, and Quintillius in on the latest details.

"Your friend Doethan managed to connect with my wife, Laetícia, earlier and she passed on the plan of attack," said Quin. "We're ready to do our part, aren't we?" he asked, looking at Bjarni and Signý. They nodded.

"It makes more sense now that I've seen how big you are with my own eyes," said King Bjarni. "If Túathal controls an even bigger dragon..."

"Zûrafiérix is slightly larger than Viridáxés in my estimation," said Nûd.

"I'm very glad this good dragon is on *our* side," said Queen Signý. "We can hope one great dragon can neutralize another."

"Something like that," said Zûrafiérix.

"The primary goal is to discredit Túathal in the eyes of the people of Tamloch," said Quintillius.

"Is it true that the handsome strawberry merchant is really the king of Tamloch, not Dâron?" asked Sigrun.

Nûd hadn't noticed the girls were now listening in on the conversation instead of watching the legionnaire's skillful work with her pilum. "Yes," he said. "And it seems that *I'm* the true king of Dâron."

"*And* you've got a dragon!" said Rannveigr.

"It's more like I have a new friend who happens to *be* a dragon," said Nûd. "Zûrafiérix doesn't belong to anyone."

"That sounds like something a king would say," said Sigrun.

"Do you plan to scout out the Tamloch fleet on your way to Riyas?" asked Quintillius. "Laetícia says Grand Admiral Sónnel may have reservations about supporting Túathal."

"Good to know," said Nûd.

Their conversation was interrupted by a bellow of alarm from Rocky. The wyvern's neck was pointing up at a robed figure on a flying disk a quarter-mile ahead of their course, silhouetted by the almost full moon.

"Speaking of the Tamloch fleet," said Quintillius.

"I'd bet a mug of mead against a tankard of sorghum beer that's an observer from Grand Admiral Sónnel," said King Bjarni.

"I won't take the bet, but I'll take the mead," said Quintillius.

"I'm going to follow that wizard back to the Grand Admiral," said Nûd. He called up to Zûrafiérix. "Do you think you can reach the Tamloch fleet swimming, or will you need to fly?"

"That depends on how far ahead they are," said Zûrafiérix. "Once this kind legionnaire hops off, I'll get some altitude and see if I can spot their ships without them seeing me, then use my best judgment on how to approach them."

"Excellent," said Nûd.

Rocky had turned to look at him, as if to say *why are you wasting time talking?*

"Good luck, Your Majesty," said Quintillius. He handed Nûd the pilum he'd borrowed from the legionnaire who'd just climbed back aboard. "Take this with you," he said. "You might find it useful."

"Uh, thanks!" said Nûd, clutching the long spear. He ran across the deck to Rocky, jumped on the wyvern's back, found a spot for the pilum in close reach, and strapped himself on. "Follow that wizard, boy. Up, up and away!"

Chapter 45

Fercha and Verro

Fercha had just finished inspecting the last segment of the wide gate from Dâron to Tamloch. It was even larger than the gate she'd helped create for the Roma and nearly the size of the one connecting the battlefield with the wisent herds in Melyncárreg. The uprights of *this* gate were formed from two huge pine trees more than a hundred feet tall. All their branches had been stripped halfway up their trunks. Heavy rope impregnated with powdered green mage-stones connected the trees a third of the way to the top. Flat pavers coated with magestone dust were laid in a channel between the trees, completing the circuit.

A few minutes ago, Fercha had confirmed the wide gate connected the Tamloch army's camp off the battlefield south of Brendinas to the marshalling field immediately west of Riyas. She'd walked through it to Riyas and back as a final test, noting that the sun was closer to setting in Tamloch than in Dâron. *The world is a sphere,* Fercha reminded herself, *like a complete shield of solidified sound. Of course the sun will be farther away from the horizon here than in Riyas.*

She felt a vibration on the third finger of her left hand and smiled, always glad to hear from the person connected to *that* ring. Fercha expanded the plain gold band and heard the standard three chimes indicating the connection was active.

"Have you completed your project, dear lady?" asked Verro.

"Yes, but I still have to report to Dârio and Duke Háiddon to let them know it's safe to use," Fercha replied. "You can come through it if you'd like. I'd love to see you."

"That's why I got in touch," said Verro. "I really don't want to haul all the drawings I've found out to the marshalling field. Can we meet at your townhouse?"

"Certainly," said Fercha, "though we won't have any time to spare for ourselves."

"I know, my love, much as I'd like to spend time in bed with you."

"With luck we'll have more chances for that soon," said Fercha. "Come through, then. I'm glad it will save you the trouble of lugging piles of parchment."

"I'll need your help," said Verro.

"With what? The code? You know it's our..."

"No, not the code for the gate to your bedchamber. That's permanently etched on my brain. I'm going to need your help finding Eynon and Merry," said Verro. "They're supposed to be practicing in the Great Hall and I can't count on word having reached the palace guards in Brendinas that I'm now an ally, not an enemy."

"I can get there faster if I gate from the inn to Brendinas then *walk* to my townhouse," said Fercha. "I'll inform Dârio and the Duke and will be in your arms in less than half an hour."

"I thought you said there wouldn't be time for us to dally?"

"My help has a price," said Fercha. "I'll accept nothing less than a proper hug and kiss."

"I was thinking of something more like an *improper* demonstration of my affection," said Verro.

"Let me see how fast I can get there," said Fercha. "Blast! If Tuto was here I could send *him* to inform Dârio, then walk through *this* gate and join you in Riyas. That would be faster still."

"Hoo!" said Verro.

"What?" asked Fercha. "You know Tuto—my owl familiar." She stopped suddenly, smiled, and wagged her index finger at Verro's image on the other side of the interface. "Oh," she said. *"Hoo* not *who.* You'll pay for that next time I have you at my mercy."

"Promises, promises," said Verro. He grinned and so did Fercha. "I'll see you at your townhouse in half an hour."

"Or less," added Fercha. She dispelled the connection and boarded her flying disk, arrowing her way down the ranks of troops arrayed to cross through the gate until she reached Dârio and Jenet.

"Aunt Fercha!" said Dârio. "Is the gate to Riyas in working order?"

"It is," said Fercha. "You can send the army through. I wish I could stay and assist you, but I can't. I have to get to Brendinas in a hurry and am taking the gate at the inn. See you. 'Bye." Fercha's flying disk and the wizard riding it disappeared toward the south without another word.

Jenet leaned close to Dârio. "What do you think *that's* about?" she whispered.

"I'm not sure," said Dârio, "but I'd guess Verro has something to do with it."

* * * * *

Fercha tapped on the leaded glass of her bedchamber's tall windows, which were locked. "Let me in!" she insisted.

Verro smiled at her from inside and put his hand to his ear. "What?" he mouthed, turning the smile into a grin. Fercha was sure he hadn't actually said anything but was simply trying to torment her.

"Open these blasted windows immediately or I'll never sleep with you again," said Fercha softly. *Two could play at this game!* she considered.

Verro leaned forward and twisted a pair of latches holding the windows tight to their frames. He gave the twin windows a delicate push with his fingertips. Fercha didn't wait for them to swing open. She stuck her hands between them and spread the tall windows wide. They flew apart so fast they almost slammed against their shutters.

"Careful, you might break a pane," said Verro, "and that would be..."

Fercha was kissing Verro before he could finish his sentence. She'd tipped her flying disk so they were both of equal height and made sure her arms were wrapped tightly around Verro's neck and shoulders. Verro used his long arms to remove any hint of distance between them. After a few timeless moments, they broke their kiss and smiled at each other.

"Thirteen years bad luck," said Verro.

"That's only for mirrors," said Fercha.

"It would be a pain, anyway," said Verro.

"But it *is* made of panes and besides, I didn't break any," answered Fercha. She sent out long cylinders of solidified sound to close and lock the windows behind her. "I'm early," she announced.

"I noticed," said Verro. "That's my *good* luck."

"And mine," said Fercha. "We'll have to hurry. Eynon and Merry and Inthíra need those drawings you brought from Riyas. They need time to practice!" She pulled her robes over her head and tossed them on a chair, then pushed past Verro to fall back on her bed.

"Why don't *we* ever get time to practice?" Verro protested, adding his green wizard's robes to Fercha's blue ones.

"Perhaps it's because we're so good at it already?" teased Fercha.

* * * * *

Twenty minutes later, Fercha and Verro were wearing their robes again and preparing to float out the windows where Fercha had recently entered her townhouse. They each had a large chest with a rounded top of the sort pirates used to bury treasure in children's stories behind them on their flying disks.

"What did you do?" asked Verro as he grinned at Fercha. "Your hair doesn't look like a dandelion."

"I poured water on it to cool off after our *exercise,*" said Fercha with a sultry smile to tease him. "You were there when I did it. My hair looks different when it's wet. I wish I *could* look like myself, but it will take an hour or so for it to dry while we're on our way."

"Maybe I can help with that," said Verro, moving closer. He created a hemisphere of solidified sound above Fercha's hair, then generated a small ball of magic that glowed red beneath it.

"Oooo! That feels wonderful," said Fercha. "I'll have to try it myself."

"Glad to be of assistance," said Verro. "Is it dry yet?"

"Oh yes," said Fercha. "Toasty."

"Good," said Verro, banishing the hemisphere and the red ball. "There's one more thing. Turn around."

"Very well," said Fercha, curious to see what her lover would do.

Verro held his hands around Fercha's dry hair and shot ten tiny bolts of lightning toward it from his fingertips. Moments later, her hair stood out from her head like the dandelion in seed Verro had referenced earlier. Fercha stepped around the chest on the back of her flying disk and crossed to the full-length mirror in her bedchamber. She smiled when she saw her hair had returned to its usual configuration.

"Was that acceptable?" asked Verro.

"Yes," said Fercha. "You can do that for me every morning."

"Of course, dear," said Verro.

Fercha smiled at Verro, reboarded her flying disk and led him out the leaded-glass windows toward the palace.

Verro extended his long arm and touched her shoulder. "Aren't you going to close and lock the windows?" he asked.

"That's taken care of," replied Fercha. "I have an enchanted broom with arms to handle such things."

"You mean you didn't need *me* to open the windows and let you in?" asked Verro.

"Of course not," said Fercha. "But where would the fun have been in that?"

Verro shook his head.

"What?" asked Fercha.

"I'm impressed, that's all."

"By an animated broom?"

"By your continuing capacity to amaze me," replied Verro. "We've been married for more than twenty years and you're still able to surprise me."

"It's not hard when we only spend one night together every two or three months," said Fercha.

"Was that an oblique complaint about my performance?" teased Verro.

"Not at all," said Fercha. "That was *quite* satisfactory as you well know." She sighed.

"What's wrong, my love?" asked Verro.

"I hope that however things sort out with Túathal and Nûd and Dârio and the dragons that the two of us can finally have a chance to live together openly..." said Fercha.

"...and share a bed *every* night," declared Verro.

Their hands reached out and clasped, bumping the edges of their flying disks together.

"Yes," said Fercha. "Exactly."

Daylight was fading, and the shadows were long between the three and four-story buildings in this part of Brendinas. Fercha and Verro were focused on each other, whispering softly and making plans for their future lives together, Fercha guiding them toward the palace by rote. They didn't see two wizards on flying disks with passengers turn a corner from a cross street and nearly collide with them. One of the wizards had shaggy hair and lightning reflexes. Before Fercha and Verro could react and raise their shields, Shaggy Hair directed a pair of transparent clubs made from solidified sound at the lovers' heads and used the generated bludgeons to smack their skulls together.

"Treasure chests!" exclaimed Fox from his spot behind Kennig.

"Looks like we won't be returning home empty-handed after all," said Kennig.

Fercha and Verro had slumped down on their flying disks. Their bodies were draped over the chests and their faces were hidden. Lacking active magical guidance, both flying disks began to descend.

"Want me t' put quarrels through their chests?" asked Fool as he raised and cocked his crossbow.

"After we take their magestones and strip their bodies," said Grúgàch, the shaggy-haired southern Clan Lands wizard. "It would be a shame to put holes in that nice fabric."

"And blood is so hard to wash out," added Fox. "How will we transport the chests?"

"Put them on our flying disks," said Kennig. "You'll have to sit on them. It will be awkward, but it's not far to the cave."

People on the street hadn't noticed the conflict above them initially, but when a pair of flying disks with unconscious wizards descended to the cobblestones, townspeople started shouting.

"Are they drunk?" asked a drayman.

"What's in the chests I wonder?" asked a young woman in a stained butcher's apron.

"Let's open them and see!" shouted a prosperous-looking man wearing a tall peaked cap.

Soon dozens of people had gathered around Fercha and Verro, poking at their bodies and trying to determine how to open the chests. Their cries brought more people and soon a substantial crowd had gathered, their excited voices carrying.

"Back away!" shouted Grúgàch, "Or I'll blast ya where ya stand!" A small fireball exploded in the air above the crowd.

"I've got this," said Kennig. He pushed a rod of solidified sound down into the assembly and transformed it into a cylinder that widened and pushed people aside.

"Nicely done," said Fox.

"I'm *so* glad I've earned your approval," said Kennig as he shook his head. "Get down there and open the chests." Kennig pushed Fox to the edge of his flying disk and the oldest Mastlands brother jumped the four remaining feet to the ground. Fool jumped before Grúgàch could do the same to him.

"Those are southern Clan Lands wizards!" shouted the man in the peaked cap. He and dozens of others began to pound on the walls of Kennig's cylindrical shield. Many in the crowd called for the city guards—some even left to find them.

Fool stood above his brother, pointing his crossbow menacingly, while Fox worked at opening the chest on Verro's flying disk. He had to push Verro's limp body off the chest before he could reach the latches and throw them. Verro's body fell face down.

"You're good with locks, brother," said Fool. "I'm sure you can get it open."

Fox, by far the smartest of the four Mastlands brothers—which wasn't saying much—tried opening the chest with*out* picking the lock. The lid swung back with only a slight protest from unhappy hinges.

"That was fast work," said Fool.

"Shut up," said Fox. He stared into the box and looked up at Kennig and Grúgàch. "It's full of paper—no jewels, no gold, no silver."

"Look them over," said Kennig. "If they're letters of credit they may still be worth something."

"They're diagrams and architects' drawings," Fox complained. "They're all related to buildings and streets and such in *Riyas*. Why would two wizards be carrying such things?"

"One of them *does* have green robes," said Kennig. "Perhaps he's a traitor delivering details about secret entrances into Tamloch's capital to spies at the king of Dâron's palace."

"Perchance th' wench is a blue-tabard spy?" suggested Grúgàch.

"Let's take them with us then," said Kennig. He now thought he knew the two wizards' identities. "We can sell them to the highest bidder later."

"Why couldn't it have been gold and silver?" muttered Fool as he put his crossbow on the ground. He shifted to his knees to remove Fercha's artifact and magestone. Before he could stick his hand down the front of her robes, a bright light appeared above the intersection, exploding into a hundred pulsing shades of angry red and orange.

"You are surrounded!" came a deep voice above them. Sizable squads of city guards with swords and truncheons marched toward the invaders along three streets leading to the intersection. Their boots hitting the cobblestones echoed off the walls of the nearby buildings. "There are a dozen wizards ready to burn you off your flying disks," the deep voice continued. "Put down your weapons. Ground your disks. Take off your magestones and put them in the center of your disks, then back away ten paces. I will count to three and if you haven't complied, you'll be incinerated."

The civilians standing nearby took that as their cue to leave. Most were too busy running to scream.

"One."

Fool shoved his crossbow away from him and Fercha. He was lucky it didn't go off as it spun around before coming to a stop. In a practiced motion, he laced his hands behind his head and stared at the dirty street.

"Two."

Fox tossed *his* crossbow toward the curb and removed his sword and three knives of assorted lengths hidden at various places on his body. Kennig lowered his flying disk to street level and dropped his artifact on top of it before backing away.

"Three."

Grúgàch launched himself straight up toward the bright light, sending fireballs ahead of him. When he rose above the light he saw a dozen wizards arrayed around him. He felt a sphere of solidified sound circling his head and knew he would soon be unconscious or asphyxiated, so he held up his hands and indicated his surrender. One of the wizards—the blasted boy with the red magestone— pointed down, so he returned to street level with his hands still above his head. He felt someone touch his wrist and remove the leather bracer there that held *his* magestone. Someone tied Grúgàch's hands behind his back.

"All clear," said Merry. "I got Shaggy Hair and two Mastlands boys."

"And I got Kennig," said Inthíra. "I'll hang on to the wizards' magestones until the city guards arrive."

The prisoners looked at each other uneasily but didn't say anything. Then the bright red-orange light, the city guards, and the wizards still circling above winked out. Eynon landed his flying disk near Fercha and Verro. He touched their throats, feeling for their pulses.

"They're hurt, but not badly damaged I think," said Eynon. "It's a good thing for them we were outside heading for the Conclave complex instead of still inside the Great Hall."

"It's a good thing for them we heard all the shouting," added Merry.

Chee nodded vigorously from Eynon's shoulder. "Cheeee," he said solemnly.

"They need healing potions," said Eynon. "Should I fly down to the inn to fetch Uirsé, so she can apply some of hers?"

"There's no need for that," said Inthíra. "There are racks of them in the vaults beneath the Conclave's octagonal hall. I know the necessary codes to access them."

"Wonderful," said Merry. "Now what are we going to with *these* idiots?" she asked, pointing to their attackers.

A squad of *real* city guards chose that moment to appear, answering her question.

Chapter 46

Túathal and Viridáxés

Túathal held on to a ridge of bone on the back of Viridáxés' skull and stared into the dusky landscape below. The sun was nearly down and Viridáxés had slowed his pace after inviting Túathal to ride high on his neck so the two of them could share a semi-private conversation. The dragon didn't want to risk losing the king if he fell from his more precarious perch. For Túathal's part, he felt warmer riding on Viridáxés' neck than he had on his back.

"There are *so* many more settlements now," said Viridáxés. "When I was buried the only population centers in Tamloch were Riyas and Bhaile Pónaire, along with Brendinas and Tyford in Dâron. There was an inn and trading post near the mouth of the Abbenoth and another south of Brendinas, but that was it. Now there are as many small settlements as there are clovers in a green meadow."

Túathal nodded, then remembered even Viridáxés' huge eyes couldn't see him on the back of the dragon's neck. "Very true," said Túathal. "Both kingdoms have grown—which is only to be expected over two thousand years."

"I expect the Roma have expanded since *they* invaded, too," said Viridáxés. "I'd like to incinerate every Roma who set foot on western shores."

"Singe the feathers of all the Eagle People, eh?" asked Túathal.

"More than that," said Viridáxés. "I want to burn them all to ash."

"Dragons *do* have a reputation for being bloodthirsty," said Túathal.

"It's well deserved, I assure you," said Viridáxés. "Look, there's the Abbenoth! It's unmistakable."

Túathal leaned to his right and saw the north-south flowing ribbon of water glinting below them. They'd made excellent time heading for Riyas and were ahead of schedule. It would be valuable for him to learn just how powerful Viridáxés could be *before* they arrived at Tamloch's capital.

"Change course," said Túathal. "Head upriver and you'll have a chance to attack the Roma now instead of later."

"Truly," said Viridáxés. "You are a most excellent king to provide such an opportunity. I hear and obey." The dragon banked left and accelerated. Túathal clutched the ridge of bone on Viridáxés' neck with greater intensity.

The sun was down now and Túathal could no longer see the ground. He wondered if Viridáxés had the same problem. "Can *you* see what's below us?" the king asked.

"Well enough," said Viridáxés. "Dragon's have excellent night vision."

"So I've heard," said Túathal. "Humans, unfortunately, do not— unless they're wizards. At times like this I miss my brother."

"A wizard?" asked Viridáxés.

"Yes," said Túathal, "and one who tried to strangle me. Quite a few wizards would prefer me dead, I understand."

"I'll burn them all," said Viridáxés.

"Don't burn my brother Verro," said Túathal. "He's family—and I'd prefer to deal with him myself."

"As you wish, Your Majesty," said Viridáxés. "I see something ahead. It's a big castle on a point on the west side of the Abbenoth where the river narrows. There's a smaller fortification on the opposite bank as well."

"I see them," said Túathal. "There are torches burning on top of the walls. Fly past them and find a place to land that seems unoccupied so we can plan our attack."

"Certainly, Your Majesty," said Viridáxés, "though I'd be glad to simply swoop down and blast the castle."

"Not with more than forty Tamloch nobles on your back," said Túathal. "You can drop us somewhere safe, *then* blast the castle."

"If I must," said Viridáxés. "I hear and obey. It *is* the sensible thing to do. I will rely on your wisdom."

"See that you do," said Túathal. "You'll be fine if you do exactly what I say at all times."

Viridáxés snorted, making his throat quiver.

Túathal could feel the vibration through the ridge of bone he grasped. "Enough of that sort of attitude," he said.

"My apologies, Your Majesty," said Viridáxés.

The dragon circled then glided down to land on a hill on the east side of the river. The Tamloch nobles and Túathal disembarked from the dragon's back and neck and stretched their legs. The rising moon allowed Túathal to see their current location had an excellent view of the castle on the point to the west and the smaller fort on this bank.

"Do you see a great chain across the river?" asked Túathal.

"I do," said Viridáxés. "Its function is stopping ships on the Abbenoth, I presume?"

"Correct," said Túathal. "I want it removed so the northern Clan Landers can sail their barges south all the way to Nova Eboracum."

"Thus harming the Roma," said Viridáxés. "I approve."

"Your approval is irrelevant," said Túathal. "As the king, I expect your obedience. Reduce the castle to rubble, if you're able."

"If I'm *able?*" roared the affronted dragon. "No stone will remain atop another."

Túathal had been thinking three steps ahead. "Try not to kill *all* the people inside," he said.

"Why *not?*" asked Viridáxés. "That's more than half the fun."

"Because the survivors will go south to Nova Eboracum," said Túathal. "They'll tell the people in the provincial capital about your magnificence and power, making it more likely they'll surrender without a fight."

"Then can I kill them?" asked Viridáxés. "Defeating the Roma is my purpose in life, or so the Founders told me."

"No, you can't kill them," said Túathal. "After they surrender, they'll cease being Roma and become citizens of Tamloch—my subjects. You will *not* kill my subjects, understand?"

"I understand," said the dragon, chuffing slowly and emitting small puffs of green smoke from his huge nostrils. "But that certainly takes the joy out of *my* role in the process. I expect it's wise, though," said Viridáxés. "That must be why I was told to serve the king, rather than follow my own judgment."

"The Founders knew what they were doing," said Túathal, not knowing or caring whether they actually did so long as Viridáxés obeyed him. He waved the dragon toward the castle. "Go!" said Túathal. "Prove that you do as well."

"Watch me, Your Majesty," said Viridáxés. The dragon took four strides down the slope, leaving deep gouges in the hillside, and launched himself into the moonlit sky. Torches were lit on the battlements of the castle on the point across the Abbenoth, but it was still difficult to see Viridáxés soaring high above, unless some alert soldier happened to spot reflected light from his polished scales.

The other Tamloch nobles kept their distance, but Duke Néillen stepped over and stood beside Túathal. They both followed the dragon's movements. "That was a bit of luck for us, wasn't it, Your Majesty?" asked the duke.

"Luck?" asked Túathal. "Or destiny?"

"Destiny, of course, Your Majesty!" said Néillen quickly. "You were destined to command a dragon."

Túathal chuckled and Néillen kept his face impassive. When Túathal sounded amused it could be either good news or bad news for anyone nearby. This time it was good news.

"No need to spread butter and jam on me like a slice of hot bread," said the king. "I know it was luck Viridáxés arrived when he did. It was also luck earlier when Uirsé got it into her head to *save* me instead of letting me die after Princess Gwýnnett tried to kill me."

"Especially after how much you used to torment her," said Duke Néillen. "Speaking of the princess, did I hear her name when you were communicating with someone by ring earlier?"

"You did," said Túathal. "Hibblig, one of her tame wizards, made a case that Gwýnnett might still be useful to me. I may need her abilities to help Dârio serve as my heir, instead of trying to depose me."

"Dârio may still try," said the duke, not mentioning the fact that Túathal had sworn fealty to Dârio on the battlefield before he'd fallen to the ground from Gwýnnett's treachery.

"He wouldn't be my son if he didn't," said Túathal.

Dârio doesn't seem much like his father as far as I can tell, thought Néillen. "Some thought Dârio *was* the king of Tamloch after you named him as your heir and collapsed," said the duke. "Many thought you were dead."

"At least you're glad I'm not," said Túathal. "You'd lose your dukedom if that happened."

Duke Néillen nodded, remembering his conversation with Dârio on that matter. Even in the dim moonlight Túathal could see a thick artery on his earl marshal's neck pulsing below his intricate tattoos. "I don't like her, Your Majesty."

"Gwýnnett?" asked Túathal. "Neither do I. But I don't have to *like* her for her to be useful to me—much the same as it is with the two of *us.*"

"Your Majesty?"

"Don't worry," said Túathal. "I'm not planning to kill you in the morning." The king made another of his hard-to-read laughs.

"That's reassuring," said the duke.

"I doubt you *like* me and I certainly don't like *you* beyond appreciating your ruthlessness and skills as a military commander," said Túathal. "I know you support me for the power my patronage gives you—and I know that the kingdom's nobility would never tolerate you, a rough soldier with a dukedom less than a decade old, as their king."

Duke Néillen performed a quick mental calculation and determined that Túathal was in the mood for plain speech before he answered. "Unlike your cousin Grand Admiral Sónnel, eh?"

Túathal glanced over at the clumps of Tamloch nobles further along the hillside. "They would have tried to replace me with Sónnel years ago if my cousin had shown the least interest in being king," he said.

"If he had shown interest, he would have soon been the *late* Grand Admiral Sónnel," replied Néillen.

"Precisely," said Túathal. "Look! Viridáxés is preparing to strike." He pointed southwest across the Abbenoth. People on the castle's walls had seen the dragon. Their combined shouts and screams were loud enough to be heard across the water. Two dozen crossbow bolts clattered against Viridáxés' scales like hail on a slate roof. They shattered whenever they struck.

"He's going for the chain first," said Duke Néillen.

They watched in awe as Viridáxés crashed like a descending thunderbolt onto a flat stretch of dressed stone by the castle's foundations next to the anchor point for one end of the chain. Each link was forged from iron as thick as a man's body. The dragon let out a roar that echoed off the walls of the castle and bounced out across the surrounding hills. Viridáxés pulled back his long neck then straightened it and shot out an impressive jet of green fire that melted the closest link like so much candle wax. Grasping one of the undamaged links in his front claws, the great dragon pulled the chain free and sent tall waves across the river from the beating of his colossal wings when he returned aloft.

"Now for the other end of the chain," said Túathal, showing a rare smile. He was pleased how well Viridáxés was following his instructions. Realizing they were overmatched, hundreds of legionnaires, slaves and families streamed out of the west point's castle. The people leaving to the south formed a well-disciplined river of refugees flowing parallel to the Abbenoth. *They may make it to the next castle south before they freeze,* he thought. *Some of them are wearing cloaks, at least.*

Viridáxés flew higher until the chain was held taut at an angle. He looked like a terrifying kite at the end of an iron string. His eyes were spinning angrily, and huge clouds of smoke formed a green nimbus around his head. Viridáxés' chest expanded, and he shifted his head to face the chain's second anchor point at the small fort on the opposite bank. Hot flames emerged from the dragon's mouth and flew like a javelin toward the eastern shore of the Abbenoth, cutting that end of the chain as easily as a sword would sever a limb. No longer a kite but a missile, Viridáxés' beating wings pulled him higher with a river's width of heavy chain dangling beneath him.

"Yes!" shouted Duke Néillen. Impressed cheers came from the other Tamloch nobles nearby, a counterpoint to the increased screams from the defenders remaining in the west point's castle.

"Watch," said Túathal. "He's going to use the chain like a whip!"

As if Viridáxés could hear his master's words, the dragon gained even more altitude, then tilted his wings and began to corkscrew down toward the fortified stronghold. Viridáxés' body's rotation transferred speed and torque to the chain. Its end struck the portcullis in the middle of the east wall—the one facing the river—demolishing both wall and entrance in one blow. Great stones toppled like piles of wooden blocks kicked by a petulant child.

Too bad the battlements were empty, thought Túathal. *A few defenders' deaths would have made the stories of the dragon's wrath more compelling. No matter,* he observed. *There are still three more walls.*

Then there were only two. Viridáxés rose back up and made three quick spins, wrapping most of the chain around his torso. Adding the mass of the chain to his own gargantuan bulk, the dragon fell at an angle toward the north wall, turning just before he struck so the momentum of his entire chain-wrapped body was transferred to the castle's wall in a single instant. Stones the size of carriages flew out from the impact. Many landed in snowbanks near escaping members of the garrison, prompting even more cries of terror.

"That was impressive," said Duke Néillen. "I don't know how I'd defend against an attack like that."

"I do," said Túathal. "You have a strong sense of self-preservation. You'd surrender when a king commanding a dragon made a polite request to do so."

"I'd strip every bed I could find and wave a hundred white flags as soon as I even *saw* a dragon the size of Viridáxés," said the duke. "Grand Admiral Sónnel will be glad he decided to stick to the fleet, not try for the throne."

"I'm more concerned about what my *son* has planned," said Túathal. "If I were Dârio I'd be moving the army of Dâron through our wide gate straight to Riyas, hoping to take the city before Viridáxés and I can get there. He'll hope I'll be reluctant to attack my own capital."

"A miscalculation on his part?" asked Néillen.

"What do *you* think?" replied Túathal.

"I think an example of what a dragon can do would be quite instructive for the people of Riyas. Particularly the nobility that have been less than happy with your draconian rule," said Duke Néillen. "They need to see that it can quickly become a lot *more* draconian. You'll have to let Viridáxés know that sometimes it *is* permitted to harm your subjects—especially when they need to be taught a lesson."

"Absolutely," said Túathal. "I'm impressed."

"By my analysis?" asked the duke.

"No," said Túathal. "By the fact that you knew the word draconian."

"Self-taught doesn't mean ignorant," said Néillen.

"A good lesson for me to learn," said Túathal. He pointed at the castle. "It's on fire!"

"Falling torches must have set it alight," said Néillen.

"Not unless you know how to make torches burn green," said Túathal.

"Soak the wood in a copper sulfate solution," said Néillen.

"You're full of surprises today, Earl Marshal," said Túathal. "I think a more likely answer is dragon fire."

"Under present circumstances, I must agree Your Majesty," said the duke, smiling. "Viridáxés is heating the foundation stones until they crack and crumble. Once that happens, the walls fall on their own."

"I did order him to leave no stone atop another," said Túathal. "But I think we've made our point."

"True," said Duke Néillen, "and we do have a schedule to keep if we want to get to Riyas by dawn."

Túathal nodded. "I wonder how I can get Viridáxés' attention?"

"You're his master," said the duke. "Call to him. He may be attuned to the sound of your voice. We can have everyone here shout his name at once if you think that will help."

"Let me try it without assistance first," said Túathal. "If your theory is correct it would be quite convenient." Túathal cupped his hands to his mouth and tried to project his voice the way the heralds at his court in Riyas made announcements. He wasn't sure the dragon would be able to hear anything softer than a peal of thunder on the other side of the river. "Viridáxés! Enough!" said Túathal. "Well done, but it's time to be on our way."

Túathal was pleased when he saw Viridáxés ascend from the center of the ruined castle and land on the hillside in front of him a few wing beats later.

"I brought the chain, Your Majesty," said the dragon. "I thought it might be useful if we need to knock down any walls in Riyas." Viridáxés practically glowed with joy from finally having a chance to use his strength against the Roma.

"Good thinking," said Túathal.

"And we don't want to leave it here," said Duke Néillen. "They might string it back across the river."

"Also good thinking," said Túathal. "And the chain might make it easier for those of us riding you to hang on."

"Very good, Your Majesty," said Viridáxés. "I'm ready to leave when you are."

Túathal, Néillen, and the Tamloch nobles resumed their spots on the dragon's back. As they flew on to Tamloch's capital, smoke from the ruined castle behind them formed a column tall enough to touch the clouds.

Chapter 47

Túathal and Néillen

"Your Majesty," said Duke Néillen from his position sitting next to Túathal on Viridáxés' back. "Have you considered the matter of troops to counter Dârio's army?"

"You don't think a dragon is enough to counter an army?" asked Túathal. "Two or three blasts of fire from Viridáxés will send Dârio's soldiers scurrying back to Dâron. Besides, the people of Riyas *love* me. I've been their king for more than a decade. I'm certain they will support me."

Duke Néillen wasn't as confident about the people of Riyas as his patron. Inexperienced townsfolk wouldn't fare well against trained troops, and Túathal vastly overestimated how much his subjects loved him. The king's public floggings for minor offenders and hangings for political malcontents ensured that.

"It might still be a good idea to collect additional forces of our own, just in case," said the duke. "We can use them to garrison key strongholds once Viridáxés convinces Dârio's army to surrender and go back to Dâron."

"What forces do you have in mind?" asked Túathal. "We can't depend on the marines with the fleet. Grand Admiral Sónnel may well decide that arriving in Riyas harbor at noon, rather than dawn, would be the best way to end up on the winning side."

"Which will be you, of course, my king," said Duke Néillen. He smiled at Túathal and received a wary look in return. *He thinks I'm up to something,* thought Néillen. *And he's right. I'm trying to figure out how to improve our chances, or more specifically* my *chances, of surviving and keeping my lands.* Duke Néillen rubbed his chin. "You know that the levies from the far north and west of the kingdom hadn't arrived for the muster on time...?"

"Yes, yes," said Túathal impatiently. "It's a long trip to Riyas from the Great Falls and the Inland Seas."

"As your earl marshal, I ordered those levies to gather at my estate ten miles to the west of Riyas," said the duke. "I'd hoped they could serve as a reserve force, if one was needed. We could stop there and see how many soldiers have arrived, then assign them to support our attack at dawn."

"So very kind of you to pay for feeding those levies from your own resources," said Túathal.

"But..." began Néillen, thinking he'd be reimbursed, then remembering Túathal's changeable moods, "...of course, Your Majesty. It's my honor."

"Good," said Túathal. "You make excellent sense—for once." Túathal cupped his hands around his mouth and shouted to Viridáxés. "When will we reach Riyas?" he asked.

"Within the hour," said the dragon, turning his head part way back. "I'm making good time, thanks to a tail wind."

Duke Néillen looked over his shoulder. The tip of Viridáxés' tail was so far behind him that he couldn't even *see* it in the moonlight. *Half the blasted dragon* is *tail,* he realized.

"There's a change in plans," said Túathal. "We're stopping at Néillen's estate ten miles west of the capital to collect more soldiers."

"As my king commands," said Viridáxés. "It's not quite midnight and the sun won't be up for more than seven hours."

"That means I can get some sleep before our dawn attack," said Túathal. "Once we arrive I'll need the softest feather bed you own, Néillen. And be sure to find Viridáxés a cow or something. He's been working hard, haven't you, my magnificent dragon? Knocking down castles can be a challenge, I imagine, and quite strenuous."

"Not for *me!*" bellowed Viridáxés. "I could push over every wall in Riyas without any rest—though come to think of it, a cow would be nice—or maybe a wisent."

"Wisents aren't common in Tamloch," said Néillen, "but I'd be glad to provide a milk cow or two."

"That would be appreciated," said Viridáxés.

"Just don't knock down the walls of any of *my* castles," said the duke.

"I can assure you I wouldn't, unless ordered by my king to do so," said Viridáxés.

Somehow, I don't find that reassuring, thought Néillen.

"How many troops do you expect will be waiting?" asked Túathal.

"Everyone the northwestern baronies can spare," said Duke Néillen. "A thousand soldiers, maybe more. At least half of them will have combat experience from border clashes with Dâron."

"That's better than I expected," said Túathal. "They should be able to quick march to Riyas in time to be useful."

"I'm glad you approve, Your Majesty," said the duke. "I'll make sure they reach the capital by dawn."

"Good, good," said Túathal. He paused to yawn without covering his mouth. "Send those useless nobles with them, and remember, I'll need the best bed in your castle for several hours."

"To yourself, Your Majesty?" asked Néillen.

"Unless that fool wizard Hibblig delivers Gwýnnett to me," said Túathal. "I'm more interested in sleep, but I'd gladly skip my rest for a chance to convince her that poisoning *me* was a big mistake."

"I could hold her prisoner for you, so you could get your rest first then deal with her later," said Duke Néillen. "And for that matter, you have chambers below the royal palace in Riyas that are far better equipped for dealing with the princess than anything I have at my estate."

"True, true," said Túathal. "It would be a shame to do less than my best work on Gwýnnett. If she ever *does* show up, it's likely to be at a time that's most advantageous to her without a thought being given for *my* destiny."

Viridáxés rumbled his support for his king.

"The woman does seem focused on her own agenda," said Néillen. *I've never seen a more perfectly matched self-centered pair,* he thought.

"Which reminds me," said Túathal. "Be sure to double the usual number of guards on the bedchamber you assign me."

"You'll be in the royal suite, Sire," said Néillen. "You found the accommodations acceptable on your previous visit."

"That was seven years ago when I first gave you your lands," said Túathal. The king smiled at Néillen in a way that made the duke uneasy. "In a way, you owe Princess Gwýnnett for them," Túathal continued. "Did you know that?"

"How so?" asked Néillen. "I thought old Duke Gériath died in his sleep without any heirs."

"Perhaps you should keep thinking that," said Túathal. "For all that Gwýnnett thinks only of herself, she *does* have her talents."

"I suppose she does," said Néillen, stroking his chin. His eyes lost focus for a moment as he considered the implications of what Túathal had revealed.

"You don't have an old wizard pensioned away at your castle who knows how to test for poisons, do you?" asked Túathal, interrupting.

"No, Your Majesty," said Duke Néillen reflexively. "Every mage in my employ went south with the army."

"That's a pity," said Túathal. "I'll need a pair of food tasters then. See that *they* eat my meal first, at least an hour before I dine." The king shook his head and grumbled. "Blast! I hate having a cold breakfast."

"We can put your food on metal plates and warm them in the oven," said the duke.

"No!" said Túathal. "I don't want my breakfast leaving my guards' sight after it's delivered to my suite. They can watch my meal *and* my tasters."

"Yes, Sire," said Néillen. "I'll have the cooks prepare something that will be as good cold as it is warm."

"We'll see," said Túathal. "If they succeed, I'll promote them to my staff at the palace."

"I'll let them know," said Néillen, reminding himself to warn his cooks not to be too creative.

"Find me a dagger as well," said Túathal. "It felt good to hold one to that traitor's throat back at the inn and I'd feel more secure if I could defend myself."

"That shouldn't be a problem, Your Majesty," said Néillen.

"See that it has a gold scabbard, so it matches my robes," barked Túathal.

"Certain, Sire," said Néillen. The only dagger at his estate with a gold scabbard was the one *he* wore opposite his sword on formal occasions.

"And a thin blade in a leather scabbard for my boot."

"I'll have them both for you at breakfast, My Liege."

"See that you do," said Túathal. The king stretched and yawned. "Are we there yet, Viridáxés?" he asked.

"Soon, my king," replied the dragon.

"Your Majesty," said Duke Néillen. "I hate to bring this up, but what about Dârio being your heir? Do you still plan to groom him to succeed you?"

"Dârio will be much more amenable to my instruction after Viridáxés has sent his army scurrying back through the gate to Dâron," said Túathal.

"I understand," said Néillen. "But what if Dârio's trickery costs you your victory?" he asked. *Again* was the word he left unspoken out of self-preservation.

"Then I will abdicate in my son's favor and declare him king of Tamloch in front of all Riyas," said Túathal. "Afterward, I'll convince him to keep me by his side as an adviser, given my vast experience ruling the kingdom. He's naive enough to go along with that, I'm sure."

"Of course, Your Majesty," said the duke. *The Dârio I've seen wouldn't tolerate Túathal within five hundred miles of him,* thought Néillen. *How can I get on Dârio's good side, so I can avoid whatever he has planned for Túathal?* He filed that question away for his mind to consider in the background.

"We're nearly there, my king," said Viridáxés. "Where would you like me to land?"

"There are fallow fields half a mile from my castle," said Duke Néillen. "That would be most convenient."

"Most convenient for *you* perhaps," said Túathal, "but I have no intention of walking half a mile. Land beside the castle wherever you can find room."

"Yes, my king," said the dragon.

"But that's where the troops will be camped," said Néillen.

"Fly over them first and bellow at them, my dragon," said Túathal. "Scare them with a quick blast of fire too. Believe me, they'll move!"

"Yes, my king," said Viridáxés.

I'm not sure what I'm going to do, thought Duke Néillen, *but whatever it turns out to be, Túathal's petty cruelty will make it easier.*

Chapter 48

The Conclave Complex

"Put them down on these," said Inthíra, waving at a pair of long marble-topped tables.

Eynon used his flying disk to lower Verro's unconscious body to the same level as the left-hand table then went to his knees and gently rolled the tall Tamloch wizard onto the slab. He watched Merry hover with Fercha at tabletop level and jumped down to help slide Merry's mentor onto the table on the right. He noticed the room was unusual—almost every surface was covered in white tiles and there were drains on the floor between the tables.

Chee seemed subdued. He held on to Eynon's hair and observed instead of climbing down and leaping from table to table as Eynon would have expected. The raconette's big eyes moved from Fercha to Verro, trying to confirm they were breathing.

"Will they recover?" asked Merry.

"Of course," said Inthíra. "As soon as I get them healing potions."

"They work well on head injuries, right?" asked Eynon. He smiled at Merry, since he'd given her one of Doethan's healing potions after she'd been smacked in the head by the flat of a sword when they'd traveled down the Rhuthro together.

"They work on most everything except severed heads, pierced hearts, and the fastest of fast-acting poisons," said Inthíra. "Fercha and Verro should be fine in a few minutes. Try not to let someone steal these drawings a second time," she added, pointing to the two large chests resting on the floor on top of her flying disk. Fercha and Verro's flying disks were on their edges, wedged between the chests.

"Yes ma'am," said Eynon.

Inthíra disappeared through a door whose inner surface was also covered in white tiles. Eynon could hear her footsteps echoing before the door shut completely.

"I had no idea the Conclave's headquarters went so far underground," said Merry. "I'd been on a lower level with Astrí when I came here from the palace, but we must have descended three levels, maybe four to get *here.*"

"It's harder to tell with ramps than with stairways," said Eynon. "Those must be more convenient for wizards on flying disks."

"I don't think the path we took had ramps," said Merry. "Stairways or ramps would be much the same on a flying disk."

"Why, then?" asked Eynon. "What am I missing?"

"Barrels," said Merry. "Believe me, I know a lot about cider barrels."

"I'll bet you do," said Eynon. "The ramps make it easier to bring in supplies? Wouldn't wizards be able to lift boxes as easily as they'd roll barrels?"

"You may be right," said Merry. "I'm extrapolating without enough information."

"Sometimes you have to do that," said Eynon. "I'm glad you're good at it." Finally taking stock of his surroundings, he noticed the temperature was unusually cold and shivered, and not just because he was chilled. "This room makes me uneasy," he said. "What do you think it's for?"

"I thought that was obvious," said Merry. "White tile walls. Drains in the floor."

"Do wizards butcher their own meat?" asked Eynon. "Are there frightening ritual sacrifices in the catacombs beneath the Conclave?"

Merry closed the distance between them and gave Eynon a peck on the nose. "Don't be silly," she said. "Think about it."

Eynon glanced around the room again and thought. "Oh," he said. "It's a morgue. I should have guessed."

"It's not like you ever encountered such a place before..." said Merry.

"...except in stories," said Eynon. "I never liked the scary ones that much. I wonder why Inthíra wanted us to take Fercha and Verro here instead of to an infirmary?"

"Because the hedge wizard running the Conclave's infirmary is a garrulous, gossiping old fool," said Inthíra as she bustled through the door carrying four small vials. "I didn't have two hours to cope with his questions and things at the morgue are usually…"

"…dead," completed Merry with a smile.

"Exactly," said Inthíra.

Eynon laughed, then yawned.

"Here," said Inthíra. She pushed one of the vials into Eynon's hands and gave a similar one to Merry. "Drink these. They'll give you energy to keep you going. I doubt either one of you has had much sleep in the past few days. You're young and healthy but pushing through without sleeping can affect your judgment and reflexes. These potions will keep you alert and energized for another twenty-four hours, then you'll need to sleep for twice that long."

"Yes, ma'am," Eynon repeated. "Let's hope things are resolved by then." He swallowed the potion, surprised it tasted like teaberries instead of fish oil. Merry drank her potion too.

"In case you're wondering, I already took my energy potion on the way here," said Inthíra. "Help me get these healing potions into Fercha and Verro. You sit them up, Eynon, while Merry holds their mouths open."

"This seems undignified," said Eynon. "It feels almost like burping a baby."

"It's different when the baby is as tall or taller than you are," said Merry.

"Tilt Fercha's head back, please," Inthíra told Merry. The older wizard poured the potion down Fercha's throat and Merry's mentor started coughing and sputtering. "Lower her back down and lift up Verro, Eynon," said Inthíra. The trio repeated the maneuver and managed to get a healing potion into Verro as well.

"What do we do now?" asked Eynon.

"Wait," said Inthíra. "It won't take long."

"Are you one of the Crown Investigators?" asked Merry. "You seem pretty comfortable down here in the morgue."

"I am," said Inthíra. "My specialty is identifying traces of poison remaining in dead bodies."

"With Princess Gwýnnett around, that must keep you busy," said Eynon.

"Not as much as you'd think," said Inthíra. "She prefers drugs that make people suggestible to ones that kill."

"Except with Túathal," said Merry.

"Even then," said Inthíra. "She could have used a poison that would have killed Túathal instantly, but she didn't."

"Probably because she didn't have anything stronger with her at the time," said Eynon. Gwýnnett and Túathal, the king's parents, were truly despicable. *They ought to be stranded together on a deserted island,* he thought. *They deserve each other's company.*

"Oooo," moaned Fercha from her marble slab. "What happened?"

"Is my skull still whole?" asked Verro. His hands were gently pressing his temples. "I haven't failed to get my shields up in time to block an attack since I was an apprentice."

Chee waggled a finger at Verro and issued an accusatory *cheee.* Verro laughed, then rubbed his head again and frowned.

Fercha rolled to face Verro and propped her head up with her palm. "We were distracted, my love," she said. "I didn't block the blow either."

"It's not like you had any cause to expect a raid by southern Clan Lands' wizards in the heart of Brendinas," said Inthíra. "You can complain about your oversights later—now you've got to show us the plans for Riyas. Eynon and Merry and I need to know the shape of the city intimately and we don't have much time to do so."

Verro sat up slowly and let his long legs dangle over the side of the table. "I can show you everything I've brought," he said, "but I'm not much good at generating solidified sound illusions. It was never one of my talents."

"You have plenty of others," said Fercha, now standing beside her table.

Eynon heard the hint of innuendo in Fercha's voice and smiled at Merry. She grinned back at him.

"We can use the Conclave's octagonal hall as our practice site," said Inthíra. She pulled Fercha and Verro's flying disks out from between the chests on her flying disk and handed them to the two wizards. "The young people can transport the chests," she said, "and the two of you can fly yourselves, just take it easy."

Eynon and Merry moved the chests full of drawings to their flying disks and hovered a foot off the floor. Chee dropped down to sit on the chest on Eynon's flying disk and rapped on the lid.

"It's full, little fellow," said Merry. "The southern Clan Landers didn't steal any drawings."

"Chee," nodded the raconette.

"Verro will be explaining all the drawings he brought while you and Eynon and Merry are learning the shape of Riyas," said Fercha to Inthíra. "I guess I know what I'll need to do."

"What's that?" asked Merry.

"Protect you while you're working," Fercha replied.

No one disagreed and a procession of five flying disks made its way to the octagonal hall.

* * * * *

"There are nine towers, not seven," said Verro. He pointed to a wizards' complex in the southwestern quadrant of the city Eynon was generating. "Here's a line drawing the architect made to guide the builders."

"Like this?" asked Eynon, modifying part of his construct.

"Exactly," said Verro. "But the third tower has a pointed green slate roof, not a flat one with a crenelated wall. The wizard living there changed his mind after the plans were completed."

"Does that sort of thing happen often?" asked Eynon, making the appropriate adjustments.

"Constantly," said Verro. "It's a rare building project that *doesn't* change during construction."

"I'm glad we have you to identify the differences then," said Eynon.

"I'll try my best to remember everything," said Verro.

"This painting you brought is a big help," said Inthíra. "It shows the skyline of Riyas from Fadacaolo Bay."

"It wasn't painted that long ago, either," said Verro. "I'm the one who sponsored the artist, Gaylissa. Charming woman. Two of my wizards kept the rain off her while she was painting," Verro added.

"She's quite talented," said Inthíra.

"How does this look?" asked Merry. She had focused on the royal palace and had added fluttering green and gold pennants on the roof line.

"Be sure to adjust the pennants to match the wind in the morning," said Inthíra.

"Right," said Merry.

"It looks good from up here," said Fercha from her vantage point keeping guard near the top of the octagonal hall's dome.

"Chee," added Chee from Fercha's shoulder. Fercha had taken charge of the raconette to keep him from scampering around the simulated scale model buildings in Riyas like some giant monster.

"I think I can manage *all* the buildings if you and Merry want to focus on details," said Eynon. "It's easier if I can do everything, instead of remembering *not* to do the ones you're practicing."

"It's one thing to generate solidified sound illusions on a small scale, and another to make them full-sized," said Inthíra. "Are you sure you can manage the entire city?"

"Eynon's wonderful with big things," said Merry. "He's an expert with massive magic."

"I wouldn't go *that* far," said Eynon. "It's more like I don't know my own magical strength sometimes."

Verro laughed and Chee joined in from the top of the dome.

"We can give it a try from the roof," said Inthíra. "You can generate a transparent full-sized version of Riyas in the sky. We'll be able to sense it and confirm its shape, without giving away what we're doing."

"Won't it show up in the moonlight?" asked Eynon.

"Who's going to be up at that time of the night to see it?" asked Inthíra.

"Oh," said Eynon. "Right. How do we get to the roof?"

Inthíra led them up a spiral stairway, which was easier to navigate on flying disks than on foot. Soon they reached the rectangular roof of the annex to the Conclave, extending off one side of the octagonal hall. Eynon stood in the center of the roof with Merry on his right and Inthíra on his left. Fercha, assisted—if you could call it that—by Chee, floated behind them, keeping careful watch. Verro found a vantage point several hundred yards above so he could effectively assess the accuracy of Eynon's huge construct.

"Here goes," said Eynon. Merry squeezed his hand, then released it and watched as her senses detected a full-sized version of Riyas forming above her. The walls and towers of the city glimmered in the moonlight but didn't stop the stars from showing through.

"Make it look like gray stone, just for a moment," said Inthíra. "On my count. Merry, you and I can add in details. You handle architectural touches—I'll generate people."

"Got it," said Merry.

"One, two, *three!*" said Inthíra.

The city of Riyas floated above Brendinas, one capital superimposed upon the other. Every foot of wall and every building was present, just like in the drawings and paintings. Pennants flapped, and torches sputtered. Throngs of people—men, women and children—peered out from battlements. For a few seconds the stars and the moon disappeared, then the complex constructs were all dispelled and Verro descended.

"I think you've got it," he said. "It would convince me, and I'm a better observer than my brother."

"I don't doubt *that,*" said Fercha. "Who will generate the fog?"

"Fog is within my capabilities," said Verro. "I'm glad to make all you'll need."

"The fog of war," said Eynon. He smiled, pleased with his accomplishment.

"*Cheeeeeeeeee!*" cheered Eynon's familiar from Fercha's shoulder. The raconette's high voice echoed in the still night. He jumped back to Eynon when Fercha joined Verro.

"I should probably contact Uirsé and have her come to Riyas as well," said Verro. "We'll need her skills as a healer if our plans don't turn out the way we expect."

"Ask her to bring Salder with her," said Merry. "Now that he's back from the dead, I like having him around."

"I can do that," said Verro. "I'll ask her to sober up my wizards in the fish-drying shed and bring *them* along too. They're personally loyal to me, not my brother."

"Tell her to get them to wash first," said Eynon.

"Good thinking," said Fercha. "What about the fussy man with the Athican name and the long black beard—the apothecary?"

"Herophilos Bodégash!" said Eynon and Merry simultaneously. They both grinned, enjoying the name.

"Send him to Riyas as well," said Fercha. "I'll have to change the code on the gate from my townhouse to Verro's suite when all this is over—and schedule a good cleaning for the place!"

"Our next stop is Riyas, I expect," said Inthíra.

"Our next stop is my townhouse—then Riyas," said Fercha.

"I'm hungry," said Eynon.

"Come to think of it, so am I," said Merry.

"I am as well," said Inthíra. "Major magic is hard work."

"I'll have food brought to my suite in the palace," said Verro.

"At three in the morning?" asked Merry.

"My brother insists on having the kitchen staffed day and night," said Verro. "It won't be a problem."

"Good," said Eynon. "How soon can we get there? I could eat a wisent."

Chapter 49

The Gates of Riyas

"The army can't stay here," said Dârio. "This is where the illusion of the city will go."

"I'd recommend marching to the *real* Riyas," said Duke Háiddon.

"Won't that be perceived as a threat?" asked Dârio.

"Isn't that the point?" asked the duke.

"I won't win the hearts of my new people by showing up with an army at their gate," said Dârio.

"No," said Duke Háiddon. "You'll do that by *not* being Túathal."

"Right," said Dârio. "Still," he said, "perhaps knocking on the gate with a small, less intimidating force first might be wise."

"You're the king," said the duke with a smile. "I'll pull together a select contingent—say a thousand or so."

"I was thinking more like a hundred, and *not* the royal guard," said Dârio. "Or maybe the royal guard *without* their blue tabards."

"I'll see if we have enough captured green tabards to equip them, Your Majesty," said Duke Háiddon.

"Excellent," said Dârio. "I'm not here as the King of Dâron ready to accept the city's surrender. I'm the rightful heir of Tamloch here to claim my birthright."

"I hope the leaders of Riyas see things that way," said the duke. "I'll see to the green tabards for the troops—and one for you as well."

"Don't forget one for yourself," said Dârio. "I don't want you attracting crossbow bolts."

"Jenet said she was getting something for us that might be helpful," said Duke Háiddon. "How much would you like to bet she's already rounding up green tabards?"

"Not a copper penny," said Dârio. "It doesn't pay to bet against your daughter."

"Is she still letting you win at *shah mat?*" asked the duke.

"What?" asked Dârio.

"Never mind," said Duke Háiddon.

* * * * *

Dârio tried not to wince when a trumpet blared in his ear and a royal herald shouted, "Open the gates for Dârio, son of Túathal and rightful king of Tamloch."

A hesitant voice called down from the battlements above the main gates of Riyas. "That's the mayor's business, not mine," said the guard on duty.

"Summon the mayor to parlay with King Dârio," said the herald, projecting her voice to be heard even beyond the city's walls.

"I'm here," came a firm but sleepy contralto from the battlements. A person's upper torso appeared on top of the wall—a middle-aged woman of middling height with mid-length graying hair. "I'm the mayor, not that Túathal allowed me much authority."

Dârio put his hand on his herald's arm before she could speak again. "I'm Dârio," he said. "Please come down so we can talk. I personally guarantee your safety."

"If you're your father's son, I don't hold much stock in your guarantees, but it doesn't seem like I have a lot of choice in the matter," said the mayor. "I'm Cáinta, by the way. I'll be down in a minute."

Dârio, resplendent in a gold and green tabard taken from a captured noble, looked at Jenet, then at Duke Háiddon, then at the gates. Duke and daughter both gave Dârio small nods of encouragement. He smiled back at them nervously. He'd seen the Old King and Queen Carys practice diplomacy, but knew it was a challenging subject, where the wrong word could put kingdoms at war. *No need to worry about that, I suppose,* thought Dârio. *We're already* at *war.*

The trumpeter and herald withdrew thirty paces to stand with the royal guards who held their weapons by their sides. A few seconds later, part of the stone wall of one of the towers flanking the gates moved outward, revealing a hidden exit. Cáinta stepped through, followed by a short man and a tall woman, both dressed like prosperous merchants. The trio stepped forward to join Dârio, Jenet and Háiddon.

Cáinta stared at Dârio's face. "You don't look much like your father," she said. Dârio's eyebrows went up. "I mean that as a compliment," she added. "You look more like Verro, actually. Are you sure *he's* not your father? That would make more sense and wouldn't affect your position in the line of succession."

"It would, actually," said Jenet. "If Dârio was Verro's son, his older cousin Nûd would be king of Dâron *and* Tamloch."

"I'm confused," said Cáinta. "Who is Nûd? For that matter, who are *you?*"

"She's my daughter," said the duke. "And I'm Háiddon, Dârio's earl marshal. Nûd is Dârianûd—Verro's son with Fercha, Princess Seren's daughter."

"Princess *Seren?*" exclaimed Cáinta. "Children's tales come to life! Next you'll be telling me made up stories about fire breathing dragons."

Dârio was about to explain about Viridáxés but stopped himself when he felt the toe of Jenet's shoe pressing on his boot.

"I *am* the rightful king of Tamloch," said Dârio. "Túathal acknowledged me as the son of his body and named me the rightful heir of Tamloch on the battlefield yesterday before he collapsed from a slow-acting poison."

"Túathal is dead then?" asked Cáinta. Her face looked hopeful.

"Alas, no," said Duke Háiddon. "He recovered. But his army has been solidly defeated on the field. We hold them all hostage."

"That's a shame," said Cáinta, shaking her head and staring at the paving stones beneath her feet.

"About the hostages?" asked Jenet.

"No, about Túathal," said Cáinta. "Too bad the poisoner wasn't more skillful." She lifted her gaze and pulled back her shoulders. "Were there many casualties in the battle?" asked Cáinta.

"Very few," said Duke Háiddon. "And no reported deaths on either side, though there were a few broken legs and cracked ribs from soldiers who couldn't run fast enough."

"We heard rumors about the wisents," said Cáinta, "but it all sounded so strange we didn't know what to believe."

"Our mages froze the Brenavon and summoned vast herds of wisents from thin air," said Dârio. "They're very powerful."

"Evidently," said Cáinta. "All I know is that thousands of families in Tamloch are grateful their sons and daughters aren't lying dead on the grass."

"I can assure you, the captured Tamloch troops are being well treated and well fed," said Duke Háiddon. "Their bellies are full of roasted wisent. There's no shortage of meat on the hoof."

"Really," said the mayor. "All the meat in Riyas was sent south with the army." Cáinta glanced at her companions then back at Dârio. "You don't suppose..." she started.

"We'll send two hundred wisents north to help feed the city after the sun comes up," said Dârio.

"That's very kind," said Cáinta. "You don't act much like Túathal," she said. "I mean that as a compliment."

"Of course," said Dârio.

"Why are you wearing Tamloch tabards if you're all from Dâron?" asked Cáinta.

"That was *my* idea, good mayor," said Jenet. "I thought it would be a sign of respect if King Dârio came to your gates as the king of Tamloch, not of Dâron."

"Huh," said Cáinta. "All it did was confuse us," she said, motioning to her companions with her hands. "Séamísh and Mags here are on the city council," she said, indicating the man and the woman. "We thought you'd escaped from the Dâron army surrounding the city."

"We *command* the Dâron army, good mayor," said Duke Háiddon.

"Then it seems like you can do anything you wish with or without our cooperation," said Cáinta, "including getting us out of bed in the middle of the night. What do you want from us?"

"Three things, good mayor," said Dârio. "First, I want everyone in the city on the western walls watching the marshalling fields at dawn."

Cáinta laughed. "Easily done," she said. "Most of the people of Riyas will be doing that anyway, once word of your army's arrival spreads."

"Thank you," said Dârio. "Second, I want free access to the top of the tallest tower on the western wall for my wizards."

"That will also be easy," said Cáinta, "since the tower's former occupant is dead."

"Oh?" asked Dârio.

"He'd been drinking too much and decided to jump from the top to see if he could fly without his flying disk," said Cáinta.

Jenet winced. Duke Háiddon kept his face expressionless. Dârio bowed his head, thinking as much of the poor people who had to clean up the mess as the late wizard.

"You said you had a third thing," said Cáinta. "I assume *this* one isn't easy."

"You'll have to tell me if it is later," said Dârio. "I want the people of Riyas to watch what happens at dawn, and if they agree, acknowledge me as their king by acclamation."

"A good portion of the city would celebrate my dog being king since he's not Túathal," said Cáinta.

Duke Háiddon smiled when Dârio glanced at him.

"Is he a good dog?" asked Dârio. "What breed?"

"Ahem," said Jenet to Cáinta as she pressed the heel of her shoe into her lover's instep. "You and Dârio can discuss matters canine in the future. For now, can you gather the leading citizens of Riyas in the next few hours before dawn and see if they're willing to acknowledge Dârio, Túathal's true son, as your new king?"

"If events at dawn warrant," added Duke Háiddon.

"Your cryptic words guarantee everyone in Riyas will be on the western walls," said Cáinta. "Will there be a mage's duel on the marshaling plain?" she asked.

"Something like that," said Jenet.

"Huh," said Cáinta. "I don't know if your third thing will be easy or not, but I'll pass the word. I can't guarantee people's reactions, however. There are still many who support Túathal, though it would be easier to get them to accept Túathal's son than anyone else as king. Tamloch's never had a usurper who wasn't at least a king or prince's bastard."

"An impressive record over two thousand years," said Dârio.

"There were a lot of bastards," said Mags, the tall woman with Cáinta.

Everyone laughed, and it seemed like the tightly wound rope powering a siege engine suddenly released. Tensions between Dârio and the Riyasans, especially the mayor, were greatly reduced.

"About your tabard," said Cáinta.

"Yes?" said Dârio and Jenet simultaneously.

"You shouldn't wear one that belonged to a repulsive minor baron. It doesn't send the right message."

"Thank you," said Dârio, looking down at his borrowed tabard. "I appreciate your advice and will see about getting a few dozen wisents to you *before* dawn, so you can get started cooking them for tonight's celebration."

"If there *is* a celebration," said Cáinta.

"Isn't that a given?" asked Jenet. *"Someone* has to win."

"Huh," said Cáinta. "You're right, now that you mention it. Does wisent taste like beef?"

"Very much so, good mayor," said Duke Háiddon. "You'll soon have a chance to taste it for yourself. Now we need to get back to the army."

"I understand," said Cáinta. She nodded left and right. "We'll get busy with your requests."

"Requirements," said Séamísh, the short man from the city council standing next to Cáinta.

"Requests," said Dârio. He turned and started to walk away, but Cáinta called to him.

"Tell me, m'lord," she said, "what's your position on merchants' tax rates?"

Chapter 50
Nûd and Sónnel

Rocky was rapidly closing the distance remaining between him and the scout wizard. Nûd leaned forward on the wyvern's neck, hoping to learn more about the object of their chase, but flapping robes and a hood prevented him from detecting nuances like the wizard's age or gender.

After an initial burst from Rocky, the pursuit found an equilibrium, with Rocky only gaining one of his body lengths every minute. Nûd wasn't sure there was enough time to catch up to the fast-moving wizard before they reached the Tamloch fleet. At that point, he and Rocky would be targets for attacks from the ships' archers and siege engines.

"Steady boy," said Nûd as he worked the pilum Quintillius had given him out of the strapping holding it in place. "Give me just a little more altitude."

Rocky obediently rose and Nûd stood up in Rocky's wyvern-equivalent of stirrups. They were more like niches carved into the sides of the padded saddle's thick leather.

"Steady," said Nûd. "Steady…"

The scout wizard's course didn't deviate and Nûd let his pilum fly with an accuracy developed spearing fish back in Melyncárreg. The point of the seven-foot javelin struck in the center of the flying disk and the length of its shaft flipped up like a rake stepped on by a careless farmer. Most of the pilum struck whatever portions of the wizard's anatomy were kept at the juncture of left and right legs.

I hope it's a woman, thought Nûd, feeling sympathetic pain.

The robed individual on the flying disk was stunned and the disk's forward motion stopped. Nûd saw the wizard kneel in pain, and probably no small degree of shock. A few wing beats later, Rocky and Nûd were even with the wizard. Nûd pulled the flying disk, the pilum, and the robed figure onto Rocky's back. While the wizard was still stunned he unbuckled the leather strap holding a bright green magestone embedded in a delicately carved wooden setting from a slim wrist. He put the setting in his belt pouch.

If you're serving on a ship, you don't want to wear a heavy artifact, Nûd realized. *Even wizards can fall overboard by accident.*

He pushed back his captive's deep hood, revealing a boy or a short-haired girl. *No, it's a woman,* Nûd determined with a closer look. *That face shows more maturity than any lad too young to shave.* Nûd couldn't stop looking at the wizard. *She's close to* my *age,* he thought. *In her early twenties.*

Nûd looped a rawhide thong around her wrists and tied them to a leather loop firmly riveted to the saddle. She was facing forward, he backward, with his spine against Rocky's neck.

"That was a lucky throw," said the wizard.

"Not at all," said Nûd. "I've been spearing trout back home for years."

"I don't suppose I could convince you to give back my magestone?" asked the wizard.

"You might," said Nûd. "But you'll have to answer my questions first."

"What kinds of questions?" asked the wizard uncertainly.

"The kind spies don't want to answer," said Nûd.

"I'm *not* a spy," said the wizard. "I'm a scout—and not a very good one, I expect. If I was good, you wouldn't have seen me."

"True enough," said Nûd. "Don't allow yourself to be backlit by the moon. You couldn't have been easier to spot if you'd been carrying a glow ball."

"Blast," said the wizard. She glared at Nûd and he could tell she was every bit as angry at herself as she was with him.

"Questions," said Nûd. "If you want your magestone back."

"Ask," said the wizard. She tried to make her face expressionless but failed when wind from Rocky's flight forced her to blink rapidly.

"Let me give you information first, so it will be more of an exchange than an interrogation. My name is Nûd."

"What kind of a name is Nûd?" asked the wizard.

"It's a nickname. What's yours?"

"Bonnie," said the wizard. "And please don't say it. I'll toss the next person who calls me a *bonnie lass* into a gate to nowhere!"

"The thought never crossed my mind," said Nûd, grinning.

"Stop that," said Bonnie.

Nûd frowned at her.

"Stop *that* too," she said.

"Very well," said Nûd. He looked very serious for a few seconds, then made the sort of odd, distorted face with wide eyes and a lolling tongue that a parent might make to amuse a small child.

"I *said* you could ask your questions," said Bonnie. "They can't be any worse than those faces." The corners of Bonnie's mouth were turning up.

"That was just my technique for loosening you up so you'd reveal the location of the pirates' treasure," said Nûd.

He made another funny face and Bonnie laughed before asking, "The *what?*"

"Pirate treasure," said Nûd. "What did you think I was going to ask you about?"

"The location of Tamloch's fleet," said Bonnie. "That's only a few..." She closed her mouth and squeezed her lips together tightly once she realized what she'd been about to reveal.

"You *aren't* very good at being a spy," said Nûd.

"Which should prove I'm not one," said Bonnie. "You can torture me if you want, but I not only won't tell you anything, I can't tell *you* anything because they don't tell *me* anything."

Privately, Nûd thought he understood why Bonnie was largely kept in the dark about strategy. She seemed to be the sort of wizard who focused on obscure magical topics to the exclusion of almost everything else. He'd met several wizards like that over the years. His grandmother Astrí—Princess Seren, he corrected—was one. His mother Fercha another. Even his grandfather Damon could get lost in his studies.

"What's your line of magical research?" Nûd asked.

Bonnie's face lit up. "Congruencies and non-Euclidean geometries," she answered. "I spent my wander year studying advanced mathematics at a small academy just north of Bhaile Pónaire before I became a wizard."

Bonnie paused for a quick breath and continued. "Did you know you can generate a bag of infinite capacity by adding a fourth direction to length, width, and height then twisting and..." She felt Nûd's hand on her bound ones and saw him smiling at her. "Sorry," she said. "You did ask."

"That's right," said Nûd, "I did. I'd love nothing more than to listen to you explain the things you've learned. I'm not a wizard, but I've grown up around them and find how they push the boundaries of magical knowledge fascinating. Unfortunately, this isn't the best time for such discussions. I need to speak to Grand Admiral Sónnel about something important as soon as possible."

"How do I know you aren't planning to kill him once you find him?" asked Bonnie. "You're pretty good at throwing that Roma spear."

"So are half the sailors in Tamloch's fleet," said Nûd.

Bonnie frowned and shrugged her shoulders, acknowledging the truth of what Nûd had said. The full moon emerged from behind thin, high clouds to the left and Nûd's face was now illuminated. "Have we met before?" asked Bonnie. "Your face looks familiar."

"I doubt it," said Nûd. "I haven't gotten out much until recently—and I'd remember *you*."

"Interesting," said Bonnie. "You look like someone from court, but I can't remember who." She closed her eyes for a moment and opened them, then smiled. "I know who it is," she said. "You remind me of a younger version of Verro."

"That makes sense," said Nûd. "Considering he's my father."

"What!" said Bonnie. "Why didn't you say so immediately? I'd be glad to escort you to the fleet and introduce you to the Grand Admiral. Sónnel is a sweetheart."

Nûd doubted Sónnel would appreciate being referred to that way, but maybe he was misjudging the man. The leader of Tamloch's fleet must be wise to survive so long as a reluctant next-in-line heir to Túathal's throne. *And now Dârio is in the middle of the mix,* thought Nûd. *For that matter, so am I.* He stared over Bonnie's shoulder at the tip of Rocky's tail as he tried to sort out *those* twists in his personal Gordian knot. On top of that, he could sense himself developing a sudden interest in non-Euclidean geometries.

"Excuse me," said Bonnie. "It's quite nice flying along holding hands with you, but do you think you could give me back my magestone?"

"Uh, sure," said Nûd. He removed his hand from on top of hers and fumbled in his belt pouch for the leather strap holding her artifact. When he reached for his knife to cut her bonds she didn't flinch. Three heartbeats later, Nûd had returned Bonnie's magestone to her wrist.

"Thank you," she said. Bonnie kissed his cheek and whispered, "You're a sweetheart too."

Then, as best Nûd could tell in the moonlight, she blushed. He felt his own ears get warm and turned around to face in the direction Rocky was flying. "So where's the Tamloch fleet?" he asked.

"Look down," said Bonnie.

Nûd did. He smiled when he saw hundreds of sails below him.

Bonnie unstowed her flying disk. "I'll go ahead and let Grand Admiral Sónnel know you're coming. He's on the *Búa Mór,* the biggest ship in the fleet, just a few rows back from the front. You can't miss it." She put her feet in the straps on the bottom of her flying disk and jumped from Rocky's back.

"That was interesting," said Nûd. Rocky's soft rumble revealed his amusement.

* * * * *

"Help me understand," said Grand Admiral Sónnel. "You ride a wyvern, but you're not a wizard and he's not your familiar?"

"That's right," said Nûd, "but both my parents are wizards."

"Verro is his father, I told you," said Bonnie. She stood next to Nûd and Sónnel in relative privacy on a raised platform at the stern of the *Búa Mór*. Captain Maírné, the Grand Admiral's second in command, was even farther back at the rudder, advising the sailor steering the flagship's course and pretending not to listen.

Sónnel smiled at Bonnie like an indulgent uncle before turning back to Nûd. "Who is your mother, if you don't mind me asking?"

"Her name is Fercha," said Nûd.

"I thought so!" said Sónnel. "When I heard rumors from the battlefield about Verro and a tall red-headed woman..."

"You know my mother?" asked Nûd.

"I do," said the Grand Admiral. "Or at least I've met her. That was back when high level relations between Tamloch and Dâron were more *cordial,* shall we say. Fercha was an impressive woman then. I'm sure she's even more so now."

"That's accurate, if you favor understatement," said Nûd. "She's Princess Seren's only child, after all." He smiled as he shook his head slowly, then found himself staring at Bonnie.

For her part, Bonnie had generated a small, dim glow ball so the three of them could see each other as they talked. Nûd saw that her hair was the same dark shade as Uirsé's, though cut shorter. She was about the same age as Uirsé, as best Nûd could tell, and was much the same height, though with a more slender figure. *From missing too many meals scribbling formulas and reading ancient tomes,* thought Nûd. Bonnie's cloistered scholar's life had probably left her as much of a misfit around others as Nûd himself. *Which must be one of the reasons I find her fascinating,* he told himself. He could still feel the spot on his cheek where she'd kissed him.

"Nûd?" said Sónnel for what clearly wasn't the first time.

Bonnie poked Nûd's shoulder with four bunched fingers. "Could you please come back to *this* side of the Ocean?"

"Sorry," said Nûd. "I was woolgathering."

"Obviously," said Bonnie. She prepared to poke Nûd again, but he stopped her by taking her hand in his and holding it down at an angle between them. Bonnie didn't try to pull away.

Sónnel smiled at their behavior. "Now that I know who you are," he said to Nûd, "what do you want from *me,* Your Majesty?" The Grand Admiral's last two words were pitched soft enough so only Nûd could hear them. "You must know I'm not a traitor," said Sónnel, loud enough to be sure Captain Maírné heard over the wind and the lapping waves. "And besides, Túathal has a dragon. Your cause is lost."

"I don't think so," said Nûd. "Turn around."

Bonnie, Grand Admiral Sónnel, and even Captain Maírné turned and followed Nûd to the stern rail. Zûrafiérix lifted her great head out of the water until her eyes were level with the observers.

"Greetings," she said, her great round orbs glowing and showing dancing azure spirals.

"Túathal has a dragon, good gentles," said Nûd, "but as you can see, I've made friends with one myself. Great timing, Zûra."

"Thank you," said the dragon. "I wanted to let you know that I spotted a second large fleet of Bifurland longships heading south past Fishhook Cape. It would be wise to investigate and block their incursion."

"We can't have that," said Grand Admiral Sónnel. "Give the orders to sail past the mouth of Fadacaolo Bay and Riyas harbor," he commanded.

Captain Maírné passed the admiral's instructions on to one of his assistants and returned. "That detour should delay us, so we won't get to Riyas until several hours past dawn," he told Sónnel.

"Can't be helped," replied the admiral.

"Good sailing," said Nûd.

"You have a *dragon!*" said Bonnie.

"We're just friends," said Nûd.

"Will I see you again?" she asked.

"Count on it," said Nûd. He reluctantly climbed on Rocky's back and stared over his shoulder at Bonnie as the wyvern leapt skyward. Zûra would find them and together they would seek a spot near Riyas to wait for dawn.

Chapter 51

Rescuing Kennig

The tavern where Hibblig and Gwýnnett waited was a ramshackle place that smelled like stale beer and fish guts. They sat at a table for two against a far wall, under an open window, as shadows were growing longer on the street outside. The air coming in from the window smelled like fish guts too, so their hope for something less unpleasant to breathe was unrealized. Gwýnnett had her cloak's hood pulled forward to hide her features, which was just as well. Hibblig had seen the look on her face and it would stop water from flowing downhill. The princess stared down into the dirty mug holding her beer, unwilling to entertain drinking even a sip.

"Why isn't he answering!" she whispered, her anger masked by two sailors trading loud insults at the bar.

"I don't know," said Hibblig. "He's not responding to requests for contact from your ring *or* mine."

"I should have used a double dose of poison and killed Túathal quickly," Gwýnnett muttered.

Hibblig nodded his agreement and tried bringing his beer to his lips but failed. Every time the mug came close to his nose, the smell of sour skunk convinced him drinking the liquid wouldn't be wise. He glanced at a small bowl of heavily salted walnuts on the tablet and thought about eating a few but thought better of that too when the nuts seemed to shift of their own accord and he realized there were bugs in the bowl beneath the surface.

"Want to try him again?" asked Hibblig. This wasn't his sort of drinking establishment at all. He sensed it was growing noisy outside the tavern, not just inside. People were shouting.

"Don't bother," said Gwýnnett. "He's trying to teach me a lesson after I tried to kill him. It's not as if he wouldn't have done the same to me."

"True," said Hibblig. *More true than Gwýnnett knew,* he considered. The shouting outside was growing louder. He heard dozens of pairs of feet running across the cobbles beyond the window. "I'm going out to see what's going on," said Hibblig.

"I'm coming with you," said Gwýnnett. She pushed her chair back.

"Absolutely not," said Hibblig.

"Don't presume to order *me,* wizard," said Gwýnnett. She stood up to emphasize her authority. Hibblig stood as well.

"You might be recognized," Hibblig protested.

"I'll keep my hood up," said Gwýnnett.

"It may not be safe on the street," Hibblig added, though he knew he'd already lost.

"It's not particularly safe here in the tavern either," said Gwýnnett, gesturing to the sailors at the bar who'd moved from trading insults to trading drunken punches.

"Very well," said Hibblig, "but do what I tell you."

"I will if it suits me," said Gwýnnett.

Realizing that would be the best he'd get, Hibblig escorted Gwýnnett out of the tavern. He'd already paid for their beers. Cash in advance was the rule in such places. No one noticed them when they left. Hibblig let his ears lead him toward the commotion, walking along with the crowd of people also headed in the same direction.

Gwýnnett soon urged Hibblig to get her out of the mob and up to somewhere she could see. He tugged her down an alley and assisted her onto his flying disk. They rose to rooftop level and hovered above a block of apartments with a clear view of the intersection where most of the noise was coming from. He lowered his flying disk behind a three-foot wall around the flat top of the building and leaned over it to watch.

"Far-seeing lenses," said Gwýnnett.

"Yes, Your Highness," said Hibblig. He constructed distance vision lenses from solidified sound and gave a pair to Gwýnnett, keeping one for himself. Then he looked down and laughed softly. His cousin Kennig was there. So were three of the other seven people he'd met in the cave a few hours ago.

Grúgàch, the senior wizard from the southern Clan Lands next to Kennig and two of the four self-exiled brothers from the Rhuthro valley were digging through the contents of a pair of wooden chests, looking at documents. Fercha and Verro's bodies lay sprawled on flying disks beside the chests.

How in the First Ships had Kennig killed Fercha and Verro? thought Hibblig. *This won't end well.*

"Do you know these people?" asked Gwýnnett.

"The relatively clean one is my cousin Kennig," said Hibblig. "He's a southern Clan Lander now."

"Oh yes, I remember him," said Gwýnnett. "A handsome fellow."

"Whatever you say," said Hibblig. "The others are all southern Clan Landers, though some started out as Dâron subjects."

"That shaggy-haired Clan Lands' wizard has fast reflexes," said Gwýnnett. "I wish I was down there with him so I could kick Fercha. There are *other* things I'd like to do with Verro."

"Which would be difficult while he's unconscious," said Hibblig.

"You never did have much imagination," said Gwýnnett.

Hibblig snorted, then his jaw dropped when the bright light appeared above the intersection. From his high vantage point, he observed guard troops march into place to surround the southern Clan Lands' raiders. Seconds later, he heard the anonymous ultimatum for Kennig and company to surrender. Hibblig watched Grúgàch zoom up and attack but was unable to see the results of his offensive. All he saw was Grúgàch returning to the street and a young wizard with red hair remove his magestone. She was the same one who'd trapped him in a web of tight light after his duel with Doethan yesterday.

"I can think of plenty of things I'd like to do to *her,*" Hibblig whispered.

"Oooo," said Gwýnnett. "Can I watch?"

Hibblig declined to answer, not sure how he felt about Gwýnnett observing. His silence held as the squads of guards disappeared, revealing themselves to be solidified sound illusions. He looked twice to confirm that a late-arriving squad of guards *were* real and watched Inthíra hand Grúgàch and Kennig's magestones to the squad's sergeant for safekeeping. Kennig and his companions were marched off toward the palace and its nearby jail for wizards. The trio of wizards flew off in the same direction with the treasure chests and Fercha and Verro's unconscious bodies.

"Back to the tavern?" asked Gwýnnett. "Maybe we could wait for Túathal to reply from up here? The air's better."

"No," said Hibblig. "There's something I need to do first."

"What's that?" asked Gwýnnett.

"Rescue my cousin from the city guards," said Hibblig.

"Why bother doing it now?" she asked. "You can do it tomorrow or the next day. I doubt he'll be going anywhere."

"Yes, but we might be," said Hibblig. "Besides, Kennig is a *very* talented wizard. He's better at generating realistic solidified sound illusions than Inthíra. I once saw him stage a play for the old king and queen where he animated over twenty characters while maintaining all the sets and scenery."

"I remember that," said Gwýnnett. "It was some sort of Athican comedy about a fat slave. There was lots of singing if I recall."

"That's the one," said Hibblig.

"Very well," said Gwýnnett. "A wizard like your cousin could be useful. And the shaggy one from the southern Clan Lands had exceptionally fast reflexes."

"Those Rhuthro valley men could serve as our bodyguards, for that matter," said Hibblig. "Let's get moving. They'll be easier to retrieve *before* they're inside their cells. Do you have anything with you to help us incapacitate the guards?"

"More of the sleeping powder that I used on the two outside the door to my suite," said Gwýnnett. "I always keep a good supply on my person."

"Good to know," said Hibblig. "That reminds me of a trick I've always wanted to try..."

Gwýnnett and Hibblig boarded his flying disk and sped off to catch up with the squad of guards and their prisoners.

* * * * *

"That was impressive," said Kennig. "How did you contrive to have all the guards fall asleep at once without affecting the rest of us?"

"Solidified sound and Princess Gwýnnett's sleeping powder," said Hibblig. "I delivered the power directly below each guard's nose on a transparent length of solidified sound so the next time they inhaled, they fell to the cobblestones."

"I'm in your debt, cousin," said Kennig. "Where are we off to now?"

"A tavern by the docks," said Gwýnnett. "There's a gate there used by Tamloch spies."

"It's lucky for us you didn't have a chance to go through it before we were captured," said Kennig.

Fox commented from his position standing behind Kennig on his flying disk. "I'm betting luck didn't have much to do with it."

"You're right about that," said Hibblig. "Túathal hasn't given us the gate code."

"I'll kill him if he's not already dead by the time we get there," said Gwýnnett.

"Are you trying to get to Riyas?" asked Kennig.

"Why? Do you know another gate that opens there?" asked Hibblig.

"No," said Kennig, "but remember years back when the leaders of Dâron and Tamloch were on much better terms than they are now?"

"I remember," said Gwýnnett.

"I was a young man in court then," said Kennig, "and quite popular. A noble's daughter from Bhaile Pónaire north of Fishhook Cape took a fancy to me and I to her. I can remember her beckoning me to bed wearing only a pair of red stockings..."

"Is there a point here?" asked Gwýnnett.

"There is," said Kennig. "I built a small gate from Brendinas to her bedchamber in Bhaile Pónaire more than twenty-five years ago. Those were the days. She was a lovely lass with long red hair down to her..."

"As nice as that may be, what are the odds of an unmaintained gate that old still working?" asked Hibblig.

"Better than you'd think," said Kennig. "The end in Brendinas is in my former bedroom in my father's townhouse here in the city. It's my brother's now, but as far as I know he's been too cheap to redecorate. The girl's father's mansion in Bhaile Pónaire has been standing for three centuries. There are decent odds that end of the gate still works, too."

"We'll have to test it," said Hibblig.

"You can send my brother through," whispered Fox. "It would be no great loss to the world if he lost an arm—or his head."

"Well then," said Kennig. "I expect we have a plan."

"There's a problem," said Gwýnnett. "Once we go through the gate, we'll be in Bhaile Pónaire, not Riyas."

"True enough," said Hibblig. "But it's a much shorter distance to fly than coming from Brendinas."

"So long as you see to my comfort," said Gwýnnett.

"Of course, my princess," said Hibblig.

"What happened with you and the redhead?" asked Fox. "How long did it last?"

"Quite some time," said Kennig. "Though I learned I wasn't the only one visiting. I came to her one night wearing the face of another man she fancied. She said, 'You were supposed to be here an hour ago.'"

"And you think she hasn't closed your gate in all that time?" asked Gwýnnett. "I would have done it the minute you broke things off."

"We never did quite end our relationship," said Kennig. "At least not until I went into exile. She liked variety in her lovers, but her father kept close watch on her after catching a young man climbing the trellis outside her bedroom window. I was useful to her and could wear a different face each time I'd visit, providing both variety and convenience."

"Hmmm..." said Gwýnnett, looking over at Kennig flying nearby. It was a good thing Hibblig couldn't see her expression. "Where's your father's townhouse?"

"Just a few blocks from here," said Kennig. "My father's old steward will be surprised to see me."

"And the rest of us, I imagine," added Fox.

"Have you ever been to Bhaile Pónaire?" Kennig asked Fox. "It's an excellent town for dining. There are dozens of fine inns with great cooks. There's a place near one of the piers that has amazing baked beans and clam chowder."

"You eat them at the same time?" asked Fox.

"No, no," said Kennig. "Chowder, then beans as a side dish with a whole lobster."

"What's a lobster?" asked Fox.

"Sort of a big crayfish," said Kennig. "They can be as large as your arm but mind their claws when you trap them."

"I'm not fond of food that fights back," said Fox.

"You might want to opt for salted cod then," said Kennig.

"Stop," said Gwýnnett. "You're making me hungry. Do you think the cook at your father's townhouse could make us something to eat?"

"I'd recommend stopping at an inn in Bhaile Pónaire instead," said Kennig.

"I don't want to eat big crayfish," said Fox.

"You won't want to eat the tasteless pap my father's cook prepares, either," said Kennig. "There's a place down by the fens that makes quite tasty beef sausages. I'm sure you'll like *them*."

"So long as there's good beer," said Fox.

Chapter 52

Duke Néillen's Estate

Duke Néillen was tired. He hadn't gotten much sleep while flying on Viridáxés. He had to attend to Túathal's every whim or risk some other noble being tossed off and falling to his death after giving an inadvertent insult to the king. Now that they had arrived at his estate and disembarked from the dragon, Néillen had even more work to do.

His first order of business was seeing that Túathal was safely parked in bed and wheels were in motion to ensure his food and his tasters would be ready when he woke. The second item on his plate—made worse by the delay to deal with Túathal—was calming down the staff of his estate, his tenants, and the troops who had arrived from the northwestern corner of Tamloch about the tower-sized dragon next to the north wall of the castle who was gnawing on a third cow from Néillen's prize-winning dairy herd.

Item three on Néillen's mental list *had* been procuring food for Viridáxés. He crossed that off, since the dragon had clearly taken that project into his own claws. Faint puffs from luminescent green flames illuminated the dragon's jaws as he cooked and masticated the remains of Néillen's best milk producers.

Néillen walked the grounds near the impressive castle he'd been given and stopped to talk to everyone he encountered. He explained that the dragon would be leaving before dawn and would likely *not* be returning. The duke wasn't so sure about that last part, but he figured hoping might make it so.

After telling senior members of his castle staff and a dozen representatives from the tenant farmers' council there was nothing to worry about, he confirmed where the newly arrived troops were encamped and headed that way. Luckily, the soldiers hadn't set up next to the castle where Viridáxés might have crushed them. Néillen spotted a large officers' tent flying flags from the distant baronies and considered how to hail its occupants.

There was a nice way, and a not-so-nice way to get their attention. It was still early, between one and two in the morning, so at first he opted for the nice way. Then he realized he hadn't been challenged when he approached the encampment and changed his mind.

"Who's in charge here?" Néillen bellowed. "Present yourself immediately, if you don't want to be digging night-soil pits for the next decade."

To the duke's surprise, no one answered. Rather than shout again, he opened the tent's flaps and stared inside. There were two desks, two sleeping cots, and no occupants. Néillen was glad he hadn't bellowed again. Then he slapped his forehead with the heel of his palm. *They're all watching the dragon,* thought Néillen. *I'll bet there aren't more than twenty sound sleepers left in the encampment.*

The duke made his way to the side of the rows of tents closest to Viridáxés. As expected, he found rank after rank of soldiers watching the dragon devour his latest snack. *Was that Elsinore?* Néillen asked himself as he tried to make out the pattern of spots on the cow's backside while her front half was being chewed. "Blast!" said Néillen under his breath. "I *liked* Elsie."

The duke put his hand on the shoulder of a woman who had the demeanor—and the scarred arms—of a professional soldier. Her white scars showed bright against her dark, sun-weathered skin in the moonlight. "Where can I find the commander of these forces?" he asked.

"You're looking at her," said the woman. "Are you Duke Néillen?"

"I am."

"I thought so," she said. "I was told you were covered with tattoos. My name's Rood. Captain Rood, if you hold much with titles."

"Not much," said Néillen.

"Neither do I," said Rood. *"Actions are lightning while words are pale starlight* my mother used to say."

"Wise mother," said Néillen. "Thanks for getting your troops here in good order," he said.

"I'm only sorry we couldn't get here soon enough to be useful," said Rood.

"You'll be *very* useful if you can get your people and the nobles who came in on dragonback last night to the hill just this side of the marshalling field west of Riyas before dawn," said Néillen. He wasn't going to tell Rood about the debacle on the field south of Brendinas yesterday if word hadn't reached her already.

"I can try," said Rood, "if I can pry their attention away from yon dragon. He must be as long or longer than the Great Falls are wide."

"I've never seen the Great Falls," said Néillen, "but if they're truly great, I expect you're right. Tell your soldiers King Túathal said he'd give Viridáxés permission to eat them if they weren't in place before dawn. Leave your tents and just bring enough food for a few meals. Move fast—travel light."

"Yes, Your Grace," said Rood. "That might also prove enough to motivate the nobles." She nodded at Néillen and started shouting at the men and women under her command. Most turned away from Viridáxés and followed her orders.

That's done, thought Néillen as he started back to his castle. *Now to grab something to eat and a short nap myself.*

The duke was only halfway to his castle's main gate when three wizards descended to land on the stone path in front of him. They each carried a passenger. He did a double take when he realized one of the passengers was Princess Gwýnnett.

"What are *you* doing here?" asked Duke Néillen.

"Visiting the father of my child," said Gwýnnett.

"The king is expecting us," said Hibblig.

Néillen remembered Túathal saying *something* about a wizard named Hibblig who was connected to Gwýnnett on their flight north, but he was too tired to remember exactly what had been said. If Túathal had just gone to bed, telling him about Gwýnnett and her associates' arrival could wait until after the king had his breakfast.

"We were flying to Riyas, but got a bit off course," said Kennig. "When we saw the dragon, we knew we were in the right place to find Túathal. Gwýnnett recognized you, so we came down to intercept you. I'm Kennig, by the way."

Hibblig introduced himself as Gwýnnett's personal wizard. Grúgàch just grunted and stared at Viridáxés munching on yet another cow not far away. Fool seemed about to say something, but Fox shut him up with a look.

"Got any grub?" asked Grúgàch.

"I do," said Néillen. "I was on my way to get something to eat when you blocked my way."

"Sorry about that," said Kennig.

"Come along then," said Duke Néillen. "There's plenty of food in the castle's larders."

"Do you have any spare beds?" asked Hibblig with a sideways glance at Gwýnnett."

"I've got beds too," said Néillen. "I'll assign you rooms and you can sort out your own sleeping arrangements."

"Thank you," said Kennig. Fox and Fool nodded. Gwýnnett glared at Hibblig. She seemed to radiate a sense of indignation over life's unfairness.

"Don't get too comfortable," said Néillen. "Everyone will be getting up at least an hour before dawn."

"We'd better eat fast then," said Fox.

"Fast," echoed Fool tentatively.

"The dragon is on *our* side, isn't he?" asked Kennig.

"He is for now," said Néillen as he led the others up the path. "We'll see about whose side he's on after I tell him he can't eat any more of my cows!"

Chapter 53

Predawn Conversations

"Try to sleep for an hour or two, my love," said Jenet. She put a warm hand on Dârio's forehead and held it there, keeping him from sitting up. They were both still dressed but rested under a thick quilt on a thin mattress in a small tent close to the main gates of Riyas. Dârio had told his soldiers earlier that they didn't need to put up the royal pavilion since he expected to be occupying *his* royal palace in the city sometime after sunrise.

"There's still so much to do," said Dârio.

"My father has things well in hand," said Jenet. "Your role is to be the sort of young, vigorous, and virtuous monarch the people of Riyas will *want* to acclaim as their king. You won't be able to do that if your eyelids won't stay open."

"You're right," said Dârio from somewhere halfway between being awake and asleep. He moved Jenet's hand from his forehead to his lips and kissed it. "How does it feel to have a father who loves you?"

Jenet waited for a few breaths before answering, hoping that Dârio's eyes would fully close, but they didn't.

"It feels centered," she said. "Losing my mother a few years ago was hard but losing my father would be harder still. I'm definitely his daughter."

"You certainly are," said Dârio softly. "Are you interested in being earl marshal of Tamloch when the position comes open?"

"Ask me later, when you're awake," she said. "And only if my plan works."

"Yes dear," said Dârio. "I'm not *my* father's son."

"Which one?" asked Jenet. "Prince Dâri or King Túathal?"

"Neither," said Dârio. "Your father was more of a father to me than Dâri, and the thought of being related to Túathal gives me an unending stomach ache."

"With good reason," said Jenet. "You know Prince Dâri loved you, right? That's why he fostered you out to our family—to get you out of the palace and away from Gwŷnnett as often as possible."

"My brain knows that," said Dârio, "but the eight-year-old boy inside me still doesn't understand why his father sent him away."

"I understand, my love," said Jenet as she nestled against Dârio and draped an arm across his chest. "You'll just have to do better with *our* children."

"Is this your way of telling me we're having a baby?" asked Dârio in a voice that sounded like he was talking in a dream.

"I certainly hope so," said Jenet. "Several babies—if you'll have me as your queen. Just not in the next nine months or so."

"Earl marshal first," said Dârio, his eyelids fluttering. "Queen second. Babies afterward."

"Yes, my love," said Jenet, though she didn't think Dârio remained awake to hear her. *I've had the past year to consider being a queen,* thought Jenet, *but I never entertained the notion of being earl marshal. That was always my father's position. Still, he can't very well be earl marshal of Dâron* and *Tamloch. I wonder if being queen would make serving as earl marshal harder or easier? Maybe if I...*

Jenet's breathing slowed and soon she joined Dârio in his all-too-brief slumbers.

* * * * *

Fercha leaned up on one elbow and watched Verro sleep. They were in his bed—their bed—in the palace in Riyas. Earlier, she had made sure everyone gated through from her townhouse. She'd had more visitors in half an hour than had come to her home in Brendinas since she'd purchased the place. Merry and Eynon and Inthíra, Salder and Uirsé and the apothecary with the long black beard whose adopted Athican name always made her smile, and Verro's collection of wizards from the fish-drying shed all trooped through her townhouse *and* her bedchamber.

She grimaced at the thought. Visitors entering her townhouse were an annoyance but having them invade her private sleeping quarters was totally disconcerting. She resolved to change the code phrase for the gate as soon as possible and to redecorate her bed-chamber back in Brendinas, perhaps after consulting with Verro, since she expected the two of them would be spending a *lot* more time together in one capital city or the other.

Inthíra had encouraged Fercha and Verro to get a few hours of sleep before dawn, saying she'd had an energy potion and had also given ones to Eynon and Merry. Someone had to be awake and alert tomorrow evening, after the trio of mages with projective illusion skills crashed for forty-eight hours. Verro and Fercha were the obvious choices.

Uirsé and Salder had a room to themselves down the hall. The young couple seemed on their way to resolving their difficulties after Merry's older brother revealed he was a Dâron spy. *Their situation is a lot like ours,* thought Fercha as she watched Verro's chest's rise and fall. *Things will be much easier for them if Dâron and Tamloch end up on better terms after everything is over.*

When a servant woke them in a few hours, they'd go to the top of the tallest western tower and support their friends. Fercha would manage their defenses, while Verro would generate fog to cover the *real* Riyas, assisted by Uirsé and the wizards from the fish-drying shed. *I'll have to learn their names I suppose,* thought Fercha. *Verro can introduce me in the morning.*

She allowed her head to descend to her pillow. Her last thoughts as she faded into sleep were *Whatever happened to Doethan?* and *I wonder what my parents are up to?*

* * * * *

The Bifurland fleet sailed north through the dark waters of Fadacaolo Bay. Quintillius sat on a barrel near the mast on King Bjarni's flagship and smiled at his wife through the circular interface of a communications ring. "How are the children?" he asked.

"Fine, as always," said Laetícia. "Primus and the girls miss their father."

"I miss them too," said Quin. "It's too bad you can't just gate to the Bifurland flagship now to keep me company."

"We'll meet soon enough," said Laetícia. "I'm planning to gate to Riyas before dawn to assist in implementing Jenet's plan however I can. Give my best to Mafuta and Felix. I'm sure you're glad to have them with you. I asked Mafuta to learn as much as possible about the hooded Bifurland wizards in the amber robes. They're odd—and they puzzle me."

"I'll pass the word," said Quintillius. "As for the Bifurlanders, you're just intrigued because the amber-robed wizards don't talk."

"I'm intrigued because we know next to nothing about their powers and abilities," said Laetícia. "I don't like not knowing."

"Understood," said Quin. "The fleet is on schedule, so I should arrive in Riyas at dawn. I want to be there for the fireworks."

"Fire at least, if not fireworks," said Laetícia. "Though dragon fire is reputed to be spectacular."

"Speaking of dragons," said Quintillius, "Did I tell you I met Zûrafiérix?"

"The *blue* dragon?" asked Laetícia.

"Yes," said Quintillius. "She swims."

"Fascinating," said Laetícia.

"She's also quite polite—and bigger than you can possibly imagine."

"I doubt that," said Laetícia. "You know I'm quite imaginative."

"Let me rephrase," said Quin. "Her head alone was the size of half the Bifurland flagship."

"I see," said Laetícia. "That would stretch the limits of my imagination."

"You should have seen Bjarni and Signý's daughter and her friends," said Quintillius.

"The young gold dragon riders?" asked Laetícia.

"Correct," said Quintillius. "Signý had to threaten to lash them to the deck to prevent them from following Zûrafiérix once she finally surfaced and flew off toward the Tamloch fleet."

"The little gold dragons?" asked Laetícia.

"No, her daughter and her niece," said Quintillius. "Sigrun and Rannveigr. I've told you about them—they're close to the same age as Primus."

"Don't agree to any marriage alliances with the Bifurlanders until we've had a chance to talk about it," said Laetícia. She smiled at Quintillius through the communication ring's interface.

"I won't," said Quin. "Stay safe."

"And you," said Laetícia. *"Ave amor meus..."*

Quintillius collapsed the communications ring down to a plain gold band, returned it to his finger, and looked forward to the dawn.

* * * * *

"How far are we from Riyas?" asked Nûd from his vantage point on Rocky's back, flying near the blue dragon's head.

"It's not far west of us, if I'm remembering properly," said Zûra. "It has been two thousand years, though. My eyes can detect light beyond those hills."

"Probably torches on the walls of the city," said Nûd.

"Unless Viridáxés decided to start his destructive rampage *before* the sun came up," said Zûra.

"Let's hope not," said Nûd. "We're counting on his attack commencing at dawn, and that's still several hours off. We're early."

"My apologies," said Zûrafiérix. "Even with our stops to visit the Bifurland and Tamloch fleets, with my increased wingspan, my speed in the air is so much greater than before. I misjudged the timing."

"If we can find a place to land, I might be able to get a nap," Nûd suggested. "Do you need to rest, Zûra?"

"No," said the dragon. "Not after sleeping for twenty centuries— but I could use some time to prepare myself for meeting Viridáxés. We haven't seen each other since we left Riyas in different directions to reach the quarries where we were to be buried."

"Your personalities are quite different," said Nûd. "Viridáxés is rather..."

"Self-centered? Impulsive? Full of himself?"

"All that, yes," said Nûd. "He seems like an adolescent version of Túathal."

"I don't know Túathal," said Zûrafiérix, "but Viridáxés was all those things *before* he was buried in a magestone quarry. Bonding with Túathal may have just made him worse."

"What do you mean?" asked Nûd.

"I paid attention to the senior mages who crossed on the First Ships," said Zûrafiérix. "They said that dragons' personalities tend to reflect the leaders they serve."

"Then why haven't you flown west to hide from your destiny?" asked Nûd.

"Don't sell yourself short, my king," said Zûrafiérix. "That was not of your choosing. If I understand things correctly, your mother and her parents decided that for you."

"I guess," said Nûd.

"In my experience, you have shown yourself to be calm in a crisis, as well as brave and resourceful. You've spent the last decade learning the history of Dâron, its laws, and its lands. You've even demonstrated wisdom—except about yourself, and that will come with age and experience," said Zûrafiérix.

"You can't be reflecting *my* personality," said Nûd. "You're wise already."

"When two thousand years you are, wise you may be," teased Zûra. "Does that sound like a proper epigram?"

"I'll have to ask my grandfather next time I see him," said Nûd. "I don't understand how dragons can reflect leaders' personalities when they don't know which king they'll be bonding with? You could have emerged when the Old King was still on the throne. I'm nothing like *him*."

"That's a puzzle for those wiser than either of us," said Zûrafiérix. "The senior mages from the time of the First Ships said that dragons' minds may be attuned to internal congruencies that look forward in time, though that notion seems strange to me. Better to accept things as they are for now."

"Does that mean Viridáxés will mirror Túathal's personality for thousands of years to come?" asked Nûd.

"Perhaps, perhaps not," said Zûrafiérix. "It is also said that mating changes dragons' priorities."

"Interesting," said Nûd. "It's a lot to think about."

"I see a clearing below us that would be a good place for you to rest," said Zûra. "Rocky can guard you."

The wyvern bobbed his head in agreement.

"I spotted black and white wolf-whales off the coast on our way here," said Zûrafiérix. "One of them would be more filling than a dozen farmers' cows."

"And far less trouble if the farmers came to me asking for payment," said Nûd.

"Sleep well," said Zûrafiérix. "I'll be back to wake you before dawn."

* * * * *

"Hello, Doethan," said Princess Rúth, Túathal's younger sister. "I wondered when you'd *ring* me."

Doethan smiled at her through their communication rings' circular interface.

"I'm in Nova Eboracum and should be in Riyas soon," he said. "May I see you?"

"I expect that depends on Túathal," said the princess. "You know I'd be glad to see you if he didn't object."

"If all goes well, your brother may not *be* in a position to object to much of anything," said Doethan. "Has word reached you to be watching from the western wall at dawn?"

"One of the servants told me," said Princess Rúth. "I'll be on the roof of one of the towers beside the main gate—and well-guarded."

"Look for me on top of the tallest tower on the western side of Riyas," said Doethan.

"The one where the drunken wizard tried to fly without his..." began Rúth.

"That's the one," said Doethan. "I'll wave to you."

"And I'll wave back," said Princess Rúth.

"I'd like that," said Doethan.

"I want to learn more about what took you to Nova Eboracum," said the princess.

"I'll be glad to tell you face to face if we have the chance," said Doethan.

"Be careful," said Princess Rúth, "and good luck. Things are never what they seem where my brother is concerned."

"I'll remember," said Doethan.

A few moments later, after smiling at Rúth and allowing his eyes to dance with hope and possibilities, he reluctantly closed the connection.

Chapter 54

On the Tallest Tower

It was an hour before dawn when Merry, Inthíra and Eynon, with Chee, floated a thousand feet above Tamloch's capital, using lenses of solidified sound adapted to see at night to take in the true shape of the city.

"There have been changes since the paintings Verro showed us were made," said Merry.

"Cities are always changing," said Inthíra. "They're living things—always growing or dying, never static."

"I think I can hold the shape of the city in my head," said Eynon. "I'm just not sure about getting the colors right. Everything looks red and gray through our lenses."

"Don't worry too much about color," said Inthíra. "Focus on shapes and shadows. The light will be different at dawn and Verro and his team will generate lots of fog. Our false version of Riyas should be enough to fool Túathal."

"It's not Túathal I'm worried about," said Merry. "It's Viridáxés."

"Our imitation doesn't have to fool the dragon for long," said Inthíra. "Just long enough for Jenet's plan to work."

"True," said Eynon.

"Chee," said Chee with the same intonation as he climbed from Eynon's shoulder to sit in the crook of his arm.

"What am I going to do about *you,* little friend?" asked Eynon. "I can't have you jogging my elbow while I'm concentrating."

"Maybe this will help?" said Merry, bringing her flying disk alongside Eynon's and offering him a small flask from her belt pouch.

"What is it?" asked Eynon.

"A half-pint of Applegarth's Finest fortified hard cider," she replied. "I was saving it for a special occasion."

"It seems a shame to waste such a drink on a raconette's unrefined palate," said Inthíra from her flying disk a few feet away.

"Do you have a better idea?" asked Merry. No suggestions were forthcoming, so Eynon handed the flask to Chee. His clever fingers deftly removed the cork stopper and sniffed it. Looking up at Eynon for confirmation, Chee took a long swallow from the flask. A second later his small head rolled back against Eynon's upper arm.

Eynon steadied the flask before Chee could drop it and with a bit of juggling, managed to replace the cork. He then deposited the raconette between his feet on his flying disk.

"Sleep well," said Eynon. Chee's eyes were already closed and the little familiar was smiling.

"It's time to get to work," said Inthíra.

"Right," said Eynon. "My part is first. I guess I'd better get started." He dove for the flat roof of the tallest tower on the city's western wall. The roof was thirty feet in diameter and surrounded by a circle of waist-high crenelations. Eynon tried not to think about which side of the roof the previous owner had jumped from. He was already concentrating on building the full-sized model of Riyas when he sensed Merry and Inthíra land behind him.

Eynon let his wizardry sense the elevations of the land around the marshalling field. *Part of what's going to make this work is that the slope of the ground is the same,* he confirmed. The gentle rise as you moved away from the harbor at Riyas was mirrored by the changes in slope leading up to the hill just north of the marshalling field. That hill looked the same as the hill inside the walls of Riyas where the royal palace and the offices of the king's ministers were located.

Taking a slow breath and remembering how the city looked from above, Eynon leaned against one of the crenelations and pressed his tongue against his upper teeth in concentration. He could feel both his magestones pulsing, sending out mixed waves of purple light. Eynon was about to generate his full-sized model of Riyas on top of the marshalling field when he had a better idea.

He began by creating a thin, flexible plane of solidified sound the same dimensions as the city, but several hundred feet above it. Oblivious to Inthíra and Merry's surprised expressions, he allowed the plane to float down and cover every street and building, like a bed sheet draped over a sleeping cat. Feeling the texture of his plane, he made adjustments here and there to capture fine details.

When his impression of Riyas in solidified sound was complete, he lifted his arms. The plane rose two hundred feet back into the sky and followed the motions of Eynon's arms as he guided the imitation city over the marshalling field and let it settle in place. He heard applause from all along the western wall of the true Riyas and realized thousands of city residents were already assembled and watching avidly.

"Nicely done," said Inthíra.

"I'm impressed," said Merry. "That was a lot easier than generating the shape of every building individually."

"And more accurate, too," said Inthíra. "See if you can make your plane the color of the limestone used for most buildings," she added. "Merry and I can work on details."

Inthíra and Merry sketched in lines of mortar on the imitation city's walls and buildings. Merry painted rooftops, shutters and doors with bright virtual colors while Inthíra lined the tops of the walls with row upon row of cheering simulated Tamloch subjects. The real Tamloch citizens cheered even louder when they saw Inthíra's simulations.

Fercha joined them on the roof of the tower. She stood on top of one of the crenelations, ready to generate a sensitive hemispherical shield around the top of the tower if necessary. Such a shield would give everyone on top of the tower some protection from inbound magical attacks while not interfering with the powerful illusion magic Eynon and Merry and Inthíra were working. Offensive spells *could* get through the three holes Fercha planned to leave in her sphere, but she had offensive magic of her own to discourage any overly brave or foolhardy wizard from trying to send any.

Fercha watched Uirsé and Salder reach the tower's roof by climbing up the flight of stairs inside it. They were holding hands and had serious looks on their faces. Young love was grand, but it could be so very very painful.

She nearly laughed when Herophilos Bodégash, the apothecary with the long black beard, reached the roof a few moments after the reconciled lovers. He carried a bulging leather bag and had the good sense to keep silent in the presence of so many powerful wizards. Fercha was pleased when he found a spot with a decent view to the west that was far from Eynon, Merry and Inthíra. Uirsé must have warned the man of dire consequences if he acted in his usual ebullient manner.

When Verro and his contingent of wizards from the fish-drying shed swept in from the east on their flying disks, Fercha smiled and waved at her husband. Uirsé and Salder moved to join Verro. Fercha could see them speak to each other but didn't want to distract herself by generating a listening spell. She wanted to stay sensitive to potential external attacks.

With a loud *pop,* a flying disk materialized through an *ad hoc* gate near the middle of the roof. Fercha nearly blasted its riders with a lightning bolt before she could tell who had arrived. To her surprise, it was Laetícia, one of the few wizards in Orluin able to create *ad hoc* gates.

Standing behind Laetícia was Doethan, and next to him was a woman a few years younger who looked enough like a female version of Verro that she had to be Princess Rúth. It struck Fercha that she hadn't seen Princess Rúth since they were both young women at court in Brendinas.

Fercha waved a greeting to Laetícia and hailed Doethan, who carried a mesh sack that bulged in odd ways. "Where have *you* been, neighbor?" she asked. "Off learning qua-qua?"

"No," said Doethan. "Buying dough rings. Would you like one? You need to keep your strength up."

"Maybe later," said Fercha. "Is that…?"

"Princess Rúth?" answered Doethan. "It is, I'm pleased to say." He put his arm around Rúth's shoulder and continued. "She was surrounded by guards a quarter mile down the wall by the main entrance to the city. Laetícia offered to gate in and help me liberate her."

"I see your rescue mission was successful," said Fercha, inclining her head to the second most powerful person in Occidens Province, or maybe the first.

"Very," said Princess Rúth, smiling broadly. "I'm in Laetícia's debt."

"I'm glad to do my part to support young love," said Laetícia.

"Not so young anymore, are we Doethan?" teased the princess.

"We were young when we started," Doethan offered.

"There you have it," said Laetícia. "What can I do to help?"

"I'm not sure," said Fercha. "You and Verro can gate where you're needed. You can be our reserves."

Verro smiled and pretended to protest. "Wasn't I supposed to be in charge of fog?" he asked.

"Doethan can lead that effort now that he's here," said Fercha. "He's foggy more than half the time anyway."

"Hey," said Doethan. "Just because you're right doesn't mean you need to *say* it." He smiled at Fercha and she grinned back. "Let's get started, good wizards," he said. "We want lots of fog in place *before* the first hint of dawn."

Doethan showed Verro's wizards how to form vast clouds of fog from the cold waters of Fadacaolo Bay and the warmer waters of the Ádhabhainn, the so-called Lucky River that emptied into the bay at Riyas. There was already plenty of fog to draw on where they met. Soon Riyas was draped in thick fog and wisps of it were encroaching onto the illusionary city. The moon had gone down and the stars were beginning to fade, so the imitation Riyas really did make a convincing facsimile of the original, even to wizardry-enhanced eyes.

"Be sure to give the people on the walls of the city a chance to see Túathal's actions when he arrives," said Fercha.

"Of course," said Doethan. "I know the plan."

"Laetícia, could you gate down to Dârio and let him know we've got everything in place up here?" asked Fercha.

"Certainly," said Laetícia. "But Doethan did just give me a communications ring paired with one he gave Dârio. I could *ring* him if you prefer."

"He may not be in a position to respond to a ring," said Fercha. "If you show up in person, you can leave word with Duke Háiddon or Jenet if that would be more appropriate."

"Understood," said Laetícia. She pulled her flying disk from her shoulders and prepared to mount it.

"Wait!" said Fercha. "Has anyone heard from Nûd?"

Eynon and Merry and Inthíra had their attentions focused elsewhere, but everyone else shook their heads.

"He and his dragon paid a call on the Bifurland fleet a few hours ago," said Laetícia. "My husband told me about it. He said Nûd and his wyvern set off after a scout wizard from the Tamloch fleet and Zûrafiérix flew after him a few minutes later."

"Oh," said Fercha. She found it hard to believe anyone with the Tamloch fleet could pose a threat to Nûd, Rocky, and Zûrafiérix.

"If it helps," said Laetícia, "my agents told me Túathal stripped the fleet of all its experienced wizards."

"Against my recommendation," said Verro. "There is one who's quite talented, but not in a way my brother would appreciate."

"Thank you for that reassurance," said Fercha. "I'm sure Nûd is fine. How much trouble can he get into with a dragon protecting him?" She eyed a communications ring on her outstretched hand, not thinking anyone would notice. Only Verro and Laetícia did.

"I'll gate down to Dârio then," said Laetícia. "Maybe he's had news." She rose a few feet from the tower's roof and disappeared with a *whoosh* of air rushing into the space where she had been.

Chapter 55

Cáinta's Gift

"Dârio, wake up!" said Jenet. She shoved his shoulder gently, then less so. "There's someone here to see you."

"Who is it?" said Dârio. "How long have I been asleep?" He sat up and swung his feet over the edge of the camp bed's folding frame, then fumbled for his boots in the dim light of a wizard lamp.

"She'd rather not say—and not much more than an hour," came Duke Háiddon's voice from outside the tent's front flaps.

"Come in then, and bring her with you," said Dârio after a silent yawn. He didn't insult the duke by asking if their visitor had been checked for weapons and poisons first.

The woman who entered seemed familiar, though her head and body were hidden by a voluminous black cloak with a deep hood. The garment looked three sizes too big for her. To further conceal her identify, she had wrapped a long green woolen scarf around her face so that only her eyes were visible. Dârio couldn't even see her hands, because she carried a large canvas bag that seemed both stuffed to bursting and light enough to lift without strain.

"Welcome," said Dârio. "Would you like some refreshment? A place to sit? Somewhere to put down your burden?"

"No," said the woman in a guttural rasp.

She's trying to disguise her voice, thought Dârio. *And not doing a good job of it.*

The woman pushed the canvas bag at him and said, "Here!"

Dârio took the bag and sensed it held fabric.

"Open it," the woman barked.

Dârio fumbled for the drawstring, so Jenet helped him. She pulled on one side of the bag mouth while Dârio held the other. The bag's contents tumbled out onto the bed where Dârio and Jenet had been sleeping. Duke Háiddon grabbed a corner of the pile of green and gold fabric that had been inside the bag and shook it gently. His other hand found a shoulder of the garment and held it up to be admired.

"That is a kingly gift, good lady," said Jenet. Her father was holding an embroidered cloth-of-gold surcoat with a four-pointed Tamloch crown outlined in black above that kingdom's symbol—the four circles of a bright green quatrefoil.

"It's not just a kingly gift," said Duke Háiddon. "It's Túathal's. I saw him wear it at a tournament held in his honor in Brendinas when we were both young."

"Were you *ever* young, father?" asked Jenet.

"Hush, daughter," said the duke. "With luck, you'll reach my advanced age yourself some day."

"You've run quite a risk to take such a treasure," said Dârio.

"I know," said the woman, not bothering to hide her true voice now. "Consider it a vote of confidence in your future leadership. I didn't tell the others I took this from the palace so that I'd be the only one for Túathal to blame if he somehow remained in power."

"I'll do my best to ensure that doesn't happen," said Dârio.

"Túathal is slippery," said the woman. "I've dealt with him for a decade and won't believe I'm finished with him until I see his head on a pike above the main gate to Riyas." She paused and sniffed behind her wool scarf. "Perhaps not even then."

"We will provide the people of Riyas with protection from Túathal," said Dârio.

"We'll need it," said the woman. "I'm sure Túathal's spies in the city have told him about the celebrations we held when word reached us of his so-called death. I'm not looking forward to the revenge he will visit upon us for that."

"Don't worry," said Dârio. "We're counting on Túathal's overreach and expect him to show his people he's unfit to rule. Return to Riyas and watch to the west."

"I will," said the woman. She bowed to Dârio and nodded to Duke Háiddon and Jenet. "I can see myself out," she said. "And don't forget those wisents you promised."

Jenet waited a few moments before speaking. "I can understand how she lasted as mayor of Riyas for a decade of Túathal's rule," she said after she was sure the mayor was far enough away not to overhear.

"And *I* can see why she's eager for Túathal's reign to be over," added Duke Háiddon. He held the elaborate surcoat higher. "Try it on, Sire. I'll bet it will look better on you than it ever did on Túathal."

"There's no question of that," said Jenet.

Dârio bent his body and used both arms to find the bottom of the surcoat then rose up and stuck his head through its square neckline. Jenet helped him smooth out the fabric once it was settled on his shoulders. Duke Háiddon found Dârio's sword and sword belt under the camp bed where they had been carefully placed earlier. He buckled the belt around Dârio's waist, then stepped back and smiled.

"You look like a proper king now," said the duke.

"I've been king of Dâron for the past two years," said Dârio.

"Yes, but now you look like a proper king of *Tamloch,*" said Háiddon.

"All those gold threads will look spectacular when the first rays of dawn catch them," said Jenet.

"It looks good even when lit by a simple wizard lamp," said her father.

"Ahem," came a guard's voice from just outside the tent. "You have another visitor, Your Majesty."

Dârio heard the sound of clacking beads and instantly guessed who was there based on stories Fercha had told him.

"Come in, Laetícia," he said. "How are things progressing on the wall?"

"Quite well," Laetícia began as she pushed aside the tent flap. When she saw Dârio in his surcoat her mouth formed a circle and whatever she'd been about to say turned into, "Oh my!"

"Do you like it?" asked Dârio. He performed a full turn so she could see the fine embroidery on both sides.

"I do," said Laetícia. "It's quite a piece of work—just like you are." The Roma spymaster smiled. "Couldn't you liberate Túathal's crown from the palace, too?"

Háiddon answered on Dârio's behalf. "We thought it better to save that for his formal coronation ceremony."

Laetícia tossed her head and laughed, leading to more beads clacking. "As I said, things are going well on the wall. The imitation of Riyas is in place on the marshalling field and fog covers the real city and the docks. Some of it has spilled over onto the illusion Riyas, too."

"Good," said Dârio. "Now we just have to hope Túathal behaves the way we expect him to."

"Yes," said Laetícia. "The odds of that are good. In my experience, I've found leopards seldom change their spots."

"What about hyenas?" asked Jenet.

"There are different sayings about them," said Laetícia. "Oh, your finery almost made me forget. Fercha wanted me to ask if any of you have heard from Nûd and Zûrafiérix? She hasn't."

Dârio looked at Jenet then at Duke Háiddon. Both shook their heads. "We haven't heard from them, but they know their part in the plan. I'm sure we can count on them."

"I heard from my husband that Dârianûd fled the battlefield when confronted with the prospect of serving as king of Dâron," said Laetícia. "Are you sure he didn't get cold feet?"

"I hope not," said Dârio. "Fighting one dragon without another would be a losing proposition."

Chapter 56

Breakfast with Túathal

Duke Néillen was *not* happy. His entreaties to get Viridáxés to stop eating his prized dairy herd were met with the dragon's equivalent of laughter. A few minutes ago, his steward had informed him that the dragon's count of bovine *snacks* was now up to twenty-three. It would take Néillen years to rebuild his stock. On top of that his estate's revenues from milk and cheese production would suffer.

On the bright side, thought Néillen, *I may not own this estate in a few hours if Túathal loses. Then it will be someone else's problem.* Somehow, despite the fact that he hadn't had a chance to sleep, that prospect cheered him.

Néillen had gotten Gwýnnett and her party squared away by assigning them a seldom-used set of rooms in his castle and having his cooks roused from their beds to deliver trays of yesterday's bread and the second-best quality cheese to each room. They could join Túathal for breakfast in a few minutes if they wanted more than that. He'd made sure not to walk or stand too close to Princess Gwýnnett when he escorted the visitors to their rooms and even though he hadn't touched her, Néillen had washed his hands at the first opportunity.

Next came the tasks he was *really* dreading—waking Túathal and informing him of Gwýnnett's arrival. Néillen was concerned that Túathal would be angry Néillen hadn't informed him about Gwýnnett flying in, but he expected Túathal would be equally angry if Néillen woke him before he'd had a chance to rest. Néillen thought it would be better to deal with a somewhat rested angry king than an utterly tired one.

Néillen tapped lightly on the door to Túathal's room. "Your Majesty," said Néillen softly. He didn't hear an answer but didn't expect to. The door was made from thick oak boards and designed to be soundproof. He wrapped on it hard with his knuckles and raised his voice. "Your Majesty! Time to get up!" Frustrated, Duke Néillen drew his sword and pounded on the door with its hilt while bellowing the way he'd learned to do when commanding troops over the tumult of battle. "YOUR MAJESTY! WAKE UP! YOUR DRAGON AND YOUR DESTINY AWAIT YOU!"

He was rewarded for his efforts by hearing the bolt drawn inside the room. Túathal opened the door a few inches and stared out at Néillen. "What was all that about?" asked the king. "You're making enough noise to wake the dead. Couldn't you just knock?"

"My apologies, Sire," said Duke Néillen. "It won't happen again."

"See that it doesn't," said Túathal. "Is my breakfast ready? Do you have the tasters I requested?"

"About that, Your Majesty..." Néillen began.

"Never mind," said Túathal. "I'll be right out. I could eat a cow."

He closed the door in the duke's face before Néillen could say what he was thinking. "If Viridáxés has left you any..." the duke muttered.

Túathal emerged a few minutes later with his face washed and his hair immaculately combed. Someone on Duke Néillen's staff had cleaned the king's fine gold robes covered in hundreds of small green quatrefoils. He wasn't smiling—Néillen knew Túathal was especially dangerous when he smiled—but he wasn't frowning either.

"Breakfast is this way, Your Majesty," said the duke. "There will be visitors joining us."

"Who?" barked the king.

"Princess Gwýnnett, three wizards, and two sons of a minor baron from western Dâron recently exiled to the southern Clan Lands," said Duke Néillen. To his astonishment, Túathal was more intrigued than incensed.

"That sounds exactly like the sort of strays Gwýnnett would attract," said the king. "I could use some wizards, since all of mine seem to be loyal to my brother, not me—and Verro wants to kill me."

"Yes, Sire," said Néillen, feeling like he'd just avoided forty lashes.

"Make sure the princess is seated as far away from me as possible," ordered Túathal. "I have no interest in having this be my last meal."

"A wise precaution, My Liege," said Néillen. He resolved not to eat or drink anything that hadn't been tested by Túathal's tasters.

In the duke's private dining room, Túathal sat at the head of the long table. The two daggers he requested were near his plate. Kennig was seated to his left and Néillen to his right. Princess Gwýnnett sat at the far end ten feet away, opposite Túathal, with Hibblig to her right and Fox to her left. Grúgàch was to Hibblig's right and Fool sat across from him. Several empty chairs separated the groups at each end of the table.

The tasters assigned to Túathal had sampled every dish he'd be eating an hour ago and still seemed healthy. For form's sake, they ate bites of cold sausage rolls and room temperature soft-boiled eggs before passing them to the king, the duke, and Kennig. Gwýnnett and those at her end of the table ate hot sausage rolls and shelled hard-boiled eggs fresh from the pot. Introductions had been made and Túathal seemed fascinated by Kennig.

"Are you the one who created an entire play from illusions of solidified sound?" asked the king. "I'd heard about that even here in Tamloch."

"I did, Your Majesty," said Kennig. "The farce itself was Athican, but I wrote the songs, designed the sets, and generated all the characters."

"That's quite a feat of wizardry," said Túathal.

"Just a minor amusement for the court," said Kennig.

"Nonsense," said Túathal. He leaned close to Kennig and whispered in his ear.

"That wouldn't be a problem, Your Majesty," said Kennig. "It's child's play. Let's hope it isn't necessary."

"Excellent," said Túathal.

The king was smiling, which made Néillen particularly nervous. As if to mirror Túathal, Gwýnnett had just whispered to Hibblig and she was smiling too.

I wonder if the southern or northern Clan Lands would be more welcoming to an experienced military commander, thought Néillen. *I hope I don't need to find out.*

"Néillen!" said Túathal. "I'm going to need the door to my room. It's quite sturdy and should work well for what I intend. See that it is brought to the castle's courtyard immediately."

"Yes, Sire," said Duke Néillen. He really liked that door and would be sorry to lose it to whatever mysterious purpose Túathal's twisted mind had devised.

Chapter 57

The Reluctant Dragon

"There you are!" said Nûd when Zûrafiérix returned to join him and Rocky in the clearing east of Riyas. "I wondered why you weren't back sooner."

"I did some thinking while I was hunting," said Zûrafiérix. "I determined that it would be better if I didn't appear shortly after Viridáxés started destroying things but waited a bit to let things play out."

"But your role is to ensure Viridáxés is kept in check," said Nûd. "What if he decides to destroy the *real* version of Riyas?"

"I would show myself, if that happened," said Zûra, "but I want to give Viridáxés a chance to do the right thing on his own."

"If you think that's wise," said Nûd.

"I do," said Zûra.

"Where can you wait and watch from where you won't be seen?" asked Nûd.

Zûra told him.

"That makes it hard for Rocky and me to stay with you," Nûd replied.

"It does, but it can't be helped," said Zûra.

"Shouldn't we tell the others about our change in plans?" asked Nûd.

"I think it best if we just allow things to play out as they will," said the dragon. "There are bigger things at stake than the fates of two kingdoms."

"I don't know if it's wise or not, but you're my friend and I'm going to trust you," said Nûd.

"Thank you for that," said Zûrafiérix. "You and Rocky should head for the highest tower on the western wall of Riyas. I flew over the city, hidden by the fog, and sensed a major collection of mages there. That must be where your friends are."

"Thank *you*," said Nûd. "The highest tower on the western wall. Did you hear that, Rocky?"

The wyvern twisted his head to look at Nûd and snorted.

"Right," said Nûd. "Of course you did. Best of luck to you, Zûra."

"And to both of you," said the dragon. Zûrafiérix launched herself into the air, flying southwest in the direction of the harbor.

Rocky glanced at Nûd as if to say *mount up,* so Nûd did. Wyvern and rider proceeded west toward Riyas. Behind them, the first rays of dawn appeared in the east.

Chapter 58

Death from Above

Duke Néillen winced with every hammer blow as long nails attached a pair of leather footstraps to the door Túathal had appropriated. Even if Néillen somehow got the well-made bedroom door back, it would never be the same. He watched the carpenters lift the door and overlap it on Kennig and Hibblig's flying disks before he realized what Túathal had in mind. He'd convinced the two wizards to fly him into battle so he could direct Viridáxés without the risks associated with *riding* a dragon bent on destruction.

A dozen feet away, Fool was standing behind Grúgàch on *his* flying disk. The youngest Mastlands brother had a stack of small crossbows at his feet. All were cocked and loaded, something Néillen would never tolerate from his own archers. It was too easy for one of them to go off by accident and hurt a friend, not an enemy.

"Joining our fun?" Túathal called to the southern Clan Lands' wizard.

"Not my fight," said Grúgàch. He rose and angled south, back toward his homeland.

"Good riddance," said Túathal. "You can't trust anyone from the Clan Lands, south *or* north." Then he noticed Fox hanging on to Hibblig's belt. "Why aren't you leaving with the other cowards?" asked the king.

"I want to see that dragon of yours in action," said Fox. "And the odds of a reward and a title seem a lot higher fighting for you than for the so-called honor of the southern Clan Lands."

"I like the way you think, young man," said Túathal.

Ten years ago, I was a lot like him, Néillen realized. *I've risen far—let's hope I don't fall.*

"Where's Gwýnnett?" asked Túathal. "She should be here to see me off, at least."

"I think she's still sleeping," said Kennig. "At least she was when I left her."

Néillen couldn't miss the daggers in the look Hibblig gave his cousin. He'd have to remember that and use it to his own advantage if an opportunity presented itself. He knew Túathal had seen Hibblig's look as well.

Túathal glared at Néillen. "Aren't you climbing on? Don't you want to witness my victory?"

"Of course, Sire," said Néillen. He hadn't spared a thought for how he'd get to the battlefield, assuming he'd be stuck riding on the dragon's back with his king.

"Snap to it and ride behind Kennig," ordered Túathal.

Néillen nodded and quick-stepped to take the indicated position.

"Now let's collect my dragon," said Túathal.

If he's not too fat to fly after eating all my cows, thought Néillen. He knew that was unlikely. A dragon the size of Viridáxés would need to eat an entire herd of wisents before it slowed him down.

Hibblig and Kennig ascended with Túathal balanced on the door between them. The leather straps over his boots made it easy for the king to keep his footing. When they were above the castle's walls, Viridáxés raised his head and dropped a well-gnawed thighbone.

"King of Tamloch, is it time?" asked the dragon.

"It is," said Túathal. "My own people have chosen to disrespect me. We must demonstrate my power—and yours—so the people of Tamloch will know that *I* am their king and that *I* am the one to lead them against the Roma!"

"Yes, my king!" roared Viridáxés. "How may I serve you?"

"We fly to Riyas, arriving with the dawn," said Túathal. "Knock down a hundred feet of city wall. Blast scores of people with your fire. Show them that none can stand before the mighty Viridáxés and the mightier king who commands him!"

"Yes, my king," said the dragon.

Néillen was pleased to hear Viridáxés' voice wasn't as confident as it was earlier. Túathal may have gone too far. He didn't think it was wise for a human king to tell a great dragon that *he* was more powerful.

Viridáxés was ready to leap skyward, but Túathal stopped him. "Aren't you forgetting something, my dragon?"

The dragon looked puzzled, then saw his chain at his feet, half-covered with cow bones.

"Sorry," said Viridáxés. He clutched the chain in his claws, launched himself up and spread his huge wings, flapping like a monstrous batsnake toward Riyas. The wizards and their passengers, royal and otherwise, kept close behind him.

Néillen held tightly to Kennig's belt and wondered where Gwýnnett really was. She was too interested in Túathal and his quest to regain power *not* to want to see Viridáxés teach the people of Riyas a lesson. A few white-knuckled minutes later—Néillen was *not* fond of heights—the flying disks descended by the hill where Captain Rood had assembled her forces that had arrived too late to take part in yesterday's battle in Dâron.

"Get off," ordered Túathal. "Your place is with your troops and you can watch my triumph from here."

"Yes, Your Majesty," said Néillen as he hopped off. He shouldn't have bothered replying. Túathal and the pair of wizards acting as his literal supporters were already back in the air, close to Viridáxés. *Something is off,* thought Néillen. *The hill where I told Captain Rood to wait was due west of the marshalling field. Now it's next to the city.* "There's not much I can do about it now," said Néillen to himself.

"What did you say?" asked Captain Rood who had come over to join him.

"There's something important I need to tell King Túathal," said Duke Néillen, "but I don't have any way to get word to him."

"I thought someone like you, the kingdom's earl marshal, would have one of them fancy magical rings that let you talk at a distance," said the captain. "Is yours broken?"

"No," said Néillen. "It's just that I know Túathal won't answer if I ring him now. He's too interested in watching Viridáxés."

"Me and my troops are interested in watchin' the big dragon, too," said Captain Rood. "It's sort of like seein' destruction personified."

"You have the soul of a poet, Captain," said Duke Néillen.

"I hope that's a compliment," said Rood.

"It is," said Néillen. "Look!" said the duke, pointing to the sky above not-quite-Riyas.

Viridáxés was circling just south of the city walls, swinging his chain. The people watching from those walls and ones nearby began screaming loud enough to be faintly heard where Néillen and Rood and her troops stood more than a mile away. Néillen had seen this before, at the castle along the Abbenoth. He knew what was in store, but not Rood and her soldiers. They began shouting. Even the rescued Tamloch nobles joined in.

The sun was more than a sliver to the east, allowing Néillen to see Túathal and Hibblig and Kennig and Fox as faint silhouettes against the brightening sky. Then their figures disappeared, displaced by a version of Túathal's head nearly as big as the head at the end of the dragon's long neck.

"People of Tamloch!" came a voice like Túathal's but a hundred times as loud. "Feel the wrath of your king!"

Kennig, thought Néillen. *The head must be one of Kennig's illusions. Is* that *what Túathal had been asking the wizard at breakfast?*

"Strike, Viridáxés!" ordered Túathal's echoing voice. "Show them the price of their defiance!"

The great green dragon ascended and corkscrewed down next to the walls by the city's gates, snapping the giant links of chain into the thick walls near their base with a force so powerful the closest stones were not displaced but disintegrated. The remaining stones above, unsupported, toppled down to fill the breach. What had been a solid stretch of wall was now so much rubble. He could make out the bodies of men, women and children, some still moving, trapped in the debris.

"By the First Ships!" said Captain Rood. Several of her soldiers echoed her words and added ones of their own.

Néillen stood transfixed. He knew what was coming next. *Dragonfire!*

Chapter 59

Not Quite as Planned

Inthíra's eyes scanned the roof for Doethan and his team. "Excellent work on the fog cover, old friend. It's thick enough to hide the city from the air, but you've left a narrow band clear so people on the walls can see what's happening to the copy of Riyas." She moved to stand between the two young wizards providing the majority of that illusion. "Nice job on the damaged wall, Eynon," she said after Viridáxés' chain struck. "Your people in the rubble look quite realistic, Merry," Inthíra added. "I'll make their screams louder so they carry to the *real* Riyas."

"There are plenty of screams coming from *these* walls already," said Princess Rúth. "How can my brother be so heartless?"

"He's doing a great job of proving he's unfit to be king," said Fercha. She'd seen Túathal riding between two wizards and recognized one of them as Hibblig—Gwýnnett's pet wizard—and hoped that didn't mean Gwýnnett herself was nearby. The giant projection of Túathal's head was facing the false Riyas, not the true one, so they couldn't see Túathal's expressions, but his words and tone of voice made his intentions clear.

"I could gate in right behind them and blast them with a fireball," said Laetícia.

"No," said Verro. "We want Túathal discredited—shown to be totally unfit to rule. The longer he keeps attacking the Riyas illusion and the more simulated people Viridáxés kills, the stronger the case against him will be."

"Eynon! Merry! Brace yourselves!" shouted Inthíra. "Viridáxés is about to spray the imitation city with dragonfire!"

Squeezing his hands into tight fists, Eynon concentrated on holding the complex patterns of solidified sound in place *and* on preparing to adjust those patterns based on where Viridáxés decided to shoot his flames. It felt like he was using his magic to lean against a tottering three-story brick wall and keep it standing through gale-force winds and pounding rain. Beside him he could feel magical energy radiating from Merry as she stretched her capacity to maintain *her* illusions.

"Here he comes!" yelled Inthíra.

Viridáxés had been high above the imitation city. Now, after a steep dive, he was heading straight for the main gates of illusionary Riyas, his mouth wide. Hundreds of simulated people were on the walls above the gates. They screamed when a hundred-foot-long jet of green fire shot from Viridáxés' mouth and played across the gates and the ersatz observers above.

Eynon, Merry, and Inthíra were ready for everything—except what actually happened. When the dragonfire touched the simulated city, the entire construct winked out. Eynon fell forward into a gap between crenelations and Merry landed on top of him. Inthíra fell forward as well, but she remained mostly standing because there was no place for her to fall.

"Ooof!" said Eynon when Merry and Inthíra's combined weights forced air out of his lungs. Both his magestones wanted to continue what they'd been doing—generating and maintaining complex patterns of solidified sound—but they couldn't. The patterns were gone.

Inthíra levered herself fully upright and stepped back so Merry could stand. Merry helped Eynon get to his feet in turn. They held each other, seeking something sure when their illusions had failed.

"Blast!" said Verro. "It wasn't long enough. The people need more proof Túathal doesn't care about his kingdom, only himself."

"Wait brother," said Princess Rúth. "Listen."

Everyone on the tallest western tower strained to hear. Merry cast a listening spell, glad to use a small bit of familiar magic that had never let her down. She heard waves of *boos* punctuated with angry shouts.

Down with Túathal!
Murderer!
Traitor!
Depose him!

Merry listened a bit longer and heard *Down with Túathal!* predominate, thanks to its rhythm. Soon, nearly everyone in Riyas was taking up the chant.

"I think your plan worked," said Princess Rúth. "Our brother's subjects have all the evidence they need that he's unfit to be their king."

"I don't think Túathal sees it that way," said Verro. "Look!"

To the west, Viridáxés was wheeling about. He seemed puzzled by his target's disappearance. Túathal's giant projected head, with Túathal, Kennig, Hibblig and Fox beneath it, turned east and approached the thick bank of fog hiding the real version of Tamloch's capital.

On orders from Túathal, Viridáxés flew back and forth along the fog bank, beating his wings to cause the low-lying clouds to dissipate. Hibblig added high winds from a large congruency and Kennig did his part by generating heat so more of the fog evaporated. Now Túathal could hear the people in the real city of Riyas chanting. The expression on the giant projection of his face turned sour, then angry, then wrathful.

"Down with Túathal?" shouted the great head. "Down with Riyas, I say! Death to everyone inside its walls! Viridáxés will tear it down and I will find more grateful subjects and rebuild a capital that's twice as grand!" Túathal's tirade continued for several minutes, making less and less sense as it went on.

Princess Rúth watched and heard her brother's initial rant from the tallest tower on the western wall. She left Doethan's side and crossed to stand next to Verro. "He's mad, you know," she said, speaking softly. "He's been on the edge for years but losing the battle yesterday must have pushed him over. You have to do something."

"I will," said Verro. "But it's not an easy matter to counter an angry dragon."

"I thought your son was supposed to have a dragon too," said Rúth. "I really want to meet him."

"The dragon is a she," said Verro. "Her name is Zûrafiérix. I can't tell you how much I wish *she* was here right now."

"Of course," said Rúth. *"It takes a dragon to match a dragon* and all that, but you know perfectly well I meant I want to meet your son—my nephew." Ruth frowned, then smiled. "I didn't think I had any nephews to dote on and now it turns out I have two."

"Dârio is not a bit like his father," said Verro. "Or his mother, if that's any consolation. He's quite sensible and level-headed if you discount his age."

"I remember *you* at that age," said Rúth. "A few years later you were impulsive enough to marry a talented Dâron mage and keep it secret from your family for decades."

"We can talk about my youthful exploits later," said Verro. He looked up at Fercha watching west and standing guard. "Now we have to stop a dragon and have Dârio proclaimed as king."

"From what I've read of dragon lore, wouldn't it work better in the other order?" asked Rúth.

"Of course it would," said Verro. "I'm an idiot." Without another word to his sister, he pulled his flying disk off his back and mounted it. He was about to leave when he saw Merry talking to Doethan and the apothecary with the long dark beard. Verro skimmed his disk along the roof to her side, hopping over Chee, who was still asleep on Eynon's flying disk. "I need your help," he said when he reached Merry. "You can project illusions. Come with me and we may be able to put an end to this mess." He leaned down and whispered something in her ear. Merry nodded.

"Of course," she said, stepping onto her own flying disk. "Glad to assist. Just a moment." She flipped her disk upside down, guided it above Eynon, who was discussing simulation nuances with Inthíra, and descended like a spider on a thread to give him an inverted kiss on the lips. She moved her head to whisper something to Eynon, then said, "Stay safe," at a normal volume. She ascended, leaving Eynon with a happy but puzzled look on his face. Merry twisted right-side up and followed Verro as he flew toward the giant projection of Túathal's head—and Túathal.

Not an idiot, thought Princess Rúth, *but still impulsive.* She walked to the edge of the tower closest to the city wall, cupped her hands around her mouth to help her voice carry farther, and shouted.

Dâr-i-o!

Dâr-i-o!

Dâr-i-o!

Below her, the well-primed crowd took up her cheer.

Chapter 60

Brother Versus Brother

"Stop!" said Verro and the giant projection of Verro's head Merry had created to match his brother's.

"I won't," said Túathal and Túathal's own projected head. "I've come too far to stop."

Every word the brothers spoke was magnified by Kennig and Merry, controlling their respective projections.

"I wasn't talking to you," said Verro. "I was talking to Viridáxés."

"Greetings O Glorious and Powerful Dragon," said Merry. "Remember me?"

"I do," said Viridáxés. "I liked your tale of the Barrel Knight. Tell me, young wizard, what does Tamloch's master mage wish to discuss with me?"

"I can speak for myself, Your Magnificence," said Verro, appreciating how Merry's compliments had been received by the dragon. "I wish to discuss the king of Tamloch."

"I'm right here, brother," said Túathal.

Verro ignored him and Viridáxés hovered closer, the better to hear what Verro had to say.

"What *is* a king, good dragon?" asked Verro. "Is that something you were taught by the senior mages who crossed on the First Ships?"

"Everyone knows what a king is," said Viridáxés in his own booming voice. "The ruler of a kingdom."

"By what right does a king rule?" asked Verro.

"By birth," said the dragon. His great green eyes were spinning.

"I am a king's son," said Verro. "Am I a king?"

"Of course not," said Viridáxés. "You're a wizard."

"Pay no attention to Verro," said Túathal. "He's just trying to confuse you. *I* am your king and your master."

"As I understand it," said Verro. "You *serve* the king of Tamloch of your own free choice. No man or woman is your master."

"There is a spell…" said Viridáxés.

"A spell that binds you to the line of kings of Tamloch, not Túathal," said Verro. "I can assure you that Túathal is no longer king of Tamloch."

"What do you mean?" asked Viridáxés.

"OF COURSE I'M THE KING!" screamed Túathal.

"Listen," said Verro. The people of Riyas were chanting *Dâr-i-o! Dâr-i-o! Dâr-i-o!* occasionally interspersed with *Death to Túathal!*

"Kings rule by right of birth, but also by the consent of their subjects," said Verro. "Our people left the White and Green Isles because they didn't want the emperor of the Roma's rule imposed upon them."

"True," said Viridáxés. "I was buried in magestones so I could protect Tamloch from rule by a hated sovereign."

"I AM *NOT* HATED!" shouted Túathal. "MY PEOPLE LOVE ME!"

Shouts of *Dâr-i-o! Dâr-i-o! Dâr-i-o!* from the walls of Riyas grew even louder.

"Look," said Verro.

Dârio stood in front of Eynon on Eynon's flying disk, close to the walls of Riyas. He was wearing his gold and green royal Tamloch surcoat and looked every inch a young king. Eynon projected an image of Dârio a hundred feet tall so everyone in the city could see him. The rhythm of the people's shouts changed from three beats to four.

KING Dâr-i-o!
KING Dâr-i-o!

"ATTEND TO *ME*, MY DRAGON!" raged Túathal.

Viridáxés turned his eyes to Dârio, then back to Túathal. "You never did treat me with respect," said the dragon. "I serve the king of Tamloch." With a flick of his massive tail in Túathal's direction he turned and flew toward Dârio.

Chapter 61

Tower of Peril

Everyone on top of the tallest tower was watching Túathal, Viridáxés, and Verro. Fercha, in particular, wanted to be with her husband, but she knew her presence would only complicate an already complex situation. She crafted far-seeing lenses of solidified sound to watch *her* Verro, not Merry's projection. The sunlight streaming over her shoulder helped her see the tension in Verro's shoulders, even if she couldn't see his face. She *could* see Túathal's face, however. It was twisted in an anger closer to pure rage. Spittle flew from Túathal's mouth as he shouted.

Ahead of her on the western side of the rooftop, the others were also observing. Uirsé stood on the left, holding Salder's hand. Beyond her, farther left and close to the stairwell, stood Herophilos Bodégash, the apothecary. Fercha imagined his long black beard was trapped against the tall stone crenelation he was leaning on. *So far, so good,* thought Fercha. *With luck we won't need his professional expertise, or Uirsé's healing skills for that matter.*

Doethan and Princess Rúth stood to Salder's right. They were also holding hands. With hopes of some sort of resolution regarding Túathal in sight, the princess had given up all pretense of *not* caring for Doethan. Inthíra stood a few paces past the princess, giving Doethan and Rúth room for private conversations. Fercha had long-suspected that Inthíra cared for Doethan as more than a friend, but Doethan's heart belonged only to Rúth from the day he'd first seen her. *Not everyone gets a happy ending,* thought Fercha.

She sniffed and smelled fish, then noted Verro's wizards were on the far right, passing around a large bottle of winter wine and discussing the quality of the ale at the Dormant Dragon. Sadly, they hadn't had a chance to wash or change their robes. They stayed downwind and kept their distance from the others.

Where was Eynon's familiar? Fercha wondered. She'd seen Eynon gently lift the sleeping raconette from his flying disk before he'd flown off to help Dârio but wasn't sure where he'd put the little beast so he wouldn't be stepped on by accident. Herophilos Bodégash chose that moment to turn and say something to Uirsé. Fercha spotted Chee in the man's arms, using the apothecary's long beard as a blanket. She smiled and returned to watching Verro's back. In hindsight, she should have been watching the stairwell.

Intense pain ripped through Fercha's side. She cried out but wasn't heard over the Verro's speech and the chanting. Her shields had been protecting the wizards on the tower from *external* attack. Fercha had neglected to consider a crossbow bolt fired from the top of the stairs *inside* her perimeter. She saw the bolt's fletching protruding under her ribs. Fercha doubled over and fell forward off her perch to crash onto the hard stones of the tower's roof. She heard a bone break in her right arm when she landed on it, but no one else on top of the tower did. The shouts of *KING Dâr-i-o!* nearby were too loud.

Her shields of solidified sound fell when Fercha did. Grúgàch emerged from his hiding place under the lip of the tower. He guided his flying disk to the spot where Fercha had been standing and gave Fool a thumbs up. The youngest Mastlands brother was standing in the stairwell, ready to fire another one of several cocked and loaded crossbows hanging from his belt. Fool aimed a bolt at Doethan's back, but Grúgàch shook his head. The southern Clan Lands' wizard wanted live captives to interrogate, enslave, or ransom.

Sensing their inebriation, Grúgàch decided to take the easiest targets off the board first. He formed bubbles of solidified sound around the heads of each of the wizards standing in a clump on the far right. He assumed the other mages on the roof would think the group had passed out from too much to drink, not from lack of air. It wasn't long before the wizards who'd been passing around bottles were all unconscious.

That done, he scanned for the young wizard with the red magestone who had caused so much trouble in the southern Clan

Lands yesterday. Capturing him and bringing him south would be a real coup, but he wasn't anywhere to be found. Grúgàch did spot a high-born woman, however. She'd be worth a sizable ransom, if he had calculated the worth of her dress accurately. As a bonus, she wasn't a wizard. That meant she'd be easier to control.

He extended his senses and counted magestones. Of the six people on the tower's roof who remained conscious, three were wizards and three were not. He'd deal with the wizards first.

Grúgàch mimed hitting the back of someone's head with an imaginary cosh and motioned Fool to strike the young woman on the left holding hands with a taller young man who was totally oblivious to anything and anyone except the young woman. Fool put down the crossbow he'd been holding and lifted his dagger from his belt. He held his dagger by its cross-guard, ready to hit the woman with the heavy hilt.

Fox had rejoined his brother and Grúgàch just south of Duke Néillen's castle on Princess Gwýnnett's instructions. He silently stepped onto the roof behind his younger brother. A crossbow hung from his belt on one side and a dagger on the other. Fox stood behind Doethan holding a dirty sock filled with smooth pebbles. He only knew Doethan as a hedge wizard with a tower farther up the Rhuthro from Mastlands. From what little Fox had heard about the man, he wasn't impressed.

Placing one foot in front of the other with exaggerated care, Grúgàch tiptoed to take a position behind the third wizard to the right of the noblewoman. He prepared a sphere of solidified sound to render *her* unconscious and was about to lower it over her head when a wyvern's thick claws dug into his back and tossed him spinning high into the air. Grúgàch's cries of pain and surprise *were* loud enough and close enough to draw the others' attention. If they hadn't been, Rocky's screeching war cry certainly would have been.

Inthíra turned in time to block Fox's blow to Doethan's head with a plane of solidified sound. His dirty sock ripped, and dozens of smooth pebbles skittered across the roof. Fox dropped and played dead, trying not to be noticed.

Warned by Rocky, Salder spun around and caught the force of Fool's hilt-strike on his crossed forearms. Fool didn't have time to recover before Salder's fists smashed into his nose with a combination of punches that caused the youngest Mastlands brother to go down and *stay* down.

Looking up, Doethan saw that the southern Clan Lands' wizard who'd been about to attack Inthíra was still spinning above the tower. Unfortunately, he was slowly regaining control of his motion. Doethan wasn't happy about that fact so he used rods of transparent solidified sound to encourage his rotation and help him spin faster.

Joining in, Inthíra slammed a hammer of force at the region around the Clan Lands' wizard's feet and ankles until his flying disk popped free and fluttered to land on the tower's roof with a resonant *clang*. Working together, Doethan and Inthíra constructed a set of tongs from solidified sound and used them to grasp the spinning wizard and slam him against the roof next to his flying disk.

As Grúgàch lay stunned, Inthíra removed his grubby brown magestone for the second time in less than twenty-four hours. Doethan used strips from the Clan Lands' wizard's own robes to secure his hands and feet. Inthíra hugged Doethan. He gave her a kind smile and returned to Princess Rúth's side. Inthíra turned away, held her nose, and moved right to check on Verro's unwashed wizards.

Nûd had vaulted off Rocky's back before the wyvern had struck. Now he was on his knees beside his mother, trying to staunch the wound from the crossbow bolt she'd taken in her side while simultaneously figuring out what to do about her fractured arm.

"Uirsé, help!" Nûd called. Two heartbeats later, Uirsé, Salder, and Herophilos Bodégash were kneeling beside Nûd, tending to Fercha.

"Her arm won't be much of a problem," said the apothecary. "I can set it so that it's as good as new after a basic healing potion is administered."

"It's not her arm we need to worry about," said Uirsé. "It's that crossbow bolt in her side. If it's punctured one of her lungs or the sack around her heart, it could be a *big* problem."

"How can I help?" asked Salder.

"Get some cloaks to help her stay warm," said Uirsé. "She's sure to be in shock."

"I have cloaks stowed on Rocky," said Nûd. "I'll get them."

Rocky was perched where Fercha had been standing guard, just above where the healers were working to save her. Nûd found the cloaks and tossed them to Salder who arranged them around Fercha to provide warmth without getting in the way of Uirsé and Herophilos. Nûd thought it was a good idea for him to stay back as well. He'd do something useful, like taking over Fercha's responsibility and guarding everyone on the tower to the best of his ability—and Rocky's.

He returned to the wyvern and smiled, noticing the small crossbow Eynon had attached to Rocky's harness weeks ago. He was sure it was Fercha's. The simple ornamentation on the stock reminded him of his mother's work. He fitted a quarrel to its string, cocked it, and began to walk the roof's circumference.

It was hard to overlook the hundred-foot projection of his cousin Dârio. Eynon had turned out to be really good at generating illusions. *Maybe I can try generating the illusion of being a competent king?* Nûd considered. *And Dârio can give me king lessons. Duke Háiddon could pitch in, and so could Queen Carys. Even Damon and Astrí's advice would be valuable if I could get Damon to treat me like a king, not a servant.* Nûd stopped pacing and considered. *Maybe Damon was trying to teach me that a king is a servant?*

Nûd took a step back when he saw Viridáxés rushing toward Dârio's oversized projection and the walls of Riyas. He shook his head in frustration. *Blast it, Zûrafiérix! By the First Ships, where are you?* He looked south toward the harbor but couldn't spot her. His mind was spinning faster than that southern Clan Lands' wizard Rocky had tossed.

He sensed more than saw Fox raise the crossbow Fool had put down before trying to knock out Uirsé. The bolt from Fercha's small crossbow hit first, striking Fox's shoulder and throwing off his aim. Nûd followed his opponent's bolt's path and saw it had

gone high. Instead of hitting Uirsé's back it had bounced off one
of the thick plates on Rocky's chest. The wyvern screeched his war
cry a second time. He plucked up the injured Fox and unconscious
Fool in his claws and launched himself from the southern edge of
the tower.

If Fox had killed Uirsé, Fercha would soon be dead as well, thought
Nûd. *Maybe Doethan also had the skill to save her, but her odds of
pulling through would be lower. Uirsé and the odd apothecary had
brought Túathal back when he was almost dead from Gwýnnett's poison.
They will save my mother.*

Nûd rolled those last two words around on his tongue a few times.
His. Mother. Fercha was *his mother. Verro was his father. The events
of the last few days had given Nûd a deeper appreciation for the
stresses both of them had been dealing with for longer than he'd been
alive. Maybe he'd been unfair to Fercha by not reaching out to her
and including her in his life, even if most of the time he felt like she'd
been treating him unfairly too? And Verro? He'd been Túathal's
strong right arm and master mage—Nûd's personification of the
enemy—while he was also sleeping with Fercha. Now Verro had
changed sides, because of* him?

"How is she doing?" Nûd asked Uirsé.

"It's too soon to tell," Uirsé replied. "Let us work."

"I'd leave for a while, but Rocky just flew off," said Nûd, as much
to himself as to anyone else.

"I can fly you down to the harbor," said Inthíra. "These wizards"—
she pointed at Verro's crew—"won't be waking up for a few hours."

"Thank you," said Nûd. "I don't want to be where I'd be in the
way. It hurts not be able to do anything to change the situation."

"That's wise," said Inthíra, glancing over at Doethan and Princess
Rúth with their heads close together. "I know how you feel,"
she said, stepping onto her flying disk. "Hop on."

Chapter 62

On the Marshalling Field

When the Riyas illusion vanished in a gout of dragonfire, Néillen ordered Captain Rood and her troops to relocate to the center of the marshalling field. It wasn't for any particular strategic reason—it was because the duke wanted a better view of Túathal, Viridáxés, Hibblig, Kennig and the man with the sharp, vulpine face flying above the field. If his patron was going to win, he wanted to be there to see it. If Túathal was going to lose, he wanted to see that, too. No dog enjoys being kicked forever.

Néillen squinted, trying to make out Hibblig and Kennig's expressions. Túathal's contorted face, ten times life size, was easy to see—until it wasn't. As best Néillen could tell from the ground, Hibblig and Kennig had conferred and Túathal's projected head had winked out. Captain Rood, from the far northwest where wizards were in short supply, had a distance vision tube with two glass lenses substituting for the superior wizard-generated lenses of solidified sound. The duke borrowed the tube and used it to read the lips of the individuals flying overhead.

"Thank you," said Hibblig. "If I had to listen to Túathal's swelled head pontificate for one more minute it would make *me* scream."

"I'm the king!" complained Túathal. "You have to do what I say."

"I'm from Dâron," said Hibblig.

"And I'm from the southern Clan Lands," said Kennig. "We're not your subjects and we don't have to do what you say."

"We're only helping you as a favor for Princess Gwýnnett since you're Dârio's father," said Hibblig. "Maybe we should just tip you off this door and see how you fly without a flying disk?"

"He *is* a king," said Fox. "Or was one, anyway. He may still have his uses—and neither one of you is a murderer, after all."

"That's not true in my case," said Kennig. "Murdering someone is why I exiled myself to the southern Clan Lands."

"I can be *very* useful," said Túathal. "I know secrets about dozens of powerful people in Dâron and hundreds in Tamloch."

"That sounds like as good a reason to kill you as keep you alive," said Hibblig. "We could take bids for the right to kill you from the people you're trying to blackmail and could raise a sizable sum."

"If you want treasure, I can provide that too," said Túathal. "I have chests filled with gold and precious gems buried in well-hidden locations from Bifurland to Dâron's provinces. I can make you all very rich men."

Captain Rood was tugging on Néillen's sleeve, but the duke didn't want to be interrupted. He'd need to know where Túathal had hidden caches of treasure in case he had to make *himself* scarce.

"Why don't you leave him with the troops down below?" said Fox. "They're surrounded, and he can be someone else's problem."

"An excellent idea," said Hibblig.

"On the count of three," said Kennig.

Néillen lowered the distance tube. He didn't need it to see Hibblig, Kennig, Fox and Túathal descending. It looked like they'd land only a few feet from where Captain Rood and Néillen were standing, next to the troops from northwestern Tamloch. Néillen was worried. He'd just parsed Fox's comment about his troops being surrounded.

Captain Rood shifted from tugging on Néillen's sleeve to pulling on his shoulder. "Your Grace," she said. "We've got trouble." She pointed south toward the harbor where Néillen saw a legion's worth of Roma and more than a thousand tough-looking Bifurlanders were forming a battle line that covered half a circle around the remnant of Tamloch's forces.

The part of Néillen's mind that kept track of troop strength noted that Quintillius had only brought one of his legions. The other must be back on the Brenavon guarding Tamloch prisoners and barbecuing wisents. Then he saw three hundred of the shaggy beasts milling about beside the city gates. "Not again," he muttered.

"It gets worse," said Captain Rood. She pointed north to where the majority of Dâron's army had occupied that side of the marshalling field, closing the remaining half of the circle. Dâron swords,

Bifurland axes and Roma javelins pounded on shields as the opposing soldiers stepped up to box in the remaining Tamloch troops who had formed a defensive square. Néillen, on the north edge of the square, watched the Dâron army stoically. He nodded to Duke Háiddon and watched as Dâron's earl marshal and his daughter Jenet crossed half the distance toward him.

Hibblig and Kennig landed close to Néillen. Fox backed off Hibblig's flying disk and escorted Túathal to the duke, staying close to the former monarch's side. The two cousins tossed their flying disks over their shoulders and joined Néillen, Fox and Túathal. Néillen stared longingly at the door to his best bedroom lying abandoned on the wet grass. He wondered if the nail holes could be filled and the door refinished, then reminded himself he had more important things to worry about.

"I don't envy your current position," said Kennig.

"My current position is still king of Tamloch!" proclaimed Túathal.

"Shut up," said Fox.

"I wasn't talking to you, ex-king," said Kennig. "I was talking to the man with all the tattoos."

"I'm not particularly fond of the way things stand myself," said Duke Néillen. "You had a good view from above. What would you say the odds against us are?"

"At least eight to one," said Kennig. "Maybe worse."

"Uh huh," said Néillen, shaking his head.

Then things got worse. Quintillius floated down to join Háiddon and Jenet thirty feet away. He was on the back of the infamous Laetícia's flying disk and accompanied by a short, round older wizard and tall, thin young one on their disks. Néillen recognized them from the battlefield on the Brenavon yesterday, but he didn't know their names. King Bjarni and Queen Signý of Bifurland landed close to Quintillius and Laetícia, transported by two silent mages wearing long amber robes with deep hoods.

"No little gold dragons today?" called Néillen.

"Sometimes they listen," said Signý.

"Sometimes they don't," added Bjarni.

Néillen shrugged in reply. Children remained a mystery to him.

Quintillius slapped King Bjarni on the back. "That was some sizable assistance we got when your ships arrived, wasn't it, my friend?"

"Absolutely," King Bjarni replied. "Sizable and scaly and blue. The biggest and fastest-built breakwater I've ever seen."

"True," said Quintillius. "It was a pleasure to land in calm water instead of heavy surf."

Néillen had no idea what the two of them were talking about and didn't try to puzzle it out. Instead, he considered who *else* might be coming. Verro proved to be the next to arrive, accompanied by a young mage with red hair who reminded Néillen of a shorter female version of the man from the *Blue Whale Inn* who used to tend bar for Verro's wizards. Someone could tell him who she was later, if there *was* a later for him.

Viridáxés flapped his great wings twice and relocated from a spot hovering above the walls of the true city of Riyas to land on the low hill at the northern end of the marshalling field, behind Dâron's forces. The dragon sat back on his haunches and patiently observed the tableau below, picking bits of Néillen's dairy herd from his imposing teeth with his front claws.

Dârio's got to be next, thought Néillen. *His victory is complete, and he'll come to gloat.* But Néillen was wrong. Eynon—the mage who'd reputedly been behind the wisent stampede and freezing the Brenavon—swooped down on his flying disk, landing close to Verro and the young red-headed wizard. Dârio's entrance was somehow more impressive because he came marching in rather than flying. Dâron's army parted and Dârio, wearing his royal green and gold Tamloch surcoat, stepped forward and stood beside Duke Háiddon.

"Is that *all* of you?" sneered Túathal as he surveyed the newcomers. "I'm still twice the king you'll ever be," he said, staring at Dârio.

"I told you to shut up," said Fox.

Dârio ignored their squabbling. Néillen watched Dârio look left and right, trying to determine if any of the others knew about additional arrivals. From their reactions, they didn't. Then Néillen saw Dârio break into a wide grin. He followed Dârio's gaze and saw a tall man who could have been Dârio's twin or a younger version of Verro flying toward the marshalling field from the south on a black wyvern. The tall man was wearing a dark blue and sky blue surcoat appropriate for the king of Dâron that was every bit as impressive as Dârio's surcoat that marked him as Tamloch's monarch. Behind the tall, regally dressed young man and his wyvern came an older mage Néillen's intelligence briefings told him was Inthíra.

The wyvern and Inthíra landed close to Dârio. The wyvern's rider—*Nûd* if Néillen remembered correctly from his reports—joined Dârio and shook his hand.

"Glad you could make it, cousin," said Dârio.

"Glad to *be* here, Your Majesty," said Nûd. He nodded to Dârio.

"Your Majesty," Dârio replied, smiling broadly. Both kings looked up to see an even newer arrival.

Duke Néillen realized he'd need a new definition of *getting worse* when he saw the colossal creature in the sky dripping more water on his troops than a summer squall. It was a great *blue* dragon every inch as large as Viridáxés. Néillen's capacity for surprise was wearing thin as he watched the blue dragon arc around the people assembled on the field and land beside Viridáxés on the hill above.

"You've grown," said the blue dragon.

"So have you, Zûrafiérix," said Viridáxés as he turned his neck to observe Zûra's size.

"No," said Zûrafiérix. "I meant you've grown in wisdom by choosing to serve a *worthy* king. Because of that, I've decided I *will* mate with you."

"Was that ever in question?" asked Viridáxés. He paused and spoke slowly. "Yes. I suppose it was. Thank you."

"See," said Zûra. "You *are* growing in wisdom. Let's see if the non-dragons are too."

Néillen couldn't help himself. He smiled, then grinned, then laughed. Laughter spread contagiously around the gathered leaders and they moved closer together so they could talk more easily. One of their number wasn't laughing, however.

"I see nothing funny about the situation," said Túathal.

"Close your trap!" said Fox angrily.

"Who are you, some minor baron's exiled son, to tell *me* not to speak?" demanded Túathal. The deposed king reached for his dagger and moved to stab Fox through his heart. Fox used his younger reflexes to pull his own dagger and block Túathal's blow, then twist his wrist and drive in a thrust of his own. Tamloch's former monarch fell, red blood staining the marshalling field's green grass.

Hibblig gathered magical energy and threw a powerful fireball at the pair. His missile was less than an inch from Fox and Túathal when Eynon's own fast reflexes popped a spherical shield around both men *and* the fireball. He wanted to isolate the fireball but couldn't. At least his efforts prevented everyone nearby from being caught by the blast when it exploded.

The interior of the spherical shield flashed with a blue-white heat that faded rapidly. Eynon canceled the spherical shield and looked in horror at what remained within. All that was left were two piles of ash.

"You *idiot!*" shouted Kennig. "He didn't tell us where he'd hidden any treasure before you killed him! I should kill *you!*"

Hibblig didn't waste a second. He launched his flying disk skyward without bothering to remove it from his shoulders. When he was fifty feet up he shot westward at high speed with Kennig right behind him.

"Would you like us to chase them?" asked Zûrafiérix, indicating herself and Viridáxés with a wing tip.

"No," said Dârio. "They may have done us all a favor."

"I'm sorry about the loss of your father," said Duke Háiddon.

"Don't be," said Dârio. "At least not right now. Accept Duke Néillen's surrender and make sure his troops are treated with all due courtesy."

After a long, stunned silence, Roma legionnaires, Bifurland warriors, Dâron soldiers and even Captain Rood's Tamloch troops began to cheer.

Chapter 63

Come Here, I Need You

"You, you, and *you*," said Princess Rúth, emphasizing her words to Verro's wizards with a stabbing finger. "Go to the Tamloch Conclave's infirmary and return with more healing potions, a stretcher, and all the talented healers you can find if any have made it back from that debacle of a battle down in Dâron. The designated individuals stared at her with glazed eyes from drinking too much winter wine. *Why did my brother settle for wizards like* these *drunken fools?* Rúth asked herself. Then she answered her own question. *Because my* elder *brother punishes any wizard who shows initiative other than Verro.*

"Doethan," said Rúth. "Go with these three and help them remember what I told them, please. They can get you into the Conclave's hall, you can help them help Uirsé help Fercha."

"Have I ever told you I love it when you take charge?" asked Doethan.

"We'll have a discussion about *that* comment later," said Rúth. "I'd do it myself except I'm worried my guards might spot me and drag me back to my rooms—and I'm not a wizard, so I can't enter the Conclave."

"Shouldn't, maybe—not can't," said Doethan. "Members of the royal family *are* allowed to enter the Conclave complex, at least in Dâron."

"We can parse fine points of grammar and discuss how customs differ between kingdoms when lives aren't at stake," said Rúth. "I wish I had a bucket of cold water."

"To sober up your three *volunteers?*" asked Doethan.

"No, to get *you* moving!" Rúth insisted. "Can you get me a bucket of cold water?" she asked.

"I don't need a bucket," said Doethan. "I can open a congruency to the Rhuthro river. With all the snow melt it carries, it's quite cold. Shall I soak my own head?"

Princess Rúth took a deep breath and then another. She composed her previously agitated face and spoke to Doethan calmly. "Please apply *small* quantities of cold Rhuthro river water to the heads of the three wizards I selected," she requested. "Don't use a lot of water. Uirsé and that apothecary fellow are kneeling, and I don't want them getting wet if it slops around the roof."

"Right," said Doethan. "Just a minute." He waved his fingers and spoke a few phrases in ancient Athican. Circular disks pierced by dozens of tiny holes appeared in space above three of the inebriated wizards. Water drizzled out of them onto the wizards' heads.

Rúth didn't have to confirm the water was cold. The wizards' reactions provided ample feedback regarding its temperature. "Quick," said Rúth. "Put up a privacy shield. We don't want their screams to disturb Uirsé."

Doethan did so and was able to drop the privacy shield soon after, once the wizards had recovered from their original shock. They seemed much more alert now. Rúth repeated her instructions and kissed Doethan on the cheek before he mounted his flying disk and jumped off the tower to follow the three wizards. The four of them stayed in close formation and flew north and east across Riyas toward the high dome of Tamloch's Conclave.

Princess Rúth approached Uirsé without getting too close. "How is Fercha doing?" she asked.

Uirsé replied without shifting her attention from her work. "Herophilos has finished setting her arm, but the crossbow bolt pierced one of Fercha's lungs *and* the sack around her heart. It even nicked one of the chambers. I'm holding the rip in the sack and the nick closed with my magic, but we don't have enough healing potions to repair all the damage fast enough. If I stop holding things closed, she'll bleed out in less than a minute."

"What can I do to help?" asked Rúth. "I sent Doethan and three of Verro's wizards to get more healing potions."

"That will be too little too late," said Uirsé. "Can you make *ad hoc* gates?"

"I'm not a wizard," said Rúth. "But my brother is a wizard and he can."

"I've been so focused on keeping Fercha alive I forgot Verro gave me a communications ring in case I had any questions about orders from Túathal," said Uirsé. "I can't stop what I'm doing, but I can tell you how to trigger it."

"You don't have to," said Rúth. "I'm his sister. He gave *me* a ring, too."

"Contact him—get him here fast," said Uirsé. "There's only one thing I can think of that can save Fercha."

"What's that?" asked Rúth.

"The Pool of Healing," said Uirsé. "Túathal was so worried about assassination attempts he had me make thousands of healing potions to fill up a pool where he could be submerged in case some assassin got lucky. He thought the healing potential in so many potions would overwhelm anything, and he's probably right."

"Where is this pool?" asked Princess Rúth.

"Three levels down from Túathal's royal suite," said Uirsé. "There's a hidden slide in a closet in his bedroom that will drop him into the pool. I helped test it."

"Right," said Rúth. She heard distant cheering from the marshalling field. "I'll contact Verro," she said.

"Hurry," said Uirsé.

Rúth recited her ring's trigger words and the gold band expanded until it enclosed a circle three feet in diameter. After far too long a wait, she heard the three chimes that signified he'd accepted the connection. She didn't wait for her brother's face to shift into focus. He knew who she was. She just said, "Verro, come here. I need you." Two breaths later a four-foot black circle appeared above her and Verro descended to the top of the tower on his flying disk. His *ad hoc* gate disappeared with a sound like a cracking whip.

"What's wrong?" he asked, closing his ring. Rúth put hers back on her finger.

"Fercha broke her arm when she fell, but I've set it," said the apothecary.

"She's been shot by a crossbow," said Rúth. "And those injuries are a lot more serious. Uirsé is keeping Fercha alive for now, but she says you need to gate her to the Pool of Healing right away."

"Túathal's Folly?" asked Verro. "I thought that was just another one of my brother's paranoid schemes. He saw assassins behind every arras and poisons in every meal."

He moved past Rúth and saw the bloody hole in Fercha's side where Uirsé had removed the crossbow bolt. "My love!" Verro shouted. He shoved Herophilos Bodégash out of the way and was about to lift Fercha to gate her out when Uirsé said, "HOLD!" in a tone that froze Verro in place. That was the word used on archery fields across Orluin to stop anyone from walking into the line of fire.

"I have to come with you," said Uirsé. "I'm holding her heart together and keeping both her lungs inflated. She'll die before she lands in the pool if I'm not with her."

Verro looked at Fercha and saw her bone-white clammy skin, her labored breathing, and her weakly pulsing magestone. "I'll have to make an *ad hoc* gate that goes sideways," he said. "I can climb through and we can float Fercha on our flying disks. You can stay close to her that way."

Verro concentrated and a new black circle appeared three feet above surface of the roof and just beyond Fercha's feet. Rúth helped them slide their flying disks under Fercha so the wizards could lift her up to the *ad hoc* gate's level. Verro backed through the gate on foot and helped slide Fercha through, legs first, along with him. Uirsé kept her hands in contact with Fercha's chest and eased her patient's body the rest of the way in. She then stepped all the way through the gate herself and the black circle disappeared with a loud snap.

Rúth found herself alone on top of the tower, with only the apothecary and nine wizards sleeping off too much to drink for company. She heard a faint sound from where Herophilos had been standing on the west side of the tower before moving to the east side to set Fercha's arm. She walked over to investigate and found a small creature who seemed to be waking from a long nap. Its face and hands resembled a raccoon, but it was smaller, and its tail was quite different.

"Chee," said the little beast. He was friendly and allowed Rúth to pick him up. The charming fellow curled into the crook of her arm, making a gentle, reassuring hum like a kitten purring. He fell back asleep with his ears near Rúth's steadily beating heart.

Chapter 64

The Pool of Healing

While everyone around them was cheering Túathal's death, Nûd stepped close to Dârio and told him about Fercha's injuries.

"My apologies, but I have to leave the festivities and get back to the tower," said Nûd after he'd finished filling Dârio in, describing the attack by Grúgàch, Fox and Fool in detail. "After that, I thought it best to get out of the way while Uirsé was working. Inthíra helped me follow Rocky and stop him before he could dump two of the would-be assassins in the center of Fadacaolo Bay."

"Were you successful in your quest, cousin?" asked Dârio.

"Not exactly," said Nûd. "Zûrafiérix was submerged in the harbor. She raised her head out of the water and told Rocky to put the men down immediately." Nûd paused for effect. "Rocky dropped them into the water at the end of the royal dock."

Dârio smiled and Nûd continued. "Inthíra and I had to fish them out of the harbor before they drowned."

"I would have enjoyed seeing Rocky drop them," said Dârio.

"I can have him do it again," said Nûd.

"Don't bother," said Dârio. "I expect I'll have plenty of other things to keep me busy now that I'm king of Tamloch."

"One of them had better be helping me be a good king for Dâron," said Nûd. "By the way, how do you like *my* surcoat? Inthíra whipped it up for me as an illusion."

"It looks a lot like *my* former surcoat," said Dârio.

Nûd nodded. "That's what Inthíra said you would say." Dâron's new and as yet uncrowned king stroked his chin with one hand, then the other. "There's something I don't understand," he said.

"What's that?" asked Dârio.

"I left the assassins we plucked from the end of the royal dock tied to chairs in a tavern by the waterfront," said Nûd. "I told a squad of Dâron troops I'd stand them a round of beers if they'd guard my prisoners."

"And?" asked Dârio.

"I don't see how one of the assassins—the one with short dark hair and a pointed beard—could be here and murder Túathal while also being tied to a chair in a tavern?"

"Say what?" said Dârio.

"I know," said Nûd, his face looking like a wizard lamp had just lit above his head. "They must be identical twins." He smiled at Dârio. "Wouldn't it be funny if *we* turned out to be identical twins?"

"Don't say things like that," said Dârio. "Our lives are complicated enough already."

"You can say that again," said Nûd. "Please tell everyone else what happened. I'll keep you posted on how Fercha is doing." He waved to Rocky, then stepped over, climbed on the wyvern's back, and set a course for the tallest tower on the western wall of Riyas.

Below him, Verro popped out through an *ad hoc* gate, leaving Merry in mid-conversation. She knew he'd just received word through a ring but couldn't see who had been calling. Eynon joined Merry, curious about Verro's disappearance as well.

"Did you hear or see anything before he gated out?" asked Eynon.

"Just a woman's voice that might have belonged to Princess Rúth," said Merry. "It said, 'Verro, come here. I need you.'"

"Princess Rúth is back at the tower, right?" asked Eynon.

"I think so," said Merry. "It looks like that's where Nûd and Rocky are headed."

"I think *we* should get back there, too," said Eynon. "I wish *I* could make *ad hoc* gates. I wish I could make *any* sort of gate for that matter. Damon hasn't even taught me how to make an emergency gate."

"I need to talk to Fercha about more training on building gates, too," said Merry.

"But for now, we fly," said Eynon. "Last one to the tower is sour milk!"

"You're on," said Merry.

The two young wizards sped off after their friend.

Back on the field, Dârio beckoned Inthíra over and started asking questions.

* * * * *

Merry reached the roof of the tower ahead of Eynon by the length of a gryffon's beak. Nûd and Rocky landed seconds later. The wyvern gave Merry and Eynon a reproachful glare since the turbulence of their speedy passage had interfered with his wing strokes.

"*CHEE!*" shouted Chee as he jumped from the top of Rúth's head to his usual spot on Eynon's shoulder.

"Did you miss me, little buddy?" asked Eynon. He rubbed a ridge on the top of Chee's skull.

"Chee," confirmed the raconette affectionately.

"Your familiar is charming," said the princess. "Let me know if you ever need someone to look after him. I'd be glad to help."

"Where's Fercha?" asked Merry. She looked around the roof of the tower and saw two patches of blood near the eastern wall. "What happened to her?"

"She was shot by a crossbow," said Nûd.

"And broke her arm," said the apothecary with the long black beard. "I set it, though."

"As you've noted several times now," said Princess Rúth.

Eynon looked from Rúth to the apothecary and back. He wisely decided not to comment.

"Who shot her?" asked Merry.

"Some simpleton around your age," said Rúth. "He was with a southern Clan Lands' wizard with a scraggly beard and someone who might have been his brother. The brother had dark hair, a sly look and a pointed beard. *He* seemed to have a clue."

"Fox and Fool and one of the wizards from Brendinas?" asked Eynon. "I thought they were on the way to jail?"

"And *I* thought it was Fox who just killed Túathal on the marshalling field," said Merry.

"Túathal is dead?" asked Princess Rúth.

"It seems so, Your Highness," said Eynon. "Sorry you couldn't get the news in a more sensitive way."

"I'm only sorry *I* wasn't the one to kill him," said the princess. "If you knew the things he..." she began. "No," said Rúth. "You don't want to hear about Túathal's many cruelties. You want to know about Fercha."

"My mother," said Nûd.

"My mentor," said Merry.

"My friend," said Eynon.

"Where is she?" asked Nûd.

"Verro and Uirsé gated Fercha to the Pool of Healing," said Rúth. "Uirsé said the bolt had hit her lung *and* damaged her heart. She said the Pool was Fercha's only hope."

The apothecary looked like he wanted to add something, but Rúth stopped him with a sharp look.

"What is the Pool of Healing?" asked Nûd.

"A tiled pool in the palace filled with three thousand healing potions," said the princess. "Túathal was so worried about being poisoned he worked one of Verro's wizards night and day for a year to make them. Uirsé said they'd heal Fercha where administering a few individual potions would not." Rúth paused and looked closely at Nûd. "If Fercha is your mother, then Verro must be your father. You look just like him. That means I'm your aunt. Everything was far too complicated when you first arrived for introductions."

"Sadly, they're still complicated," said Nûd. "Excuse me for a moment. I need to make them even more so."

"What?" asked Rúth. Nûd wasn't listening. He'd turned his back and had moved to the far side of the tower near Verro's odoriferous wizards. Rúth looked at Eynon and Merry. "I thought he was in a hurry?" she said. Then they heard the three distinctive chimes of a communications ring. "What is he *doing?*" asked Rúth.

"Shhh…" said Merry. "I still have a listening spell in place."

"Isn't it wrong to invade Nûd's privacy?" asked Eynon.

"Blast!" said Merry. "I couldn't hear what Nûd was saying because you were talking, and now he's finished."

"Sorry," said Eynon.

"Sorry," said Nûd as he took ten steps to return to Rúth and the others. "There was something I had to do." He looked at Rúth and held his hands out to her in supplication. "Can you help us get to the Pool of Healing? Quickly?"

"I can, and I will," said Rúth. "Is there room on that handsome wyvern of yours for another rider?"

"Certainly," said Nûd. Rocky bobbed his head in confirmation. Nûd helped the princess mount and positioned her in front of him. "Just tell him where to go and he'll take us there," said Nûd. "He's a fast flier."

"What if it turns out the crossbow bolt was poisoned?" interrupted Herophilos Bodégash. "I wrote the book on poisons, you know. And I'm good at setting bones."

"Get on," said Merry, pointing to the back of her flying disk. "Eynon already has a passenger."

"Chee!" said Chee as they left the tower and made good time toward Tamloch's royal palace. Four wizards on their way back from Tamloch's Conclave spotted them and shifted course to intercept.

* * * * *

"Try not to get any of the liquid on your skin," said Uirsé. "You'll remove healing potential that way." Verro was slipping Fercha's body into the Pool of Healing legs first while Uirsé continued to hold Fercha's pierced heart together with her magical constructs.

"How can I avoid it?" asked Verro.

Verro is too worried to think straight, thought Uirsé. *He should have already figured out three or four ways to do it by now.*

"Use bands of solidified sound," suggested Uirsé. "Like you were lowering a horse into a ship's hold."

"Of course," said Verro. "I can do that. I'll support her shoulders and head, too."

"Good," said Uirsé. "Submerge her in the liquid but keep her mouth and nose up so she can breathe."

The liquid in the Pool of Healing was iridescent and polychromatic, like dragon scales in a rainbow of colors. It circled the pool in a pattern that reminded Verro of the wise spinning eyes of Zûrafiérix. The tiled pool was shaped like half an egg cut lengthwise. It was seven feet long and five wide, with a polished marble slide leading down to the narrower end from above. The room housing the pool was also egg-shaped, but much larger, with a vaulted ceiling and a single door in one long wall. Three wizard lamps in the center of the vaults provided illumination. The air inside the chamber smelled like mint and summer thunderstorms.

Verro, Uirsé, and Fercha were at the end of the pool opposite the slide. Manipulating his broad bands of solidified sound with great care, Verro allowed Fercha's body to enter the liquid, not wanted to risk blocking her mouth or nose. Soon she was almost completely covered.

"That's it," said Uirsé. "Hold her there, just like that. Watch her arm where the sleeve of her robe is pushed up. You can see the bones knitting and the broken skin healing."

"I can," said Verro. "It's amazing. I'm surprised my brother's twisted obsession could lead to something so beautiful. I called it Túathal's Folly and never assigned him any wizards to help with it."

"He's not responsible for the Pool of Healing," said Uirsé. "Oh, he had this chamber built, and provided the specifications for the tiled pool itself, but he didn't fill it. I did."

"What?" asked Verro.

"I think it may have been my skill with healing potions that gave Túathal the idea such a thing was even possible," said Uirsé. "You didn't need to assign him wizards. He made me his prisoner last summer, locking me in down here with food, water, a congruent chamber pot, and raw materials for healing potions. He said he wouldn't release me until the pool was full."

"I'd thought you'd gone to visit your cousin studying in Bhaile Pónaire. That's what Túathal told me," said Verro.

"He lied," said Uirsé.

"He does that," said Verro. "Did that, I mean. He's dead."

"Túathal is dead?" asked Uirsé. A smile lit up her face like a sunbeam. "How did it…?" she began. "No. Tell me later. You have no idea how difficult it was for me to heal your brother instead of letting him die when Princess Gwýnnett poisoned him. There are times when I regret having professional ethics." Uirsé seemed to center herself and returned to her original train of thought. "Let me finish *my* story," she said.

"It's a good thing he *is* dead, or I'd be tempted to kill him," muttered Verro as he watched the pool's strange liquid work its magic on Fercha. Then he nodded and Uirsé continued, still focusing most of her attention on Fercha's heart.

"You know how hard it is to create *one* healing potion, right?"

"Of course," said Verro as he watched Fercha's chest slowly rise and fall. "It took hours and left me so tired I wished I could drink it after I made it. I've created several, but I'm not particularly good at them."

"That must be one of the few kinds of magic you *can't* do well," said Uirsé. "I, on the other hand, am *very* good at making healing potions."

"Which is one of the reasons I assigned you to protect my brother, given his paranoia," said Verro.

"It's also why he imprisoned me, I expect," said Uirsé. "For the first month I made potion after potion, each one just a few ounces, until I was utterly exhausted." She sighed. "The bottom of the pool was barely wet. I asked myself what my cousin would do—she's a wizard and studies advanced mathematics. I remembered that she'd taught me how to calculate the volume of an egg just for fun when we were girls. This pool is more like half an egg, so I followed her steps then cut the results in half when I finished and divided that by the two ounces of liquid in a typical healing potion. You can still see my calculations scratched on the wall behind us."

Verro didn't turn. He just nodded to let Uirsé know he'd heard.

Uirsé moved her head slowly left and right, remembering her frustration. "I determined I'd need six hundred and eighty-eight *gallons* of potion to fill the pool," she said.

"That would take lifetimes," said Verro.

"That's what I figured as well," said Uirsé. "I spent the next week rethinking the problem and finally came up with a literal solution." Uirsé shared a small smile but Verro wasn't watching her face so she went on. "I filled the pool with the relevant ingredients and transformed it into something resembling a standard healing potion all at once."

"That's impressive," said Verro.

"Thank you," said Uirsé. "I thought so too when I woke up after passing out from the strain. Túathal was pleased enough by the news to release me. I told him it took only three thousand potions to fill the pool."

"So *you* lied to *him*," said Verro with a smile.

"I did," said Uirsé. "Túathal certainly was calculating, but mathematics was never his *forte*." Uirsé shifted position a few inches. "Could you make a tube of solidified sound and slide it between Fercha's ribs so the liquid can reach her heart faster?" she asked. "It's getting harder for me to keep the hole closed."

Verro could see Fercha's arm had already healed. The skin was whole and looked healthy. Her face still had an unhealthy pallor, however. Crafting a needle of solidified sound, Verro opened a connection between the liquid in the pool and Fercha's heart.

"Perfect," said Uirsé. "Her punctured lung has healed and the hole in her heart is already closing." She sat back and smiled a broader smile at Verro. This time, he *did* see it. "I lied to Túathal about something else, too," said Uirsé.

"Oh?" asked Verro.

"I didn't tell him the Pool of Healing would only work once."

Fercha surprised both Uirsé and Verro by standing up in the pool, splashing healing potion everywhere. Her eyes were wild, and she shouted, "Look out! He's got a crossbow!"

"Looks like once was enough," said Uirsé.

Verro wasn't paying attention, though. He'd jumped into the pool and was too busy hugging his wife.

Chapter 65

Making a Splash

Uirsé stood up and turned her back on the Pool of Healing to give Fercha and Verro more privacy. That meant she was facing the chamber's door when it opened, admitting Nûd, Eynon, Merry, Doethan, Princess Rúth and Herophilos Bodégash, the man who had helped Uirsé heal Túathal the previous morning.

"Watch your step," said Uirsé. "The floor is wet. I don't want anyone slipping and falling."

"Someone might break an arm," said Princess Rúth, "and Herophilos would have to set it." She smiled at the apothecary and raised an eyebrow, reminding Uirsé ever so sightly of Rúth's older brother.

"A broken arm wouldn't need to be set," said Doethan. He'd just seen Fercha restored to health and was smiling more sincerely than the princess. He held up a mesh bag so its contents—a dozen small flasks—clinked like muffled bells. "I've got enough healing potions here to deal with anything." Doethan noticed the contents of the pool that weren't Fercha and Verro. "An entire pool full of healing potions?" he asked, looking at Uirsé. "How did...?"

"It's a long story," Uirsé replied.

Fercha and Verro separated at that point and acknowledged the existence of the universe beyond their own embrace. Nûd helped his parents step out of the pool and hugged them both before stepping back. "I'm *so* glad you're healed!" he told Fercha.

"So am I," she replied.

"Wow!" said Merry, examining Fercha. "That liquid is *really* powerful. It even got the blood out of your robes and closed the hole in the fabric."

Fercha looked down. "So it did," she said. "Where are we?"

"That's a long story too, my love," said Verro.

"We sent three of your wizards to tell Dârio and the others where to find you," said Eynon. Verro nodded absentmindedly.

The chamber suddenly grew more crowded when Dârio, Inthíra, Salder, Laetícia, Quintillius, Mafuta, Felix, Bjarni, Signý and two of their amber-robed wizards bustled in. "We were already at the tower when we met the wizards you sent," said Dârio. "As soon as I told everyone about your injury, Aunt Fercha, they all wanted to come to see how you were doing."

Fercha laughed, her melodic voice echoing from the chamber's roof. Quintillius, Felix and Bjarni, the tallest people in the room, moved closer to the pool where the ceiling was higher. Everyone spread out to ease the crush of people by the door.

"Where's that wyvern of yours?" asked Signý. "I'm surprised *he's* not here. It seems like the rest of the world is in attendance."

"I left him on the roof," said Nûd.

"We know," said Signý. "He met us there and pointed out the best stairway for us to use to get here."

"Good wyvern," said Nûd. "We're lucky there's not enough room here for Zûrafiérix and Viridáxés or they'd try to join us too."

Damon and Astrí chose that moment to enter the chamber. "Good job, grandson," said Damon, using the same tone Nûd had used to praise his wyvern. "Thanks for letting us know about Fercha."

Nûd nodded.

"I'm glad to see you're healed, dear," said Astrí.

"Thank you, mother," said Fercha. "So am I." She smiled at Uirsé. "Thank you, too, good mage. I owe you my life."

"I was glad to help," said Uirsé.

Damon, Astrí and Fercha shared a three-way hug, then Verro bent down and joined in to make it four-ways.

Salder surprised Uirsé by stepping behind her and wrapping his arms around her.

"That had better be you," she said.

"It is," Salder replied.

Merry chuckled softly as she watched her brother and Uirsé, then realized she and Eynon probably looked every bit as sappy much of the time. She moved in front of Eynon and he obligingly put his arms around her, imitating Salder. It wasn't quite as intimate because Merry still had her flying disk strapped to her back, but Eynon had long arms. "Where's Chee?" asked Merry softly. "I'm surprised he's not trying to stand on my head."

"I left him upstairs," whispered Eynon. "He wanted to explore Túathal's suite."

"I hope he doesn't get into any trouble," said Merry.

They both stopped talking when Dârio raised his arms. "I'm sure we're all glad to be together and know that Fercha is whole," said Dârio, "but we have a lot to talk about and I can think of better places to gather than *here*. Why don't we leave this damp subterranean chamber and relax somewhere more comfortable."

"The sooner the better!" Uirsé agreed. She wrinkled her nose at not-so-fond memories of her imprisonment by Túathal.

"I have a perfect room for that sort of discussion in my suite," said Princess Rúth. "Shall we adjourn upstairs?"

A high wordless cry came from the far end of the room. Everyone present turned to stare at the marble slide where the cry echoed from.

"CHEEEEEE!" shouted Chee as the raconette slid down the last length of slide and hit the potion-filled pool, sending liquid everywhere.

"I hope you have plenty of towels in your suite, my princess," said Doethan.

Chapter 66

Princess Rúth's Sitting Room

"That's it then," said King Dârio. Everyone from the chamber holding the Pool of Healing was in Princess Rúth's spacious sitting room. Duke Háiddon and Jenet were there as well. The sitting room was high in a tower in the southeast corner of the palace with a wide balcony overlooking a twenty-acre royal park. Opening the doors to the balcony allowed Viridáxés and Zûrafiérix to listen and participate, though the gardeners responsible for maintaining the park objected to a pair of dragons trampling their topiaries. Rocky was on one side of the balcony gnawing a wild boar that had been hanging in the palace kitchen's larder an hour earlier.

"Yes," said Quintillius, raising his wine glass for emphasis. He was lying sideways on a comfortable sofa next to Laetícia, using it like one of the Roma's dining couches. "We're all agreed to meet in Nova Eboracum in a week to sign a formal treaty of friendship among our respective realms."

"It can't happen soon enough," whispered Laetícia so that only her husband could hear.

"Why not just sign it now?" asked Nûd. "We're all in one place."

"You're new at being a king, cousin," said Dârio. "It will take the heralds that long just to work out the details of the signing ceremony."

"I guess the timing doesn't matter, so long as we're all agreed," said Nûd. "It's going to feel every bit as odd having Tamloch as an ally as it does being king." He paused. "Well, maybe not *that* odd."

Dârio laughed. "Tell me about it," he said. "It will be strange for me to dress in green and gold instead of in two shades of blue."

"Our hearts weep for your hardships," said King Bjarni. "I'm looking forward to seeing these fine dragons"—he waved toward the balcony—"every time I sail between Bjarniston and my new territories on the eastern half of Insula Longa."

"You don't mind me providing a home for our large friends, do you Nûd?" asked Dârio. "Bucket Island east of the Isle of Vines is an uninhabited royal Tamloch hunting preserve. They won't be disturbed there."

"I don't mind in the least, cousin," said Nûd. "In fact, I think it's a brilliant idea, because it solves our biggest problem—feeding them. Viridáxés still owes one of the farmers in the Coombe the price of a sheep."

"Let me know how much a sheep costs and I'll make sure the farmer is paid back," said Dârio.

"About three..." began Eynon. He stopped when Merry put her hand on his arm. He leaned closer to whisper in her ear. "Rocky stole the ewe, not Viridáxés."

"Worry about those details later," said Merry. "Let them talk."

"Are whales tasty?" asked Viridáxés.

"Very," said Zûrafiérix. "And they're filling. I'm sure Bucket Island will be quite suitable."

"It has a number of rock formations that would be suitable for laying clutches," said Verro.

"Excellent," said Zûrafiérix.

"More great dragons in Orluin," said Astrí. "What a lovely thought—but I must admit, the very idea of having offspring when you're over two thousand years old is rather daunting."

"Don't get any ideas about *us* having more children," said Damon. "After spending a night getting pleasantly reacquainted at that inn overlooking the Great Falls, I'm ready to spend the rest of my life with you back in Melyncárreg."

"Think again, darling," said Astrí. "We're getting two townhouses, one here in Riyas, one in Brendinas, so we can enjoy our great-grandchildren."

"What?" said Dârio.

"Oh my!" said Jenet who was cuddled next to Dârio on a padded armchair.

"Huh?" said Nûd.

"No hurry, dears," said Astrí. "But I won't live forever, and neither will Queen Carys."

"Want to get started tonight?" teased Jenet, poking Dârio in the ribs and making his ears turn red.

"I'll take it under advisement," Dârio answered.

"That's an excellent universal answer," Damon told Nûd.

Nûd stuck out his tongue at Damon, then smiled.

"I'll make sure all the Tamloch soldiers willing to accept you as king are returned to Riyas," said Nûd, changing the subject. "I expect that will be most of them."

"I hope so," said Dârio.

"What are you going to do about Duke Néillen?" asked Duke Háiddon.

"That's a very good question," Dârio answered. "I told Néillen he could keep his lands and titles if he gave me his support, but he didn't, so he'll have to be exiled. Do you have any convenient uninhabited islands off the coast of Dâron where I can stash him?"

Duke Háiddon shook his head, but Nûd nodded.

"I remember some islands several hundred miles east of Dâron's southern provinces. They showed up as tiny squiggles on the wall of the Map Room back in Melyncárreg."

"I know the ones you're talking about," said Laetícia. "Those are the Tempest Islands. The biggest one has an excellent anchorage. My ship took shelter from a hurricane there on the way back from a trip to the Imperial capital on the other side of the Ocean. I could gate him there and transport enough supplies for Néillen to survive for a year or so. Long enough for him to learn how to live off the land, anyway. I'll give him a communications ring so he can contact me if he gets into trouble."

"If you could do that for me, I'd be in your debt," said Dârio.

"You already are, King of Tamloch," said Laetícia. "You agreed to give us control of the Five Lakes region west of the Abbenoth and gate access to the black rock mines near the upper reaches of the Brenavon."

"I made that agreement when I was king of Dâron," said Dârio. "I'm not sure if it's still binding."

"I'm the king of Dâron now, so I'll stand behind your agreement," said Nûd with a smile.

"But I, I mean you, have now agreed to hand over *Tamloch* territory!" Dârio protested, though everyone could see he was smiling too.

"What does it matter?" asked Verro. "Those lands have changed hands so many times we might as *well* let the Roma have their turn."

Laetícia nudged her husband. "There's also the matter of the Roma castle Viridáxés destroyed," said Quintillius to Dârio.

"What? Where?" asked Dârio.

"At the point on the west bank of the river where it narrows, sixty-odd miles north of Nova Eboracum," said Quintillius.

"That's where Viridáxés got his chain," said Laetícia. "If Viridáxés would be kind enough to help us deal with the northern Clan Landers' attack, Occidens Province would consider the scales in balance."

"I'm sure that can be arranged," said Dârio. "Viridáxés would probably enjoy it."

"So would we," said Laetícia.

"I still don't like giving up Tamloch lands," said Dârio, returning to his initial subject. "It sets a poor precedent." He waved his free hand at Nûd and grinned. "I demand compensation."

"I'll send your soldiers back. Will that do?" Nûd replied.

"It's not good enough," said Dârio. "You'll have to make some sort of payment."

"I'll take it under advisement," said Nûd.

Everyone laughed, even the dragons.

"You'll make a good king," said Dârio.

"Thank you," said Nûd. "I do want everyone to know I have four conditions before I formally accept the job."

"A little late for that, isn't it?" Merry whispered to Eynon. They were sitting together in their own big padded armchair, while Chee sat playing with a ball of yarn on Princess Rúth's lap. The princess was on a loveseat she occupied with Doethan. Eynon squeezed Merry's hand. She could tell he was smiling even though she couldn't see his face.

"First," said Nûd. "I require Duke Háiddon to serve as my earl marshal."

"It would be my honor to serve you and continue serving Dâron, Sire," said the duke.

"Thank you," said Nûd. "Dârio had your help and seems to be managing this king business reasonably well."

"A very *large* payment," teased Dârio.

Nûd continue to enumerate his conditions. "Second," he said. "I want Fercha and Verro to split their time between Dâron and Tamloch. I need to get to know you both a lot better and don't want to gate up to Riyas every time I want to see you. Agreed?"

Fercha and Verro were on a pair of tall stools placed behind the sofa occupied by Quintillius and Laetícia. Their hips were touching and Verro had his arm draped over Fercha's shoulders.

"We can make that sacrifice," said Fercha.

"If we must," added Verro.

The two of them broke into wide grins and began to rise to give Nûd hug, but he waved them back down. "I have two other conditions," he said. "Third..." Nûd paused for dramatic effect. "I want *Eynon* as my master mage."

"Excellent, excellent!" exclaimed Damon who jumped from his seat next to Astrí. "I can finally fob the job off on someone else."

"But..." said Eynon.

Merry stood and pulled Eynon to his feet. "Take a bow, Master Mage," she said. Everyone else in the room started clapping, including Chee. Both dragons bugled outside the balcony.

"I can't," Eynon protested. "I just learned how to work magic. I have eleven months left in my wander year."

"It was your idea to stampede the wisents across the battlefield," said Fercha.

"You froze the Brenavon when I lacked the strength to do it," said Damon.

"You made the gold we used to recruit the Bifurlanders," said Nûd.

King Bjarni and Queen Signý gave Eynon small bows from their seats.

"And you carried the heaviest load of constructing the illusion of Riyas that proved Túathal unfit," said Inthíra. "I support you as master mage."

"Ummm," said Eynon. "Doesn't Dâron's master mage have to be selected by a vote of the kingdom's Conclave?"

"Correct," said Damon. "But if I support you…"

"And I support you," said Inthíra.

"And we support you…" said Fercha and Doethan.

"And you're the king's choice as well," said Nûd, "Your election shouldn't be a problem."

"I don't understand," said Eynon. "Why choose me?"

"Let me explain," said Damon. "Once in every generation or two, a wizard appears with a particularly powerful talent. This wizard can be from a royal family, like Verro, or a small fishing village up the Moravon, like me."

"My parents herded goats," said Laetícia.

"Long-haired or…" began Eynon before he saw the look Merry was giving him. "Sorry," he said.

"Don't say, '*Sorry*,'" said Merry. "Say, 'Thank you, Your Majesty. I accept.'"

"Let me finish explaining," said Damon. "That might make it easier." He moved to stand in front of Eynon. "You are a phenomenal talent," Damon stated. "Everyone can see wizards with such talents will be master mages. I knew that from your first day in Melyncárreg. You reminded me a lot of, well, *me* actually. When I came to court I ended up performing feats of wizardry no one else could, simply because I didn't know I *couldn't* do them. You're the same way." Damon put his hands on Eynon's shoulders. "There are plenty of us who can teach you more types of magic," he said. "You'll pick most of it up fast, I'm sure, like you did with illusion magic. Right, Inthíra?"

"Absolutely," Inthíra replied. "Eynon and Merry both impressed me. I've never seen anyone pick up illusion magic as fast as they did."

"There you have it," said Damon. "What's your answer?"

"If you all agree…" said Eynon. "But I don't know if I *really* have what it takes. You can form *ad hoc* gates. So can Verro and Laetícia." Eynon looked toward King Bjarni and Queen Signý. The wizard in amber robes behind the king gave a slight bow. "Every kingdom has a master mage who can create *ad hoc* gates. I don't want to let Dâron down, since I can't create any sort of gate at all."

The room was silent for the space of a long breath, then Nûd's new and improved sulphur-free voice rang out.

"Fourth and finally," said the King of Dâron, "would one of you talented wizards *please* teach Eynon how to make *ad hoc* gates— and all the other kinds of gates for that matter? He's going to need that talent since I'm keeping his wyvern."

Rocky inserted his head into the sitting room and nodded at Nûd and Eynon.

"That's settled then," said Nûd.

Zûrafiérix gently nudged Rocky out of the way so the tip of her snout was near the balcony doors and her huge swirling blue eyes could see into the room through tall windows. "Good gentles," she said. "The Tamloch fleet is entering the harbor and a young wizard has arrived. She says Grand Admiral Sónnel would like to give King Dârio his fealty at the king's earliest convenience. She also told me I have fascinating eyes and said she'd dreamed of a whole new sort of dancing numbers to describe their patterns."

"Bonnie!" Nûd exclaimed as he hurried to the balcony.

"Is it safe to come in?" asked a slim, short-haired wizard peering around the edge of the balcony door.

Astrí caught Fercha's eye and smiled.

Outside, Zûrafiérix moved closer to Viridáxés. "Why don't *you* ever tell me I have fascinating eyes?" she asked.

Viridáxés had no idea how to answer.

Chapter 67

Epilogue

The Treaty of Friendship signing ceremony in Nova Eboracum was every bit as formal as the discussions in Princess Rúth's sitting room a week earlier had been informal. Nûd and Dârio were wearing elaborate robes of state instead of martial surcoats, and Nûd's ensemble had the advantage of being real, not an illusion this time.

Quintillius wore a purple toga and a small gold circlet bearing an eagle like the one on the Roma's battle standards affixed to its band. King Bjarni and Queen Signý wore saffron-dyed sleeveless wool robes with fur trim. Their arms were covered with engraved gold bands from their shoulders to their wrists.

The ceremony was taking place in an amphitheater cut into the solid rock of a prominent hill on *Insula Montes,* the island at the mouth of the Abbenoth where Nova Eboracum was located. Eynon and Merry were standing on stage at the bottom of the amphitheater's bowl, wearing new sky-blue wizard's robes with dark blue dragons appliqued on their shoulders. Silver piping on Eynon's robes marked his pending status as Dâron's master mage following what he had been assured would be a perfunctory ratification. His sister Braith had presented Eynon with a flat round cap made from the same material as his new robes, but stiffened to hold its shape. A sprig of green holly stuck out from the cap at a jaunty angle.

As Inthíra had promised, he and Merry had slept for two days straight once the energy potions they'd taken wore off. Princess Rúth had found them comfortable quarters with a large feather bed a few hours before their deadline. The two young wizards had found several ways to amuse themselves in the meantime. Now, five days later, after lessons from Damon, Verro, and Laetícia, Eynon had learned how to create *ad hoc* gates and had used them to transport a select group of people close to him and Merry to Nova Eboracum.

"You look good," said Eynon, admiring Merry as they waited for the last preparations for the ceremony to finish. She smiled and turned all the way around, letting the gathers in her new robes billow out and swirl around her legs.

"You painted the bottom of your flying disk," said Eynon as he saw Merry's back. "White, with a wavy blue line between two red apples. That's Applegarth's flag."

"Technically, it's not *Applegarth's* flag," said Merry. "It belongs to the Upper Rhuthro barony, but everyone *calls* it Applegarth."

"That's what I'm going to do," said Eynon. "Applegarth sounds much nicer than Upper Rhuthro."

"Maybe we can ask someone to petition the king to let us change its name?" said Merry. "I wonder if we know anyone with royal connections?"

"I'm sure we can find *someone* to plead our case," teased Eynon. He ran his finger along the outer rim of Merry's flying disk. "Hey," he said. "This isn't painted. It's a canvas cover."

"Technically," said Merry, "the design *is* painted, just on canvas, not directly on my flying disk. It comes off. Let me show you." She shrugged off her flying disk and removed the cover, revealing that the bottom of her flying disk had been painted sky blue.

"Sky blue for Dâron?" asked Eynon.

"Sky blue so I'm harder to see overhead," said Merry. "Now watch this." She turned her cover inside out and fit it around the edges of her flying disk. This side was jet black.

"I get it," said Eynon. "Black so you're not seen at night."

"There are times when I think there might be hope for you after all, Master Mage Designate," said Merry, smiling.

"Hey!" said Eynon. "I'm nervous enough about having to stand next to Nûd and sign copies of the treaty as a witness."

Merry reversed her cover so the apple-side showed and stretched it around her flying disk. "Don't worry," she said. "Nûd doesn't know what he's doing either."

"You're not helping," said Eynon as he assisted Merry with slipping her flying disk over her shoulders. She pulled him behind a tall piece of wood painted to resemble a Doric column and kissed him.

"Is *that* helping?" asked Merry.

"Yes," said Eynon, "though I think I'll need more encouragement like that before I'm sure."

Merry kissed him again. They laughed and returned to the stage holding hands.

"Do you think I should get a cover?" asked Eynon.

"You don't really need one," said Merry. "I don't either, but my parents made this for me. They didn't know I have a talent for illusions."

"Ah," said Eynon. "We can make our flying disks look like whatever we want, can't we?"

"Like I said, there's hope for you yet," said Merry. "We'd better get into our places. The ceremony is about to start."

They dropped hands and Eynon moved up to stand near the monarchs. Nûd stood between Eynon and Duke Háiddon, while Dârio found his position between Verro and Jenet. Beyond them were two trios: Laetícia, Quintillius and Mafuta, followed by Signý, Bjarni, and Bifurland's master mage in her amber robes. *I'll have to find out her name,* thought Eynon.

Almost everyone from Princess Rúth's sitting room was on the stage, as far as Eynon could tell. Damon and Astrí weren't, however. An hour before the ceremony, Eynon's mentor had shared a completely inappropriate epigram about a man from an isle known as Bucket and gated out with Astrí for parts unknown. Eynon was on his own as Dâron's designated master mage.

He looked over his shoulder and saw Merry standing a few paces back next to Salder and Uirsé and Bonnie. He saw Uirsé smile and Salder wince, then wondered which embarrassing story Merry had just told about her older brother. High above, at the back of the stage, Rocky was watching everything from atop a sturdy stone arch. Chee was perched on the wyvern's head, observing the scene intently. Two dragons, blue and green, soared more than a thousand feet above the amphitheater on rising thermals. They were a colorful collection of friends, dragons, wizards and monarchs.

The spectators filling the amphitheater's seats were a diverse lot. Many were Roma, but several hundred Bifurlanders from their fleet were present, including all of the young golden dragon riders. Eynon saw a nearly naked Bifurland woman balancing on two tall warriors' shoulders and waving at a Roma woman a dozen rows back. There were sizable contingents of guests from Tamloch and Dâron in attendance as well. Eynon's parents, his sister, and Merry's parents were in the front row of the Dâron section near Queen Carys.

I'll have to tell Braith about Bonnie, thought Eynon. Then he remembered how his sister had been eying Felix, the tall young Roma wizard much closer to her age, when she'd come to the stage to deliver Eynon's new hat three-quarters of an hour ago. Somehow, he didn't think the news about Nûd and Bonnie would break her heart.

A Roma wizard Eynon didn't recognize had the job of projecting speakers' voices so everyone present could hear, though the amphitheater's natural acoustics made that easy. From his spot in the middle of things, Eynon heard everything, except when something distracted him and tugged at the back of his mind about what Nûd had told him at breakfast that morning. Apparently, Fox from the Mastlands had an identical twin brother. It was odd that Merry hadn't mentioned that before they'd arrived at the Mastlands dock on their first day down the Rhuthro.

Despite Eynon's nerves and the warm spring sun, time continued to flow. The treaty was ready. Four copies of it were signed by five rulers and four master-mage witnesses. Eynon contributed Dâron's part to the four-ply magical shield verifying the signatures were true, valid, and not delivered under duress. He was ready for a mug of cold Applegarth cider—the plain kind, not the hard stuff—by the time everything was over. The cheering lasted for a long time. Eynon was glad everyone was happy all four realms had agreed to peace, friendship and mutual support. He did his own share of cheering, but Eynon was pleased when the people on stage got to walk a short block to the site of the party Laetícia and Quintillius had organized.

The party was in a walled garden, Eynon wasn't sure quite where. He just followed the others and enjoyed Merry tugging him when he started to make a wrong turn. Eynon sat on a stone bench next to Merry and got his mug of cider at long last, gratefully lifting it from a servant's tray.

"What now?" Eynon asked Merry. "Some new adventure?"

"If you mean getting married, I think we should wait," said Merry. "Once we're married there will be all that pressure, and we don't need that."

"Pressure?" asked Eynon.

"For grandchildren," said Merry. "My parents are already hinting."

"Mine aren't," said Eynon. "Not yet, anyway." He put down his mug and took Merry's hand. "You'll still live with me, won't you?"

"Try and stop me," Merry replied. They laughed. Eynon picked his mug back up and took a long swallow.

"What sort of wizardry do you want to focus on first?" Eynon asked. "Stick with illusions? Healing, maybe, like Uirsé? Battle magic?"

"I don't know if I want to have a single specialty," said Merry. "I like using my imagination and channeling it through wizardry."

"So do I," said Eynon.

Merry made her *don't be an idiot, I know that already* face.

Eynon tried a more pragmatic question. "Where do you want to live?" he asked. "I don't think I can afford a townhouse in Brendinas."

"Do you still have a ball of gold the size of a plum in your belt pouch?" asked Merry. "Do you remember how to get more gold from the river back in Melyncárreg?" She smiled over at Eynon and stroked the back of his hand. "I don't think buying a townhouse in Brendinas will be a problem. And besides, you're the kingdom's master mage now, or will be as soon as the Conclave votes on it. Doesn't some sort of tower come with the job?"

"I have no idea," said Eynon. "But I'll find out."

"Good," said Merry.

"Does Fox from the Mastlands have an identical twin?"

"Where did *that* question come from?" asked Merry.

Eynon explained, his expression serious.

"I've got a bad feeling about this," said Merry.

"Now I'm wondering where Princess Gwýnnett has disappeared to," said Eynon. "I haven't seen her since she flew out the window of the Dormant Dragon with Hibblig."

"I know more than that," said Merry. "Gruffyd and Nyssia told me she tried to kidnap Queen Carys, but they stopped her and locked her in her apartments, but Hibblig helped her escape."

"What?" said Eynon. "When did you have a chance to pick up news from Gruffyd and Nyssia?"

"Gruffyd told his mother who told Maddolyn at Flying Frog Farms who told my mother who told me," said Merry.

"Oh," said Eynon.

"That reminds me," said Merry. "Maybe I can spend time with Laetícia and learn a few things. With Damon retired and Queen Carys slowing down, Nûd's going to need a new spymaster. From what I hear, my brother's good at that sort of thing. I expect I am, too."

"That makes great sense," said Eynon. "You should talk to Laetícia tonight and see if she's agreeable."

They looked over toward the center of the garden where Laetícia was laughing with Dârio, Nûd and Bjarni. Figuring that serious business wasn't being discussed, they walked over to see if Laetícia could spare a minute for Merry. They heard Laetícia saying, "...and then he tried to do it with an *elephant*." Everyone began to laugh again.

"Excuse me," said Merry. "Could you spare a minute for a question?"

"Certainly," said Laetícia. "Private or public?"

"Public is fine," said Merry. She didn't say more because she heard buzzing from Laetícia's left hand.

"Just a second," said Laetícia. "I should take this. It's Duke Néillen. I dropped him off on the Tempest Islands yesterday and told him to ring if he was missing any critical supplies." Three chimes sounded. Beads clacked at the end of dark braids when Laetícia turned around and opened the communications ring to its full diameter. Duke Néillen's face filled the interface. Merry waved to Dârio, Nûd and Bjarni so they'd follow the conversion.

"What did I forget?" asked Laetícia.

"You forgot to tell us about the two thousand ships in a Roma invasion force," said Duke Néillen. "Look!"

He adjusted the interface on his ring to show a wide harbor below his high vantage point. It was filled with too many ships and sails to count. Circling above the anchored fleet were seven obsidian-colored dragons, each the size of a Bifurland longship.

"Thunder and lightning," said Laetícia. "She's done it."

"I thought so," said Duke Néillen. "You knew about this. That makes you a far-greater traitor than I am, forgetting to mention a little thing like an imperial invasion."

"No," said Laetícia. "It's *not* an invasion from the empire of the Roma. It's an attempt to create a rival empire on this side of the Ocean. She must have pushed too far. The other emperors in her ruling Tetrarchy must have forced her into exile and she decided to come west to establish her own empire in Orluin."

"With a fleet *that* size?" exclaimed Duke Néillen.

"It's less than a quarter of the empire's full strength," said Laetícia. "They must be waiting for a storm to pass before sailing for Occidens Province."

"Who is *she?*" asked Dârio, who had stepped close to the ring's interface to count ships.

"I can answer that," responded Quintillius, who'd just come to join them. "Laetícia is referring to Sírénae Accipiter, the Siren Hawk. She makes Túathal look like a sparrow."

"I don't like the sound of that," said Merry.

"At least *we* have bigger dragons," said Eynon.

TO BE CONTINUED IN *The Congruent Emperor*

Please visit

www.CongruentMage.com

for more information about
Eynon, Merry and their friends

Sign up for the Congruent Mage mailing list
on the web site to get advance notice of publication
and receive a free short story set in the author's
Xenotech Support universe.

XenotechSupport.com/mailing-list

Additional Material

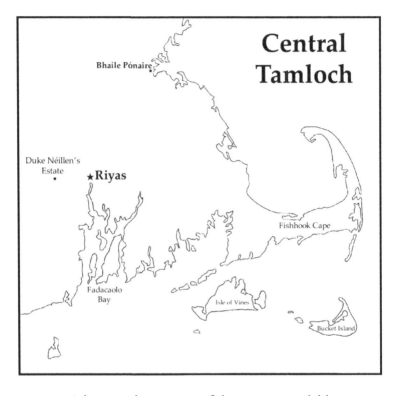

A larger color version of this map is available at:

CongruentMage.com/maps.html

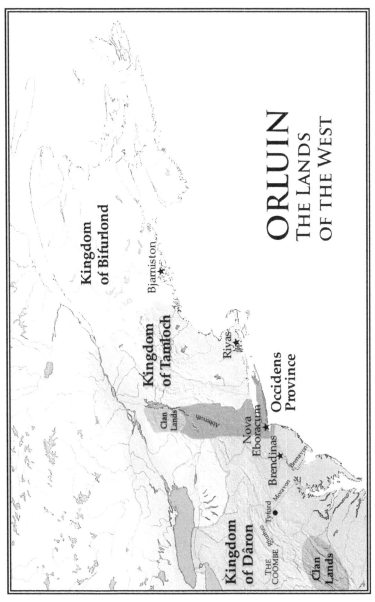

A larger color version of this map is available at:

CongruentMage.com/maps.html

Royal Tamloch Family Tree

Dates are recorded from the year the First Ships landed

Túanath
1973–2018

Túan
1995–2057

Túath
2017–2053

Sónnath
1976–2059

Two Generations

Sónnel
2033–

Daughters

Túathal
2032–

Gwýnnett
2038–

Dário
2062–

Verro
2035–

Fercha
2035–

Rúth
2038–

Dárionûd
2058–

Made in the USA
Columbia, SC
06 July 2020